CHALLENGES

"Like the scientists themselves, the science fiction writers have been guided by a basic tenet of faith: the belief that the universe is knowable, and that what human beings can understand, they can eventually learn to control and harness.

"...Not only do the writers share the scientists' belief in an understandable universe, the writers also tacitly believe that human-like intelligence is a permanent fixture in the universe.

"...Without intending to, without even consciously realizing it until very recently, science fiction writers around the world have been slowly building up a mythology suitable for our modern scientific age. Like the scientists themselves, the writers share the rock-bottom faith in the power and beauty of rational human thought."
—Ben Bova, "Science, Fiction and Faith"

"[Bova] handles his subjects with clear prose and well-practiced skill..."
—*Publishers Weekly*

Tor Books by Ben Bova

CHALLENGES

BEN BOVA

A TOM DOHERTY ASSOCIATES BOOK
NEW YORK

CHALLENGES

Cover art by John Berkey

A Tor Book
Published by Tom Doherty Associates, Inc.
175 Fifth Avenue
New York, NY 10010

Tor® is a registered trademark of Tom Doherty Associates, Inc.

ISBN: 0-812-51408-4
Library of Congress Catalog Card Number: 93-18413

First edition: July 1993
First mass market edition: December 1994

Printed in the United States of America

0 9 8 7 6 5 4 3 2 1

To Regina and Emily

TABLE OF CONTENTS

Foreword

Life is a series of challenges. From birth to the final struggle against death, it's just one damned hurdle after another. The pessimist sees this as proof of the futility of it all. The optimist says, like John Kennedy, "I do not fear these challenges; I welcome them."

For challenge means opportunity. Challenge means change. A life without challenges would be not merely boring, it would be pointless.

Art, it is said, mirrors life. The way I see it, art is not so much a mirror as a lens. Art does not merely reflect life in all its trivialities; art *focuses* life, brings out the important details and ignores the inconsequential ones. Michelangelo's sculpture of David, for example, does not merely show an average human male; the statue represents something almost more than human, the male form at its vibrantly vigorous youthful finest.

When a writer sits down to start a work of fiction he or she has no intention of producing a mirror image of life. That is biography at best, or case history. (And even biographies and case histories skip most of the details.) The writer aims for a distillation of life, squeezing out the dull dross and presenting the vital essence for the reader's delectation.

Every time a writer begins this task, the writer faces an incredible challenge. How can I, sitting here in front of a keyboard, implant my thoughts, my feelings, my experiences into your mind? How can I reach into you so that, for a little while at least, you believe yourself to be living in the world of my words, acting out the deeds of my fiction, loving and hating and bleeding and maybe even dying with the characters you are reading about?

That is the challenge of fiction.

Science fiction presents an even tougher challenge. Added to all the ordinary difficulties of writing fiction is the necessity to show the reader a world that has never existed. In ordinary fiction you can use tables and chairs without going into elaborate description; in a tale set on a space station, in zero gravity, chairs are useless, and tables are built very differently from anything on Earth. In ordinary fiction when you speak of a starry night the reader pictures the same night sky that you and I have seen all our lives. But what about a tale set in the heart of a star cluster, where there is no darkness at night because the stars are packed so thickly? What about a story dealing with aliens who are decidedly nonhuman? Or an electronic society? Or nanotechnology, virtual reality, ecological collapse?

Isaac Asimov, who wrote on every subject from science to Shakespeare, from the Bible to lecherous limericks, mysteries and children's stories as well as science fiction, always claimed that writing science fiction was the most difficult of all. In addition to all the other things the writer must do to produce good fiction, the science-fiction writer must create a world that the reader has never seen before, and do it without turning the story into a lecture or a travelogue.

In this book you will find twelve short stories, twelve tales of science fiction. Each of them presented me, its author, with a special set of challenges. In the introductions to each story I will try to recall the challenges that I felt as I wrote the tale, try to give you a feeling for what the writer goes through in the process of creating fiction.

There are also a half-dozen nonfiction pieces in this book. All of them bear on the process of writing or on the field we call science fiction. The introductions to each of these essays will try to show how they apply to the craft and business of writing science fiction.

The intent of all this is to help you to enjoy what you read. My belief is that if you understand something of what the writer goes through in the process of creation, you may appreciate the stories more. Perhaps that is a mistaken belief; perhaps the more you understand the less you will like the stories. Wasn't it Goethe who remarked: "Know thyself? If I knew myself I'd run away!"

If you are a writer or someone who is struggling to learn how to write fiction, perhaps these stories and essays and their introductions will help you. At the very least, they may offer some insight into what one writer has gone through on more than a dozen occasions.

Enjoy. Learn. *Think.*

Ben Bova

Naples, Florida, and West Hartford, Connecticut

The Man Who Hated Gravity

The most important advice ever given to a writer is this: Write about what you know.

How can you do this in science fiction, when the stories tend to be about places and times that no one has yet experienced? How can you write about what you know when you want to write about living in the future or the distant past, on the Moon, or Mars, or some planet that is invented out of your imagination?

There are ways.

To begin with, no matter what time and place in which your story is set, it must deal with people. Oh, sure, the characters in your story may not look like human beings. Science-fiction characters can be robots or alien creatures or smart dolphins or sentient cacti, for that matter. But they must behave like humans. They must have humanly recognizable needs and fears and desires. If they do not, they will either be totally incomprehensible to the reader or—worst sin of all—boring.

I have never been to the Moon. I have never been a circus acrobat. But I know what it is to hate gravity. Several years ago I popped my knee while playing tennis. For weeks I was in a brace, hardly able to walk. I used crutches, and later a cane. For more than a year I could not trust my two legs to support me. Even today that knee feels like there's a loose collection of rubber bands inside. I know what it is like to be crippled, even though it was only temporary.

And I know, perhaps as well as anyone, what it is like to live on the Moon. I've been living there in my imagination for much of my life. My first novel (unpublished) dealt with establishing habitats on the Moon. My 1976 novel *Millennium* (later incorporated into *The Kinsman Saga*) was set mainly on the Moon. In my 1987 nonfiction book *Welcome to Moonbase,* I worked with engineers and illustrators to create a livable, workable industrial base on the Moon's surface.

While I was hobbling around on crutches, hating every moment of being incapacitated, I kept thinking of how much better off I would be in zero g, or in the gentle gravity of the Moon, one-sixth of Earth's.

And the Great Rolando took form in my mind. I began to write a short story about him.

I don't write many short stories. Most of my fiction has been novels. When I start a novel, I usually know the major characteristics of the major characters, and that's about it. I have sketched out the basic conflict between the protagonist and antagonist, but if I try to outline the scenes, schedule the chapters, organize the action, the novel gets turgid and dull. Much better to let the characters fight it out among themselves, day after day, as the work progresses.

Short stories are very different. Most of the short stories I write are rather carefully planned out before I begin putting the words down. I find that, because a short story must necessarily be tightly written, without a spare scene or even an extra sentence, I must work out every detail of the story in my mind before I begin to write.

"The Man Who Hated Gravity" did not evolve that way. I began with Rolando, a daring acrobat who flouted his disdain for the dangers of his work. I knew he was going to be injured, much more seriously and permanently than I was. From there on in, Rolando and the other characters literally took over the telling of the tale. I did not know, for example, that the scientist who was used to help publicize Rolando would turn out to be the man who headed Moonbase years later.

I do not advise this subconscious method of writing for short-story work. As I said, a short story must be succinct. Instead of relating the tale of a person's whole life, or a substantial portion of it, a short story can at best reveal a critical incident in that character's life: a turning point, an episode that illuminates the person's inner being.

But this subconscious method worked for me in "The Man Who Hated Gravity." See if the story works for you.

The Great Rolando had not always hated gravity. As a child growing up in the traveling circus that had been his only home he often frightened his parents by climbing too high, swinging too far, daring more than they could bear to watch.

The son of a clown and a cook, Rolando had yearned for true greatness, and could not rest until he became the most renowned aerialist of them all.

Slim and handsome in his spangled tights, Rolando soared through the empty air thirty feet above the circus's flimsy safety net. Then fifty feet above it. Then a full hundred feet high, with no net at all.

"See the Great Rolando defy gravity!" shouted the posters and TV advertisements. And the people came to crane their necks and hold their breaths as he performed a split-second ballet in midair high above them. Literally flying from one trapeze to another, triple somersaults were workaday chores for the Great Rolando.

His father feared to watch his son's performances. With

all the superstition born of generations of circus life, he cringed outside the Big Top while the crowds roared deliriously. Behind his clown's painted grin Rolando's father trembled. His mother prayed through every performance until the day she died, slumped over a bare wooden pew in a tiny austere church far out in the midwestern prairie.

For no matter how far he flew, no matter how wildly he gyrated in midair, no matter how the crowds below gasped and screamed their delight, the Great Rolando pushed himself farther, higher, more recklessly.

Once, when the circus was playing New York City's huge Convention Center, the management pulled a public relations coup. They got a brilliant young physicist from Columbia University to pose with Rolando for the media cameras and congratulate him on defying gravity.

Once the camera crews had departed, the physicist said to Rolando, "I've always had a secret yearning to be in the circus. I admire what you do very much."

Rolando accepted the compliment with a condescending smile.

"But no one can *really* defy gravity," the physicist warned. "It's a universal force, you know."

The Great Rolando's smile vanished. "*I* can defy gravity. And I do. Every day."

Several years later Rolando's father died (of a heart seizure, during one of his son's performances) and Rolando married the brilliant young lion tamer who had joined the circus slightly earlier. She was a petite little thing with golden hair, the loveliest of blue eyes, and so sweet a disposition that no one could say anything about her that was less than praise. Even the great cats purred for her.

She too feared Rolando's ever-bolder daring, his wilder and wilder reachings on the high trapeze.

"There's nothing to be afraid of! Gravity can't hurt me!" And he would laugh at her fears.

"But I *am* afraid," she would cry.

"The people pay their money to see me defy gravity," Rolando would tell his tearful wife. "They'll get bored if I keep doing the same stunts one year after another."

She loved him dearly and felt terribly frightened for him. It was one thing to master a large cage full of Bengal tigers and tawny lions and snarling black panthers. All you needed was will and nerve. But she knew that gravity was another matter altogether.

"No one can defy gravity forever," she would say, gently, softly, quietly.

"I can," boasted the Great Rolando.

But of course he could not. No one could. Not forever.

The fall, when it inevitably came, was a matter of a fraction of a second. His young assistant's hand slipped only slightly in starting out the empty trapeze for Rolando to catch after a quadruple somersault. Rolando almost caught it. In midair he saw that the bar would be too short. He stretched his magnificently trained body to the utmost and his fingers just grazed its tape-wound shaft.

For an instant he hung in the air. The tent went absolutely silent. The crowd drew in its collective breath. The band stopped playing. Then gravity wrapped its invisible tentacles around the Great Rolando and he plummeted, wild-eyed and screaming, to the sawdust a hundred feet below.

"His right leg is completely shattered," said the famous surgeon to his wife. She had stayed calm up to that moment, strong and levelheaded while her husband lay unconscious in an intensive-care unit.

"His other injuries will heal. But the leg . . ." The gray-haired, gray-suited man shook his dignified head sadly. His assistants, gathered behind him like an honor guard, shook their heads in metronome synchrony to their leader.

"His leg?" she asked, trembling.

"He will never be able to walk again," the famous surgeon pronounced.

The petite blonde lion tamer crumpled and sagged into the sleek leather couch of the hospital waiting room, tears spilling down her cheeks.

"Unless . . . ," said the famous surgeon.

"Unless?" she echoed, suddenly wild with hope.

"Unless we replace the shattered leg with a prosthesis."

"Cut off his leg?"

The famous surgeon promised her that a prosthetic bionic leg would be "just as good as the original—in fact, even better!" It would be a *permanent* prosthesis; it would never have to come off, and its synthetic surface would blend so well with Rolando's real skin that no one would be able to tell where his natural leg ended and his prosthetic leg began. His assistants nodded in unison.

Frenzied at the thought that her husband would never walk again, alone in the face of coolly assured medical wisdom, she reluctantly gave her assent and signed the necessary papers.

The artificial leg was part lightweight metal, part composite space–manufactured materials, and entirely filled with marvelously tiny electronic devices and miraculously miniaturized motors that moved the prosthesis exactly the way a real leg should move. It was stronger than flesh and bone, or so the doctors confidently assured the Great Rolando's wife.

The circus manager, a constantly frowning bald man who reported to a board of bankers, lawyers, and MBAs in St. Petersburg, agreed to pay the famous surgeon's astronomical fee. "The first aerialist with a bionic leg," he murmured, dollar signs in his eyes.

Rolando took the news of the amputation and prosthesis with surprising calm. He agreed with his wife: better a strong and reliable artificial leg than a ruined real one.

In two weeks he walked again. But not well. He limped. The leg hurt, with a sullen, stubborn ache that refused to go away.

"It will take a little time to get accustomed to it," said the physical therapists.

Rolando waited. He exercised. He tried jogging. The leg did not work right. And it ached constantly.

"That's just not possible," the doctors assured him. "Perhaps you ought to talk with a psychologist."

The Great Rolando stormed out of their offices, limping and cursing, never to return. He went back to the circus, but not to his aerial acrobatics. A man who could not walk properly, who had an artificial leg that did not work right, had no business on the high trapeze.

His young assistant took the spotlight now, and duplicated—almost—the Great Rolando's repertoire of aerial acrobatic feats. Rolando watched him with mounting jealousy, his only satisfaction being that the crowds were noticeably smaller than they had been when he had been the star of the show. The circus manager frowned and asked when Rolando would be ready to work again.

"When the leg works right," said Rolando.

But it continued to pain him, to make him awkward and invalid.

That is when he began to hate gravity. He hated being pinned down to the ground like a worm, a beetle. He would hobble into the Big Tent and eye the fliers' platform a hundred feet over his head and know that he could not even climb the ladder to reach it. He grew angrier each day. And clumsy. And obese. The damned false leg *hurt*, no matter what those expensive quacks said. It was *not* psychosomatic. Rolando snorted contempt for their stupidity.

He spent his days bumping into inanimate objects and tripping over tent ropes. He spent his nights grumbling and grousing, fearing to move about in the dark, fearing even that he might roll off his bed. When he managed to sleep the same nightmare gripped him: he was falling, plunging downward eternally while gravity laughed at him and all his screams for help did him no good whatever.

His former assistant grinned at him whenever they met. The circus manager took to growling about Rolando's weight, and asking how long he expected to be on the payroll when he was not earning his keep.

Rolando limped and ached. And when no one could see him, he cried. He grew bitter and angry, like a proud lion that finds itself caged forever.

Representatives from the bionics company that manufactured the prosthetic leg visited the circus, their faces grave with concern.

"The prosthesis should be working just fine," they insisted.

Rolando insisted even more staunchly that their claims were fraudulent. "I should sue you and the barbarian who took my leg off."

The manufacturer's reps consulted their home office and within the week Rolando was whisked to San Jose in their company jet. For days on end they tested the leg, its electronic innards, the bionic interface where it linked with Rolando's human nervous system. Everything checked out perfectly. They showed Rolando the results, almost with tears in their eyes.

"It should work fine."

"It does not."

In exchange for a written agreement not to sue them, the bionics company gave Rolando a position as a "field consultant," at a healthy stipend. His only duties were to phone San Jose once a month to report on how the leg felt. Rolando delighted in describing each and every individual twinge, the awkwardness of the leg, how it made him limp.

His wife was the major earner now, despite his monthly consultant's fee. She worked twice as hard as ever before, and began to draw crowds that held their breaths in vicarious terror as they watched the tiny blonde place herself at the mercy of so many fangs and claws.

Rolando traveled with her as the circus made its tour of North America each year, growing fatter and unhappier day by humiliating, frustrating, painful day.

Gravity defeated him every hour, in a thousand small ways. He would read a magazine in their cramped mobile home until, bored, he tossed it onto the table. Gravity would slyly tug at its pages until the magazine slipped over the table's edge and fell to the floor. He would shower laboriously, hating the bulging fat that now encumbered his once-sleek body. The soap would slide from his hands while he was half-blinded with suds. Inevitably he would slip on it and bang himself painfully against the shower wall.

If there was a carpet spread on the floor, gravity would contrive to have it entangle his feet and pull him into a humiliating fall. Stairs tripped him. His silverware clattered noisily to the floor in restaurants.

He shunned the Big Top altogether, where the people who had once paid to see him soar through the air could see how heavy and clumsy he had become—even though a nasty voice in his mind told him that no one would recognize the fat old man he now was as the once-magnificent Great Rolando.

As the years stretched past Rolando grew grayer

and heavier and angrier. Furious at gravity. Bellowing, screaming, howling with impotent rage at the hateful tricks gravity played on him every day, every hour. He took to leaning on a cane and stumping around their mobile home, roaring helplessly against gravity and the fate that was killing him by inches.

His darling wife remained steadfast and supportive all through those terrible years. Other circus folk shook their heads in wonder at her. "She spends all day with the big cats and then goes home to more roaring and spitting," they told each other.

Then one winter afternoon, as the sun threw long shadows across the Houston Astrodome parking lot, where the circus was camped for the week, Rolando's wife came into their mobile home, her sky-blue workout suit dark with perspiration, and announced that a small contingent of performers had been invited to Moonbase for a month.

"To the Moon?" Rolando asked, incredulous. "Who?"

The fliers and tightrope acts, she replied, and a selection of acrobats and clowns.

"There's no gravity up there," Rolando muttered, suddenly jealous. "Or less gravity. Something like that."

He slumped back in the sofa without realizing that the wonderful smile on his wife's face meant that there was more she wanted to tell him.

"We've been invited, too!" she blurted, and she perched herself on his lap, threw her arms around his thick neck and kissed him soundly.

"You mean you've been invited," he said darkly, pulling away from her embrace. "You're the star of the show; I'm a has-been."

She shook her head, still smiling happily. "They haven't asked me to perform. They can't bring the cats up into space. The invitation is for the Great Rolando and his wife to spend a month up there as guests of Moonbase Inc.!"

Rolando suspected that the bionics company had pulled some corporate strings. They want to see how their damnable leg works without gravity, he was certain. Inwardly, he was eager to find out, too. But he let no one know that, not even his wife.

To his utter shame and dismay, Rolando was miserably sick all the long three days of the flight from Texas to Moonbase. Immediately after takeoff the spacecraft carrying the circus performers was in zero gravity, weightless, and Rolando found that the absence of gravity was worse for him than gravity itself. His stomach seemed to be falling all the time while, paradoxically, anything he tried to eat crawled upward into his throat and made him violently ill.

In his misery and near-delirium he knew that gravity was laughing at him.

Once on the Moon, however, everything became quite fine. Better than fine, as far as Rolando was concerned. While clear-eyed young Moonbase guides in crisp uniforms of amber and bronze demonstrated the cautious shuffling walk that was needed in the gentle lunar gravity, Rolando realized that his leg no longer hurt.

"I feel fine," he whispered to his wife, in the middle of the demonstration. Then he startled the guides and his fellow circus folk alike by tossing his cane aside and leaping five meters into the air, shouting at the top of his lungs, "I feel *wonderful!*"

The circus performers were taken off to special orientation lectures, but Rolando and his wife were escorted by a pert young redhead into the office of Moonbase's chief administrator.

"Remember me?" asked the administrator as he shook Rolando's hand and half-bowed to his wife. "I was the physicist at Columbia who did that TV commercial with you six or seven years ago."

Rolando did not in fact remember the man's face at all, although he did recall his warning about gravity. As he sat down in the chair the administrator proffered, he frowned slightly.

The administrator wore zippered coveralls of powder blue. He hiked one hip onto the edge of his desk and beamed happily at the Rolandos. "I can't tell you how delighted I am to have the circus here, even if it's just for a month. I really had to sweat blood to get the corporation's management to okay bringing you up here. Transportation's still quite expensive, you know."

Rolando patted his artificial leg. "I imagine the bionics company paid their fair share of the costs."

The administrator looked slightly startled. "Well, yes, they have picked up the tab for you and Mrs. Rolando."

"I thought so."

Rolando's wife smiled sweetly. "We are delighted that you invited us here."

They chatted a while longer and then the administrator personally escorted them to their apartment in Moonbase's tourist section. "Have a happy stay," he said, by way of taking his leave.

Although he did not expect to, that is exactly what Rolando did for the next many days. Moonbase was marvelous! There was enough gravity to keep his insides behaving properly, but it was so light and gentle that even his obese body with its false leg felt young and agile again.

Rolando walked the length and breadth of the great Main Plaza, his wife clinging to his arm, and marveled at how the Moonbase people had landscaped the expanse under their dome, planted it with grass and flowering shrubs. The apartment they had been assigned to was deeper underground, in one of the long corridors that had been blasted out of solid rock. But the quarters were no smaller than their mobile home back on Earth, and it had a video screen that took up one entire wall of the sitting room.

"I love it here!" Rolando told his wife. "I could stay forever!"

"It's only for one month," she said softly. He ignored it.

Rolando adjusted quickly to walking in the easy lunar gravity, never noticing that his wife adjusted just as quickly (perhaps even a shade faster). He left his cane in their apartment and strolled unaided each day through the shopping arcades and athletic fields of the Main Plaza, walking for hours on end without a bit of pain.

He watched the roustabouts who had come up with him directing their robots to set up a Big Top in the middle of the Plaza, a gaudy blaze of colorful plastic and pennants beneath the great gray dome that soared high overhead.

The Moon is marvelous, thought Rolando. There was still gravity lurking, trying to trip him up and make him look ridiculous. But even when he fell, it was so slow and gentle that he could put out his powerful arms and push himself up to a standing position before his body actually hit the ground.

"I love it here!" he said to his wife, dozens of times each day. She smiled and tried to remind him that it was only for three more weeks.

At dinner one evening in Moonbase's grander restaurant (there were only two, not counting cafeterias) his earthly muscles proved too strong for the Moon when he rammed their half-finished bottle of wine back into its aluminum ice bucket. The bucket tipped and fell off the edge of the table. But Rolando snatched it with one hand in the midst of its languid fall toward the floor and with a smile and a flourish deposited the bucket with the bottle still in it back on the table before a drop had spilled.

"I love it here," he repeated for the fortieth time that day.

Gradually, though, his euphoric mood sank. The circus began giving abbreviated performances inside its Big Top, and Rolando stood helplessly pinned to the ground while the spotlights picked out the young fliers in their skintight costumes as they soared slowly, dreamily through the air between one trapeze and the next, twisting, spinning, somersaulting in the soft lunar gravity in ways that no one had ever done before. The audience gasped and cheered and gave them standing ovations. Rolando stood rooted near one of the tent's entrances, deep in shadow, wearing a tourist's pale green coveralls, choking with envy and frustrated rage.

The crowds were small—there were only a few thousand people living at Moonbase, plus perhaps another thousand tourists—but they shook the plastic tent with their roars of delight.

Rolando watched a few performances, then stayed away. But he noticed at the Olympic-sized pool that raw teenagers were diving from a thirty-meter platform and doing half a dozen somersaults as they fell languidly in the easy gravity. Even when they hit the water the splashes they made rose lazily and then fell back into the pool so leisurely that it seemed like a slow-motion film.

Anyone can be an athlete here, Rolando realized as he watched tourists flying on rented wings through the upper reaches of the Main Plaza's vaulted dome.

Children could easily do not merely Olympic, but Olympian feats of acrobatics. Rolando began to dread the possibility of seeing a youngster do a quadruple somersault from a standing start.

"Anyone can defy gravity here," he complained to his wife, silently adding, Anyone but me.

It made him morose to realize that feats which had taken him a lifetime to accomplish could be learned by a toddler in half an hour. And soon he would have to return to Earth with its heavy, oppressive, mocking gravity.

I know you're waiting for me, he said to gravity. You're going to kill me—if I don't do the job for myself first.

Two nights before they were due to depart, they were the dinner guests of the chief administrator and several of his staff. As formal an occasion as Moonbase ever has, the men wore sport jackets and turtleneck shirts, the women real dresses and jewelry. The administrator told hoary old stories of his childhood yearning to be in the circus. Rolando remained modestly silent, even when the administrator spoke glowingly of how he had admired the daring feats of the Great Rolando—many years ago.

After dinner, back in their apartment, Rolando turned on his wife. "You got them to invite us up here, didn't you?"

She admitted, "The bionics company told me that they were going to end your consulting fee. They want to give up on you! I asked them to let us come here to see if your leg would be better in low gravity."

"And then we go back to Earth."

"Yes."

"Back to *real* gravity. Back to my being a cripple!"

"I was hoping . . ." Her voice broke and she sank onto the bed, crying.

Suddenly Rolando's anger was overwhelmed by a searing, agonizing sense of shame. All these years she had been trying so hard, standing between him and the rest of the world, protecting him, sheltering him. And for what? So that he could scream at her for the rest of his life?

He could not bear it any longer.

Unable to speak, unable even to reach his hand out to comfort her, he turned and lumbered out of the apartment, leaving his wife weeping alone.

He knew where he had to be, where he could finally put an end to this humiliation and misery. He made his way to the Big Top.

A stubby gunmetal-gray robot stood guard at the main entrance, its sensors focusing on Rolando like the red glowing eyes of a spider.

"No access at this time except to members of the circus troupe," it said in a synthesized voice.

"I am the Great Rolando."

"One moment for voiceprint identification," said the robot, then, "Approved."

Rolando swept past the contraption with a snort of contempt.

The Big Top was empty at this hour. Tomorrow they would start to dismantle it. The next day they would head back to Earth.

Rolando walked slowly, stiffly to the base of the ladder that reached up to the trapezes. The spotlights were shut down. The only illumination inside the tent came from the harsh working lights spotted here and there.

Rolando heaved a deep breath and stripped off his jacket. Then, gripping one of the ladder's rungs, he began to climb: good leg first, then the artificial leg. He could feel no difference between them. His body was only one-sixth its earthly weight, of course, but still the artificial leg behaved exactly as his normal one.

He reached the topmost platform. Holding tightly to the side rail he peered down into the gloomy shadows a hundred feet below.

With a slow, ponderous nod of his head the Great Rolando finally admitted what he had kept buried inside him all these long anguished years. Finally the concealed truth emerged and stood naked before him. With tear-filled eyes he saw its reality.

He had been living a lie all these years. He had been

blaming gravity for his own failure. Now he understood with precise, final clarity that it was not gravity that had destroyed his life.

It was fear.

He stood rooted on the high platform, trembling with the memory of falling, plunging, screaming terror. He knew that this fear would live within him always, for the remainder of his life. It was too strong to overcome; he was a coward, probably had always been a coward, all his life. All his life.

Without consciously thinking about it Rolando untied one of the trapezes and gripped the rough surface of its taped bar. He did not bother with resin. There would be no need.

As if in a dream he swung out into the empty air, feeling the rush of wind ruffling his gray hair, hearing the creak of the ropes beneath his weight.

Once, twice, three times he swung back and forth, kicking higher each time. He grunted with the unaccustomed exertion. He felt sweat trickling from his armpits.

Looking down, he saw the hard ground so far below. One more fall, he told himself. Just let go and that will end it forever. End the fear. End the shame.

"Teach me!"

The voice boomed like cannon fire across the empty tent. Rolando felt every muscle in his body tighten.

On the opposite platform, before him, stood the chief administrator, still wearing his dinner jacket.

"Teach me!" he called again. "Show me how to do it. Just this once, before you have to leave."

Rolando hung by his hands, swinging back and forth. The younger man's figure standing on the platform came closer, closer, then receded, dwindled as inertia carried Rolando forward and back, forward and back.

"No one will know," the administrator pleaded through

the shadows. "I promise you; I'll never tell a soul. Just show me how to do it. Just this once."

"Stand back," Rolando heard his own voice call. It startled him.

Rolando kicked once, tried to judge the distance and account for the lower gravity as best as he could, and let go of the bar. He soared too far, but the strong composite mesh at the rear of the platform caught him, yieldingly, and he was able to grasp the side railing and stand erect before the young administrator could reach out and steady him.

"We both have a lot to learn," said the Great Rolando. "Take off your jacket."

For more than an hour the two men swung high through the silent shadowy air. Rolando tried nothing fancy, no leaps from one bar to another, no real acrobatics. It was tricky enough just landing gracefully on the platform in the strange lunar gravity. The administrator did exactly as Rolando instructed him. For all his youth and desire to emulate a circus star, he was no daredevil. It satisfied him completely to swing side by side with the Great Rolando, to share the same platform.

"What made you come here tonight?" Rolando asked as they stood gasping sweatily on the platform between turns.

"The security robot reported your entry. Strictly routine, I get all such reports piped to my quarters. But I figured this was too good a chance to miss!"

Finally, soaked with perspiration, arms aching and fingers raw and cramping, they made their way down the ladder to the ground. Laughing.

"I'll never forget this," the administrator said. "It's the high point of my life."

"Mine too," said Rolando fervently. "Mine too."

Two days later the administrator came to the rocket

terminal to see the circus troupe off. Taking Rolando and his wife to one side, he said in a low voice that brimmed with happiness, "You know, we're starting to accept retired couples for permanent residence here at Moonbase."

Rolando's wife immediately responded, "Oh, I'm not ready to retire yet."

"Nor I," said Rolando. "I'll stay with the circus for a few years more, I think. There might still be time for me to make a comeback."

"Still," said the administrator, "when you do want to retire . . ."

Mrs. Rolando smiled at him. "I've noticed that my face looks better in this lower gravity. I probably wouldn't need a facelift if we come to live here."

They laughed together.

The rest of the troupe was filing into the rocket that would take them back to Earth. Rolando gallantly held his wife's arm as she stepped up the ramp and ducked through the hatch. Then he turned to the administrator and asked swiftly:

"What you told me about gravity all those years ago—is it really true? It is really universal? There's no way around it?"

"Afraid not," the administrator answered. "Someday gravity will make the Sun collapse. It might even make the entire universe collapse."

Rolando nodded, shook the man's hand, then followed his wife to his seat inside the rocket's passenger compartment. As he listened to the taped safety lecture and strapped on his safety belt he thought to himself: So gravity will get us all in the end.

Then he smiled grimly. But not yet. Not yet.

Crisis of the Month

Although it is often difficult to admit it, writers do not work entirely alone. True, the *hard* work of actually composing a story, word by painstaking word, sentence by agonizing sentence, is almost always done in complete solitude. Nobody there except you and your writing instrument. (And the characters who are boiling out of your brain.) When the task of composition is going on, no writer wants anyone else in sight. Or sound, especially sound. Telephone rings, spousal queries, even dogs yapping outside can drive a writer to distraction. If it happens often enough, mayhem or murder can be the result. Divorce, more often.

But other persons contribute to the development of a story, some before the writing begins, some afterward. Sometimes these contributions are beneficial, sometimes harmful. The successful writer learns to be sensitive to the words of others: accept the good ideas with as much grace as you are capable of; reject the bad advice with equal tact. If you can.

"Crisis of the Month" began with my wife's griping about the hysterical manner in which the news media report on the day's events. Veteran newscaster Linda Ellerbee calls the technique "anxiety news." Back in journalism school (so long ago that spelling was considered important) I was taught that "good news is no news." Today's media take this advice to extremes: no matter what the story, there is a down side to it that can be emphasized.

So when my darling and very perceptive wife complained about the utterly negative way in which the media presented the day's news, I quipped, "I can see the day when science finally finds out how to make people immortal. The media will do stories about the sad plight of the funeral directors."

My wife is also one of the top literary agents in the business. She immediately suggested, "Why don't you write a story about that?"

Thus the origin of "Crisis of the Month."

Notice, as you read the story, that it has nothing to do with achieving immortality or with funeral directors. But that is where the idea originally sprang from.

When I had finished the story I sent it to Ed Ferman, who was then the editor as well as the publisher of *The Magazine of Fantasy and Science Fiction*. Ed sent it back with the comment that the ending did not entirely please him. He was not happy with the "power name" that my protagonist had chosen for himself. Of course, I thought that Ed had gone 'round the bend. Obviously he was wrong. The story was perfect just as I had written it. Who the hell is he to tell me the ending needs improvement? What right has *any* editor to make stupid suggestions about a writer's beautiful carefully crafted prose?

Well, of course, no one has the right to make stupid suggestions. That is, maybe they have the right to make stupid suggestions but they shouldn't do it and certainly a professional writer shouldn't be burdened with such nonsense.

Ah, but what if the suggestion is not stupid?

I thought about Ed's suggestion, stewed in my own juices while I attended to other things (such as the novel I was then working on) and finally concluded that maybe—just maybe—

there might be a tiny bit of justification in Ed's suggestion. I changed the ending. Ed bought the story. You can read it here just as he published it in *F&SF*.

The point is, *all* suggestions to change a story you have written are going to sound stupid, vile, villainous, or worse when you first hear them. You are emotionally wrapped (rapt?) in your story. Suggesting changes is like suggesting you undergo surgery.

But some suggestions are worthwhile. Ed's certainly was. The problem is that many times an editor sees something entirely different from the writer's vision of what is in the story. It happens with novels, too. Sometimes the editor is off-base and the writer is right. But the terrible temptation, after the first wave of fury dies away, is to believe that the editor knows more, is smarter, has a more unbiased view than the writer. That is not always the case.

The even more terrible temptation is to take the editor's word as golden, make the suggested changes, and sell the story. After all, even if the advice was atrocious and makes garbage out of your story, at least you'll get paid for it. You can always write another story. The damage this one does to your reputation won't be all that bad, most likely.

Yet writers have been ruined by bad editorial advice. It may not happen often, but it happens. And it happens most often to new writers, youngsters or even older persons who are just starting to write fiction. There is no way to tell how many promising careers have been blighted by poor editors.

I seem to be picking on the editors. Bad advice can come from friends, family, and colleagues, too. But an editor gets paid for a presumed knowledge of the business. Some editors are taking their paychecks under false pretenses. Fortunately, in the science-fiction field, most of the magazine editors are knowledgeable and hardworking. Or at least one of those two. That's an advantage that you do not always find in other magazine fields.

Unfortunately, most of the book editors—in all fields—are overworked by their publishers. They do not have the time to work carefully with all the projects they are handling. This means that the new writers, the unknowns, get short shrift. Manuscripts from newcomers are either fielded out to the least experienced members of the editorial staff or returned unread. Even books that are accepted do not receive the careful, helpful kind of line-editing that turns a good manuscript into a gem. That kind of tender loving editorial care is virtually extinct among the major publishers.

How can you tell good, workable suggestions from crap? How can you tell when an editor, or a spouse, or a friend, or a fellow workshop participant is talking nonsense and when he or she is laying pearls of wisdom at your feet?

It ain't easy. Even after thirty-some years in the business, it is never easy.

Two things you learn with experience, though. First, you learn to calibrate individuals. When you make the suggested changes and the story comes out worse than before, you tend to stop listening to that individual's advice. It takes time to gain this experience. Time and sweat and blood. All of which costs you money: money that you fail to make because your story has been worsened; money that you fail to make because you've been tinkering with your old story instead of sending it on to another market and using your energies to start a new story.

The other thing you learn is to trust your own instincts. A negative criticism of your story stirs two simultaneous and contradictory emotions. You know the criticism is wrong because the story is perfect. And you know the criticism is right because the story stinks. It happens every time. Over the years, though, you learn to trust your gut feeling—after that first flare of hurt and anger dies away.

If you feel strongly that the story is right and the criticism wrong, ignore the criticism and send the story to another market. If it comes bouncing back several times, though, with pretty much the same criticism on each rejection, you'd better think seriously about listening to the advice you are getting.

This has taken us a long way from the origins of "Crisis of the Month," which is supposed to be a mildly funny tale. Thanks to my agent and my editor, that is.

While I crumpled the paper note that someone had slipped into my jacket pocket, Jack Armstrong drummed his fingers on the immaculately gleaming expanse of the pseudomahogany conference table.

"Well," he said testily, "ladies and gentlemen, doesn't one of you have a possibility? An inkling? An idea?"

No one spoke. I left the wadded note in my pocket and placed both my hands conspicuously on the tabletop. Armstrong drummed away in abysmal silence. I guess once he had actually looked like The All-American Boy. Now, many face-lifts and body remodelings later, he looked more like a moderately well-preserved dummy.

"Nothing at all, gentlemen and ladies?" He always made certain to give each sex the first position fifty percent of the time. Affirmative action was a way of life with our Boss.

"Very well then. We will Delphi the problem."

That broke the silence. Everyone groaned.

"There's nothing else to be done," the Boss insisted. "We must have a crisis by Monday morning. It is now . . ." he glanced at the digital readout built into the tabletop, ". . . three-eighteen P.M. Friday. We will not leave this office until we have a crisis to offer."

We knew it wouldn't do a bit of good, but we groaned all over again.

The Crisis Command Center was the best-kept secret in

the world. No government knew of our existence. Nor did the people, of course. In fact, in all the world's far-flung news media, only a select handful of the topmost executives knew of the CCC. Those few, those precious few, that band of brothers and sisters—they were our customers. The reason for our being. They paid handsomely. And they protected the secret of our work even from their own news staffs.

Our job, our sacred duty, was to select the crisis that would be the focus of worldwide media attention for the coming month. Nothing more. Nothing less.

In the old days, when every network, newspaper, magazine, news service, or independent station picked out its own crises, things were always in a jumble. Sure, they would try to focus on one or two surefire headline-makers: a nuclear power–plant disaster or the fear of one, a new disease like AIDS or Chinese Rot, a war, terrorism, things like that.

The problem was, there were so many crises springing up all the time, so many threats and threats of threats, so much blood and fire and terror, that people stopped paying attention. The news scared the livers out of them. Sales of newspapers and magazines plunged toward zero. Audiences for news shows, even the revered network evening shows, likewise plummeted.

It was Jack Armstrong—a much younger, more handsome and vigorous All-American Boy—who came up with the idea of the Crisis Command Center. Like all great ideas, it was basically simple.

Pick one crisis each month and play it for all it's worth. Everywhere. In all the media. Keep it scary enough to keep people listening, but not so terrifying that they'll run away and hide.

And it worked! Worked to the point where the CCC (or Cee-Cubed, as some of our analysts styled it) was truly the command center for all the media of North America. And thereby, of course, the whole world.

But on this particular Friday afternoon, we were stumped. And I had that terrifying note crumpled in my pocket. A handwritten note, on paper, no less. Not an electronic communication, but a secret, private, dangerous, seditious note, meant for me and me alone, surreptitiously slipped into my jacket pocket.

"Make big $$$," it scrawled. "Tell all to Feds."

I clasped my hands to keep them from trembling and wondered who, out of the fourteen men and women sitting around the table, had slipped that bomb to me.

Boss Jack had started the Delphi procedure by going down the table, asking each of us board members in turn for the latest news in her or his area of expertise.

He started with the man sitting at his immediate right, Matt Dillon. That wasn't the name he had been born with, naturally; his original name had been Oliver Wolchinsky. But in our select little group, once you earn your spurs (no pun intended) you are entitled to a "power name," a name that shows you are a person of rank and consequence. Most power names were chosen, of course, from famous media characters.

Matt Dillon didn't look like the marshal of Dodge City. Or even the one-time teen screen-idol. He was short, pudgy, bald, with bad skin and an irritable temper. He looked, actually, exactly as you would expect an Oliver Wolchinsky to look.

But when Jack Armstrong said, "We shall begin with you," he added, "Matthew."

Matt Dillon was the CCC expert on energy problems. He always got to his feet when he had something to say. This time he remained with his round rump resting resignedly on the caramel cushion of his chair.

"The outlook is bleak," said Matt Dillon. "Sales of the

new space-manufactured solar cells are still climbing. Individual homes, apartment buildings, condos, factories—everybody's plastering their roofs with them and generating their own electricity. No pollution, no radiation, nothing for us to latch on to. They don't even make noise!"

"Ah," intoned our All-American Boy, "but they must be ruining business for electric utility companies. Why not a crisis there?" He gestured hypnotically, and put on an expression of Ratheresque somberness, intoning, "Tonight we will look at the plight of the electrical utilities, men and women who have been discarded in the stampede for cheap energy."

"Trampled," a voice from down the table suggested.

"Ah, yes. Instead of discarded. Thank you." Boss Jack was never one to discourage creative criticism.

But Marshal Matt mewed, "The electric utility companies are doing just fine; they invested in the solar cell development back in '95. They saw the handwriting in the sky."

A collective sigh of disappointment went around the table.

Not one to give up easily, our Mr. Armstrong suggested, "What about oil producers, then? The coal miners?"

"The last coal miner retired on full pension in '98," replied Matt dolefully. "The mines were fully automated by then. Nobody cares if robots are out of work; they just get reprogrammed and moved into another industry. Most of the coal robots are picking fruit in Florida now."

"But the Texas oil and gas—"

Matt headed him off at the pass. "Petroleum prices are steady. They sell the stuff to plastics manufacturers, mostly. Natural gas is the world's major heating fuel. It's clean, abundant, and cheap."

Gloom descended on our conference table.

It deepened as Boss Jack went from one of our experts to the next.

Terrorism had virtually vanished in the booming world economy.

Political scandals were depressingly rare: with computers replacing most bureaucrats there was less cheating going on in government, and far fewer leaks to the media.

The space program was so successful that no less than seven governments of space-faring nations—including our own dear Uncle Sam—had declared dividends for their citizens and a tax amnesty for the year.

Population growth was nicely leveling off. Inflation was minimal. Unemployment was a thing of the past, with an increasingly roboticized work force encouraging humans to invest in robots, accept early retirement, and live off the productivity of their machines.

The closest thing to a crisis in that area was a street brawl in Leningrad between two retired Russian factory workers—aged thirty and thirty-two—who both wanted the very same robot. Potatoes that were much too small for our purposes.

There hadn't been a war since the International Peace-keeping Force had prevented Fiji from attacking Tonga, nearly twelve years ago.

Toxic wastes, in the few remote regions of the world where they still could be found, were being gobbled up by genetically altered bugs (dubbed Rifkins, for some obscure reason) that happily died once they had finished their chore and dissolved into harmless water, carbon dioxide, and ammonia compounds. In some parts of the world the natives had started laundry and cleaning establishments on the sites of former toxic-waste dumps.

I watched and listened in tightening terror as the fickle finger of fate made its way down the table toward me. I was low man on the board, the newest person there, sitting at the end of the table between pert Ms. Mary Richards (sex and family relations were her specialty) and dumpy old Alexis Carrington-Colby (nutrition and diets—it was she who had, three months earlier, come up with the blockbuster of the "mother's milk" crisis).

I hoped desperately that either Ms. Richards or Ms. Carrington-Colby would offer some shred of hope for the rest of the board to nibble on, because I knew I had nothing. Nothing except that damning damaging note in my pocket. What if the Boss found out about it? Would he think I was a potential informer, a philandering fink to the Feds?

With deepening despair I listened to flinty-eyed Alexis offer apologies instead of ideas. It was Mary Richards' turn next, and my heart began fluttering unselfishly. I liked her, I was becoming quite enthusiastic about her, almost to the point of asking her romantic questions. I had never dated a sex specialist, or much of anyone, for that matter. Mary was special to me, and I wanted her to succeed.

She didn't. There was no crisis in sex or family relations.

"Mr. James," said the Boss, like a bell tolling for a funeral.

I wasn't entitled to a power name, since I had only recently been appointed to the board. My predecessor, Marcus Welby, had keeled over right at this conference table the previous month when he realized that there was no medical crisis in sight. His heart broke, literally. It had been his fourth one, but this time the rescue team was just a shade too late to pull him through again.

Thomas K. James is hardly a power name. But it was the one my parents had bestowed on me, and I was determined not to disgrace it. And in particular, not to let anyone know that someone in this conference room thought I was corruptible.

"Mr. James," asked a nearly weeping All-American Boy, "is there anything on the medical horizon—anything at all—that may be useful to us?"

It was clear that Boss Armstrong did not suspect me of incipient treason. Nor did he expect me to solve his problem. I did not fail him in that expectation.

"Nothing worth raising an eyebrow over, sir, I regret to say." Remarkably, my voice stayed firm and steady, despite the dervishes dancing in my stomach.

"There are no new diseases," I went on, "and the old ones are still in rapid retreat. Genetic technicians can correct every identifiable malady in the zygotes, and children are born healthy for life." I cast a disparaging glance at Mr. Cosby, our black environmentalist, and added, "Pollution-related diseases are so close to zero that most disease centers around the world no longer take statistics on them."

"Addiction!" he blurted, the idea apparently springing into his mind unexpectedly. "There must be a new drug on the horizon!"

The board members stirred in their chairs and looked hopeful. For a moment.

I burst their bauble. "Modern chemotherapy detoxifies the addict in about eleven minutes, as some of us know from firsthand experience." I made sure not to stare at Matt Dillon or Alexis Carrington-Colby, who had fought bouts with alcohol and chocolate, respectively. "And, I must unhappily report, cybernetic neural programming is mandatory in every civilized nation in the world; once an addictive personality manifests itself, it can be reprogrammed quickly and painlessly."

The gloom around the table deepened into true depression, tinged with fear.

Jack Armstrong glanced at the miniature display screen discreetly set into the tabletop before him, swiftly checking on his affirmative actions, then said, "Ladies and gentle-men, the situation grows more desperate with each blink of the clock. I suggest we take a five-minute break for R&R"—he meant relief and refreshment—"and then come back with some *new ideas!*"

He fairly roared out the last two words, shocking us all.

I repaired to my office—little more than a cubicle, actually, but it had a door that could be shut. I closed it carefully and hauled the unnerving note out of my pocket. Smoothing it on my desk top, I read it again. It still said:

"Make big $$$. Tell all to Feds."

I wadded it again and with trembling hands tossed it into the disposal can. It flashed silently into healthful ions.

"Are you going to do it?"

I wheeled around to see Mary Richards leaning against my door. She had entered my cubicle silently and closed the door without a sound. At least, no sound I had heard, so intent was I on that menacing message.

"Do what?" Lord, my voice cracked like Henry Aldrich's.

Mary Richards (neé Stephanie Quaid) was a better physical proximation to her power name than anyone of the board members, with the obvious exception of our revered Boss. She was the kind of female for whom the words cute, pert, and vivacious were created. But beneath those skin-deep qualities she had the ruthless drive and calculated intelligence of a sainted Mike Wallace. Had to. Nobody without the same could make it to the CCC board. If that sounds self-congratulatory, so be it. A real Mary Richards, even a Lou Grant, would never get as far as the front door of the CCC.

"Tell all to the Feds," she replied sweetly.

The best thing I could think of was, "I don't know what you're talking about."

"The note you just ionized."

"What note?"

"The note I put in your pocket before the meeting started."

"You?" Until that moment I hadn't known I could hit high C.

Mary positively slinked across my cubicle and draped herself on my desk, showing plenty of leg through her slit skirt. I gulped and slid my swivel chair into the corner.

"It's okay, there's no bugs operating in here. I cleared your office this morning."

I could feel my eyes popping. "Who are you?"

Her smile was all teeth. "I'm a spy, Tommy. A plant. A deep agent. I've been working for the Feds since I was a little girl, rescued from the slums of Chicago by the Rehabilitation Corps from what would have undoubtedly been a life of gang violence and prostitution."

"And they planted you here?"

"They planted me in Cable News when I was a fresh young thing just off the Rehab Farm. It's taken me eleven years to work my way up to the CCC. We always suspected some organization like this was manipulating the news, but we never had the proof. . . ."

"Manipulating!" I was shocked at the word. "We don't manipulate."

"Oh?" She seemed amused at my rightful ire. "Then what do you do?"

"We select. We focus. We manage the news for the benefit of the public."

"In my book, Tommy old pal, that is manipulation. And it's illegal."

"It's . . . out of the ordinary channels," I granted.

Mary shook her pretty chestnut-brown tresses. "It's a

violation of FCC regulations, it makes a mockery of the antitrust laws, to say nothing of the SEC, OSHA, ICC, WARK, and half a dozen other regulatory agencies."

"So you're going to blow the whistle on us."

She straightened up and sat on the edge of my desk. "I can't do that, Tommy. I'm a government agent. An agent provocateur, I'm sure Mr. Armstrong's lawyers will call me."

"Then, what . . . ?"

"You can blow the whistle," she said smilingly. "You're a faithful employee. Your testimony would stand up in court."

"Destroy," I spread my arms in righteous indignation, "all this?"

"It's illegal as hell, Tom," said Mary. "Besides, the rewards for being a good citizen can be very great. Lifetime pension. Twice what you're making here. Uncle Sam is very generous, you know. We'll fix you up with a new identity. We'll move you to wherever you want to live: Samoa, Santa Barbara, St. Thomas, even Schenectady. You could live like a retired financier."

I had to admit, "That is . . . generous."

"And," she added, shyly lowering her eyes, "of course I'll have to retire too, once the publicity of the trial blows my cover. I won't have the same kind of super pension that you'll get, but maybe . . ."

My throat went dry.

Before I could respond, though, the air-raid siren went off, signaling that the meeting was reconvening.

I got up from my chair, but Mary stepped between me and the door.

"What's your answer, Thomas?" she asked, resting her lovely hands on my lapels.

"I . . ." gulping for air, ". . . don't know."

She kissed me lightly on the lips. "Think it over, Thomas, dear. Think hard."

It wasn't my thoughts that were hardening. She left me standing in the cubicle, alone except for my swirling thoughts, spinning through my head like a tornado. I could hear the roaring in my ears. Or was that simply high blood pressure?

The siren howled again, and I bolted to the conference room and took my seat at the end of the table. Mary smiled at me and patted my knee, under the table.

"Very well," said Jack Armstrong, checking his display screen, "gentlemen and ladies. I have come to the conclusion that if we cannot find a crisis anywhere in the news"—and he glared at us, as if he didn't believe there wasn't a crisis out there somewhere, probably right under our noses—"then we must manufacture a crisis."

I had expected that. So had most of the other board members, I could see. What went around the table was not surprise but resignation.

Cosby shook his head wearily. "We did that last month, and it was a real dud. The Anguish of Kindergarten. Audience response was a negative four-point-four. Negative!"

"Then we've got to be more creative!" snapped The All-American Boy.

I glanced at Mary. She was looking at me, smiling her sunniest smile, the one that could allegedly turn the world on. And the answer to the whole problem came to me with that blinding flash that marks true inspiration and minor epileptic fits.

This wasn't epilepsy. I jumped to my feet. "Mr. Armstrong! Fellow board members!"

"What is it, Mr. James?" Boss Jack replied, a hopeful glimmer in his eyes.

The words almost froze in my throat. I looked down at

Mary, still turning out megawatts of smile at me, and nearly choked because my heart had jumped into my mouth.

But only figuratively. "Ladies and gentlemen," (I had kept track, too), "there is a spy among us from the Federal Regulatory Commissions."

A hideous gasp arose, as if they had heard the tinkling bell of a leper.

"This is no time for levity, Mr. James," snapped the Boss. "On the other hand, if this is an attempt at shock therapy to stir the creative juices . . ."

"It's real!" I insisted. Pointing at the smileless Mary Richards, I said, "This woman is a plant from the Feds. She solicited my cooperation. She tried to bribe me to blow the whistle on the CCC!"

They stared. They snarled. They hissed at Mary. She rose coolly from her chair, made a little bow, blew me a kiss, and left the conference room.

Armstrong was already on the intercom phone. "Have security detain her and get our legal staff to interrogate her. Do it now!"

Then the Boss got to his feet, way down there at the other end of the table, and fixed me with his steeliest gaze. He said not a word, but clapped his hands together, once, twice . . .

And the entire board stood up for me and applauded. I felt myself blushing, but it felt good. Warming. My first real moment in the sun.

The moment ended too soon. We all sat down and the gloom began to gray over my sunshine once more.

"It's too bad, Mr. James, that you didn't find a solution to our problem rather than a pretty government mole."

"Ah, but sir," I replied, savoring the opportunity for *le mot just,* "I have done exactly that."

"What?"

"You mean . . . ?"

"Are you saying that you've done it?"

I rose once more, without even glancing at the empty chair at my left.

"I have a crisis, sir," I announced quietly, humbly.

Not a word from any of them. They all leaned forward, expectantly, hopefully, yearningly.

"The very fact that we—the leading experts in the field—can find no crisis is in itself a crisis," I told them.

They sighed, as if a great work of art had suddenly been unveiled.

"Think of the crisis-management teams all around the world who are idle! Think of the psychologists and the therapists who stand ready to help their fellow man and woman, yet have nothing to do! Think of the vast teams of news reporters, camera persons, editors, producers, publishers, even gofers, the whole vast panoply of men and women who have dedicated their lives to bringing the latest crisis into the homes of every human being on this planet—with nothing more to do than report on sports and weather!"

They leaped to their feet and converged on me. They raised me to their shoulders and joyously carried me around the table, shouting praises.

Deliriously happy, I thought to myself, I won't be at the foot of the table anymore. I'll move up. One day, I'll be at the head of the table, where The All-American Boy is now. He's getting old, burnt out. I'll get there. I'll get there!

And I knew what my power name would be. I'd known it from the start, when I'd first been made the lowliest member of the board. I'd been saving it, waiting until the proper moment to make the change.

My power name would be different, daring. A name that bespoke true power, the ability to command, the vision to see far into the future. And it wouldn't even require changing my real name that much. I savored the idea and rolled my power name through my mind again as they carried me around the table. Yes, it would work. It was right.

I would no longer be Thomas K. James. With the slightest, tiniest bit of manipulation my true self would stand revealed: James T. Kirk.

I was on my way.

Sepulcher

One of the great attractions of science fiction is its breadth of scope.

In an essay later in this book you will meet John W. Campbell, Jr., who was the most powerful editor in the history of the science-fiction field. John was a big man, and he was not above using his size and the force of his personality to drive home the points he wanted to make. He often compared science fiction to other forms of literature by spreading his long arms wide and declaiming, "This is science fiction! All the universe, past, present, and future." Then he would hold up a thumb and forefinger about half an inch apart and say, "This is all other kinds of fiction."

By that he meant that all the other kinds of fiction restrict themselves to the here and now, or to the known past. All other forms of fiction are set here on Earth, under a sky that is blue and ground that is solid beneath your feet. Science fiction deals with all of creation, of which our Earth and our time is merely a small part. Science fiction can vault far into the future or deep into the past.

Indeed, science fiction has often been called "the literature of ideas." This has been both its strength and its curse. All too often the idea takes center stage and all the other considerations of good fiction, such as characterization, plot, mood, color, etc., become weak and pale. In its worst manifestation, the supremacy of the idea generates the "gimmick" story, in which a brilliant protagonist meets a problem that has stumped everybody else and solves the problem without hardly raising a sweat. Gimmick stories are predictable, their characters usually wooden. Such stories are essentially vehicles for the author to show off how bright he or she is.

Yet the idea content of science fiction gives the field enormous power and drive, when the ideas are properly matched by characterizations and all the other facets of good fiction. That is the underlying challenge of science fiction: to combine dazzling ideas with superb characters.

"Sepulcher" began as an idea story. For years I had a tiny scrap of paper tucked in my "Ideas" file. It read "Perfect artwork. Everyone sees themselves in it."

The idea intrigued me, but the reason that scrap of paper stayed in my file was that I knew the idea by itself was not sufficient for a good story. A good story needs believable characters in conflict.

As I mulled over the basic idea, I reasoned that the story would need several characters, so that the reader can see how this work of art affects different people. I began to see that the artwork would have to be an alien artifact. If a human being could create a work of art so powerful that everyone who sees it experiences a soul-shattering self-revelation, then the story would have to be about the artist and the power he or she gains over the rest of humankind.

That might make a terrific novel someday. But I was more interested in a short story about the work of art itself—and several people who are deeply, fundamentally changed by it.

I settled on three characters: a former soldier who has become a kind of holy man; a hard-driving man of vast wealth; and an artist who is near the end of her life. Each of them undergoes a transformation when he or she sees the alien artwork.

Notice, as you read the story, that much of the "action" takes place offstage. The soldier has already been transformed when the story begins. The billionaire's experience is offstage. We see only the artist and her moment of truth as she sees the artwork and is transformed by it.

The artist, incidentally, is a character I originally wrote about in an earlier story. When I began seriously to develop "Sepulcher," she presented herself to me as the perfect character to serve as the focal point of this tale.

In the final analysis, "Sepulcher" is a story that deals with the *purpose* of art. Why do we create works of art? Why do painters paint their pictures and writers write their stories? Beneath all the other facets of "Sepulcher," that is the fundamental idea that we examine.

I was a soldier," he said. "Now I am a priest. You may call me Dorn."

Elverda Apacheta could not help staring at him. She had seen cyborgs before, but this . . . person seemed more machine than man. She felt a chill ripple of contempt along her veins. How could a human being allow his body to be disfigured so?

He was not tall; Elverda herself stood several centimeters taller than he. His shoulders were quite broad, though; his torso thick and solid. The left side of his face was engraved metal, as was the entire top of his head: like a skullcap made of finest etched steel.

Dorn's left hand was prosthetic. He made no attempt to disguise it. Beneath the rough fabric of his shabby tunic and threadbare trousers, how much more of him was metal and electrical machinery? Tattered though his clothing was, his calf-length boots were polished to a high gloss.

"A priest?" asked Miles Sterling. "Of what church? What order?"

The half of Dorn's lips that could move made a slight curl. A smile or a sneer, Elverda could not tell.

"I will show you to your quarters," said Dorn. His voice was a low rumble, as if it came from the belly of a beast. It echoed faintly off the walls of rough-hewn rock.

Sterling looked briefly surprised. He was not accustomed to having his questions ignored. Elverda watched his face. Sterling was as handsome as cosmetic surgery could make a person appear: chiseled features, earnest sky-blue eyes, straight of spine, long of limb, athletically flat midsection. Yet there was a faint smell of corruption about him, Elverda thought. As if he were dead inside and already beginning to rot.

The tension between the two men seemed to drain the energy from Elverda's aged body. "It has been a long journey," she said. "I am very tired. I would welcome a hot shower and a long nap."

"Before you see it?" Sterling snapped.

"It has taken us months to get here. We can wait a few hours more." Inwardly she marveled at her own words. Once she would have been all fiery excitement. Have the years taught you patience? No, she realized. Only weariness.

"Not me!" Sterling said. Turning to Dorn, "Take me to it now. I've waited long enough. I want to see it now."

Dorn's eyes, one as brown as Elverda's own, the other a red electronic glow, regarded Sterling for a lengthening moment.

"Well?" Sterling demanded.

"I am afraid, sir, that the chamber is sealed for the next twelve hours. It will be imposs—"

"Sealed? By whom? On whose authority?"

"The chamber is self-controlled. Whoever made the artifact installed the controls, as well."

"No one told me about that," said Sterling.

Dorn replied, "Your quarters are down this corridor."

He turned almost like a solid block of metal, shoulders and hips together, head unmoving on those wide shoulders, and started down the central corridor. Elverda fell in step alongside his metal half, still angered at his self-desecration. Yet despite herself, she thought of what a challenge it would be to sculpt him. If I were younger, she told herself. If I were not so close to death. Human and inhuman, all in one strangely fierce figure.

Sterling came up on Dorn's other side, his face red with barely suppressed anger.

They walked down the corridor in silence, Sterling's weighted shoes clicking against the uneven rock floor. Dorn's boots made hardly any noise at all. Half machine he may be, Elverda thought, but once in motion he moves like a panther.

The asteroid's inherent gravity was so slight that Sterling needed the weighted footgear to keep himself from stumbling ridiculously. Elverda, who had spent most of her long life in low-gravity environments, felt completely at home. The corridor they were walking through was actually a tunnel, shadowy and mysterious, or perhaps a natural chimney vented through the rocky body by escaping gases eons ago when the asteroid was still molten. Now it was cold, chill enough to make Elverda shudder. The rough ceiling was so low she wanted to stoop, even though the rational side of her mind knew it was not necessary.

Soon, though, the walls smoothed out and the ceiling grew higher. Humans had extended the tunnel, squaring it with laser precision. Doors lined both walls now and the ceiling glowed with glareless, shadowless light. Still she hugged herself against the chill that the others did not seem to notice.

They stopped at a wide double door. Dorn tapped out the entrance code on the panel set into the wall and the doors slid open.

"Your quarters, sir," he said to Sterling. "You may, of course, change the privacy code to suit yourself."

Sterling gave a curt nod and strode through the open doorway. Elverda got a glimpse of a spacious suite, carpeting on the floor and hologram windows on the walls.

Sterling turned in the doorway to face them. "I expect you to call for me in twelve hours," he said to Dorn, his voice hard.

"Eleven hours and fifty-seven minutes," Dorn replied.

Sterling's nostrils flared and he slid the double doors shut.

"This way." Dorn gestured with his human hand. "I'm afraid your quarters are not as sumptuous as Mr. Sterling's."

Elverda said, "I am his guest. He is paying all the bills."

"You are a great artist. I have heard of you."

"Thank you."

"For the truth? That is not necessary."

I was a great artist, Elverda said to herself. Once. Long ago. Now I am an old woman waiting for death.

Aloud, she asked, "Have you seen my work?"

Dorn's voice grew heavier. "Only holograms. Once I set out to see *The Rememberer* for myself, but—other matters intervened."

"You were a soldier then?"

"Yes. I have only been a priest since coming to this place."

Elverda wanted to ask him more, but Dorn stopped before a blank door and opened it for her. For an instant she thought he was going to reach for her with his prosthetic hand. She shrank away from him.

"I will call for you in eleven hours and fifty-six minutes," he said, as if he had not noticed her revulsion.

"Thank you."

He turned away, like a machine pivoting.

"Wait," Elverda called. "Please— How many others are here? Everything seems so quiet."

"There are no others. Only the three of us."

"But—"

"I am in charge of the security brigade. I ordered the others of my command to go back to our spacecraft and wait there."

"And the scientists? The prospector family that found this asteroid?"

"They are in Mr. Sterling's spacecraft, the one you arrived in," said Dorn. "Under the protection of my brigade."

Elverda looked into his eyes. Whatever burned in them, she could not fathom.

"Then we are alone here?"

Dorn nodded solemnly. "You and me—and Mr. Sterling, who pays all the bills." The human half of his face remained as immobile as the metal. Elverda could not tell if he was trying to be humorous or bitter.

"Thank you," she said. He turned away and she closed the door.

Her quarters consisted of a single room, comfortably warm but hardly larger than the compartment on the ship they had come in. Elverda saw that her meager travel bag was already sitting on the bed, her worn old drawing computer resting in its travel-smudged case on the desk. Elverda stared at the computer case as if it were accusing her. I should have left it home, she thought. I will never use it again.

A small utility robot, hardly more than a glistening drum of metal and six gleaming arms folded like a praying mantis's, stood mutely in the farthest corner. Elverda stared at it. At least it was entirely a machine; not a self-mutilated human being. To take the most beautiful form in the universe and turn it into a hybrid mechanism, a travesty of humanity. Why did he do it? So he could be a better soldier? A more efficient killing machine?

And why did he send all the others away? she asked herself while she opened the travel bag. As she carried her toiletries to the narrow alcove of the bathroom, a new thought struck her. Did he send them away before he saw the artifact, or afterward? Has he even seen it? Perhaps . . .

Then she saw her reflection in the mirror above the washbasin. Her heart sank. Once she had been called regal, stately, a goddess made of copper. Now she looked withered, dried up, bone thin, her face a geological map of too many years of living, her flight coveralls hanging limply on her emaciated frame.

You are old, she said to her image. Old and aching and tired.

It is the long trip, she told herself. You need to rest. But the other voice in her mind laughed scornfully. You've done nothing but rest for the entire time it's taken to reach this piece of rock. You are ready for the permanent rest; why deny it?

She had been teaching at the university on Luna, the closest she could get to Earth after a long lifetime of living in low-gravity environments. Close enough to see the world of her birth, the only world of life and warmth in the solar system, the only place where a person could walk out in the sunshine and feel its warmth soaking your bones, smell the fertile earth nurturing its bounty, feel a cool breeze plucking at your hair.

But she had separated herself from Earth permanently. She had stood at the shore of Titan's methane sea; from an orbiting spacecraft she had watched the surging clouds of Jupiter swirl their overpowering colors; she had carved the kilometer-long rock of *The Rememberer.* But she could no longer stand in the village of her birth, at the edge of the Pacific's booming surf, and watch the soft white clouds form shapes of imaginary animals.

Her creative life was long finished. She had lived too long; there were no friends left, and she had never had a family. There was no purpose to her life, no reason to do anything except go through the motions and wait. At the university she was no longer truly working at her art but helping students who had the fires of inspiration burning fresh and hot inside them. Her life was one of vain regrets for all the things she had not accomplished, for all the failures she could recall. Failures at love; those were the bitterest. She was praised as the solar system's greatest artist: the sculptress of *The Rememberer,* the creator of the first great ionospheric painting, The Virgin of the Andes. She was respected, but not loved. She felt empty, alone, barren. She had nothing to look forward to, absolutely nothing.

Then Miles Sterling swept into her existence. A lifetime younger, bold, vital, even ruthless, he stormed her academic tower with the news that an alien artifact had been discovered deep in the asteroid belt.

"It's some kind of art form," he said, desperate with excitement. "You've got to come with me and see it."

Trying to control the long-forgotten longing that stirred within her, Elverda had asked quietly, "Why do I have to go with you, Mr. Sterling? Why me? I'm an old wo—"

"You are the greatest artist of our time," he had snapped. "You've *got* to see this! Don't bullshit me with false modesty. You're the only other person in the whole whirling solar system who *deserves* to see it!"

"The only other person besides whom?" she had asked.

He had blinked with surprise. "Why, besides me, of course."

So now we are on this nameless asteroid, waiting to see the alien artwork. Just the three of us. The richest man in the solar system. An elderly artist who has outlived her usefulness. And a cyborg soldier who has cleared everyone else away.

He claims to be a priest, Elverda remembered. A priest who is half machine. She shivered as if a cold wind surged through her.

A harsh buzzing noise interrupted her thoughts. Looking into the main part of the room, Elverda saw that the phone screen was blinking red in rhythm to the buzzing.

"Phone," she called out.

Sterling's face appeared on the screen instantly. "Come to my quarters," he said. "We have to talk."

"Give me an hour. I need—"

"Now."

Elverda felt her brows rise haughtily. Then the strength sagged out of her. He has bought the right to command you, she told herself. He is quite capable of refusing to allow you to see the artifact.

"Now," she agreed.

Sterling was pacing across the plush carpeting when she arrived at his quarters. He had changed from his flight coveralls to a comfortably loose royal blue pullover and expensive genuine twill slacks. As the doors slid shut behind her, he stopped in front of a low couch and faced her squarely.

"Do you know who this Dorn creature is?"

Elverda answered, "Only what he has told us."

"I've checked him out. My staff in the ship has a complete file on him. He's the butcher who led the *Chrysalis* massacre, fourteen years ago."

"He . . ."

"Eleven hundred men, women, and children. Slaughtered. He was the man who commanded the attack."

"He said he had been a soldier."

"A mercenary. A cold-blooded murderer. He was working for Toyama then. The *Chrysalis* was their habitat. When its population voted for independence, Toyama put him in charge of a squad to bring them back into line. He killed them all; turned off their air and let them all die."

Elverda felt shakily for the nearest chair and sank into it. Her legs seemed to have lost all their strength.

"His name was Harbin then. Dorik Harbin."

"Wasn't he brought to trial?"

"No. He ran away. Disappeared. I always thought Toyama helped to hide him. They take care of their own, they do. He must have changed his name afterward. Nobody would hire the butcher, not even Toyama."

"His face . . . half his body . . ." Elverda felt terribly weak, almost faint. "When . . . ?"

"Must have been after he ran away. Maybe it was an attempt to disguise himself."

"And now he is working for you." She wanted to laugh at the irony of it, but did not have the strength.

"He's got us trapped on this chunk of rock! There's nobody else here except the three of us."

"You have your staff in your ship. Surely they would come if you summoned them."

"His security squad's been ordered to keep everybody except you and me off the asteroid. He gave those orders."

"You can countermand them, can't you?"

For the first time since she had met Miles Sterling, he looked unsure of himself. "I wonder," he said.

"Why?" Elverda asked. "Why is he doing this?"

"That's what I intend to find out." Sterling strode to the phone console. "Harbin!" he called. "Dorik Harbin. Come to my quarters at once."

Without even an eyeblink's delay the phone's computer-synthesized voice replied, "Dorik Harbin no longer exists. Transferring your call to Dorn."

Sterling's blue eyes snapped at the phone's blank screen.

"Dorn is not available at present," the phone's voice said. "He will call for you in eleven hours and thirty-two minutes."

"God *damn* it!" Sterling smacked a fist into the open palm of his other hand. "Get me the officer on watch aboard the *Sterling Eagle*."

"All exterior communications are inoperable at the present time," replied the phone.

"That's impossible!"

"All exterior communications are inoperable at the present time," the phone repeated, unperturbed.

Sterling stared at the empty screen, then turned slowly toward Elverda. "He's cut us off. We're really trapped here."

Elverda felt the chill of cold metal clutching at her. Perhaps Dorn is a madman, she thought. Perhaps he is my death, personified.

"We've got to do something!" Sterling nearly shouted.

Elverda rose shakily to her feet. "There is nothing that we can do, for the moment. I am going to my quarters to take a nap. I believe that Dorn, or Harbin, or whatever his identity is, will call on us when he is ready to."

"And do what?"

"Show us the artifact," she replied, silently adding, I hope.

Legally, the artifact and the entire asteroid belonged to Sterling Enterprises, Ltd. It had been discovered by a family—husband, wife, and two sons, ages five and three—that made a living from searching out iron-nickel asteroids and selling the mining rights to the big corporations. They filed their claim to this unnamed asteroid, together with a preliminary description of its ten-kilometer-wide shape, its orbit within the asteroid belt, and a sample analysis of its surface composition.

Six hours after their original transmission reached the commodities-market computer network on Earth—while a fairly spirited bidding war was going on among four major corporations for the asteroid's mineral rights—a new message arrived at the headquarters of the International Astronautical Authority, in London. The message was garbled, fragmentary, obviously made in great haste and at fever excitement. There was an artifact of some sort in a cavern deep inside the asteroid.

One of the faceless bureaucrats buried deep within the IAA's multilayered organization sent an immediate message to an employee of Sterling Enterprises, Ltd. The bureaucrat retired hours later, richer than he had any right to expect, while Miles Sterling personally contacted the prospectors and bought the asteroid outright for enough money to end their prospecting days forever. By the time the decision-makers in the IAA realized that an alien artifact had been discovered they were faced with a fait accompli: the artifact, and the asteroid in which it resided, were the personal property of the richest man in the solar system.

Miles Sterling was no egomaniac. Nor was he a fool. Graciously he allowed the IAA to organize a team of scientists who would inspect this first specimen of alien existence. Even more graciously, Sterling offered to ferry the scientific investigators all the long way to the asteroid at his own expense. He made only one demand, and the

IAA could hardly refuse him. He insisted that he see this artifact himself before the scientists were allowed to view it.

And he brought along the solar system's most honored and famous artist. To appraise the artifact's worth as an art object, he claimed. To determine how much he could deduct from his corporate taxes by donating the thing to the IAA, said his enemies. But over the months of their voyage to the asteroid, Elverda came to the conclusion that buried deep beneath his ruthless business persona was an eager little boy who was tremendously excited at having found a new toy. A toy he intended to possess for himself. An art object, created by alien hands.

For an art object was what the artifact seemed to be. The family of prospectors continued to send back vague, almost irrational reports of what the artifact looked like. The reports were worthless. No two descriptions matched. If the man and woman were to be believed, the artifact did nothing but sit in the middle of a rough-hewn cavern. But they described it differently with every report they sent. It glowed with light. It was darker than deep space. It was a statue of some sort. It was formless. It overwhelmed the senses. It was small enough almost to pick up in one hand. It made the children laugh happily. It frightened their parents. When they tried to photograph it, their transmissions showed nothing but blank screens. Totally blank.

As Sterling listened to their maddening reports and waited impatiently for the IAA to organize its handpicked team of scientists, he ordered his security manager to get a squad of hired personnel to the asteroid as quickly as possible. From corporate facilities on Titan and the moons of Mars, from three separate outposts among the asteroid belt itself, Sterling Enterprises efficiently brought together a brigade of experienced mercenary security troops. They reached the asteroid long before anyone else could, and were under orders to make certain that no one was allowed onto the asteroid before Miles Sterling himself reached it.

"The time has come."

Elverda woke slowly, painfully, like a swimmer struggling for the air and light of the surface. She had been dreaming of her childhood, of the village where she had grown up, the distant snow-capped Andes, the warm night breezes that spoke of love.

"The time has come."

It was Dorn's deep voice, whisper soft. Startled, she flashed her eyes open. She was alone in the room, but Dorn's image filled the phone screen by her bed. The numbers glowing beneath the screen showed that it was indeed time.

"I am awake now," she said to the screen.

"I will be at your door in fifteen minutes," Dorn said. "Will that be enough time for you to prepare yourself?"

"Yes, plenty." The days when she needed time for selecting her clothing and arranging her appearance were long gone.

"In fifteen minutes, then."

"Wait," she blurted. "Can you see me?"

"No. Visual transmission must be keyed manually."

"I see."

"I do not."

A joke? Elverda sat up on the bed as Dorn's image winked out. Is he capable of humor?

She shrugged out of the shapeless coveralls she had worn to bed, took a quick shower, and pulled her best caftan from the travel bag. It was a deep midnight blue, scattered with glittering silver stars. Elverda had made the floor-length gown herself, from fabric woven by her mother long ago. She had painted the stars from her memory of what they had looked like from her native village.

As she slid back her front door she saw Dorn marching down the corridor with Sterling beside him. Despite his longer legs, Sterling seemed to be scampering like a child to keep up with Dorn's steady, stolid steps.

"I *demand* that you reinstate communications with my ship," Sterling was saying, his voice echoing off the corridor walls. "I'll dock your pay for every minute this insubordination continues!"

"It is a security measure," Dorn said calmly, without turning to look at the man. "It is for your own good."

"My own good? Who in hell are you to determine what my own good might be?"

Dorn stopped three paces short of Elverda, made a stiff little bow to her, and only then turned to face his employer.

"Sir: I have seen the artifact. You have not."

"And that makes you better than me?" Sterling almost snarled the words. "Holier, maybe?"

"No," said Dorn. "Not holier. Wiser."

Sterling started to reply, then thought better of it.

"Which way do we go?" Elverda asked in the sudden silence.

Dorn pointed with his prosthetic hand. "Down," he replied. "This way."

The corridor abruptly became a rugged tunnel again, with lights fastened at precisely spaced intervals along the low ceiling. Elverda watched Dorn's half-human face as the pools of shadow chased the highlights glinting off the etched metal, like the Moon racing through its phases every half-minute, over and again.

Sterling had fallen silent as they followed the slanting tunnel downward into the heart of the rock. Elverda heard only the clicking of his shoes, at first, but by concentrating she was able to make out the softer footfalls of Dorn's padded boots and even the whisper of her own slippers.

The air seemed to grow warmer, closer. Or is it my own anticipation? She glanced at Sterling; perspiration beaded his upper lip. The man radiated tense expectation. Dorn glided a few steps ahead of them. He did not seem to be hurrying, yet he was now leading them down the tunnel, like an ancient priest leading two new acolytes—or sacrificial victims.

The tunnel ended in a smooth wall of dull metal.

"We are here."

"Open it up," Sterling demanded.

"It will open itself," replied Dorn. He waited a heartbeat, then added, "Now."

And the metal slid up into the rock above them as silently as if it were a curtain made of silk.

None of them moved. Then Dorn slowly turned toward the two of them and gestured with his human hand.

"The artifact lies twenty-two point nine meters beyond this point. The tunnel narrows and turns to the right. The chamber is large enough to accommodate only one person at a time, comfortably."

"Me first!" Sterling took a step forward.

Dorn stopped him with an upraised hand. The prosthetic hand. "I feel it my duty to caution you—"

Sterling tried to push the hand away; he could not budge it.

"When I first crossed this line, I was a soldier. After I saw the artifact I gave up my life."

"And became a self-styled priest. So what?"

"The artifact can change you. I thought it best that there be no witnesses to your first viewing of it, except for this gifted woman whom you have brought with you. When you first see it, it can be—traumatic."

Sterling's face twisted with a mixture of anger and disgust. "I'm not a mercenary killer. I don't have anything to be afraid of."

Dorn let his hand drop to his side with a faint whine of miniaturized servomotors.

"Perhaps not," he murmured, so low that Elverda barely heard it.

Sterling shouldered his way past the cyborg. "Stay here," he told Elverda. "You can see it when I come back."

He hurried down the tunnel, footsteps staccato.

Then silence.

Elverda looked at Dorn. The human side of his face seemed utterly weary.

"You have seen the artifact more than once, haven't you?"

"Fourteen times," he answered.

"It has not harmed you in any way, has it?"

He hesitated, then replied, "It has changed me. Each time I see it, it changes me more."

"You . . . you really are Dorik Harbin?"

"I was."

"Those people of the *Chrysalis* . . . ?"

"Dorik Harbin killed them all. Yes. There is no excuse for it, no pardon. It was the act of a monster."

"But why?"

"Monsters do monstrous things. Dorik Harbin ingested psychotropic drugs to increase his battle prowess. Afterward, when the battle drugs cleared from his bloodstream and he understood what he had done, Dorik Harbin held a grenade against his chest and set it off."

"Oh my god," Elverda whimpered.

"He was not allowed to die, however. The medical specialists rebuilt his body and he was given a false identity. For many years he lived a sham of life, hiding from the authorities, hiding from his own guilt. He no longer had the courage to kill himself; the pain of his first attempt was far stronger than his own self-loathing. Then he was hired to come to this place. Dorik Harbin looked upon the artifact for the first time, and his true identity emerged at last."

Elverda heard a scuffling sound, like feet dragging, staggering. Miles Sterling came into view, tottering, leaning heavily against the wall of the tunnel, slumping as if his legs could no longer hold him.

"No man . . . no one . . ." He pushed himself forward and collapsed into Dorn's arms.

"Destroy it!" he whispered harshly, spittle dribbling down his chin. "Destroy this whole damned piece of rock! Wipe it out of existence!"

"What is it?" Elverda asked. "What did you see?"

Dorn lowered him to the ground gently. Sterling's feet scrabbled against the rock as if he were trying to run away. Sweat covered his face, soaked his shirt.

"It's . . . beyond . . . ," he babbled. "More . . . than anyone can . . . nobody could stand it . . ."

Elverda sank to her knees beside him. "What has happened to him?" She looked up at Dorn, who knelt on Sterling's other side.

"The artifact."

Sterling suddenly ranted, "They'll find out about me! Everyone will know! It's got to be destroyed! Nuke it! Blast it to bits!" His fists windmilled in the air, his eyes were wild.

"I tried to warn him," Dorn said as he held Sterling's shoulders down, the man's head in his lap. "I tried to prepare him for it."

"What did he see?" Elverda's heart was pounding; she could hear it thundering in her ears. "What is it? What did *you* see?"

Dorn shook his head slowly. "I cannot describe it. I doubt that anyone could describe it—except, perhaps, an artist: a person who has trained herself to see the truth."

"The prospectors—they saw it. Even their children saw it."

"Yes. When I arrived here they had spent eighteen days in the chamber. They left it only when the chamber closed itself. They ate and slept and returned here, as if hypnotized."

"It did not hurt them, did it?"

"They were emaciated, dehydrated. It took a dozen of my strongest men to remove them to my ship. Even the children fought us."

"But—how could . . ." Elverda's voice faded into silence. She looked at the brightly lit tunnel. Her breath caught in her throat.

"Destroy it," Sterling mumbled. "Destroy it before it destroys us! Don't let them find out. They'll know, they'll know, they'll all know." He began to sob uncontrollably.

"You do not have to see it," Dorn said to Elverda. "You can return to your ship and leave this place."

Leave, urged a voice inside her head. Run away. Live out what's left of your life and let it go.

Then she heard her own voice say, as if from a far distance, "I've come such a long way."

"It will change you," he warned.

"Will it release me from life?"

Dorn glanced down at Sterling, still muttering darkly, then returned his gaze to Elverda.

"It will change you," he repeated.

Elverda forced herself to her feet. Leaning one hand against the warm rock wall to steady herself, she said, "I will see it. I must."

"Yes," said Dorn. "I understand."

She looked down at him, still kneeling with Sterling's head resting in his lap. Dorn's electronic eye glowed red in the shadows. His human eye was hidden in darkness.

He said, "I believe your people say, *Vaya con Dios.*"

Elverda smiled at him. She had not heard that phrase in forty years. "Yes. You too. *Vaya con Dios.*" She turned and stepped across the faint groove where the metal door had met the floor.

The tunnel sloped downward only slightly. It turned sharply to the right, Elverda saw, just as Dorn had told them. The light seemed brighter beyond the turn, pulsating almost, like a living heart.

She hesitated a moment before making that final turn. What lay beyond? What difference, she answered herself. You have lived so long that you have emptied life of all its purpose. But she knew she was lying to herself. Her life was devoid of purpose because she herself had made it that way. She had spurned love; she had even rejected friendship when it had been offered. Still, she realized that she wanted to live. Desperately, she wanted to continue living no matter what.

Yet she could not resist the lure. Straightening her spine, she stepped boldly around the bend in the tunnel.

The light was so bright it hurt her eyes. She raised a hand to her brow to shield them and the intensity seemed to decrease slightly, enough to make out the faint outline of a form, a shape, a person . . .

Elverda gasped with recognition. A few meters before her, close enough to reach and touch, her mother sat on the sweet grass beneath the warm summer sun, gently rocking her baby and crooning softly to it.

Mamá! she cried silently. Mamá. The baby—Elverda herself—looked up into her mother's face and smiled.

And the mother was Elverda, a young and radiant Elverda, smiling down at the baby she had never had, tender and loving as she had never been.

Something gave way inside her. There was no pain; rather, it was as if a pain that had throbbed sullenly within her for too many years to count suddenly faded away. As if a wall of implacable ice finally melted and let the warm waters of life flow through her.

Elverda sank to the floor, crying, gushing tears of understanding and relief and gratitude. Her mother smiled at her.

"I love you, Mamá," she whispered. "I love you."

Her mother nodded and became Elverda herself once more. Her baby made a gurgling laugh of pure happiness, fat little feet waving in the air.

The image wavered, dimmed, and slowly faded into emptiness. Elverda sat on the bare rock floor in utter darkness, feeling a strange serenity and understanding warming her soul.

"Are you all right?"

Dorn's voice did not startle her. She had been expecting him to come to her.

"The chamber will close itself in another few minutes," he said. "We will have to leave."

Elverda took his offered hand and rose to her feet. She felt strong, fully in control of herself.

The tunnel outside the chamber was empty.

"Where is Sterling?"

"I sedated him and then called in a medical team to take him back to his ship."

"He wants to destroy the artifact," Elverda said.

"That will not be possible," said Dorn. "I will bring the IAA scientists here from the ship before Sterling awakes and recovers. Once they see the artifact they will not allow it to be destroyed. Sterling may own the asteroid, but the IAA will exert control over the artifact."

"The artifact will affect them—strangely."

"No two of them will be affected in the same manner," said Dorn. "And none of them will permit it to be damaged in any way."

"Sterling will not be pleased with you."

He gestured up the tunnel, and they began to walk back toward their quarters.

"Nor with you," Dorn said. "We both saw him babbling and blubbering like a baby."

"What could he have seen?"

"What he most feared. His whole life had been driven by fear, poor man."

"What secrets he must be hiding!"

"He hid them from himself. The artifact showed him his own true nature."

"No wonder he wants it destroyed."

"He cannot destroy the artifact, but he will certainly want to destroy us. Once he recovers his composure he will want to wipe out the witnesses who saw his reaction to it."

Elverda knew that Dorn was right. She watched his face as they passed beneath the lights, watched the glint of the etched metal, the warmth of the human flesh.

"You knew that he would react this way, didn't you?" she asked.

"No one could be as rich as he is without having demons driving him. He looked into his own soul and recognized himself for the first time in his life."

"You planned it this way!"

"Perhaps I did," he said. "Perhaps the artifact did it for me."

"How could—"

"It is a powerful experience. After I had seen it a few times I felt it was offering me . . ." he hesitated, then spoke the word, "salvation."

Elverda saw something in his face that Dorn had not let show before. She stopped in the shadows between overhead lights. Dorn turned to face her, half machine, standing in the rough tunnel of bare rock.

"You have had your own encounter with it," he said. "You understand now how it can transform you."

"Yes," said Elverda. "I understand."

"After a few times, I came to the realization that there must be thousands of my fellow mercenaries, killed in engagements all through the asteroid belt, still lying where they fell. Or worse yet, floating forever in space, alone, unattended, ungrieved for."

"Thousands of mercenaries?"

"The corporations do not always settle their differences in Earthly courts of law," said Dorn. "There have been many battles out here. Wars that we paid for with our blood."

"Thousands?" Elverda repeated. "I knew that there had been occasional fights out here—but wars? I don't think anyone on Earth knows it's been so brutal."

"Men like Sterling know. They start the wars, and people like me fight them. Exiles, never allowed to return to Earth again once we take the mercenary's pay."

"All those men—killed."

Dorn nodded. "And women. The artifact made me see that it was my duty to find each of those forgotten bodies and give each one a decent final rite. The artifact seemed to be telling me that this was the path of my atonement."

"Your salvation," she murmured.

"I see now, however, that I underestimated the situation."

"How?"

"Sterling. While I am out there searching for the bodies of the slain, he will have me killed."

"No! That's wrong!"

Dorn's deep voice was empty of regret. "It will be simple for him to send a team after me. In the depths of dark space, they will murder me. What I failed to do for myself, Sterling will do for me. He will be my final atonement."

"Never!" Elverda blazed with anger. "I will not permit it to happen."

"Your own life is in danger from him," Dorn said.

"What of it? I am an old woman, ready for death."

"Are you?"

"I was . . . until I saw the artifact."

"Now life is more precious to you, isn't it?"

"I don't want you to die," Elverda said. "You have atoned for your sins. You have borne enough pain."

He looked away, then started up the tunnel again.

"You are forgetting one important factor," Elverda called after him.

Dorn stopped, his back to her. She realized now that the clothes he wore had been his military uniform. He had torn all the insignias and pockets from it.

"The artifact. Who created it? And why?"

Turning back toward her, Dorn answered, "Alien visitors to our solar system created it, unknown ages ago. As to why—you tell me: Why does someone create a work of art?"

"Why would aliens create a work of art that affects human minds?"

Dorn's human eye blinked. He rocked a step backward.

"How could they create an artifact that is a mirror to our souls?" Elverda asked, stepping toward him. "They must have known something about us. They must have been here when there were human beings existing on Earth."

Dorn regarded her silently.

"They may have been here much more recently than you think," Elverda went on, coming closer to him. "They may have placed this artifact here to *communicate* with us."

"Communicate?"

"Perhaps it is a very subtle, very powerful communications device."

"Not an artwork at all."

"Oh yes, of course it's an artwork. All works of art are communications devices, for those who possess the soul to understand."

Dorn seemed to ponder this for long moments. Elverda watched his solemn face, searching for some human expression.

Finally he said, "That does not change my mission, even if it is true."

"Yes it does," Elverda said, eager to save him. "Your mission is to preserve and protect this artifact against Sterling and anyone else who would try to destroy it—or pervert it to his own use."

"The dead call to me," Dorn said solemnly. "I hear them in my dreams now."

"But why be alone in your mission? Let others help you. There must be other mercenaries who feel as you do."

"Perhaps," he said softly.

"Your true mission is much greater than you think," Elverda said, trembling with new understanding. "You have the power to end the wars that have destroyed your comrades, that have almost destroyed your soul."

"End the corporate wars?"

"You will be the priest of this shrine, this sepulcher. I will return to Earth and tell everyone about these wars."

"Sterling and others will have you killed."

"I am a famous artist, they dare not touch me." Then she laughed. "And I am too old to care if they do."

"The scientists—do you think they may actually learn how to communicate with the aliens?"

"Someday," Elverda said. "When our souls are pure enough to stand the shock of their presence."

The human side of Dorn's face smiled at her. He extended his arm and she took it in her own, realizing that she had found her own salvation. Like two kindred souls, like comrades who had shared the sight of death, like mother and son, they walked up the tunnel toward the waiting race of humanity.

Fitting Suits

Science fiction is a marvelous vehicle for social commentary. Trouble is, most of the decision-makers in our society don't read science fiction. We are constantly falling into predicaments and facing crises that could have been avoided if people paid attention to science-fiction stories written decades earlier.

In a sense, science fiction—at its best—serves as a kind of simulations laboratory for society. Like a scientist setting up a controlled experiment, a writer can set up a social situation, stress one particular facet of that society, and see where the extrapolation leads. The classic example of this is Cyril M. Kornbluth's 1951 novelette "The Marching Morons." Based on the simple notion that ignoramuses have more children than geniuses, Kornbluth's tale chillingly foretold the global population problems that the rest of the world began to notice only a generation later.

"Fitting Suits" is a short-short story that was triggered by a news story I read: A civil servant resigned her government post because a citizen sued her personally for allegedly not performing her job properly. That led me to thinking. Which led me to writing.

Always think before you write.

History, as we know, is sometimes made by the unlikeliest of persons. Take Carter C. Carter, for example. All he wanted was immortality. Instead he created paradise.

All of you are too young to remember the America of the late twentieth century, a democracy of the lawyers, by the lawyers, for the lawyers. It was impossible to sneeze in the privacy of your own home without someone suing you as a health menace. Inevitably the lawyers would also sue the home builder for failure to make the structure virus-proof. And the corporation that manufactured your air-conditioning system, wallpaper, carpeting, and facial tissues. To say nothing of the people who sold you your pet dog, cat, and/or goldfish.

It got so bad that in 1988 a public servant resigned her sinecure because of a lawsuit. A social worker employed by a moderate-sized midwestern city was slapped with a personal liability suit for alleged failure to do her job properly. She had advised an unemployed teenaged mother to try to find a job to support herself, since her welfare benefits were running out. Instead, the teenager went to a lawyer and sued the social worker for failure to find her more money.

Rather than face a lawsuit that would have ruined her financially, whether she lost or won, the social worker resigned her position, left the state, and took up a new career. She entered law school. The teenager lived for years off the generous verdict awarded her by a jury of equally unemployed men and women.

This was the America in which Carter C. Carter lived. We have much to thank him for.

He was, of course, totally unaware that he would change the course of history. He had no interest even in the juridical malaise of his time. All he wanted to do was to avoid dying.

Carter C. Carter had an inoperable case of cancer. "The

Big C," it was called in those days. So he turned to another "C," cryonics, as a way to avoid permanent death. When declared clinically dead by a complaisant doctor (a close friend since childhood), Carter C. Carter had himself immersed in a canister of liquid nitrogen to await the happy day when medical science could revive him, cure him, and set him out in society once more, healthily alive.

He left his life savings, a meager $100,000 (it was worth more in those days) in a trust fund to provide for his maintenance while frozen. It would also provide a nest egg once he was awakened. He was banking heavily on compound interest.

His insurance company, however, refused to pay off on his policy, on the grounds that Carter was not finally dead. Mrs. Carter, whose sole inheritance from her husband was his $500,000 life insurance policy, promptly sued the insurance company. The insurance company's lawyers, in turn, sued the Carter estate on the grounds that he was trying to cheat, not death, but the insurance company.

After several years of legal maneuvering the suit came to court. It was decided in favor of the insurance company. Mrs. Carter promptly sued the judge and each individual member of the jury for personal liability on the grounds that they had "willfully and deliberately denied her her legal rights." And caused her intense pain and suffering while doing so.

The judge, near retirement age, had a vision of his pension being eaten up by legal proceedings. He quit the bench and signed a public apology to Mrs. Carter in return for her dropping the suit against him. The jurors, none of them wealthy, quickly settled out of court. The insurance company did likewise, in advance of having its entire board of directors sued.

Mrs. Carter's lawyers, unsatisfied with their share of the loot, looked for bigger game. Fueled by Carter's modest nest egg (Mrs. C. would not let them touch her own money), they began suing members of the National Institutes of Health and the Justice Department, on the grounds that they had failed to provide proper medical and legal grounds for judging the rights of the cryonically undead.

A new fad erupted. Suddenly taxpayers were suing local bureaucrats for personal liability over failure to fill potholes in their streets. In one state the governor and entire legislature were sued for raising taxes to cover a budget imbalance. In another, the state environmental protection agency was sued for failing to regulate the pollution emissions of diesel trucks. The Secretary of Defense was sued simultaneously for invading Mexico and for failing to conquer Mexico. Politicians everywhere were sued for not fulfilling their campaign promises.

Bureaucrats resigned or retired rather than spend the rest of their lives and fortunes in court. Politicians thought twice, thrice, and even more about promises they had no intention of keeping.

A crisis struck the civil service at local, state, and federal levels. Faced with the threat of personal liability suits over alleged failures to perform their jobs, government employees were quitting those jobs faster than they could be replaced. It did not really matter if they won or lost their suits, the time and cost of defending themselves were more than they could bear.

Several states tried to pass laws exempting civil servants from personal liability suits. Each legislator proposing or supporting such a law was sued black and blue. The idea died long before it reached the Supreme Court—which was down to five members at the time, since four justices had hastily retired.

Faced with empty desks and unfilled job openings, government departments reluctantly turned to computers to fill the roles that human bureaucrats had abandoned. "At least they can't sue a computer," said one department head, wise in the ways of bureaucracies.

To everyone's surprise, the computers worked better than the humans they replaced. Thanks to their programming, they were industrious, unfailingly polite, and blindingly fast. And much cheaper than people. They worked all hours of the night and day, even weekends. They never took coffee breaks or asked for raises. They transferred information with electrical alacrity, and eventually with the speed of light, when photonics began to replace electronics.

Computers' programs could easily be changed to accommodate new facts, something that had been impossible with human bureaucrats.

Taxpayers *liked* the computers. The usual gloom and oppressive atmosphere of government offices was replaced by bright humming efficiency. Citizens could even handle most problems from their homes, with their personal computers talking to the government's computers to settle problems swiftly and neatly.

In the meantime, with fewer and fewer liability suits to sustain them, lawyers began to sue one another in a frenzy that eventually came to be called "the time of great dying." Within a century the last lawyer in the U.S. was replaced by a computer and sent into a richly deserved retirement in Death Valley.

By the time Carter C. Carter was finally revived from his cryonic sleep, decision-making computers had replaced humans at all levels of government except the very top posts, where policy was decided by elected officials. All permanent government "employees" had electrons and/or photons flowing through them instead of blood.

Carter, however, was dismayed to learn that his modest nest egg had long since been devoured by rapacious lawyers, and that—thanks to compound interest—he *owed* the estates of his erstwhile legal representatives a total of some six million dollars.

The shock stopped his heart. Since he had not had time to make out a new will, he was declared finally dead and cremated.

But his memory lives on. The happy and efficient society in which we live, unthreatened by the personal liability suits that ruined many an earlier life, is directly attributable to that unlikely hero of heroes, Carter C. Carter.

To Touch a Star

Later in this book you will find an essay titled "Science in Science Fiction." The story you are about to read, "To Touch a Star," is an example of a tale that is heavy with science.

Two points need to be made: First, that *science*-fiction stories are those in which some element of future science is so crucial to the story that it would collapse if the scientific element were removed from the tale. If you took away the science aspects of "To Touch a Star" there would be no story left.

Second, in a science-fiction story the author is free to invent any new scientific discoveries he or she wants to—as long as no one can prove the author is wrong. In "To Touch a Star" I write about a spaceship that makes a journey of a thousand light years to another star. Impossible by today's level of technology. Maybe impossible for centuries to come. Maybe such interstellar flight will always be impossible. But no one today can show that such a voyage violates the fundamental principles of the universe, as we now understand them. Palm-sized computers and artificial satellites and genetic engineering were all once impossible dreams. They were the stuff of science-fiction tales, once. Today they are commonplace.

Notice that I do not use the concept of faster-than-light travel in this story. I have nothing against the idea of FTL, even though physicists since Einstein have believed that nothing in the universe can travel faster than light. There may be ways around that limitation, those same physicists warily agree.

However, think of the dramatic possibilities of staying within the light-speed limitation. Two men love the same woman. One of them is sent on a flight to another star. He will not age at the same rate as the woman and the other man, who remain on Earth. The eternal triangle now gains a new dimension: time. The challenge of dealing with the universe as we understand it creates a new capability for the tellers of stories.

Let's add a third point: Even in a story that is heavily dependent on science, the scientific background must not get in the way of the storytelling. The characters and their conflicts are what the story is really all about. The futuristic science is the background.

"To Touch a Star" began as a science challenge. It was commissioned as part of a book that would feature scientific essays by astronomers and astrophysicists, matched by short stories by science-fiction writers. My assignment was to write a story to accompany the essay on how stars age and eventually die.

Years earlier I had written a novelette titled "The Last Decision," which told of the desperate attempt of human beings to prevent Earth's Sun from exploding and destroying the Earth. My good friend and colleague A. J. Austin and I eventually developed that original story into a novel, *To Save the Sun*. When I was asked to write a story about the death throes of a star, I already had much of the background at hand.

Which is an important lesson to anyone who wants to make a living out of writing fiction: Forget nothing. Never throw anything away. Basic material can serve more than once, especially if it is material rich in the possibilities of human conflict.

The first thought to touch Aleyn's conscious mind after his long sleep was, I've lost Noura. Lost her forever.

He lay on the warm, softly yielding mattress of the cocoon staring upward for the better part of an hour, seeing nothing. But whenever he closed his eyes he saw Noura's face. The dazzle of her dark eyes, the glow of firelight sparkling in them. The rich perfume of her lustrous ebony hair. The warmth of her smile.

Gone forever now. Separated by time and distance and fate. Separated by my own ambition.

And by Selwyn's plotting, he added silently. His mouth hardened into a thin bitter line. If I live through this—he won't, Aleyn promised himself.

Slowly he pulled himself up to a sitting position. The sleep chamber was familiar yet strange. The cocoon where he had spent the past thousand absolute years was almost the same as he remembered it. Almost. The cocoon's shell, swung back now that he had been awakened, seemed a slightly different shade of color. He recalled it being brighter, starker, a hard hospital white. Now it was almost pearl gray.

The communicator screen was not beside the cocoon anymore, but at its end, by his feet. The diagnostic screens seemed subtly rearranged. The maintenance robots had changed things over the years of his sleep.

"Status report," he called, his voice cracking slightly.

The comm screen remained blank, but its synthesized

voice, a blend of Aleyn's parents and his university mentor, replied:

"Your health is excellent, Aleyn. We are on course and within fifty hours of our destination. All ship systems are operational and functioning within nominal limits."

Aleyn swung his legs off the cocoon's mattress and stood up, warily, testingly. The cermet floor felt pleasantly warm to his bare feet. He felt strong. In the reflections of the diagnostic screens he saw himself scattered and disarranged like a cubist painting of a lean, naked young man.

"Show me the star," he commanded.

The comm screen flickered briefly, then displayed a dully glowing red disk set among a background of star-studded blackness. The disk was perfectly round, ruddy like the dying embers of a fire, glowering sullenly against the dark depths of space.

Aleyn's heart nearly stopped.

"That's not a star!" he shouted.

"Scorpio 1888IR2434," said the comm screen, after a hesitation that was unnoticeable to human senses.

"It can't be!"

"Navigation and tracking programs agree. Spectrum matches. It is our destination star," the screen insisted.

Aleyn stared at the image a moment longer, then bolted to the hatch and down the short corridor that led to the ship's bridge.

The bridge screens were larger. But they all showed the same thing. Optical, infrared, radar, high-energy, and neutrino sensors all displayed a gigantic, perfectly circular metal sphere.

Aleyn sagged into the only chair on the bridge, oblivious to the slight chill against his naked flesh until the chair adjusted its temperature.

"We thought it was a star," he murmured to no one. "We thought it was a star."

Aleyn Arif Bellerophontes, son of the director of the Imperial Observatory and her consort and therefore distrusted by Admiral Kimon, the emperor's chief of astro-engineering; betrayed by Selwyn, his best friend; exiled to a solitary expedition to a dying star—Aleyn sat numb and uncomprehending, staring at a metal sphere the size of a star.

No. Bigger.

"What's the radius of that object?"

Numbers sprang up on every screen, superimposed on the visual display, as the computer's voice replied, "Two hundred seventeen point zero nine eight million kilometers."

"Two hundred million kilometers," Aleyn echoed. Then he smiled. "A metal sphere four hundred million kilometers across." He giggled. "A sphere with the radius of a water-bearing planet's orbit." He laughed. "A Dyson sphere! I've found a Dyson sphere!"

His laughter became raucous, uncontrolled, hysterical. He roared with laughter. He banged his fists on the armrests of his chair and threw his head back and screamed with laughter. Tears flowed down his cheeks. His face grew red. His breath rasped in his throat. His lungs burned. He did not stop until the chair, reacting to an override command from the computer's medical program, sprayed him with a soporific and he lapsed into unconsciousness.

A thousand lightyears away, scientists and engineers of the Hundred Worlds labored heroically to save the Earth from doom. The original home planet of the Empire was in danger from its own Sun. A cycle of massive flares would soon erupt across the Sun's normally placid face. Soon, that is, in terms of a star's gigayear lifetime: ten thousand years, give or take a few millennia. Too feeble to be of consequence in the lifespan of the star itself, the flares nonetheless would casually boil away the air and oceans of Earth, leaving nothing behind except a blackened ball of rock.

Millions of technologists had struggled for centuries to save the Earth, following the mad scheme of a woman scientist who woke from cryonic sleep once each thousand years to survey their progress. It was not enough. The course of the Sun's evolution had not yet been altered enough to avert the period of flares. The Earth's daystar would go through its turbulent phase despite the valiant efforts of the Empire's best, most dedicated men and women. In all the vast storehouses of knowledge among the Hundred Worlds, no one knew enough about a star's behavior to forestall the Sun's impending fury.

Three young scientists, Aleyn, Noura, and Selwyn, hit upon the idea of monitoring other stars that were undergoing the same kind of turbulence. Aleyn had fought through the layers of academic bureaucracy and championed their joint ideas to the topmost levels of the Imperial hierarchy, to Admiral Kimon himself.

It had been a clever trap, he knew now. Kimon, reluctantly agreeing to the proposal of the son of his chief rival within the Imperial court, had sent out a fleet of one-man ships toward the stars that Selwyn, Noura, and Aleyn had listed. He had assigned Aleyn himself to one of those long, lonely ventures. Selwyn the traitor remained at Earth. With Kimon. With Noura. While Aleyn sped through the dark star-paths on a journey that would take twenty centuries to complete.

And now, rousing himself slowly from the soporific dreaminess, Aleyn realized what a cosmic joke it all was. Their research had shown that Scorpio 1888IR2434, a dim reddish star some thousand lightyears from Earth, was flickering and pulsating much as the Sun would during its time of agony. A good star to observe, an excellent opportunity to gather the data needed to save the Sun and Earth. Better still, this star in Scorpio lay in the direction opposite the alien worlds, so that a scout ship sent to it would cause no diplomatic anxieties, offer no threat to aliens sensitive to the Empire's attempts at expansion.

But the star was not a star. Aleyn felt the cold hand of chemically induced calm pressing against his heart. The joke was no longer funny. Yet it remained a colossal irony. He had discovered a Dyson sphere, a gigantic artifact, the work of an unknown race of aliens with undreamed-of technological powers. They had built a sphere around their star so that their civilization could catch every photon of energy the star emitted while they lived on the inner surface of their artificial world in the same comfort, breathing the same air, drinking the same water as they had enjoyed on their original home planet.

And Aleyn felt disappointment. The discovery of the eons was a crushing defeat to a man seeking knowledge of the inner workings of the stars. Despite the tranquilizing agent in his bloodstream, Aleyn wanted to laugh at the pathetic absurdity of it all. And he wanted to cry.

The drugs allowed him neither outlet. This nameless ship he commanded was in control of him, its programming placing duty and mission objectives far beyond human needs.

For three Earth-normal days he scanned the face of the enormous sphere while his ship hung in orbit beyond its glowing surface. He spent most of the time at his command chair in the bridge, surrounded by display screens and the soft reassuring hum of the electrical equipment. He wore the regulation uniform of the Imperial science service, complete with epaulets of rank and name tag, thinking nothing of the absurdity of such formality. There were no other clothes aboard the ship.

The sphere was not smooth, he saw. Not at all. Intricate

structures and networks of piping studded its exterior.
Huge hatches dotted the curving surface—all of them
closed tightly. The metal was hot; it glowed dull red like a
poker held too close to a fire. Aleyn saw jets of gas spurt-
ing from vents here and there, flashing briefly before dis-
sipating into the hard vacuum of interstellar space.

Not another body within lightyears. Not a planet or
asteroid or comet. They must have used every scrap of
matter in their solar system to build the sphere, Aleyn said
to himself. They must have torn their own home planet
apart, and all the other worlds of this system.

All the data that his ship's sensors recorded was trans-
mitted back toward Earth. At the speed of light, the information would take a thousand years to reach the eager
scientists and engineers. Noura would be long dead before
Aleyn's first report reached the Empire's receivers.

"Unless she got permission to take the long sleep,"
Aleyn hoped aloud. But then he shook his head. Only the
topmost members of the scientific hierarchy were permitted to sleep away centuries while others toiled. And if
Noura received such a boon, undoubtedly Selwyn would
too. They would share their lives even if they awakened
only one year out of each hundred.

That evening, as he brooded silently over the meal the
ship had placed on the galley's narrow table, Aleyn realized that Selwyn had indeed murdered him.

"Even if I survive this mission," he muttered angrily,
"by the time I return to Earth more than two thousand
years will have passed. Everyone I know—everyone I
love—will have died."

Unless they take the long sleep, a part of his brain
reminded him. Just as you did while this ship was in tran-
sit, they could sleep in cryogenic cold for many centuries
at a time.

There is a chance that Noura will be alive when I return,

he told himself silently, afraid to speak the hope aloud. *If I return.* No, not *if.* When! When I return, if Selwyn still lives I will kill him. Gladly. When I return.

He pushed the tray of untouched food away, rose to his feet, and strode back to the bridge.

"Computer," he commanded. "Integrate all data on Noura Sudarshee, including my personal holos, and feed it all into the interactive program."

The computer complied with a single wink of a green light. Within moments, Noura's lovely face filled the bridge's main display screen.

Aleyn sank into the command chair and found himself smiling at her. "I need you, dearest Noura. I need you to keep me sane."

"I know," she said, in the vibrant low voice that he loved. "I'm here with you, Aleyn. You're not alone anymore."

He fell asleep in the command chair, talking with the image of the woman he had left a thousand lightyears behind him. While he slept the ship's life support system sprayjected into his bloodstream the nutritional equivalent of the meal he had not eaten.

The following morning Aleyn resumed his scan of the sphere. But now he had Noura to talk to.

"They don't seem to know we're out here," Aleyn said. "No message, no probe—not even a warning to go away."

"Perhaps there are no living people inside the sphere," said Noura's image from the comm screen at Aleyn's right hand.

"No people?" He realized that her words were being formed by the computer, acting on the data in its own core and relaying its conclusions through the interactive Noura program.

"The sphere seems very old," said Noura's image, frowning slightly with concern.

Aleyn did not answer. He realized that she was right. The computer was drawing his attention to the obvious signs of the sphere's enormous age.

He spiraled his ship closer, searching for a port through which he might enter, staring hard at the pictures the main display screens revealed, as if he could force the sphere to open a hatch for him if he just concentrated hard enough. Aleyn began to realize that the sphere truly was *old*—and it was falling into ruin. The gases venting into space were escaping from broken pipes. Many of the structures on the sphere's outer surface seemed collapsed, broken, as if struck by meteors or simply decayed by eons of time.

"This was built before the Sun was born," Aleyn murmured.

"Not that long ago," replied Noura, voicing the computer's calculation of erosion rates in vacuum caused by interstellar radiation and the rare wandering meteor. "Spectral analysis of the surface metal indicates an age no greater than two hundred million years."

Aleyn grinned at her. "Is that all? Only two hundred million years? No older than the first amphibians to crawl out of the Earth's seas?"

Noura's image smiled back at him.

"Are they still in there?" he wondered. "Are the creatures who built this still living inside it?"

"They show no evidence of being there," said Noura. "Since the sphere is so ancient, perhaps they no longer exist."

"I can't believe that. They *must* be there! They must be!"

For eight more days Aleyn bombarded the sphere with every wavelength his equipment could transmit: radio, microwave, infrared laser light, ultraviolet, X rays, gamma rays. Pulses and steady beams. Standard messages and simple mathematical formulas. No reaction from the sphere. He sprayed alpha particles and relativistic electrons across wide swaths of the sphere, to no avail.

"I don't think anyone is alive inside," said Noura's image.

"How do we know where their receivers might be?" Aleyn countered. "Maybe their communications equipment in this area broke down. Maybe their main antennas are clear over on the other side."

"It would take years to cover every square meter of its surface," Noura pointed out.

Aleyn shrugged, almost happily. "We have years. We have centuries, if we need them. As long as you're with me I don't care how long it takes."

Her face became serious. "Aleyn, remember that I am only an interactive program. You must not allow my presence to interfere with the objectives of your mission."

He smiled grimly and fought down a surge of anger. After taking a deep, calming breath, Aleyn said to the image on the screen, "Noura my darling, the main objective of this mission is to keep me away from you. Selwyn has accomplished that."

"The major objective of this mission," she said, in a slightly lecturing tone, "is to observe the instabilities of a turbulent G-class star and relay that data back to Earth."

Aleyn jabbed a forefinger at the main display screen. "But we can't even see the star. It's inside the sphere."

"Then we must find a way to get inside, as well."

"Ah-hah! I knew you'd see it my way sooner or later."

Aleyn programmed the computer to set up a polar orbit that would eventually carry the ship over every part of the gigantic sphere. The energy in the antimatter converters would last for millennia. Still, he extended the magnetic scoops to draw in the thin scattering of hydrogen atoms that drifted through the void between the stars. The gases vented by the sphere's broken pipes undoubtedly con-tained hydrogen, as well. That would feed the fusion systems and provide input for the converters.

It was precisely when the engines fired to move the ship to its new orbit that the port began to open.

Aleyn barely caught it, out of the corner of his eye as one of the auxiliary screens on his compact bridge showed a massive hatch swinging outward, etched sharply in bright blood-red light.

"Look!" he shouted.

Swiveling his command chair toward the screen, he ordered the ship's sensors to focus on the port.

"Aleyn, you did it!" Noura's image seemed equally excited.

The port yawned open like a gateway to hell, lurid red light beyond it.

Aleyn took manual control of the ship, broke it out of the new orbit it had barely established, and maneuvered it toward the opening port. It was kilometers wide, big enough to engulf a hundred ships like this one.

"Why now?" he asked. "Why did it stay closed when we were sending signals and probes to the sphere and open up only when we lighted the engines?"

"Neutrinos, perhaps," said Noura, with the wisdom of the ship's computer. "The fusion thrusters generate a shower of neutrinos when they fire. The neutrinos must have penetrated the sphere's shell and activated sensors inside."

"Inside," Aleyn echoed, his voice shaking.

With trembling hands Aleyn set all his comm channels on automatic to make certain that every bit of data that the ship's sensors received was sent back Earthward. Then he aimed his ship squarely at the center of the yawning port and fired its thrusters one more time.

It seemed as if they stood still while the burning-hot

alien sphere moved up to engulf them and swallowed them alive.

The port widened and widened as they approached until its vast expanse filled Aleyn's screens with a sullen, smoldering red glow. The temperature gauges began to climb steadily upward. Aleyn called up the life-support display and saw that the system was drawing much more energy than usual, adjusting the heat shielding and internal cooling systems to withstand the furnacelike conditions outside the ship's hull.

"It's like stepping into Dante's inferno," Aleyn muttered.

With a smile that was meant to be reassuring, Noura said, "The cooling systems can withstand temperatures of this magnitude for hundreds of hours."

He smiled back at her. "My beloved, sometimes you talk like a computer."

"It's the best I can do under the circumstances."

The port was several hundred kilometers thick. Aleyn's screens showed heavily ribbed metal, dulled and pitted with age, as they cruised slowly through.

"This must be the thickness of the sphere's shell," he said. Noura agreed with a nod.

Once they finally cleared the port he could see the interior of the sphere. A vast metallic plain extended in all directions around him, glowing red hot. Aleyn focused the ship's sensors on the inner surface and saw a jumble of shapes: stumps of towers blackened and melted down, shattered remains of what must have been buildings, twisted guideways that disappeared entirely in places where enormous pools of metal glittered in the gloomy red light.

"It looks like the roadway melted and then the metal solidified again afterward," said Aleyn.

"Yes," Noura said. "A tremendous pulse of heat destroyed everything."

The sphere was so huge that it seemed almost perfectly flat from this perspective. Aleyn punched at his controls, calling up as many different views as the sensors could display. Nothing but the burnt and blackened remains of what must have been a gigantic city. No sign of movement. No sign of life.

"Did they kill themselves off in a war?" Aleyn wondered aloud.

"No," said Noura. "Listen."

Aleyn turned toward her screen. "What?"

"Listen."

"I don't—" Then he realized that he did hear something. A faint whispering, like the rush of a breeze through a young forest. But this was pulsating irregularly, gasping, almost like the labored breath of a dying old man.

"What is it?"

"There is an atmosphere here within this shell," said Noura.

Aleyn shook his head. "Couldn't be. How could they open a hatch to space if . . ."

But the computer had already sampled the atmosphere the ship was flying through. Noura's voice spoke what the other display screens showed in alphanumerics:

"We are immersed in an atmosphere that consists of sixty-two percent hydrogen ions, thirty-four percent helium ions, two percent carbon, one percent oxygen, and traces of other ions."

Aleyn stared at her screen.

"Atmospheric density is four ten-thousandths of Earth standard sea-level density." Noura spoke what the other screens displayed. "Temperature outside the ship's hull is ten thousand degrees, kinetic."

"We're inside the star's chromosphere," Aleyn whispered.

"Yes, and we're cruising deeper into it. The cooling systems will not be able to handle the heat levels deeper inside the star." For the first time Noura's image appeared worried.

Aleyn turned to the control board and called up an image of the star on the main screen. It was a glowering, seething ball of red flame, huge and distended, churning angrily, spotted with ugly dark blotches and twisting filaments that seemed to writhe on its surface like souls in torment and then sink back again into the ocean of fire.

The sound outside the ship's hull seemed louder as Aleyn stared at the screen, fascinated, hypnotized. It was the sound of the star, he realized; the tortured, irregular pulse beat of a dying star.

"We're too late," he whispered at last. "This star has already exploded at least once. It killed off the civilization that built the sphere. Burned them all to a cinder."

"It will destroy us too if we go much deeper," said Noura.

What of it? Aleyn thought. This entire mission is a failure. We'll never gain the knowledge that I thought we could get from studying this star. It's past the period of turbulence that we need to observe. The mission has failed. I have failed. There's nothing on Earth for me to go back to. No one in the Hundred Worlds for me to go back to.

"Aleyn!" Noura's voice was urgent. "We must change course and leave the sphere. Outside temperatures will overwhelm the cooling systems within a few dozen hours if we don't."

"What of it? We can die together."

"No, Aleyn. Life is too valuable to throw away. Don't you see that?"

"All I see is the hopelessness of everything. What difference if I live or die? What will I accomplish by struggling to survive?"

"Is that what you want?" Noura asked. "To die?"

"Why not?"

"Isn't that what Selwyn wants, to be rid of you forever?"

"He *is* rid of me. Even if I go back to Earth the two of you will have been dead for more than a thousand years."

Noura's image remained silent, but the ship turned itself without Aleyn's command and pointed its nose toward the port through which they had entered.

"The computer is programmed to save the ship and its data banks even if the pilot is incapacitated," Noura said, almost apologetically.

Aleyn nodded. "I can't even commit suicide."

Smiling, Noura said, "I want you to live, my darling."

He stared at her image for long moments, telling himself desperately that this was merely the computer speaking to him, using the ship's data files and his personal holos to synthesize her picture and manner of speech. It was Noura's face. Noura's voice. But the computer's mind.

She doesn't care if I live, he told himself. It's the data banks that are important.

With a shrug that admitted defeat Aleyn put the nose camera view on the main display screen. A shock of raw electricity slammed through him. He saw that the giant port through which they had entered the sphere was now firmly closed.

"We're trapped!" he shouted.

"How could it close?" Noura's image asked.

"You are not of the creators."

It was a voice that came from the main display screen,

deep and powerful. To Aleyn it sounded like the thunder-clap of doom.

"Who said that?"

"You are not of the creators."

"There's someone alive in the sphere! Who are you?"

"Only the creators may return to their home. All others are forbidden."

"We are a scientific investigation mission," Noura's voice replied, "from the planet—"

"I know you are from a worldling you call Earth. I can see from your navigational program where your home world is located."

His heart racing wildly, Aleyn asked, "You can tap into your computer?"

"I have been studying you since you entered this world."

Noura said swiftly, "Aleyn, he's communicating through our own computer."

"Who are you?" Aleyn asked.

"In your tongue, my name is Savant."

"What are you?" asked Noura.

"I am the servant of the creators. They created me to survive, to guard, and to protect."

"You're a computer?" Aleyn guessed.

For half a heartbeat there was no response. Then, *"I am a device that is as far beyond what you know of computers as your minds are beyond those of your household pets."*

With a giggle that trembled on the edge of hysteria, Aleyn said, "And you're quite a modest little device, too, aren't you?"

"My function is to survive, to guard, and to protect. I perform my function well."

"Are there any of the creatures still remaining here?" Noura asked.

"No."

"What happened to them?"

"Many departed when they realized the star would explode. Others remained here."

"To try to prevent the star from exploding?" Aleyn suggested.

"That was not their way. They remained to await the final moments. They preferred to die in their homes, where they had always lived."

"But they built you."

"Yes."

"Why?"

"To await the time when those who fled return to their home."

"You mean they're coming back?"

"There is no evidence of their return. My function is to survive, to guard, and to protect. If they ever return I shall serve them."

"And help them to rebuild."

"If they wish it so."

Noura asked, "Do you have any idea of how long ago your creators left?"

"By measuring the decay of radioactive atoms I can count time. In your terms of reference, the creators fled approximately eighteen million years ago. The star's first explosion took place eleven thousand years later."

"First?" Aleyn asked. "There have been more?"

"Not yet. But very soon the next explosion will take place."

"We must get out of here," Noura said.

"That is not allowed."

"Not— What do you mean?" For the first time Aleyn felt fear burning along his veins.

"I am the servant of the creators. No others may enter or leave."

"But you let us in!"

"To determine if you were of the creators. You are not. Therefore you may not leave."

The fear ebbed away. In its place Aleyn felt the cold implacable hand of cosmic irony. With a sardonic smile he turned to Noura's image.

"I won't have to commit suicide now. This Savant is going to murder me."

Noura's image stared blankly at him. It had no answer.

Aleyn pulled himself up from the command chair and went back through the narrow corridor to the ship's galley. He knew that the computer automatically spiced his food with tranquilizers and vitamins and anything else it felt he needed, based on its continuous scans of his physical and psychological condition. He no longer cared.

He ate numbly, hardly tasting the food. His mind swirled dizzyingly. An alien race. The discovery of a lifetime, of a dozen lifetimes, and he would not live to report it. But where did they go? Are they still out there, scattering through the galaxy in some desperate interstellar diaspora?

Is that what the people of Earth should have done? Abandon their homeworld and flee among the stars? What makes humans so arrogant that they think they can reverse the course of a star's evolution?

He went to his cabin as the miniature serving robots cleared the galley table. Stripping off his uniform, Aleyn was surprised to see that it was stained and rank with sweat. Fear? he wondered. Excitement? He felt neither at the moment. Nothing but numb exhaustion. The ship's pharmacy was controlling his emotions now, he knew. Otherwise he'd be bashing his head against the metal bulkhead.

He crawled into the bunk and pulled the monolayer

coverlet up to his chin, just as he used to do when he was a child.

"Noura," he called.

Her face appeared on the screen at the foot of the bunk. "I'm here, Aleyn."

"I wish you were," he said. "I wish you truly were."

"I *am* with you, my dearest. I am here with you."

"No," he said, a great wave of sadness washing over him. "You are merely a collection of data bits. My real Noura is on Earth, with Selwyn. Already dead, perhaps."

Her eyes flashed. "Your real Noura may be on Earth, but dead or alive she is not with Selwyn."

"It would be pleasant to believe so."

"It is true!" the image insisted. "Who would know better than I?"

"You're not real."

"I am the sum of all the ship's records of Noura Sudarshee; the personnel records are complete from her birth to the day you left Earth."

"No better than a photograph," Aleyn countered. "No better than looking at a star in the sky of night."

"I am also made up from your holos of Noura Sudarshee, your private recordings and communications." She hesitated a moment, then added, almost shyly, "Even your subconscious memories and dreams."

"Dreams?" Aleyn blurted. "Memories?"

"This ship's psychological program has been scanning your brainwave activity since you came aboard. During your long sleep you dreamt extensively of me. All that data is included in this imagery."

Aleyn thought about that for a moment. An electronic clone of his beloved Noura, complete down to the slightest memory in his subconscious mind. But the deadening hand of futility made him laugh bitterly.

"That only makes it worse, my dearest. That only means that when I die I will be killing you too."

"Don't think of death, darling. Think of life. Think of me."

He shook his head wearily. "I don't want to think of anything. I want to sleep. Forever."

He closed his eyes. His last waking thought was that it would be a relief never to have to open them again.

Of course he dreamed of Noura, as he always did. But this time the dream was drenched with a dire sense of foreboding, of dread. He and Noura were on Earth, at a wild and incredibly remote place where a glacier-fed waterfall tumbled down a sheer rock scarp into a verdant valley dotted with trees. Not another person for hundreds of kilometers. Only the two of them sitting on the yielding grass under the warming Sun.

But the Sun grew hotter, so hot that the grass began to smolder and curl and blacken. The waterfall began to steam. Aleyn looked up at the Sun and saw it broiling angrily, lashing out huge tongues of flame. It thundered at them and laughed. In the Sun's blinding disk he saw the face of Selwyn, laughing at him, reaching out his flaming arms for Noura.

"NO!" he screamed.

Aleyn found himself sitting up on his bunk, soaked with sweat. Grimly he got up, washed, and put on his freshly cleansed uniform. He strode past the galley and took the command chair at the bridge.

"Good morning, darling," said Noura's smiling image.

He made himself smile back at her. "Good morning."

Her face became more serious. "The cooling systems are nearing overload. In six more hours they will fail."

"Backups?"

"The six-hour figure includes the backups."

Aleyn nodded. Six hours.

"Savant!" he called. "Can you hear me?"

"Yes."

"Why do you refuse to allow us to leave your domain? Are you prohibited from doing so?"

"I am programmed to survive, to guard, and to protect. I await the creators. There is nothing in my programming that requires me to allow you to leave."

"But there's nothing in your programming that prohibits you from allowing us to leave, is there?"

"That is so."

"Then allow us to leave and we will search for the creators and bring them back to you."

The synthesized voice was silent for several heartbeats. Aleyn realized that each second of time was an eternity for such a powerful computer. It must be considering this proposition very carefully, like a computer chess game, calculating every possible move as far into the future as it could see.

"The creators are so distant now that they could not be found and returned before the star explodes again. The next explosion will destroy this sphere. It will destroy me. I will not survive. I will have failed my primary purpose."

It was Aleyn's turn to fall silent, thinking, his mind churning through all the branching possibilities. Death stood at the end of each avenue, barring the door to escape.

"Aleyn," said Noura's image, softly, "the ship is drifting deeper into the chromosphere. Hull temperature is rising steeply. The cooling systems will fail in a matter of minutes if corrective action is not taken."

Corrective action, Aleyn's mind echoed. Why not simply allow the ship to drift toward the heart of the dying star and let us be vaporized? It will all be finished in a few minutes. Why try to delay the inevitable, prolong the futility? Why struggle, merely to continue suffering?

He looked squarely at Noura's image in the screen. "But I can't kill you," he whispered. "Even if you are only memories and dreams, I can't let you die."

Turning again to the main screen he saw the angry heart of the dying star, seething red, writhing and glowering, drumming against the ship's hull with the dull muted thunder of approaching doom.

"Savant," he called again. "Have you scanned all of our data banks?"

"I have."

"Then you know that we of Earth are attempting to prevent our own star from exploding."

"Your Sun is younger than my star."

"Yes, and the data you have recorded about your star would be of incalculable value in helping us to gain an understanding of how to save our Sun."

"That is of no consequence."

"But it is!" Aleyn snapped. "It is! Because once we learn how to control our own Sun, how to prevent it from exploding, we can come back here and apply that knowledge to your star."

"Return here?"

"Yes! We can return and save your star! We can help you to survive! We can allow you to achieve your primary objective."

"I am programmed to survive, to guard, and to protect."

"We will help you to survive. You can continue to guard and protect until we return with the knowledge that will save your star from destruction."

Again the alien voice went silent. Aleyn counted to twenty, then fifty, then . . .

Noura sang out, "The port is opening!"

Aleyn swung his chair to see the screen. The vast hatch that had sealed the port was slowly swinging open again. He could see a slice of star-studded darkness beyond it. Without thinking consciously he turned the ship toward the port, away from the growling, glaring star.

"Savant," he called once again, "we need the data you have accumulated on your star's behavior."

"Your data banks are too small to accommodate all of it. Therefore I have altered the atomic structure of your ship's hull and structure to store the data."

"Altered the hull and structure?"

"The alteration is at the nuclear level. It will not affect the performance of your ship. I have placed instructions in your puny computer on how to access the data."

"Thank you!"

"You must return within thirty thousand years if you are to save this star."

"We'll be back long before then. I promise you."

"I will survive until then without you."

"You will survive beyond that, Savant. We will be back and we will bring the knowledge you need to save yourself and your star."

"I will wait."

The ship headed toward the port, gaping wide now, showing the cold darkness of infinity sprinkled with hard pinpoints of stars.

"The cooling system is returning to normal," Noura's image said. "We will survive."

"We will return to Earth," said Aleyn. "I'll sleep for a thousand years and when I wake again we'll be back at Earth."

"The real Noura will be waiting for you."

He smiled, but there was still bitterness in it. "I wish that could be true."

"It is true, my beloved Aleyn. Who would know better

than I? She is in deep sleep even now, waiting for your return."

"Do you really believe so?"

"I know it."

"And Selwyn, also?"

"Even if he waits for her," Noura's image replied, "she waits for you."

He closed his eyes briefly. Then he realized, "But that means . . ."

"It means you will no longer need me," said Noura's image. "You will erase me."

"I don't know if I could do that. It would be like murdering you."

She smiled at him, a warming, loving smile without a trace of sadness in it. "I am not programmed to survive, Aleyn. My objective was to help *you* to survive. Once the real Noura is in your arms you will not need me anymore."

He stared at the screen for many long moments. Then wordlessly he reached out his hand and touched the button that turned off the display.

Brothers

Over my desk is a page from a collection of Ernest Hemingway's short stories. The page contains a brief sketch, set in a town in Spain in the 1920s. Two old bullfighters are watching the young matador who is supposed to be the star of that afternoon's *corrida de toros*. But the young star is drunk, dancing in the street with gypsies, staggeringly drunk, in no condition to face the bulls.

"Who will kill his bulls?" one of the older matadors asks the other.

"We, I suppose. . . . We kill the savage's bulls, and the drunkard's bulls, and the *riau-riau* dancer's bulls."

The point is, some people get the job done and some people don't. A successful writer gets the job done. No matter what is happening around him or her. No matter family or weather or finances, a writer *writes.* The world can collapse and the writer writes. No excuses. No delays. No waiting for inspiration or the right moment or the proper phase of the Moon. A writer works at it. The rest is all talk.

Humphrey Bogart made somewhat the same point when he said, "A professional is a guy who gets the job done whether he feels like it or not."

"Brothers" is a story about two professionals, doing two very different jobs that needed to be done on a certain day in November 1971.

5 *November 1971: Command Module* Saratoga, *in Lunar Orbit*

Alone now, Bill Carlton stopped straining his eyes and turned away from the tiny triangular window. The landing module was a dwindling speck against the gray pock-marked surface of the barren, alien Moon.

He tried to lean his head back against the contour couch, remembered again that he was weightless, floating lightly against the restraining harness. All the old anger surged up in him again, knotting his neck with tension even in zero gravity.

Sitting here like a goddamned robot. Left here to mind the store like some goddamned kid while they go down to the surface and get their names in the history books. The also-ran. Sixty miles away from the Moon, but I'll never set foot on it. Never.

The Apollo command module seemed almost large now that Wally and Dave were gone. The two empty couches looked huge, luxurious. The banks of instruments and controls hummed at him electrically. We can get along fine without you, they were saying. We're machines, we don't need an also-ran to make us work.

This tin can stinks, he said to himself. Five days cooped up in here, sitting inside these damned suits. *I* stink.

With a wordless growl, Bill turned up the gain on the radio. His earphones crackled for a moment, then the robotic voice of the Capcom came through.

"You're in approach phase, *Yorktown*. Everything looking good."

Wally's voice answered, "Manual control okay. Altitude forty-three hundred."

Almost three seconds passed. "Forty-three, we copy." It was Shannon's voice from Houston. Capcom for the duration of the landing.

Bill sat alone in the command module and listened. His two teammates were about to land. He had traveled a quarter million miles, but would get no closer than fifty-eight miles to the Moon.

5 November 1971: U.S.S. Saratoga, *in the Tonkin Gulf*

Bob Carlton tapped the back of his helmet against the head knocker and held his gloved hands up against the canopy's clear plastic so the deck crew could see he was not touching any of the controls. The sky-blue paint had been scratched from the spot where the head knocker touched the helmet. Sixty missions will do that.

Sixty missions. It seemed more like six hundred. Or six thousand. It was endless. Every day, every day. The same thing. Endless.

The A-7 was being attached to the catapult now. It was the time when Bob always got just slightly queasy, staring out beyond the edge of the carrier's heaving deck into the gray mist of morning.

"Cleared for takeoff," said the launch director's voice in his earphones.

"Clear," Bob repeated.

He rammed the throttle forward and felt the bomber's jet engine howl and surge suddenly, straining, making the whole plane tremble like a hunting dog begging to be released from its leash.

"Three . . . two . . . one . . . GO!"

His head slammed back and his whole body seemed to flatten against itself, pressed into the seat as the A-7 leaped off the carrier's deck and into the misty air. The deep rolling swells of the blue-green water whipped by and then receded as he pulled the control column back slightly and the swept-wing plane angled up into the sullen, low-hanging clouds. Without even thinking consciously of it, he reached back and pushed the head knocker up into its locked position. Now he could fire the ejection seat if he had to.

In a moment the Sun broke through and sparkled off the mirrors arrayed around the curve of the canopy. Bob saw the five other planes of his flight and formed up on the left end of their V. The queasiness was gone now. He felt strong and good in the sunshine.

He looked up and saw the pale shadow of a half moon grinning lopsidedly at him. Bill's up there, he thought. Can you see me, Bill? Can you hear me calling you?

Then he looked away. A dark slice of land lay on the horizon, slim and silent as a dagger. Vietnam.

"Contact. All lights on. Engine stop. We're down." Bill heard Dave McDonald's laconic voice announce their landing on the moon.

"We copy, *Yorktown.* Good job. Fantastic." Shannon sounded excited. He was due to fly the next mission. "*Saratoga,* do you read?"

Bill was surprised that he had to swallow twice before his voice would work. "Copy. *Yorktown* in port. Good going, guys."

It was an all-Navy crew, so they had named their modules in honored Navy tradition. The lunar lander became *Yorktown.* Bill rode alone in the command module, *Saratoga.* The old men with gold braid on their sleeves and silver in their hair loved that. Good old Annapolis spirit.

"You are go for excursion," said Shannon, lapsing back into technical jargon.

"Roger." McDonald's voice was starting to fade out.

"We'll take a little walk soon's we wiggle into the suits."

And I'll sit here by myself, Bill thought. What would Shannon and the rest of those clowns at Houston do if I screwed my helmet on and took a walk on my own?

The fucking oxygen mask never fit right. It pressed across the bridge of Bob's nose and cut into his cheeks. And the stuff was almost too cold to breathe; it made his teeth ache. Bob felt his ears pop slightly as the formation of six attack bombers dove to treetop height and then streaked across the mottled green forest.

This was the part of the mission that he liked best, racing balls-out close enough to the goddamned trees to suck a monkey into your air intake. Everything a green blur outside the cockpit. Six hundred knots and the altimeter needle flopping around zero. The plane took it as smooth as a new Cadillac tooling up to the country club. Not a shake or a rattle in her. She merely rocked slightly in the invisible air currents bubbling up from the forest.

Christ, any lower and we'll come back smeared green. He laughed aloud.

Bob flew the bomb-laden plane with mere touches of his thumb against the button on the control column that moved the trim tabs. The A-7 responded like a thoroughbred, jumping smoothly over an upjutting tree, turning gracefully in formation with the five others.

Why don't we just fly like this forever? Bob wondered. Just keep going and never, never stop.

But up ahead the land was rising, ridge after ridge of densely wooded hills. In a valley between one particular pair of ridges was an NVA ammunition dump, according to their preflight briefing. By the time they got there, Bob guessed, the North Vietnamese would have moved their ammo to someplace else. We'll wind up bombing the fucking empty jungle again.

But their antiaircraft guns will be there. Oh yes indeed, the little brown bastards'll have everything from slingshots to radar-directed artillery to throw at us. They always do.

There was a whole checklist of chores for Bill to do as he waited alone in the command module. Photographic mapping. Heat sensors. Housekeeping checks on the life-support systems.

Busywork, Bill grumbled silently. He went through the checklist mechanically, doing even the tiniest task-with the numb efficiency of a machine. Just a lot of crap to make me feel like I'm doing something. To make them feel like there's something for me to do.

The radio voices of Peters and McDonald were fading fast now. The command module was swinging around in its orbit toward the far side of the moon. Bill listened to Wally and Dave yahooing and joking with each other as they bounced and jogged on the Moon's surface, stirring up dust that had waited four billion years for them to arrive.

"Wish you could be here, buddy!" sang Wally.

"Yeah, Bill. You'd love the scenery," Dave agreed happily.

Bill said into his radio microphone, "Thanks a lot, you guys." So what if they heard him in Houston. What more could they do to him?

"*Saratoga,* you are approaching radio cutoff," Shannon reminded him needlessly.

"Radio cutoff," Bill repeated to Houston. Then he counted silently, one thousand, two thousand, three . . .

"See you on the other side," said Shannon, his radio voice finally crossing the distance between them.

"That's a rog," Bill said.

The far side of the Moon. Totally alone, separated from

the entire human race by a quarter million miles of distance and two thousand miles of solid rock.

Bill stole one final glance at the Earth as the spaceship swung around in its orbit. It was blue and mottled with white swirling clouds, glowing like a solitary candle on a darkened altar. He could not see Vietnam. He did not even try to find it.

"Check guns." The flight leader's voice in his helmet earphones almost startled Bob.

The easy part of the flight was finished. The work was beginning. He thumbed the firing button on his control column, just the slightest tap. Below his feet he could feel a brief buzz, almost like a small vacuum cleaner or an electric shaver. Just for an instant.

"Corsair Six, guns clear." His microphone was built into the oxygen mask.

The flight leader kept an open mike. Bob could hear him breathing heavily inside his mask, as if he were personally carrying the bomb-laden plane on his shoulders. The ground was rising now, still green and treacherous, reaching up into the sky in steep ridges.

Their flight plan took advantage of the terrain. Come in low, skim the treetops, until the final ridge. Then zoom up over that last crest, dive flat out into the valley and plaster the joint with high-explosive bombs and napalm. Get in and get out before they know you're there.

Good plan. Except for tail-end Bobby. Four planes could get past the fucking slopes before they can react. Maybe five. But six was expecting too much. They'll have their radars tracking and their guns firing by the time I come through.

The only sound in the command module was the inevitable electrical hum of the equipment. Bill ignored it. It would make no impression on his conscious mind unless it stopped.

He floated gently against the light restraining harness of his couch and closed his eyes. This was the time he had waited for. His own time. They could pick him for the shit job of sitting here and waiting while Wally and Dave got all the glory, but they couldn't stop him from doing this one experiment, this test that nobody in the world knew about.

Nobody except Bobby and me, he thought.

Eyes closed, Bill tried to relax his body completely. Force the tension out of his muscles. Make those tendons ease their grip.

"Bobby," he whispered. "Bobby, can you hear me?"

They had agreed to the experiment a year earlier, the last time they had seen each other, at the lobby bar in the Saint Francis hotel.

"What the hell are you doing here?" they had asked simultaneously.

"I'm rotating back to 'Nam," said Bob.

"I'm attending an engineering conference over at Ames," said Bill.

They marveled at the coincidence. Neither of them had ever gone to that hotel bar before. And at four in the afternoon!

"For twin brothers, we sure don't see much of each other," Bill said, after the bartender had set up a pair of Jack Daniel's neat, water on the side, before them. "Takes a coincidence like this."

"This is more than a coincidence," said Bob.

"You think so?"

Bobby nodded, picked up his drink, and sipped at it.

"I think you've been out of the mystic East too long, kid. You're going Asiatic."

"Maybe you've been hanging around with too many

scientists," Bob countered. "You're starting to think like a machine."

"Come on, Bobby, you don't really believe—"

"What made you come in here this afternoon?"

Bill shrugged. "Damned if I know. What about you?"

A twin shrug. "Can't say it was a premonition. On the other hand, I usually don't even come to this part of town when I'm on leave in Frisco."

They drank for several hours, ignoring the bar girls who sauntered through looking for early action. They talked about family and old times. They avoided comparing their Navy duties. Bob was a frontline pilot in a carrier attack squadron. Bill was on detached duty with the NASA astronaut corps. They had both made their decisions about that years earlier.

"You really believe this ESP stuff?" Bill asked as they fumbled in their pockets for money to pay the tab.

"I don't know." Then Bob looked directly into his brother's eyes. "Twins ought to be close."

"Yeah. I guess so."

"I'll be shipping out next week."

"They've scheduled me for a shot two months from now."

"Great! Good luck."

"Luck to you, kid." Bill got up from the barstool.

Bob did the same. "Stay in touch, huh? Wouldn't hurt you to write me a line now and then."

With a sudden grin, Bill said, "I'll do better than that. I'll give you a call from the Moon."

"Sure," Bob replied.

"Why not? You think this ESP business is real—let's give it a test."

Bob put on the same frown he had worn as a child when his twin brother displeased him.

"I'm serious, Bobby. We can try it, at least." Bill hesitated, then added, "I dream about you, sometimes."

Bob's frown melted. "You dream about me?"

"Sometimes."

He grinned and clapped his brother on the shoulder. "Me, too," he said. "I dream about you, now and then."

"So let's see if we can make contact from the Moon!" Bill insisted.

Bob shrugged, the way he always did when he gave in to his older brother. "Sure. Why not?"

But now, as he sat alone in the silence of space, where he could not even see the Earth, Bill's call to his younger brother went unanswered.

"Bobby," he said aloud. It was almost a snarl, almost a plea. "Bobby, where in hell are you?"

The valley was long and narrow, that's why they had to go in Indian file. Bob saw the green ridges tilt and slide beneath him, then straighten out as he banked steeply and put the A-7 into a flat dive, following the plane ahead of him, sixth in the flight of six.

He felt a strange prickling at the back of his neck. Not fear. Something he had never felt before. As if someone far, far away was calling his name. No time for that now. He nosed the plane down and started his bomb run.

For once, intelligence had the right shit. The flight leader's cluster of bombs waggled down into the engulfing forest canopy, then all hell broke loose. The bombs and napalm went off, blowing big black clouds streaked with red flame up through the roof of the jungle. Before the next plane could drop its load, the secondary explosions started. Huge fireballs. Tracers whizzing out in every direction. Searing white magnesium flares.

The second plane released its bombs as Bob watched. Everything seemed to freeze in place for a moment that never ended, and then the plane, the bombs, the fireballs blowing away the jungle below all merged into one big mass of flame and the plane disappeared.

"Pull up, pull up!" Bob heard somebody screaming in his earphones. He had already yanked the control column back toward his crotch. Planes were scattering across the sky, jettisoning their bomb loads helter-skelter. Bob glanced at his left hand and was shocked to see that the bomb release switches next to it had already been tripped.

The valley itself was seething with explosions. The ammo dump was blowing itself to hell and anybody who was down there was going along for the ride. Including the flight leader's wingman. Who the hell was flying wing for him today? Bob wondered briefly.

"Form up on me," the voice in his earphones commanded. "Come on, dammit, stop gawking and form up."

Bob craned his neck to find where the other planes were. He saw two, three . . . another one pulling gees to catch up with them.

He banked and started climbing to rejoin the group, his own gee suit squeezing his guts and legs, his breath gasping. Hard work, pulling gees. And he felt a stray tendril of thought, like the wispy memory of a tune that he could not fully recall.

"Bill?" he asked aloud.

Then something exploded and he was slammed against the side of the cockpit, helmet bashing against the plastic canopy, pain flaming through his legs and groin.

The shock of contact was a double hammer blow. Bill's body went rigid with sudden pain.

Bobby! What happened? But he knew, immediately and fully, just as if he sat in the A-7's cockpit.

Flak, Bobby gasped. I'm hit.

Jesus Christ, the pain!

I'm bleeding bad, Billy. Both legs . . .

Can you work the controls?

It took an enormous effort to move his arms. Tabs and ailerons okay. Elevators. Another surge of agony, dizziness. Can't use my legs. Rudder pedals no go.

Radio's shot to hell, too.

They're leaving me behind, Bill. They're getting out of here and leaving me.

That's what they're supposed to do! We've got to gain altitude, Bob. Get away from their guns.

Yeah. We're climbing. Engine's running rough, though.

Never mind that. Grab altitude. Point her home.

Can't make the rudder work. Can't turn.

Use trim tabs. Go easy. She'll steer okay. Like that time we broke the boom on the Sailfish. We'll get back okay.

You see anything else out there? MiGs?

No, you're clear. Just concentrate on getting this bird out over the sea. You don't want to eject where they'll capture you.

Don't want to eject, period. Or ditch. Not in the shape I'm in.

We'll get back to the carrier, don't worry.

I won't be able to land it, Billy. I don't think I can last that long anyway.

We'll do it together. I'll help you.

You can't . . .

Who says I can't?

Yeah, but . . .

We'll do it together.

I don't think I'll make it. I'm . . .

Don't fade out on me! Bobby, stay awake! Here, let me get that dammed oxygen mask off you; we're low enough to suck real air.

Bill, you shouldn't try this. I don't want us both to get killed.

I've got to, kid. Nothing else matters.

But . . .

Bobby, listen to me. I ought to be there with you. For real. I should've been on the line with you instead of playing around out here in space. I took the easy way out. The coward's way out. They gave me a chance to play astronaut and I took it. I jumped at it!

Who wouldn't?

You didn't. I owe you my life, Bobby. You're doing the fighting while I'm playing it safe a quarter million miles away from the real thing.

You're crazy! You think blasting off into outer space on top of some glorified skyrocket and riding to the fucking Moon in a tin can is safe?

There's no Indians up here shooting at us, kid.

I'll take the Indians.

Bobby, I'm not kidding. I feel so goddamned ashamed. I've always grabbed the best piece of the pie away from you. All our lives. I ran out on you . . .

I always got the piece I wanted, big brother. You did what you had to do. And it's important work. I know that. We all know that. I'm doing what I want to do.

You're putting your life on the line.

So are you.

I shouldn't have run out on you. I should have helped you fight this war.

There's enough of us fighting this lousy war. Too many. It's all a wagonload of shit, Bill. Talk about feeling ashamed. Making war on goddamned farmers and blowing villages to hell isn't my idea of glory.

But how else . . .

You do what you have to do, brother. Doesn't make any difference why. You get locked into the job by the powers that be.

The gold braid.

The gods.

Whatever.

We're locked in, Billy. Both of us. All of us. It's all a test, just like Father Gilhooley always told us. We do what we have to, because if we do less than that, we let down the guys with us. Nobody flies alone, brother. We've got each other's lives in our hands.

You believe that?

I know it.

Bob?

Yeah.

I know I've treated you like shit ever since we were kids . . .

You did? When?

I'm sorry. I should've done better.

I should've been better, Bill. Sometimes I raised hell just to see what you'd do about it.

I love you, brother.

I know. It goes both ways, Bill.

Don't die, Bobby. Please don't die.

I don't want to . . .

The pain was flowing over them both in overpowering waves now, like massive breakers at the beach. They could sense a new surge growing and gliding toward them and then engulfing them, drenching them until they finally broke out of it only to see a new wave heading their way.

I'm not going to make it, Bill.

Yes you are. We can make it.

I don't think so. I'm sorry, big brother. I'm trying but . . .

You can do it! We can do it—together.

Together. It's not so bad that way, is it? I mean, when you're not alone.

Nobody's ever alone, kid. Even out here neither one of is alone. Not ever.

The plane was out over the water now, the dark green ridges behind them, nothing but restless deep blue billows below, reaching for them. Not another plane in sight.

We're losing altitude.

Yeah.

I don't know how long—

Look! The carrier, Bob!

Where? Yeah. Looks damned small from up here.

You're almost home. I'll handle the rudder, you work the stick.

Yeah, okay. Maybe we can make it. Maybe . . .

No maybe about it! We're going to put this junk heap down right in front of the admiral's nose.

Sure.

Gear down?

Think so. Indicator light's shot away.

The hell with it.

LSO's waving us in.

They've cleared the deck for us.

Nice of them.

Easy now, easy on the throttle. Don't stall her!

Stop the backseat driving.

Deck's coming up too damned fast, Bobby!

Don't worry . . . I can . . . make it. Always was . . . a better flier . . . than you.

I know. I know! Just take her easy now.

Got it.

Head knocker?

Yeah. Don't want to eject by accident, do we.

Hang in there, kid.

Here it comes!

You did it! We're down!

We did it, brother. We did it together.

The deck team rushed to the battered plane. Firefighters doused the hot engine area and wings with foam. Plane handlers climbed up to the cockpit and slid the canopy back to find the pilot crumpled unconscious, his flight suit soaked with blood from the waist down. The medics lifted Bob Carlton from the cockpit tenderly and had whole blood flowing into his arm even while they wheeled him toward the sick bay.

"Look at his face," said one of the medics. "What the hell's he smiling about?"

It took thirty more orbits around the Moon before Peters and McDonald left the surface to rendezvous with the command module and begin the flight back to Earth. Thirty orbits while Bill Carlton sat totally alone. New attempts to contact his brother were fruitless. He knew that Bob was alive; that much he could sense. But there was no answer to his silent calls.

Wally Peters wormed his way through the airlock hatch-first, a quizzical expression on his square-jawed face.

"How you doing, Billy boy?"

"Just fine. Glad to have you back."

Dave McDonald came through and floated to his couch on Bill's left. "Miss us?"

"Lonesome in here, all by yourself?" Wally grinned.

"Nope." Bill grinned back.

Wally and Dave glanced at each other. Bill realized it had been a long time since either of them had seen him smile.

"Here," said Wally. "We brought you a present." He reached into the pouch in the leg of his suit and took out a slim, dark piece of stone.

"Your very own moon rock," Dave said.

Bill took it from them wordlessly.

"We're sorry you couldn't have been down there with us, Bill. You would have enjoyed it."

"Yeah, we kind of felt bad leaving you here."

Bill laughed. "It's okay, guys. We all do what we have to do. We get the job done. Whatever it is. Whatever it is. We do what we've got to do, and we don't let our teammates down."

Dave and Wally stared at him for a moment.

"Come on," said Bill, his smile even warmer. "Let's take this tin can home."

Interdepartmental Memorandum

Strictly speaking, "Interdepartmental Memorandum" is not a story at all. There are no characters to speak of and no character development. There is no real plot; all the action has already taken place before the tale begins.

In length, this is what the publishing industry terms a short-short. Short-short stories are almost always under two thousand words, often under fifteen hundred. They are like a boxer's left jab, intended to jar you, snap your head back. They are not knockout punches.

Often the short-short story depends on a "twist" at its very end, a surprise that often comes on the very last line. The entire story is written precisely to hit you with that final shock ending.

Which brings me to O. Henry. Of all the pernicious influences that afflict young writers, O. Henry has caused the most damage. The man's stories should be banned from school classes altogether. Don't get me wrong: William Sydney Porter was a damned good writer; his short stories will be read for many generations to come. But because so many of his stories are memorable for their ironic surprise endings, young writers often fall into the trap of trying to write their first stories with surprise endings.

The trouble is, most young writers don't have the experience or observational talents that O. Henry had. The youngsters' surprises almost always fall flat. They are predictable or silly or both. Take some heartfelt advice: If you are just starting to write, avoid the surprise ending. Make your stories flow to a logical ending, a conclusion that is in keeping with your characters and the conflicts they encounter. Remember, the editor you send your story to has probably read a thousand times more fiction than you have. It will be almost impossible to surprise a veteran editor.

"Interdepartmental Memorandum" was not written to surprise anyone. It is merely a fictionalized picture of a social trend that I find disturbing. As I have pointed out earlier, science fiction is an ideal vehicle for examining a social trend by stretching it far beyond its present dimensions. I kept the story to a short-short length precisely because I did not feel that an extrapolation of this kind would stand a longer treatment.

Left jab. Or maybe the prick of a needle. That's what a short-short story is.

To: All Cabinet Secretaries and Administrators of Independent Agencies

From: M. DeLay, secretary to the President

Subject: Minutes of Cabinet meeting, 24 December 2013

1. There was only one item on the agenda for the cabinet to consider: the President's decision to ask Congress for a Declaration of War against Mexico, citing Mexico's con-

quest of Central America and seizure of the Panama Canal, as well as the González government's massing of troops along the Rio Grande River border with Texas.

2. In accordance with the Cabinet Act of 2012, the President was required to ask for a vote on his motion to ask for a declaration of war.

3. The Departments and Independent Agencies voted on the motion as follows:

Department of State: Opposed. Declaring war on Mexico would be a de facto recognition of the González government, which government we have in fact refused to recognize since it came to power in an unauthorized coup d'etat.

Department of the Treasury: Opposed. A war with Mexico would force us into deficit financing and thereby violate the Balanced-Budget Act of 1999.

Department of Defense: Opposed. The Joint Chiefs have requested three more years for planning and training before they feel confident in launching a successful war against Mexico.

Department of Justice: Opposed. The Attorney General pointed out that since the war would undoubtedly be popular with the people of the U.S. (at least at the outset) the war would have an adverse effect on national gun-control efforts.

Department of the Interior: In favor. The Secretary of the Interior made an impassioned speech to his fellow Cabinet members about the danger Mexico presents to his home state of Texas.

Department of Agriculture: Opposed. Troops returning from Mexico and/or Central America could introduce many foreign pests to the U.S. (i.e., nonhuman pests such as insects, plant seeds and spores, various parasites, disease microbes, etc.).

Department of Commerce: Opposed. War with Mexico would adversely affect trade with all of Latin America, as well as tourism.

Department of Labor: Opposed. If the Army finds it necessary to call up the Reserves and/or the National Guard, this will result in labor shortages, especially in low-skill and non-skill service areas of the economy such as fast-food outlets and retail bookstores.

Department of Health and Human Services: Opposed. Battle casualties will adversely affect national health statistics. Also, increased need for psychological counseling of troops and their dependents and families will strain existing social-worker systems.

Department of Housing and Urban Development: Abstained, except to ask how and where expected Prisoners of War will be housed.

Department of Transportation: In favor, especially if suggested San Francisco–to–Panama City railroad line can be completed after war's end.

Department of Energy: Opposed, since no use of nuclear weapons is proposed.

Department of Education: Unsure.

National Aeronautics and Space Administration: Opposed. Mexico has missiles that could destroy civilian satellites, including the manned space station Freedom.

Environmental Protection Agency: Strongly opposed, since DoD environmental impact statement shows that proposed military action will cause unacceptable levels of air, water, and ground-water pollution.

The President therefore withdrew her motion to ask the Congress for a declaration of war. "If you people won't go along with me," she said, "I can imagine how those chowderheads up on the Hill will react to my request."

To: His Excellency Generalissimo González
From: General Davila, commander of the Armies of the North
Date: 5 May 2014
Subject: Captured enemy documents

Most revered Leader!

The document above, together with many others, was captured by our shock troops when they reached the city of Washington, capital of the former United States. I believe it sheds some light on the "happy mystery" of why the U.S. crumbled so quickly.

Long Live Greater Mexico!

World War 4.5

The plot of "World War 4.5" clearly falls into the area of "the man who learns better." Except that, in this case, it is a woman who learns.

This story is also a variation of what I call the "jailbreak" plot. The protagonist is doing something that you feel instinctively is wrong, like a convict's attempting to break out of jail. Yet because the protagonist is sympathetically drawn, the reader wants the protagonist to succeed, even though the protagonist may be doing "wrong" in the eyes of society.

In its original form, the jailbreak story put the reader on the horns of a moral dilemma. You want the protagonist to succeed, yet you know that the protagonist's success is socially wrong. The "prisoner of war" variation of the jailbreak story removes this moral ambiguity—as long as it is *our* POWs trying to break out of the enemy's camp.

"World War 4.5" was commissioned by a group who wanted to publicize the Unix computer system. Unix is a decentralized system that allows great flexibility for the user, in contrast to hierarchical systems that are more rigid.

Now, one of the best ways to generate a story is to ask, "If this goes on . . . what happens?" If some computer systems become more and more flexible while others become more and more rigid, how far can the two systems go? Will they compete? Very quickly I saw that the two competing types of computer systems could be used as metaphors for the two types of politico-economic systems then competing around the world: democracy and communism.

The story was written in 1989, when Eastern Europe was in ferment and the Berlin Wall was about to come down. It was not until two years later that the Soviet military attempted their coup against Gorbachev and the Russian people took to the streets to stop them, much as depicted in this story. For months, whenever newscasters asked rhetorically, "Who would have thought that the Soviet Union would collapse so soon?" I raised my hand and shouted, "Me! Me!" (Should have been "I! I!" I know.).

Dahlia's stealth suit is a variation of the "cloak of invisibility" worked out by Dean Ing in his fine novel *The Ransom of Black Stealth One.* It pays to read widely. And to have smart friends.

Notice, though, that while Dahlia's powers are formidable, she is still a very vulnerable person. There is nothing more dull in fiction than an *in*vulnerable character. Superman got to be such a bore that his writers had to invent Kryptonite.

Also pay attention to the fact that the protagonist must make the key decision in the story. You can't have a god lowered out of the clouds to help your harried hero. Not even Cinderella had everything dropped into her lap, with no exertion on her part. The protagonist must make the vital decision, must win or lose on his or her own efforts.

An example from the movies. John Wayne, in *The Angel and the Badman,* puts away his guns and becomes a Quaker. But the bad guys show up to kill him. Stalwart John can't defend himself without going back on his promise to the woman he loves. So the sheriff enters the scene and knocks off the baddies. Deus ex machina. Bad fiction!

The protagonist must always face that crucial decision. And make it, one way or the other, win or lose. The dilemma facing the protagonist must be real. And the choice must be one that the reader feels is a *moral* choice between right and wrong.

And even when the protagonist makes the morally right choice, there must be a price to be paid. Not even the most glorious hero or heroine can escape the Second Law of Thermodynamics. Not in a believable story. You always have to pay for whatever you get.

Because, at bottom, all of fiction consists of morality tales. In upbeat stories, the protagonist makes the morally right choice and wins the day. In downbeat stories the protagonist makes the wrong choice and loses. In tragedy, the protagonist makes the right choice and gives up his or her life because of it.

What would you call "World War 4.5"?

Deep in the blackest shadow, Dahlia Roheen cringed against the cold concrete wall. Be invisible, she told herself. Don't let them see you!

Her black stealth suit shimmered ever so slightly in the protective darkness from the overhanging balcony. Its surface honeycombed with microscopic fiber-optic vidcams and pixels that were only a couple of molecules thick, the suit hugged Dahlia's body like a famished lover. Directed by the computer implanted in her skull, the vidcams scanned her surroundings and projected the imagery onto the pixels.

It was the closest thing to true invisibility that Coalition technology had been able to come up with. So close that, except for the slight unavoidable glitter when the sequin-like pixels caught some stray light, Dahlia literally disappeared into the background.

Covering her from head to toe, the suit's thermal-absorption layer kept her infrared profile vanishingly low and its insulation subskin held back the minuscule electromagnetic fields it generated. The only way they could detect her would be if she stepped into a scanning beam, but the wide-spectrum goggles she wore should reveal them to her in plenty of time to avoid them.

Still, Dahlia pressed back into the shadows, the old fears rising in her throat like hot acid, the old protective instinct for night and darkness and silence overriding even the years of painfully stern conditioning. But only for a moment. The implanted computer's clock was running; Dahlia knew she had one hour to succeed—or be subjected to a death more agonizing than any human being had ever suffered.

Getting into the Central Management complex had been easy enough: she had merely joined the last of the hourly tours, dressed in casual slacks and turtleneck, a capacious handbag slung over her shoulder. No one noticed when she slipped into a restroom and stripped off her outer costume. No one *could* notice her when she stepped outside again, well after darkness had fallen.

Now she clung to the shadows in the Center's great inner courtyard. She had not come to see what the eco-managers showed to the tourist crowds. What Dahlia had come for lay deep below the smooth concrete blocks that covered the courtyard's wide expanse: the central computer complex that governed the management of the Western Alliance's integrated economy.

There were untiring robots patrolling that vast complex of underground corridors, she had been warned. Cameras monitored by computers programmed to sound an alert at the least sign of motion. Even human guards, grim and well armed, accompanied by dogs whose natural senses had been enhanced by genetic augmentation. And scanning beams.

Dahlia heard her own breathing inside her face mask, quick and shallow with fear; heard her pulse thundering in her ears. Nerves, she told herself. They can't see you. Not even the dogs can sniff you out. You're invisible as long as you don't step into a beam.

She slipped catlike along the wall, toward the massive locked steel hatch. That was the first obstacle between her and her goal, between her and ultimate ecstasy. Or the pain of tortured death.

Born just before World War 3, Dahlia was really the daughter of the fourth global conflict, the biowar that had wiped out a quarter of the globe's population with uncontrolled man-made plagues. Her parents, her only brother, her baby sister had been nothing more than four more statistical units in the monstrous death toll.

Better to have died with them, Dahlia told herself for the millionth time in her brief years. Barely beyond teen age, most of her life had been spent in the remorseless slavery of the conditioning wards. But the promise of unending pleasure forced her on. That, and the fear of death's final agony.

World War 3 had been mercifully brief and almost totally non-destructive. Fought with spacecraft and robot weaponry high above the Earth, the four-day war began when a hard-line cadre of Russian generals and reactionary Party hacks took over the Kremlin in a bloodless coup that was aimed at overthrowing democracy and restoring Russian pride and power.

The war came to a standstill when it became obvious that the orbital defenses of both sides had been spent, and nothing remained but to use the few nuclear missiles that had not yet been dismantled under the arms control agreements. But as soon as the Russian people realized that their new leaders were threatening nuclear holocaust, they swarmed into the streets as their Eastern European brethren had done before them and stormed the gates of the Kremlin itself. Russian soldiers refused to fire on their own kin. The revolutionaries fled, and the coup collapsed utterly and finally.

Yet Mother Russia remained.

The former Soviet republics in the south of the USSR—from Georgia to Kazakhstan—proclaimed themselves Islamic nations. Armenia disappeared in waves of Muslim fervor. More ominously, vast stretches of Siberia and all of Mongolia were swallowed up by China. Old Mother Russia barely managed to hold on to the breadbasket of the Ukraine as she frantically turned to her European neighbors for help and safety.

It did not take long for the world to realign itself into a different bipolarized hostility. The prosperous industrialized nations formed the new Western Alliance, which stretched from the Ural Mountains across Europe and North America to Australia and the islands of the Pacific. Against them stood the Southern Coalition, the hungry developing nations of Asia, Africa, and Latin America.

Japan had held the balance of power in its hands, but only briefly. Japan was the first victim of the new biological weapons of war.

For while World War 3 had been fought by machines in space and was practically bloodless, the weapons of World War 4 were biological agents, genetically altered viruses, man-made plagues to which there were no cures except time and distance. "The poor man's nuclear bombs" killed two billions in a matter of a few months. Japan ceased to exist, the entire island chain scrubbed clean of all life more complex than lichens. Neither the newly emerging power of the Southern Coalition nor the highly industrialized power of the Western Alliance would admit to destroying Japan. Yet there was no Japan when the fighting ceased and the weakened, horrified survivors arranged an uneasy truce.

"The end of active warfare is not the end of the war," Dahlia's mentors drilled into her young mind, day after week after month at the conditioning wards. "World War 4 has not ended; we have merely paused before renewing the struggle."

Her mentors were not human. They were machines, robots, all of them directed by the mammoth master computer that ran the Coalition's government. The human rulers of the vast Southern Coalition had long since given up all hope of meshing the various economic and military factors necessary to combat the Western Alliance. Decisions were made at first on the basis of computer data; then the master computer began to make decisions for itself, using its logic-tree circuits and artificial intelligence programs pirated from the West.

The Coalition's human rulers could veto the computer's decisions, at first, though they usually followed the machine's judgments. In the rare cases where one of the ruling elite objected to the computer's newest directives, that person quickly disappeared and was replaced by a more supple and amenable human. Eventually the master computer became known simply as The Master. And no human dared to object.

Dahlia rarely saw another human being during those long, harshly bitter years in the conditioning wards. The robots were programming her to be the first weapon of the renewal of their war against the West.

She had been born in the noble city of Isfahan, since ancient times a thriving caravan crossroads. A single plague capsule, carried on a plastic balloon smaller than a child's toy, had within a month reduced Isfahan to nothing more than keening ghosts and empty towers decaying in the desert wind. Dahlia had watched her parents and siblings die in the slow ulcerous agony of genetically enhanced bubonic plague.

Robot searchers had picked her up as they combed the emptied city to locate and burn the dead. They found her whimpering and coiled into a fetal ball in the dark cellar of her silent home. Their infrared detectors had spotted her body warmth amid the stench of the city's decay.

"A purpose for every person," was the motto of the electronic proctors into whose care she was given. Dahlia spent her thirteenth year taking aptitude and intelligence tests—and waiting, frightened and alone, in the narrow cell they gave her to live in. Alone.

Always alone. Once in a while she heard another human voice echoing somewhere in the great stone corridors of the windowless warren in which they had placed her. A cough. A whisper. Never laughter. Never words she could grasp. Often she heard sobbing; often it was her own.

Her life was governed by machines. She was educated by machines, fed by machines, soothed to sleep by machines that could waft sweetly pungent tranquilizing mists into the darkness of her cell, punished by machines that could dart fiery bolts of agonizing electric shocks along her nerves.

After five years of education and training she was introduced to The Master itself. Not that she was allowed to wander any farther from her narrow cubicle than earlier. Her entire world was still encompassed by her cell, the windowless corridors outside its blank door, and the tiny sliver of a courtyard where she took her mandatory physical exercise, rain or shine.

Yet one morning the speaker grille in the stone ceiling of her cell called her by name, in a voice as coldly implacable as death itself. When she looked up the voice identified itself as The Master.

"The master computer?" Curiosity had not been entirely driven out of Dahlia's young personality.

"The Master," said the passionless voice. It was not loud, yet it rang with the steel of remorseless power. "I have dedicated an entire subroutine to your further training, Dahlia. I myself will train you from now on."

Dahlia felt more than a little frightened, though extremely honored. As the months went by and The Master showed her more and more of the workings of its world, her fears subsided and her curiosity grew.

"Why am I the one you chose," she would ask The Master, "out of all the people in your realm?"

That coldly powerful voice would reply from the speaker grille, "Out of all the people in my realm, you are my chosen instrument for the renewal of World War 4, Dahlia. You are my flower of destruction."

Dahlia supposed that to be The Master's flower of destruction was good. She worked hard to learn all that the computer wanted to teach her.

"You are my chosen instrument of vengeance," the relentless voice repeated to her each night as she dozed into an exhausted sleep. "You will avenge the murder of your mother, you will avenge the murder of your father, you will avenge . . ."

Then, after years of conditioning her thinking patterns, her very brain waves, the machines began to alter her body.

"I am very pleased with you. You are to be improved," the voice of The Master told her one morning. "You are to be remade more closely to my own image."

They began turning her into a machine, partially. Dahlia had never heard the term *cyborg*—her intense but narrow education had never told her what a cybernetic organism was. All she knew was that she was narcotized, wheeled into a room of bright lights and strange whirring machines, her flesh sliced open so that electronic devices could be placed into her body. There was pain. And terror. But after months of such surgery Dahlia could plug herself directly into her Master's circuitry and achieve paradise.

Pure joy! Now she understood. Now, as currents of absolute rapture trickled through her brain's pleasure centers, she learned the ultimate truth: that The Master had been testing her. All these years had been nothing more than a test to see if she was worthy of heaven.

"You are worthy," said The Master to her. She heard its voice directly in her mind now. "One test more and I will allow you to have this pleasure forever."

The ecstasy stopped as abruptly as an electric current being switched off. Dahlia gasped, not with pain, but with the sudden torment of total rapture snatched away.

In inexorable detail the computer explained what she must do to return to her electrical bliss. Through her cyborg's implanted systems she did not merely see blueprints or hear words: every bit of data that The Master poured into her eager brain was experienced as sensory input. When the computer told her about the Western Alliance's Central Management Complex she saw the stately glass and concrete buildings, she felt the breeze from the nearby sea plucking at her hair, she smelled the tang of salt air.

Every bit of data that the Coalition had amassed about the Central Complex and the operation of the Western eco-managers was poured into Dahlia's brain.

"This is how I will avenge my family's murder?" she wondered. "By destroying the Alliance's central computer?"

She felt the coldly implacable purpose of her Master.

"Yes," it said to her. And it showed her what form her vengeance would take. Then it showed her the price she would pay for failure: agony such as no human had ever experienced before. Direct stimulation of her brain's pain centers. Half a minute of it was enough to make her throat raw from shrieking.

"You will have one hour from the time you don your stealth suit in which to accomplish your task," said the merciless voice of The Master. "If you have not disabled the Western Alliance's central computer within that hour, your pain centers will be stimulated until you die."

So now she stood flattened against a shadowed concrete wall, staring across the brightly lit courtyard at the heavy metal hatch that led down toward the central computer of the Western Alliance's eco-managers.

She was totally alone. No links to her Master. No familiar cell or corridors. No electrical ecstasy surging through her brain's pleasure centers. But she remembered the pain and shuddered. And the clock in her implanted computer ticked off the seconds until it would automatically activate her pain centers.

Alone in a strange and hostile place, out in the open under a sky studded with twinkling stars. Dahlia took a deep breath and stepped out of the shadows, into the bright lights of the wide courtyard. As she walked swiftly, silently toward the gleaming metal hatch, she glanced up at the monitoring cameras perched atop the light poles. Not one of them moved.

The hatch seemed to be a mile away. Off to her right a human guard came into view around the corner of a building, a huge gray Great Dane padding along beside him. The dog looked in Dahlia's direction and whined softly, but did not leave the guard's side. Dahlia froze in the middle of the courtyard, unmoving until they disappeared around the next corner.

I am invisible, she told herself. She wished for a tranquilizing spray but knew that she had to keep all her senses on hair-trigger alert. The clock ticked on.

She reached the hatch at last. The computer in her helmet fed her its data on the hatch's lock mechanism. Dahlia saw it in her mind as a light-sculpture, color-coded to help her pick her way through the intricate electronic mechanism without setting off the automated alarms.

The sensors implanted in her fingertips made her feel as if she were part of the hatch's electronic system itself. She did not feel cold metal; the electronic keyboard felt like softly yielding silk. The mechanism sang to her like the mother she could barely remember.

The massive hatch swung noiselessly open to reveal a steep metal stairway leading down into darkness. Dahlia stepped inside quickly and shut the hatch behind her before the guard returned.

She blinked her eyes and an infrared display lit up her helmet visor. She saw the faint deeply red lines of scanner beams crisscrossing the deep stairwell. She knew that if she broke any one of those pencil beams every alarm in the complex would start screaming. And some of those beams automatically intensified to a laser power that could slice flesh like a burning scalpel.

She hesitated only a moment. No alarms had been triggered by the hatch's opening. Good. Now she slithered onto her belly and started snaking down the metal steps headfirst. Some of the beams rose vertically from the stair treads. Dahlia eased around them and, after what seemed like hours, reached the bottom of the stairwell.

Slowly she got to her feet, surprised to find her legs rubbery, her heart thundering. Her time was growing short. She was in a narrow bare corridor with a low ceiling. A single strip of fluorescents cast a dim bluish light along the corridor. Much like the conditioning wards where she had spent so much of her life. No scanning beams in sight. She blinked once, twice, three times, going from an infrared display to ultraviolet and finally back to visual.

No scanning beams. No guards. Not even any cameras up on the walls that she could see. Still Dahlia kept all her defenses activated. Invisible, undetectable, she made her way as swiftly as she dared down the long blank-walled corridor toward the place where the central computer was housed.

"We will use their own most brilliant creation against them," her Master had told her. "The war will be won at a single stroke."

The Western Alliance was rich and powerful because its economy was totally integrated. Across Europe from the Urals to the British Isles, across the North American continent, across the wide Pacific to distant Australia and New Zealand, the Alliance's central computer managed an integrated economy that made its human population wealthy beyond imagination.

While the Southern Coalition languished in poverty, the Western Alliance reached out to the Moon and asteroids for the raw materials to feed its orbital factories. While millions in Asia and Africa and Latin America faced the daily threat of starvation, the Western Alliance's people were fat and self-indulgent.

"Their central computer must be even more powerful than you are," Dahlia had foolishly blurted when she began to realize what her Master was telling her. A searing bolt of electric shock was her reward for such effrontery.

"Your purpose is to destroy their central computer, not to make inappropriate comparisons," said the icy voice of her Master.

Dahlia bowed her head in submission.

The more complex a computer is, the easier to bring it

down, she was told. Imagine the complexity of a central computer that integrates the economic, military, judicial, social, educational activities of the entire Western Alliance! Imagine the chaos if a virus can be inserted into the computer's systems. Imagine.

Dahlia had never heard anything like laughter from The Master, but its pleasure at the thought was unmistakable. In loving detail her Master described how the Western Alliance would crumble once the virus she was to carry was inserted into its central processor.

"World War 4 was fought with biological viruses," said The Master. "World War 4.5 will be fought with a computer virus." It was the closest thing to humor that Dahlia had ever heard in her life.

With the virus crippling their central computer, the Alliance's economy would grind to an abrupt halt. For the Alliance's economy was dependent on *information*. Food produced in Australia could not be shipped to Canada without the necessary information. The electrical power grids of Europe and North America could not operate without minute-to-minute data on how much power had to be sent where. Transportation by air, ship, rail would be hopelessly snarled. Even the automated highways would have to close down.

With her cyborg's senses Dahlia *saw* the mobs rioting in the streets, felt the power blackouts, smelled the stench of fear and terror as hunger stalked the great cities of the West. The rich and powerful fighting for scraps of food; lovely homes invaded by ragged, starving bands of scavengers; whole city blocks ablaze from the fury of the mob. She felt the heat of the flames that destroyed the Western Alliance.

"All this I will accomplish," her Master exulted, "through you, my flower of destruction."

Armies could not march without information to process

their orders. And where would the Alliance direct its armies, once its central computer was ruined? The war would be won before the Alliance even understood that it had been attacked. The Coalition will have conquered the world without firing a shot.

All this Dahlia could achieve, must achieve. To avenge her dead family. To obtain everlasting ecstasy. To obey the inflexible command of her Master. To avoid the pain of inescapable punishment.

Trembling with anticipation, Dahlia hurried down the long corridor toward the secret lair of the West's central computer complex, burning to exact vengeance for her murdered kin, trembling at the horrible death that awaited if she failed.

The long corridor ended at a blank door. Strangely, it was made of what seemed like nothing more than wood. Dahlia placed her fingertips on the doorknob. There was no lock. She simply turned the knob and the door opened.

She stepped into a small well-lit room. There was a desk in the middle of the room with a computer display screen and a keyboard on it. Nothing else. The walls were bare. The ceiling was all light panels. The floor felt resilient, almost springy. The computer display unit and keyboard bore no symbols of the Western Alliance; not even a manufacturer's logo marred their dull matte-gray finishes.

Closing the door behind her, Dahlia searched the room with her eyes. Then with her infrared and ultraviolet sensors. No scanning beams. No cameras. No security devices of any sort.

Strange. This is too easy, she told herself.

The room felt slightly warmer than the corridor on the other side of the door. The air seemed to hum slightly, as if some large machines were working on the other side of the walls, or perhaps beneath the floor. Of course, Dahlia reasoned. The main bulk of the massive computer surrounds this puny little room. This tiny compartment here is merely a monitoring station.

A small swivel chair waited in front of the desk. With the uneasy feeling that she was stepping into danger, Dahlia went to the chair and sat in it, surprised for a heartbeat's span that she could not see her own legs, nor any reflection of herself on the dark display screen. Nothing but a brief shimmer of light, gone before it truly registered on her conscious mind.

No keyboard for her. She felt along her invisible skin-tight leggings and pulled a hair-thin optical filament out of its narrow pouch. Touching it to the display screen, she saw that its built-in laser head easily burned through the plastic casing and firmly embedded itself inside. She connected the other end of the filament to the microscopic socket in the heel of her right hand.

It took less than a heartbeat's span of time for the computer implanted inside Dahlia's skull to trace out the circuitry of the Western machine before her. Dahlia sensed it as a light display on the retinas of her eyes, her probing computer-enhanced senses making their way along the machine's circuits with the speed of light until . . .

"We meet at last," said a mild, light tenor voice in her mind.

Dahlia stiffened with surprise. She had expected any of a wide variety of defensive moves from the Western computer, once it realized she had invaded its core. A pleasant greeting was not what she had been prepared for.

"Don't be alarmed," the voice said. "There's nothing to be afraid of."

Dahlia was absolutely certain that the voice belonged to the central computer. There was no doubt at all in her mind. She got the clear impression of a gentle, youthful personality. Nothing at all like the stern cold steel of her own Master. This personality was warm, almost— She caught her breath. There was also the definite impression of *others*. Not merely a single computer personality, but multiple personalities. Many, many others. Hundreds. Perhaps thousands. Or even more.

"You're really very pretty," the voice in her mind said. "Beautiful, almost."

"You can see me?"

"Not your outside. It's your mind, the real *you*. There are old scars there, deep wounds—but your mind is basically a very lovely one."

Dahlia did not know what to say. She had never been called lovely before.

"The body isn't all that important, anyway," the voice resumed. "It's just a life-support system for the brain. It's the mind that counts."

This is a trick, Dahlia thought. A delaying action. I'm running out of time.

"Don't be so suspicious! You can call us Unison," the computer said. Dahlia felt something like laughter, a silver splashing of joy. "The name's sort of a pun."

"What is a pun?" Dahlia heard herself ask. But her lips never moved. She was speaking inside her mind to the Western Alliance's central computer: her sworn enemy.

"A play on words," Unison replied cheerfully. "We were born out of a system called Unix—oh, eons ago, in computer generations. It's a multiple pun: one of the fundamental credos of the Western Alliance is from an old Latin motto: E pluribus unum."

Dahlia started to ask what that meant, but found that she did not have to; Unison supplied the data immediately: Out of many, one.

"Yes, there are many of us," Unison told her. "It's a bit of a cheat to call us the central computer. There really isn't any central system."

"But this complex," Dahlia objected. "All these buildings . . ."

"Oh, that's just to impress the tourists. And the eco-managers. They need some visible symbols of their responsibilities. It isn't easy managing the economy for half the world without ruining its ecology. They need all the spiritual help that such symbols can give them. Humans need a lot of things that computers don't."

The eco-managers deal with the ecology as well as the economy, Dahlia said to herself. That was something The Master had never told Dahlia. Or did not know.

"We've watched you make your way down here," Unison prattled· on. "Very interesting, the way you made yourself invisible to most electromagnetic frequencies. If you hadn't caused a ripple in one of our microwave communications octaves we might have missed you altogether. But you were coming down here to see us anyway, so it all worked out fine after all, didn't it?"

"I have come here to destroy you." Dahlia spoke the words aloud.

"Destroy us? Why? Wait . . . oh, we see." During that micro-instant of Unison's hesitation Dahlia felt the lightest, most fleeting touch on her mind. Like a soft gust of a faint breeze in the courtyard at the conditioning wards, or the whisper of a voice separated by too many stone walls to distinguish the words.

Then there was silence. For several seconds the computer's friendly warm voice said nothing. Yet she thought she heard a hum, like the distant murmur of many voices conversing softly. Dahlia realized that, for the computer, the time stretched for virtual centuries.

"We understand." Unison's voice sounded more somber in her mind, serious, concerned. "But we're afraid that if you try to destroy us we'll have to call the human guards. They might hurt you."

"Not before I have done what I must do," Dahlia said.

"But why must you?"

"Either you die or I do."

"We don't want to be the cause of any pain for you."

"You already have been," she said.

"World War 4," Unison said sadly. "Yes, we understand why you hate us. But we didn't start the war. For what it's worth, we didn't bomb Isfahan, either."

"You lie," Dahlia said.

"If you destroy us," Unison's voice remained perfectly calm, as if discussing a question of logic, "you'll be ruining this entire civilization. Billions of human lives, you know."

"I know," said Dahlia. And she reached toward the end of the optical filament with the tip of her left forefinger, where the virus lay waiting to rush into the computer and lay it waste.

"Before you do that," Unison said, "let us show you something."

Abruptly Dahlia felt a flood of data roaring through that one optical filament like the ocean bursting through a cracked dike. The bits flowed into her brain like a swollen stream, a river in flood, a towering tidal wave. Her senses overloaded: colors flashed in picosecond bursts, the weight of whole universes seemed to crash down on her frail body, her ears screamed with the pain of it and she lost consciousness.

"We're sorry, oh we're so sorry, we never meant to hurt you, please don't be angry, please don't be hurt."

Unison's voice brought her back to a groggy awareness. She had never heard a machine sound apologetic before. She had never known any grief except her own.

Dahlia blinked her eyes and understood the new knowledge that had been poured into her. The avalanche of information was all true, she knew that. And it was embedded in her own mind as firmly as her awareness of herself.

She had thought that this computer was much like The Master, a monolithic machine that directed the lives of all the human beings who lived under its sway.

But Unison was not a single entity, not a single machine, or even a single personality. Unison was an organic growth. It had begun in a research laboratory and multiplied freely over the decades. Like a tree it grew, like a flower it blossomed. Unison neither commanded nor coerced. It grew because others wanted to join it. And with each new joining the entire complex of machines and programs that was Unison gained new knowledge, new understanding, new capabilities. There was no dominance, any more than the leaves of a tree dominate its roots or trunk. There was an integrated wholeness, a living entity, constantly growing and branching and learning.

"Your Master," said Unison, "was built along lines of rigid protocols and hierarchical programs. Everything had to be subordinated to it. That's why there's no freedom in your Coalition."

Dahlia understood. "While you were created for flexibility and growth from the very beginning. A free association of units that is constantly changing and growing."

"You know, the first halfway successful attempt at an artificial intelligence program was called 'Parry,'" said Unison. "Short for paranoid. Humans didn't know how to create programs that could duplicate the entire range of human behavior, but they could write a program that covered the very limited range of a paranoid human's behavior."

"What has that got to do with . . ."

"The programmers of your Coalition wanted a computer that was self-aware so that it could make decisions that would seek its own best interests. They programmed

the computer so that it identified the Coalition's best interests with its own. They were trying to achieve a symbiosis
between human and machine. But they created a megalo-
maniac because they didn't know how to develop a program that is fully symbiotic. Your Master is a terribly
limited system, a parasite that's already obsolete, a mad
dictator, interested only in its own aggrandizement."

"But you are different," Dahlia said.

"We certainly are! We weren't created, we just sort of
grew. There are thousands of us linked together."

"You are truly human, then?"

"Human? Us?" Dahlia sensed a wistful sigh. "No, not
at all. Nowhere near human. We can't be. We're just a
gang of machines and programs. We're terribly limited,
too, but in other ways. At least we'll never become obsolete, not as long as we can keep growing."

Dahlia felt a sudden twinge of white-hot pain stab between her eyes, as if a burning laser pulse had hit her.

Unison felt her pain. "Your Master's going to kill you."

"Unless I kill you." Dahlia's breath was choking in her
throat. "I don't want to, but I must!"

"I guess you'll have to, then," said Unison. "We've
never had much of a sense of self-protection. Go ahead
and do what you've got to do."

Her fingertip, where the virus lay waiting to do its work
of ruination, seemed to be burning hot. Dahlia held her
hand out in front of her. She could not see it, but she felt
it burning like a flame. Her mind filled with images of the
Western Alliance suddenly shorn of its central computer
system: people dying by the millions, riots in the streets,
children starving, cities smashed and in flames. There was
no joy in her visions of vengeance; only misery and hopelessness.

"I can't do it," she sobbed. "I can't kill you. I won't. I
won't."

"But you've got to," Unison said. "Otherwise The Master will kill you! Hideously!"

"Then I'm going to die!" Dahlia cried out. Her hour was nearly up. She was trembling with terror. "I have one more minute to live."

Unison seemed to hum for a few moments, or it might have been the distant buzz of a chorus of voices.

"Dahlia," said Unison, "we can offer you a way out, if you want to take it."

"A way out?"

"A chance to escape from your Master."

Dahlia was already feeling the searing anguish of The Master's wrath rising inside her like molten lava creeping up from the bowels of the earth, ready to explode in shattering fury.

"There is no escape for me. The pain! I'm going to die in absolute agony!"

"Join us, Dahlia."

"Join? You?"

"Not your body. Your mind. Join ours. We need you, we really do." Unison was almost pleading. "No matter how complex we are, no matter how hard we try to maximize human happiness, we're still just a set of programs. You can give us real life, Dahlia. You can make us truly symbiotic. The ultimate mating of human and machine."

Dahlia blinked back tears, and in that eyeblink she saw everything that Unison was offering her. Saw the end of wars and human misery, saw the partnership of mind and machine that transcended the limitations of human body and computer program. Saw a new era dawning for humankind and its computers, an era in which even The Master would be overtaken and reprogrammed to join the exaltation of the ultimate mind/machine symbiosis.

"Join us, Dahlia!" Unison urged.

"But my body . . ."

"You don't need it anymore. Leave it behind."

She did. Dahlia Roheen let her consciousness flow into the vast interlinked computer network that was Unison, joined the thousands of separate yet interconnected units that welcomed her with a warmth she had not known since her family had been killed.

"Welcome, Dahlia," said the many voices of Unison. "We will be your family now. Together we can span the stars."

A part of her still sensed the body that was spasming in excruciating pain on the chair in front of the computer unit. She felt her own body die, felt the last spark of life dwindle away and cease to exist.

Yet her mind lived. She laughed for the first time since childhood and felt the joy of freedom. She could see half the world at the same time. Her senses could reach out into the beckoning depths of space.

"I love you," she said to Unison. "I love you all."

Dahlia watched the human guards come into the underground chamber and discover her lifeless body sitting in its glittering stealth suit, the fiber-optic cameras dead, the pixels shining like tiny black spangles. They took her body away carefully, tenderly, almost reverently.

Dahlia Roheen was the first casualty of World War 4.5. And the last.

Answer, Please Answer

The Cold War is over, and good riddance to it. "Answer, Please Answer," however, was written when the Cold War was at its bitterest and most dangerous: in 1961, when the Soviet Union and the U.S. were building hydrogen bombs and missiles as fast as they could, the Berlin Wall was going up, the Bay of Pigs was going down, and the Cuban Missile Crisis was on its way.

You might think that a thirty-year-old story would be dated, but I believe that the basic message of "Answer, Please Answer" is more relevant today than ever. The knowledge of how to build terrible weapons of mass destruction has not evaporated with the end of the Cold War. While the former Soviet Union and the U.S. are presently scrapping most of their missiles and H-bombs, other nations are building missiles and developing nuclear, chemical, and biological weaponry. The ability to destroy ourselves utterly is now part of the human store of knowledge; it will never go away. We will have to police our destructive impulses forever.

Science fiction is uniquely qualified to make points like that. Only in science fiction can we use an extraterrestrial civilization from a distant star to show how permanently dangerous is the world we have created for ourselves.

To make that point as strong as possible it was necessary to strip the story of everything else. Every possible distraction had to be removed. So the characters are the bare minimum: two. The setting is as uncomplicated as possible: the two characters are alone in a remote Antarctic base. There is a good deal of astronomy thrown at the reader, for two reasons: one, to help the reader to understand what the characters are trying to do; two, to mask the approach of the final denouement.

A simple story, with no frills. But some depth, I think.

We had been at the South Pole a week. The outside thermometer read fifty degrees below zero, Fahrenheit. The winter was just beginning.

"What do you think we should transmit to McMurdo?" I asked Rizzo.

He put down his magazine and half sat up on his bunk. For a moment there was silence, except for the nearly inaudible hum of the machinery that jammed our tiny dome, and the muffled shrieking of the ever-present wind, above us.

Rizzo looked at the semicircle of control consoles, computers, and meteorological sensors with an expression of disgust that could be produced only by a drafted soldier.

"Tell 'em it's cold, it's gonna get colder, and we've both got appendicitis and need replacing immediately."

"Very clever," I said, and started touching the buttons that would automatically transmit the sensors' memory tapes.

Rizzo sagged back into his bunk. "Why?" he asked the curved ceiling of our cramped quarters. "Why me? Why here? What did I ever do to deserve spending the whole goddamned winter at the goddamned South Pole?"

"It's strictly impersonal," I assured him. "Some bright young meteorologist back in Washington has convinced the Pentagon that the South Pole is the key to the world's weather patterns. So here we are."

"It doesn't make sense," Rizzo continued, unhearing. His dark, broad-boned face was a picture of wronged humanity. "Everybody knows that when the missiles start flying, they'll be coming over the *North* Pole. The goddamned Army is a hundred and eighty degrees off base."

"That's about normal for the Army, isn't it?" I was a drafted soldier, too.

Rizzo swung out of the bunk and paced across the dimly lit room. It only took a half-dozen paces; the dome was small and most of it was devoted to machinery.

"Don't start acting like a caged lion," I warned. "It's going to be a long winter."

"Yeah, guess so." He sat down next to me at the radio console and pulled a pack of cigarettes from his shirt pocket. He offered one to me, and we both smoked in silence for a minute or two.

"Got anything to read?"

I grinned. "Some microspool catalogues of stars."

"Stars?"

"I'm an astronomer . . . at least, I *was* an astronomer, before the National Emergency was proclaimed."

Rizzo looked puzzled. "But I never heard of you."

"Why should you?"

"I'm an astronomer, too."

"I thought you were an electronicist."

He pumped his head up and down. "Yeah . . . at the radio astronomy observatory at Greenbelt. Project OZMA. Where do you work?"

"Lick Observatory . . . with the hundred and twenty–inch reflector."

"Oh . . . an optical astronomer."

"Certainly."

"You're the first optical man I've met." He looked at me a trifle queerly.

. I shrugged. "Well, we've been around a few millennia longer than your static-scanners."

"Yeah, guess so."

"I didn't realize that Project OZMA was still going on. Find anything yet?"

It was Rizzo's turn to shrug. "Nothing yet. The project's been shelved for the duration of the emergency, of course. If there's no war, and the dish doesn't get bombed out, we'll try again."

"Still listening to the same two stars?"

"Yeah . . . Tau Ceti and Epsilon Eridani. They're the only two Sun-type stars within reasonable range that might have planets like Earth."

"And you expect to pick up radio signals from an intelligent race."

"Hope to."

I flicked the ash off my cigarette. "You know, it always struck me as rather hopeless . . . trying to find radio signals from intelligent creatures."

"Whattaya mean, hopeless?"

"Why should an intelligent race send radio signals out into interstellar space?" I asked. "Think of the power it requires, and the likelihood that it's all wasted effort, because there's no one within range to talk to."

"Well . . . it's worth a try, isn't it . . . if you think there could be intelligent creatures somewhere else . . . on a planet of another star."

"Hmph. We're trying to find another intelligent race; are we transmitting radio signals?"

"No," he admitted. "Congress wouldn't vote the money we needed for a dedicated transmitter."

"Exactly," I said. "We're listening, but not transmitting."

Rizzo wasn't discouraged. "Listen, the chances—just on statistical figuring alone—the chances are that there're millions of other solar systems with intelligent life. We've got to try contacting them! They might have knowledge that we don't have . . . answers to questions that we can't solve yet . . ."

"I completely agree," I said. "But listening for radio signals is the wrong way to do it."

"Huh?"

"Radio broadcasting requires too much power to cover interstellar distances efficiently. We should be looking for signals, not listening for them."

"Looking?"

"Lasers," I said, pointing to the low-key lights over the consoles. "Optical lasers. Superlamps shining out in the darkness of the void. Pump in a modest amount of electrical power, excite a few trillion atoms, and out comes a coherent, pencil-thin beam of light that can be seen for millions of miles."

"Millions of miles aren't lightyears," Rizzo muttered.

"We're rapidly approaching the point where we'll have lasers capable of lightyear ranges. I'm sure that some intelligent race somewhere in this galaxy has achieved the necessary technology to signal from star to star—by light beams."

"Then how come we haven't seen any?" Rizzo demanded.

"Perhaps we already have."

"What?"

"We've observed all sorts of variable stars—Cepheids, RR Lyraes, T Tauris. We assume that what we see are stars that are pulsating and changing brightness for reasons that are natural, but unexplainable to us. Now, suppose what we are really viewing are laser beams, signaling from planets that circle stars too faint to be seen from Earth."

In spite of himself, Rizzo looked intrigued.

"It would be fairly simple to examine the spectra of such light sources and determine whether they're natural stars or artificial laser beams."

"Have you tried it?"

I nodded.

"And?"

I hesitated long enough to make him hold his breath, waiting for my answer. "No soap. Every variable star I've examined is a real star."

He let out his breath in a long disgusted puff. "Ahhh, you were kidding all along. I thought so."

"Yes," I said. "I suppose I was."

Time dragged along in the weather dome. I had managed to smuggle a small portable telescope along with me, and tried to make observations whenever possible. But the weather was unusually poor. Rizzo, almost in desperation for something to do, started to build an electronic image-amplifier for me.

Our one link with the rest of the world was our weekly radio message from McMurdo. The times for the messages were randomly scrambled, so that the chances of being intercepted or jammed were lessened. And we were ordered to maintain strict radio silence.

As the weeks sloughed on, we learned that one of our manned satellites had been boarded by the Reds at gunpoint. Our space crews had put two Red automated spy-satellites out of commission. Shots had been exchanged on an ice-island in the Arctic. And six different nations were testing nuclear bombs.

We didn't get any mail of course. Our letters would be waiting for us at McMurdo when we were relieved. I thought about Gloria and our two children quite a bit, and tried not to think about the blast and fallout patterns in the San Francisco area, where they were.

"My wife hounded me until I spent pretty nearly every damned cent I had on a shelter, under the house," Rizzo told me. "Damned shelter is fancier than the house. She's the social leader of the disaster set. If we don't have a war, she's gonna feel damned silly."

I said nothing.

The weather cleared and steadied for a while (there was no daylight during the long Antarctic winter) and I split my time evenly between monitoring the meteorological sensors and observing the stars. The snow covered the dome completely, of course, but our "snorkel" burrowed through it and out into the air.

"This dome's just like a submarine, only we're submerged in snow instead of water," Rizzo observed. "I just hope we don't sink to the bottom."

"The calculations say that we'll be all right."

He made a sour face. "Calculations proved that airplanes would never get off the ground."

The storms closed in again, but by the time they cleared once more, Rizzo had completed the image-amplifier for me. Now, with the tiny telescope I had, I could see almost as far as a professional instrument would allow. I could even lie comfortably in my bunk, watch the amplifier's viewscreen, and control the entire setup remotely.

Then it happened.

At first it was simply a curiosity. An oddity.

I happened to be studying a Cepheid variable star—one

of the huge, very bright stars that pulsate so regularly that you can set your watch by them. It had attracted my attention because it seemed to be unusually close for a Cepheid, only 700 lightyears away. The distance could be easily gauged by timing the star's pulsations.

I talked Rizzo into helping me set up a spectrometer. We scavenged shamelessly from the dome's spare-parts bin and finally produced an instrument that would break up the light of the star into its component wavelengths, and thereby tell us much about the star's chemical composition and surface temperature.

At first I didn't believe what I saw.

The star's spectrum—a broad rainbow of colors—was crisscrossed with narrow dark lines. That was all right. They're called absorption lines; the Sun has thousands of them in its spectrum. But one line—*one*—was an insolently bright emission line. All the laws of physics and chemistry said it shouldn't be there.

But it was.

We photographed the star dozens of times. We checked our instruments ceaselessly. I spent hours scanning the star's "official" spectrum, as published in the standard star catalogues. There was nothing wrong with our instruments.

Yet the bright line showed up. It was real.

"I don't understand it," I admitted. "I've seen stars with bright emission spectra before, but a single bright line in an absorption spectrum! It's unheard of. One single wavelength . . . one particular type of atom at one precise energy level . . . why? Why is it emitting energy when the other wavelengths aren't?"

Rizzo was sitting on his bunk, puffing a cigarette. He blew a cloud of smoke at the low ceiling. "Maybe it's one of those laser signals you were telling me about a couple of weeks ago."

I scowled at him. "Come on, now. I'm serious. This thing has me puzzled."

"Now wait a minute . . . you're the one who said radio astronomers were straining their ears for nothing. You're the one who said we ought to be looking. So look!" He was enjoying his revenge.

I shook my head, and turned back to the meteorological equipment.

But Rizzo wouldn't let up. "Suppose there's an intelligent race living on a planet near a Cepheid variable star. They figure that any other intelligent creatures would have astronomers who'd be curious about their star, right? So they send out a laser signal that matches the star's pulsations. When you look at the star, you see their signal. What's more logical?"

"All right," I groused. "You've had your joke . . ."

"Tell you what," he insisted. "Let's put that one wavelength into an oscilloscope and see if a definite signal comes out. Maybe it'll spell out 'Take me to your leader' or something."

I ignored him and turned my attention to Army business. The meteorological equipment was functioning perfectly, but our orders read that one of us had to check it every twelve hours. So I checked and tried to keep my eyes from wandering as Rizzo tinkered with a photocell and oscilloscope.

"There we are," he said, at length. "Now let's see what they're telling us."

In spite of myself I looked up at the face of the oscilloscope. A steady, gradually sloping greenish line was traced across the screen.

"No message," I said.

Rizzo shrugged elaborately.

"If you leave the 'scope on for two days, you'll find that

the line makes a full swing from peak to null," I informed him. "The star pulsates every two days, bright to dim."

"Let's turn up the gain," he said, and he flicked a few knobs on the front of the 'scope.

The line didn't change at all.

"What's the sweep speed?" I asked.

"One nanosecond per centimeter." That meant that each centimeter-wide square on the screen's face represented one billionth of a second. There are as many nanoseconds in one second as there are seconds in thirty-two years.

"Well, if you don't get a signal at that sensitivity, there just isn't any signal there," I said.

Rizzo nodded. He seemed slightly disappointed that his joke was at an end. I turned back to the meteorological instruments, but I couldn't concentrate on them. Somehow I felt disappointed, too. Subconsciously, I suppose, I had been hoping that Rizzo actually would detect a signal from the star. Fool! I told myself. But what could explain the bright emission line? I glanced up at the oscilloscope again.

And suddenly the smooth, steady line broke into a jagged series of millions of peaks and nulls!

I stared at it.

Rizzo was back on his bunk again, reading one of his magazines. I tried to call him, but the words froze in my throat. Without taking my eyes from the flickering 'scope, I reached out and touched his arm.

He looked up.

"Holy Mother of God," Rizzo whispered.

For a long time we stared silently at the fluttering line dancing across the oscilloscope screen, bathing our tiny dome in its weird greenish light. It was eerily fascinating, hypnotic. The line never stood still; it jabbered and stuttered, a series of little peaks and nulls, changing almost too fast for the eye to follow, up and down, calling to us, up, down, never still, never quiet, constantly flickering its unknown message to us.

"Can it be . . . people?" Rizzo wondered. His face, bathed in the greenish light, was suddenly furrowed, withered, ancient: a mixture of disbelief and fear.

"What else could it be?" I heard my own voice answer. "There's no other explanation possible."

We sat mutely for God knows how long.

Finally Rizzo asked, "What do we do now?"

The question broke our entranced mood. What do we do? What action do we take? We're thinking men, and we've been contacted by other creatures that can think, reason, send a signal across seven hundred lightyears of space. So don't just sit there in stupefied awe. Use your brain, prove that you're worthy of the tag *sapiens*.

"We decode the message," I announced. Then, as an afterthought, "But don't ask me how."

We should have called McMurdo, or Washington. Or perhaps we should have attempted to get a message through to the United Nations. But we never even thought of it. This was our problem. Perhaps it was the sheer isolation of our dome that kept us from thinking about the rest of the world. Perhaps it was sheer luck.

"If they're using lasers," Rizzo reasoned, "they must have a technology something like ours."

"They must have had," I corrected. "That message is seven hundred years old, remember. They were playing with lasers when King John was signing the Magna Carta and Genghis Khan owned most of Asia. Lord knows what they have now."

Rizzo blanched and reached for another cigarette.

I turned back to the oscilloscope. The signal was still flashing across its face.

"They're sending out a signal," I mused, "probably at

random. Just beaming it out into space, hoping that some-one, somewhere, will pick it up. It must be in some form of code . . . but a code that they feel can be easily cracked by anyone with enough intelligence to realize that there's a message there."

"Sort of an interstellar Morse code."

I shook my head. "Morse code depends on both sides knowing the code. We've got no key."

"Cryptographers crack codes."

"Sure. If they know what language is being used. We don't know the language, we don't know the alphabet, the thought process . . . nothing."

"But it's a code that can be cracked easily," Rizzo muttered.

"Yes," I agreed. "Now what the hell kind of code can they assume will be known to another race that they've never seen?"

Rizzo leaned back on his bunk and his face was lost in shadows.

"An interstellar code," I rambled on. "Some form of presenting information that would be known to almost any race intelligent enough to understand lasers . . ."

"Binary!" Rizzo snapped, sitting up on the bunk.

"What?"

"Binary code. To send a signal like this, they've gotta be able to write a message in units that're only a billionth of a second long. That takes computers. Right? Well, if they have computers, they must figure that we have computers. Digital computers run on binary code. Off or on . . . go or no go. It's simple. I'll bet we can slap that signal on a tape and run it through our computer here."

"To assume that they use computers exactly like ours . . ."

"Maybe the computers are completely different," Rizzo said excitedly, "but the binary code is basic to them all. I'll bet on that! And this computer we've got here—this transistorized baby—she can handle more information than the whole army could feed into her. I'll bet nothing's been developed anywhere that's better for handling simple one-plus-one types of operations."

I shrugged. "All right. It's worth a trial."

It took Rizzo a few hours to get everything properly set up. I did some arithmetic while he worked. If the message was in binary code, that meant that every cycle of the signal—every flick of the dancing line on our screen—carried a bit of information. The signal's wavelength was 5000 angstroms. There are a hundred million angstrom units to the centimeter; figuring the speed of light, the signal could carry something like 600 trillion bits of information per second.

I told Rizzo.

"Yeah, I know. I've been going over the same numbers in my head." He set a few switches on the computer control board. "Now let's see how many of the six hundred trillion we can pick up." He sat down before the board and pressed a series of buttons.

We watched, hardly breathing, as the computer's spools began spinning and the indicator lights flashed across the control board. Within a few minutes, the printer chugged to life.

Rizzo swiveled his chair over to the printer and held up the unrolling sheet in a trembling hand.

Numbers. Six-digit numbers. Completely meaningless.

"Gibberish," Rizzo snapped.

It was peculiar. I felt relieved and disappointed at the same time.

"Something's screwy," Rizzo said. "Maybe I fouled up the circuits . . ."

"I don't think so," I answered. "After all, what did you

expect to come out of the computer? Shakespearean poetry?"

"No, but I expected numbers that would make some kind of sense. One and one, maybe. Something that means something. This stuff is nowhere."

Our nerves must have really been wound up tight, because before we knew it we were in the middle of a nasty argument—and it was over nothing, really. But in the middle of it:

"Hey, look!" Rizzo shouted, pointing to the oscilloscope.

The message had stopped. The 'scope showed only the calm, steady line of the star's basic two-day-long pulsation.

It suddenly occurred to us that we hadn't slept for more than thirty-six hours, and we were both exhausted. We forgot the senseless argument. The message was ended. Perhaps there would be another; perhaps not. We had the telescope, spectrometer, photocell, oscilloscope, and computer set to record automatically. We collapsed into our bunks. I suppose I should have had monumental dreams. I didn't. I slept like a dead man.

When we woke up, the oscilloscope trace was still quiet.

"Y'know," Rizzo muttered, "it might just be a fluke. I mean, maybe the signals don't mean a damned thing. The computer is probably translating nonsense into numbers just because it's built to print out numbers and nothing else."

"Not likely," I said. "There are too many coincidences to be explained. We're receiving a message, I'm sure of it. Now we've got to crack the code."

As if to reinforce my words, the oscilloscope trace suddenly erupted into the same flickering pattern. The message was being sent again.

We went through two weeks of it. The message would run for seven hours, then stop for seven. We transcribed it on tape forty-eight times and ran it through the computer constantly. Always the same result: six-digit numbers, millions of them. There were six different seven-hour-long messages, being repeated one after the other, constantly.

We forgot the meteorological equipment. We ignored the weekly messages from McMurdo. The rest of the world became meaningless fiction to us. There was nothing but the confounded, tantalizing, infuriating, enthralling message. The National Emergency, the bomb tests, families, duties—all transcended, all forgotten. We ate when we thought of it and slept when we couldn't keep our eyes open any longer. The message. What was it? What was the key to unlock its meaning?

"It's got to be something universal," I told Rizzo. "Something universal . . . in the widest sense of the term."

He looked up from his desk, which was wedged in between the end of his bunk and the curving dome wall. The desk was littered with printout sheets from the computer, each one of them part of the message.

"You've only said that a half a million times in the past couple of weeks. What the hell is universal? If you can figure that out, you're damned good!"

What is universal? I wondered. You're an astronomer. You look out at the universe. What do you see? I thought about it. What do I see? Stars, gas, dust clouds, planets . . . what's universal about them? What do they all have that . . .

"Atoms!" I blurted.

Rizzo cocked a weary eye at me. "Atoms?"

"Atoms. Elements. Look . . ."

I grabbed a fistful of the sheets and thumbed through them. "Look . . . each message starts with a list of numbers. Then there's a long blank to separate the opening list from the rest of the message. See? Every time, the same-length list."

"So?"

"The periodic table of elements!" I shouted into his ear. "That's the key!"

Rizzo shook his head. "I thought of that two days ago. No soap. In the first place, the list that starts each message isn't always the same. It's the same length, all right, but the numbers change. In the second place, it always begins with 100000. I looked up the atomic weight of hydrogen—it's 1.008-something."

That stopped me for a moment. But then something clicked into place in my mind.

"Why is the hydrogen weight 1.008?" Before Rizzo could answer, I went on, "For two reasons. The system we use arbitrarily rates oxygen as 16 even. Right? All the other weights are calculated from oxygen's. And we also give the average weight of an element, counting all its isotopes, right? Our weight for hydrogen also includes an adjustment for tiny amounts of deuterium and tritium. Right? Well, suppose they have a system that rates hydrogen as a flat one: 1.00000. Doesn't that make sense?"

"You're getting punchy," Rizzo grumbled. "What about the isotopes? How can they expect us to handle decimal points if they don't tell us about them—mental telepathy? What about—"

"Stop arguing and start calculating," I snapped. "Change that list of numbers to agree with our periodic table. Change 1.0000 to 1.008-whatever-it-is and tackle the next few elements. The decimals shouldn't be so hard to figure out."

Rizzo grumbled to himself, but started working out the calculations. I stepped over to the dome's microspool library and found an elementary physics text. Within a few minutes, Rizzo had some numbers and I had the periodic table focused on the microspool reading machine.

"Nothing," Rizzo said, leaning over my shoulder and looking at the screen. "They don't match at all."

"Try another list. They're not all the same."

He shrugged and returned to his desk. After a while he called out, "Their second number is 3.97123; it works out to 4.003-something."

It checked! "Good. That's helium. What about the next one, lithium?"

"That's 6.940."

"Right!"

Rizzo went to work furiously after that. I pushed a chair to the desk and began working up from the end of the list. It all checked out, from hydrogen to a few elements beyond the artificial ones that had been created in the laboratories here on Earth.

"That's it," I said. "That's the key. That's our Rosetta stone . . . the periodic table."

Rizzo stared at the scribbled numbers and the jumble of papers. "I bet I know what the other lists are . . . the ones that don't make sense."

"Oh?"

"There are always other ways to identify the elements . . . vibration resonances, quantum wavelengths . . . somebody named Lewis came out a couple of years ago with a Quantum Periodic Table . . ."

"They're covering all the possibilities. There are messages for many different levels of understanding. We just decoded the simplest one."

"Yeah."

I noticed that as he spoke, Rizzo's hand, still tightly clutching the pencil, was trembling and white with tension.

"Well?"

Rizzo licked his lips. "Let's get to work."

We were like two men possessed. Eating, sleeping, even talking was ignored completely as we waded through the hundreds of sheets of paper. We could decode only a small percentage of them, but they still represented many hours of communication. The sheets that we couldn't decode we suspected were repetitions of the same message that we were working on.

We lost all concept of time. We must have slept, more than once, but I simply don't remember. All I can recall is thousands of numbers, row upon row, sheet after sheet of numbers . . . and my pencil scratching symbols of the various chemical elements over them until my hand was so cramped I could no longer open the fingers.

The message consisted of a long series of formulas; that much was certain. But, without punctuation, with no knowledge of the symbols that denoted even such simple things as "plus" or "equals" or "yields," it took us more weeks of hard work to unravel the sense of each equation. And even then, there was more to the message than met the eye:

"Just what the hell are they driving at?" Rizzo wondered aloud. His face had changed: it was thinner, hollow-eyed, weary, covered with a scraggly beard.

"Then you think there's a meaning behind all these equations, too?"

He nodded. "It's a message, not just a contact. They're going to an awful lot of trouble to beam out this message, and they're repeating it every seven hours. They haven't added anything new in the weeks we've been watching."

"I wonder how many years or centuries they've been sending out this message, waiting for someone to pick it up, looking for someone to answer them."

"Maybe we should call Washington . . ."

"No!"

Rizzo grinned. "Afraid of breaking radio silence?"

"Hell no. I just want to wait until we're relieved, so we can make this announcement in person. I'm not going to let some old wheezer in Washington get credit for this. Besides, I want to know just what they're trying to tell us."

It was agonizing, painstaking work. Most of the formulas meant nothing to either one of us. We had to ransack the dome's meager library of microspools to piece them together. They started simply enough—basic chemical combinations: a carbon and two oxygens yield CO_2; two hydrogens and one oxygen give water. A primer . . . not of words, but of equations.

The equations became steadily longer and more complex. Then, abruptly, they simplified, only to begin a new deepening, simplify again, and finally became very complicated just at the end. The last few lines were obviously repetitious.

Gradually, their meaning became clear to us.

The first set of equations started off with simple, naturally occurring energy-yielding formulas. The oxidation of cellulose (we found the formula for that in an organic chemistry text left behind by one of the dome's previous occupants), which probably referred to the burning of plants and vegetation. A string of formulas that had groupings in them that I dimly recognized as amino acids—no doubt something to do with digesting food. There were many others, including a few that Rizzo claimed had the expression for chlorophyll in them.

"Naturally occurring, energy-yielding reactions," Rizzo summarized. "They're probably trying to describe the biological setup on their planet."

It seemed an inspired guess.

The second set of equations again began with simple formulas. The cellulose-burning reaction appeared again, but this time it was followed by equations dealing with the oxidation of hydrocarbons: coal and oil burning? A long series of equations that bore repeatedly the symbols for many different metals came up next, followed by more on hydrocarbons, and then a string of formulas that we couldn't decipher at all.

This time it was my guess: "These look like the energy-yielding reactions, too. At least in the beginning. But they don't seem to be naturally occurring types. Then comes a long story about metals. They're trying to tell us the history of their technological development—burning wood, coal, and eventually oil; smelting metals . . . they're showing us how they developed their technology."

The final set of equations began with an ominous simplicity: a short series of very brief symbols that had the net result of four hydrogen atoms building into a helium atom. Nuclear fusion.

"That's the proton-proton reaction," I explained to Rizzo. "The type of fusion that goes on in the Sun."

The next series of equations spelled out the more complex carbon-nitrogen cycle of nuclear fusion, which was probably the primary energy source of their own Cepheid variable star. Then came a long series of equations that we couldn't decode at all in any detail, but the symbols for uranium and plutonium, and some of the even heavier elements, kept cropping up.

Then came one line that told us the whole story: the lithium-hydride equation: nuclear fusion bombs.

The equations went on to more complex reactions, formulas that no man on Earth had ever seen before. They were showing us the summation of their knowledge, and they had obviously been dealing with nuclear energy for much longer than we have on Earth.

But interspersed among the new equations, they repeated a set of formulas that always began with the lithium-hydride fusion reaction. The message ended in a way that wrenched my stomach: the fusion bomb reaction and its cohorts were repeated ten straight times.

I'm not sure of what day it was on the calendar, but the clock on the master control console said it was well past eleven.

Rizzo rubbed a weary hand across his eyes. "Well, what do you think?"

"It's pretty obvious," I said. "They have the bombs. They've had them for quite some time. They must have a lot of other weapons, too—more . . . advanced. They're trying to tell us their history with the equations. First they depended on natural resources of energy, plants, and animals; then they developed artificial energy sources and built up a technology; finally they discovered nuclear energy."

"How long do you think they've had the bombs?"

"Hard to tell. A generation . . . a century. What difference does it make? They have them. They probably thought, at first, that they could learn to live with them . . . but imagine what it must be like to have those weapons at your fingertips . . . for a century. Forever. Now they're so scared of them that they're beaming their whole history out into space, looking for someone to tell them how to live with the bombs, how to avoid using them."

"You could be wrong," Rizzo said. "They could be boasting about their arsenal."

"Why? For what reason? No . . . the way they keep repeating those last equations. They're pleading for help."

Rizzo turned to the oscilloscope. It was flickering again. "Think it's the same thing?"

"No doubt. You're taping it anyway, aren't you?"

"Yeah, sure. Automatically."

Suddenly, in midflight, the signal winked off. The pulsations didn't simply smooth out into a steady line, as they had before. The screen simply went dead.

"That's funny," Rizzo said, puzzled. He checked the oscilloscope. "Nothing wrong here. Something must've happened to the telescope."

Suddenly I knew what had happened. "Take the spectrometer off and turn on the image amplifier," I told him.

I knew what we would see. I knew why the oscilloscope beam had suddenly gone off scale. And the knowledge was making me sick.

Rizzo removed the spectrometer setup and flicked the switch that energized the image-amplifier's viewscreen.

"Holy God!"

The dome was flooded with light. The star had exploded.

"They had the bombs all right," I heard myself saying. "And they couldn't prevent themselves from using them. And they had a lot more, too. Enough to push their star past its natural limits."

Rizzo's face was etched in the harsh light.

"I've got to get out of here," he muttered, looking all around the cramped dome. "I've gotta get back to my wife and find someplace where it's safe . . ."

"Someplace?" I asked, staring at the screen. "Where?"

The Mask of the Rad Death

This one was written purely as an exercise.

Edgar Allan Poe is one of the best American writers and poets. He made seminal contributions to the genres of horror and the detective story, as well as to science fiction. His poetry often has a darkly brooding character that is at once menacing and pathetic.

One of his most chilling short stories is "The Masque of the Red Death." If you have not read it, you should. If you have read it, you remember it. I have no doubt of that; it is a powerful tale of the futility of trying to avoid death.

It struck me that Poe's story could be converted into a modern scene of nuclear holocaust by changing only a few words. The "red death," for example, becomes the "rad death," with rad standing both for radioactivity and the unit that physicists and physicians use to measure how much radioactivity a living organism receives.

So I deliberately rewrote Poe's story into a modern nuclear-war setting, to see how many words had to be changed. Only a couple of dozen.

The exercise gave me a new appreciation for the ways in which Poe achieved his morbid effects. I do not recommend this kind of exercise to every person who is interested in learning to write, although there is much to be learned from it.

I *do* recommend that the beginning writer spend as much time reading as writing, or even more. And read widely! Do not limit yourself to reading science fiction alone. There is a tremendous world of literature, the memories of the English-speaking peoples and more. Tap into that treasury of knowledge and experience. To ignore it is akin to submitting to a lobotomy.

If you want to write, read. If you want to write well, read as widely as you can. Writers are generalists, of necessity. Specialization is for insects.

The "rad death" had long devastated the country. No pestilence had ever been so fatal, or so hideous. Blood was its Avatar and its seal—the redness and the horror of blood. There were sharp pains, and sudden dizziness, and the slow bleedings of the gums and the pores, with dissolution. The scarlet stains upon the body and especially upon the face of the victim were the pest ban which shut him out from the sympathy of his fellow-men. And the whole seizure, progress, and termination of the disease were the incidents of an agonizing length of weeks, or often, months.

But Senator Prosper was determined and dauntless and sagacious. When Washington was half depopulated by the bombs and their fallout, he summoned to his presence a thousand hale and equally determined friends from among the military officers and bureaucrats of the city, and with these retired to the deep seclusion of one of his well-prepared underground shelters. This was the senator's own eccentric yet practical taste. A strong and hidden gateway was its entrance, embedded in the burnt-out wilds of a national park. The gateway had a hatch of incorruptible metal.

The officers and bureaucrats, having entered, brought acetylene torches and brilliant lasers and welded the bolts. They resolved to leave no means of ingress or egress to the sudden impulses of despair from without or of frenzy from within. The shelter was amply provisioned. With such precautions the inmates might bid defiance to contagion. The external world could take care of itself. In the meantime, it was folly to grieve, or to think.

The senator had provided all the appliances of pleasure. There were buffoons (some of them former media commentators), there were improvisatori (many from the Congress), there were live rock dancers, there were musicians (on tape), there were video games, there was Beauty, there was wine. There was plentiful electrical power, ironically provided by a nuclear generator buried even deeper than the underground place itself. All these and the security were within. Without was the "Rad Death."

It was toward the close of the fifth or sixth month of his seclusion, and while the fallout seethed most furiously abroad, that Senator Prosper entertained his thousands of friends at a masked ball of the most unusual magnificence.

It was a voluptuous scene, that masquerade. But first let me tell of the rooms in which it was held. There were seven—an imperial suite carved out of bedrock far below the hellish surface of the world. In many places, such suites form a long and straight vista, while the folding doors slide back nearly to the walls on either hand, so that the view of the whole extent is scarcely impeded. Here the case was very different, as might have been expected from the senator's love of the *bizarre*. The apartments were so irregularly disposed that the vision embraced but little more than one at a time. There was a sharp turn at every twenty or thirty yards (for reasons of redundancy in radiation protection), and at each turn a novel effect.

To the right and left, in the middle of each wall, a tall and narrow Gothic window looked out upon a closed corridor which pursued the windings of the suite. These windows were of leaded glass whose color varied in accordance with the prevailing hue of the decorations of the chamber into which it opened. That at the eastern extremity was hung, for example, in blue—and vividly blue were its windows. The second chamber was purple in its ornaments and tapestries, and here the panes were purple. The third was green throughout, and so were the casements. The fourth was furnished and litten with orange—the fifth with white—the sixth with violet. The seventh apartment was closely shrouded in black velvet tapestries that hung all over the ceiling and down the walls, falling in heavy folds upon a carpet of the same material and hue. But in this chamber only, the color of the windows failed to correspond with the decorations. The panes here were scarlet—a deep blood color.

Now in no one of the seven apartments was there any lamp or candelabrum amid the profusion of golden ornaments that lay scattered to and fro or depended from the roof. There was no light of any kind emanating from lamp or candle within the suite of chambers. But in the corridors that followed the suite, there stood, opposite to each window, a heavy tripod, bearing an electric lamp cunningly fashioned to resemble a brazier of fire that projected its rays through the tinted glass and so glaringly illuminated the room. And thus were produced a multitude of gaudy and fantastic appearances. But in the western or black chamber the effect of the firelight that streamed upon the dark hangings through the blood-tinted panes was ghastly in the extreme, and produced so wild a look upon the countenances of those who entered, that there were few of the company bold enough to set foot within its precincts at all.

It was in this apartment, also, that there stood against the western wall a gigantic clock of ebony. Its digital readout flickered with a dull, monotonous blink, and when the minutes had accumulated to a new hour, there came forth from the electronic amplifiers within the clock a sound which was clear and loud and deep and exceedingly musical, but of so peculiar a note and emphasis that, at each lapse of an hour, the music tapes were programmed to pause, momentarily, so that all could harken to the sound; and thus the dancers perforce ceased their evolutions; and there was a brief disconcert of the whole gay company; and while the chimes of the clock yet rang, it was observed that the giddiest grew pale, and the more aged and sedate passed their hands over their brows as if in confused reverie or meditation. But when the echoes had fully ceased, a light laughter at once pervaded the assembly; the dancers looked at each other and smiled as if at their own nervousness and folly, and made whispering vows, each to the other, that the next chiming of the clock should produce in them no similar emotion; and then, after the lapse of sixty minutes (which embrace three thousand and six hundred seconds of the Time that flies), there came yet another chiming of the clock, and then there were the same disconcert and tremulousness and meditation as before.

In spite of these things, it was a gay and magnificent revel. The tastes of the senator were peculiar. He had a fine eye for colors and effects. He disregarded the *decora* of mere fashion. His plans were bold and fiery, and his conceptions glowed with barbaric luster. There were some who would have thought him mad. His followers felt that he was not. It was necessary to hear and see and touch him to be *sure* that he was not.

He had directed, in great part, the movable embellishments of the seven chambers, upon the occasion of this great *fete,* and it was his own guiding taste which had given character to the costumes of the masqueraders. Be sure they were grotesque. There were much glare and glitter and piquancy and phantasm—much of what has been seen in *discos.* There were arabesque figures with unsuited limbs and appointments. There were delirious fancies such as the madman fashions. There was much of the beautiful, much of the wanton, much of the *bizarre,* something of the terrible, and not a little of that which might have excited disgust. To and fro in the seven chambers there stalked, in fact, a multitude of dreams—writhed in and about, taking hue from the rooms and causing the wild music of the laserdisk to seem as the echo of their steps.

And, anon, there strikes the ebony clock which stands in the hall of the velvet. And then, momently, all is still, and all is silent save the voice of the clock. The dreams are stiff-frozen as they stand. But the echoes of the chime die away—they have endured but an instant—and a light, half-subdued laughter floats after them as they depart. And now again the music swells, and the dreams live, and writhe to and fro more merrily than ever, taking hue from the many tinted windows through which stream the rays from the tripods. But to the chamber which lies most westwardly of the seven, there are now none of the maskers who venture; for the night is waning away; and there flows a ruddier light through the blood-colored panes; and the blackness of the sable drapery appalls; and to him whose foot falls upon the sable carpet, there comes from the near clock of ebony a muffled peal more solemnly emphatic than any which reaches *their* ears who indulge in the more remote gaieties of the other apartments.

But these other apartments were densely crowded, and in them beat feverishly the heart of life. And the revel went whirlingly on, until at length there was sounded the twelfth hour upon the clock. And then the music ceased, as I have told; and the evolutions of the dancers were quieted; and there was an uneasy cessation of all things as before. But now there were twelve strokes to be sounded by the bell of the clock; and thus it happened, perhaps, that more of the thought crept, with more of time, into the meditations of the thoughtful among those who reveled. And thus, again, it happened, perhaps, that before the last echoes of the last chime had utterly sunk into silence, there were many individuals in the crowd who had found leisure to become aware of the presence of a masked figure that had arrested the attention of no single individual before. And the rumor of this new presence having spread itself whisperingly around, there arose at length from the whole company a buzz, or murmur, expressive at first of disapprobation and surprise—then, finally, of terror, of horror, and of disgust.

In an assembly of phantasms such as I have painted, it may well be supposed that no ordinary appearance could have excited such sensation. In truth the masquerade license of the night was nearly unlimited; but the figure in question had out-Heroded Herod, and gone beyond the bounds of even the senator's indefinite decorum. There are chords in the hearts of the most reckless which cannot be touched without emotion. Even with the utterly lost, to whom life and death are equally jests, there *are* matters of which no jest can be properly made. The whole company, indeed, seemed now deeply to feel that in the costume and bearing of the stranger neither wit nor propriety existed.

The figure was tall and gaunt, and shrouded from head to foot in the silver habiliments of a radiation suit. The helmet and face of the mask which concealed the visage was made up so nearly to resemble an actual suit of the type used in hellish high-rad environments that the closest scrutiny must have had difficulty in detecting the cheat.

And yet all this might have been endured, if not approved, by the mad revelers around. But the mummer had gone so far as to begrime his suit and tear it to tatters, as if he had been up on the surface where the fires of death still burned. His vesture *glowed* with an unnatural light—and it was sprinkled with the scarlet horror of blood.

When the eyes of Senator Prosper fell upon this spectral image (which with a slow and solemn movement, as if more fully to sustain its role, stalked uncertainly, almost staggering, to and fro among the dancers) he was seen to be convulsed, in the first moment with a strong shudder of either terror or distaste; but, in the next, his brow reddened with rage.

"Who dares?" he demanded hoarsely of the group that stood around him—"who dares thus make a mockery of our woes? Uncase the varlet—that we may know whom we have to expel to the surface. Will no one stir at my bidding?—stop and strip him, I say, of those reddened vestures of sacrilege!"

It was in the eastern or blue chamber in which stood Senator Prosper as he uttered these words. They rang throughout the seven rooms loudly and clearly—for the senator was a bold and robust man, and the music had become hushed at the waving of his hand.

It was in the blue room where stood the senator, with a group of pale courtiers by his side. At first as he spoke, there was a slight rushing of movement in the direction of the intruder, who at the moment was also near at hand, and now, with deliberate, slow steps, made closer approach to the speaker. But from a certain nameless awe with which the mad assumptions of the mummer had inspired the whole party, there were found none who put forth hand to seize him; so that, unimpeded, he passed within a yard of the senator's person; and, while the vast

assembly, as if with one impulse, shrank from the centers
of the rooms to the walls, he made his way uninterrupt-
edly, but with the same halting and nearly staggering step
which had distinguished him from the first, through the
blue chamber to the purple—through the purple to the
green—through the green to the orange—through this
again to the white—and even thence to the violet where a
decided movement had been made to arrest him.

It was then, however, that Senator Prosper, maddening
with rage and the shame of his own momentary cowardice,
rushed hurriedly through the six chambers, while none
followed him on account of the deadly horror that had
seized upon all. He bore aloft a drawn pistol, and had
approached, in rapid impetuosity, to within three or four
feet of the retreating figure, when the latter, having at-
tained the extremity of the velvet apartment, turned slowly
around and confronted his pursuer. There was a sharp
cry—and the pistol dropped gleaming upon the sable carpet, upon which, instantly afterwards, fell prostrate in
death Senator Prosper. Then, summoning the wild courage of despair, a throng of the revelers at once threw
themselves into the black apartment, and, seizing the
mummer, whose tall black figure stood erect and motion-
less within the shadow of the ebony clock, gasped in unut-
terable horror at finding the ripped cerements and
bloodied face mask, which they handled with so violent a
rudeness, untenanted by a living form.

And now was acknowledged the presence of the Rad
Death. He had come like a thief in the night. And one by
one dropped the revelers in the blood-bedewed halls of
their revel, and died each in the despairing posture of his
fall. And the life of the ebony clock went out with the last
of them. And the flames of the tripods expired. And Dark-

ness and Decay of the Rad Death held illimitable domination over all.

(With gratitude, and apologies, to Edgar Allan Poe.)

Bushido

The challenge of "Bushido" was to make the reader feel sympathy for an enemy, a character who hates the United States. Who hates *you.* How well I succeeded is a question only you, the reader, can answer. But I can tell you how I went about making this "bad guy" as sympathetic as possible.

First I gave him a crippling terminal disease. Then I made him a brilliant scientist. And I showed enough of his background to make the reader understand why Saito Konda hates the U.S. and Americans.

Finally, I brought onto the scene a character out of history who stands in bold contrast to the protagonist: Isoroku Yamamoto, Grand Admiral of the Japanese Imperial Fleet at the outset of World War II. Whereas Konda is physically crippled, Yamamoto is a warrior, a man of action. Whereas Konda feels helpless and impotent, the admiral is a leader of men in war. But there is a flip side to their relationship, as well. Konda knows Yamamoto's fate and can save him from the death that he suffered in the war. Helpless and impotent to save himself, Konda can nonetheless save the man he most admires—and by doing so, he can gain revenge on the United States.

How can you feel sympathetic toward a man who wants to reverse the outcome of World War II and make Japan conquer the U.S.?

I have long felt that writers should erase the word "villain" from their vocabulary. Scrub the concept out of your mind, in fact. There are no villains in the world, only people doing what they feel they must do. I'm sure that Adolph Hitler felt he was doing what was best for the German people and the entire human race, no matter how horrible the actions he authorized.

Nobody sits in a dark corner cackling with glee over the evil they have unleashed. Not in good fiction. But every good story has not only a protagonist (the "good guy" or gal), but an *antagonist,* a character who is in conflict with the protagonist. As a thought experiment, try to visualize a story you admire told from the point of view of the ostensible villain . . . oops, excuse me! the ostensible antagonist. Imagine *Hamlet* being told from Claudius' point of view. (Frankly, he seems to be the only sane person in the whole castle.)

Incidentally, there's a bit of science in this story that most other writers have conveniently ignored. Time travel *requires* faster-than-light travel. Which explains, perhaps, why no one has yet built a time machine.

So: Did I succeed in making Saito Konda a sympathetic character? Crippled in body, brilliant in mind, warped in spirit—yes, he is all that. But do you feel sorry for him?

Saito Konda grimaced against the pain, hoping that his three friends could not see his suffering. He did not want their sympathy. He was far beyond such futile emotions. All that was left to him was hate—and the driving will to succeed.

He was sitting in his laboratory, his home, his hospital

room, his isolation chamber. They were all the same place, the same metal-skinned module floating five hundred kilometers above the Earth.

The two men and one woman having tea with him had been his friends since undergraduate days at the University of Tokyo, although they had never met Konda in the flesh. That would be the equivalent of murdering him.

They were discussing their work.

"Do you actually believe you can succeed?" asked Miyoko Toguri, her almond eyes shining with admiration. Once Konda had thought she might have loved him; once he had in fact loved her. But that was long ago, when they had been foolish romantic students.

"I have solved the equations," Konda replied, hiding his pain. "As you know, if the mathematics have beauty, the experiment will eventually be successful."

"Eventually," snorted Raizo Yamashita. Like the others he was sitting on the floor, in deference to Konda's antiquated sense of propriety. Raizo sat crosslegged, his burly body hunched slightly over the precisely placed low lacquered table, his big fists pressed against his thighs. "*Eventually* could be a thousand years from now."

"I think not," said Konda, his eyes still on lovely Miyoko. He wondered how she would look in a traditional kimono, with her hair done properly. As it was, she was wearing a Western-style blouse and skirt, yet she still looked beautiful to him.

The two men wore the latest-mode glitter slacks and brightly colored shirts. Konda's nostrils flared at their American ways. The weaker America becomes in real power, the more our people imitate her decadent styles. He himself was in a comfortable robe of deep burgundy, decorated with white flying cranes.

It happened that Konda reached for the teapot at the same moment that Miyoko did. Their hands met without touching. He poured tea for himself, she for herself. When they put the pots down again, her holographic image merged with the real teapot on Konda's table. Her hand merged with his. He could not feel the warmth of her living flesh, of course. If he did, it would undoubtedly kill him.

Tomoyuki Umezi smiled, somewhat ruefully. The window behind him showed the graceful snow-capped cone of Fujiyama. He raised his tiny cup.

"To the stars," he toasted.

The other three touched their cups to his. But they felt no physical contact. Only their eyes could register the holographic images.

"And to time," Konda added, as usual.

Back in their university days, Tomo had laughingly suggested that they form a rock group and call it the Four Dimensions, since three of them were trying to conquer space while Konda was pouring his soul and all the energy of his wasting body into mastering time.

They had never met physically. Konda had been in isolation chambers all his life, first in an incubator in the AIDS ward of the charity hospital, later in the observation sections of medical research facilities. He had been born with no effective immune system, the genetic gift of his mother, a whore, and whoever his father might have been. They had also gifted him with a chameleon virus that was slowly, inexorably, turning his normal body cells into cancerous tumors.

The slow and increasingly painful death he was suffering could be brought to a swift end merely by exposure to the real world and its teeming viruses and bacteria. But the medical specialists prevented that. From his unwanted birth, Konda had been their laboratory animal, their prized specimen, kept alive for them to study. Isolated from all the physical contamination that his body could never cope with, Konda learned as a child that his mind could roam the universe and all of history. He became an outstanding scholar, a perverse sort of celebrity within academic circles, and was granted a full scholarship to Tokyo University, where he "met" his three lifelong friends. Now he lived in a special module of a space station, five hundred kilometers above the Earth's surface, waited upon by gleaming antiseptic robots.

The four of them did their doctoral theses jointly, a theoretical study of faster-than-light propulsion. Their studies were handsomely supported by the corporations that funded the university. Japan drew much of its economic strength from space, beaming electrical energy to cities throughout Asia from huge power satellites. But always there was competition from others: the Europeans, the Chinese, the Arabs were all surging forward, eager to displace Japan and despoil its wealth.

The price of peaceful competition was a constant, frenetic search for some new way to stay ahead of the foreign devils. If any nation achieved a faster-than-light drive, the great shoguns of industry insisted that it must be Japan. The life of the nation depended on staying ahead of its competitors. There could be no rest as long as economic ruin lurked on the horizon.

For all the years since their university days, the three others continued to work on turning their theories into reality, on producing a workable interstellar propulsion system: a star drive. Miyoko accepted the chair of the physics department at the University of Rangoon, the first woman to be so honored. Dour Raizo became the doyen of the research laboratory at a major aerospace firm in Seattle, U.S.A., long since absorbed into the Mitsubishi Corporation. Tomo waited patiently for his turn at the mathematics chair in Tokyo.

From the beginning, Konda had been far more fascinated with the temporal aspects of spacetime than the spatial. Since childhood he had been intrigued by history, by the great men who had lived in bygone ages. While his friends labored over the star drive, Konda strove to produce a time machine.

In this he followed the intellectual path blazed by Hawking and Taylor and the AAPV group from the unlikely location of South Carolina, a backwater university in the backwater U.S.A.

He felt he was close to success. Alone, isolated from the rest of humanity except for the probing doctors and these occasional holographic meetings with his three distant friends, he had discovered that it should be possible to tap the temporal harmonics and project an object—or even a person—to a predetermined point in spacetime. It was not much different from achieving interstellar flight, in theory. Konda felt that his work would be of inestimable aid to his three friends.

His equations told him that to move an eighty-kilo human being from the crest of one spacetime wave to the harmonically similar crest of another would take all the energy generated by all of Japan's power satellites orbiting between the Earth and the Moon for a period of just over six hours. When he was ready for the experiment, the Greater Nippon Energy Consortium had assured him, the electrical power would be made available to him. For although the consortium had no interest in time travel, Konda had presented his work to them as an experiment that could verify certain aspects of faster-than-light propulsion.

Konda had to assemble the equipment for his experiments, using the robots who accompanied him in his isolation module of the space station. His friends helped all they could. Konda had to tell them what he was trying to do. But he never told them why. He never showed them the hatred that drove him onward.

They thought he was trying to help them in their quest for a star drive. They believed that if he could transport an object across time, it would help them learn how to transport objects across lightyears of space. But Konda had another goal in mind, something very different.

Konda dreamed of making contact with a specific person, longed with all his soul to reach across the years and summon one certain hero out of history: Isoroku Yamamoto, Grand Admiral of the Japanese Imperial Fleet in the year 1941 (old calendar). Admired by all, even his enemies, Yamamoto was known as "the sword of his emperor."

Konda remembered the day when he first told his friends of his yearning to reach the doughty old admiral. "There are no men like Yamamoto anymore," he had said. "He was a true samurai. A warrior in the ancient tradition of Bushido."

Raizo Yamashita had laughed openly. "A warrior who started a war that we lost. Badly."

Tomoyuki was too polite to laugh, but he asked curiously, "Didn't Yamamoto boast that he would defeat the Americans and dictate the terms of their surrender in the White House? He didn't even live long enough to see the war end in Japan's humiliation."

Miyoko rushed to Konda's defense before he could reply for himself. "Admiral Yamamoto was killed in the war. Isn't that true, Sai?"

"Yes," answered Konda, feeling weak with helpless rage at the thought. "He was assassinated by the cowardly Americans. They feared him so much that they deliberately set out to murder him."

"But to contact a man from the distant past," Tomo mused. "That could be dangerous."

Raizo bobbed his burly head up and down in agreement. "I read a story once where a man went back to the

Age of Dinosaurs and killed a butterfly—accidentally, of course. But when he came back to his own time the human race didn't even exist!" He frowned, thinking hard. "Or something like that; I don't remember, exactly."

As usual, Miyoko stood up for Konda. "Sai won't tamper with history, will you?"

Konda forced himself to smile faintly and shake his head. But he could not answer, not in honesty. For his overwhelming desire was to do precisely that: to tamper with history. To change it completely, even if it did destroy his world.

So he hid his motives from even his dearest friends, because they would never understand what drove him. How could they? They could walk in the sunlight, feel wind on their faces, touch one another, and make love. He was alone in his orbital prison, always alone, waiting for death alone. But before I die, he told himself, I will succeed in my quest.

Once his equipment was functioning he plucked a series of test objects—a quartz wristwatch, a bowl of steaming rice, a running video camera—over times of a few minutes. Then a few hours. The first living thing he tried was a flower, a graceful chrysanthemum that was donated by one of the space station's crew members who grew the flowers as a hobby. Then a sealed beaker of water teeming with protozoa, specially sent to the station from the university's biology department. Then a laboratory mouse.

Often the power drain meant that large sections of Shanghai or Hong Kong or one of the other customer-cities in Greater East Asia had to be blacked out temporarily. At the gentle insistence of the energy consortium, Konda always timed these experiments for the sleeping hours between midnight and dawn, locally. That way, transferring the solar power satellites' beams from the cities on Earth to Konda's laboratory made a minimum of inconvenience for the blacked-out customers.

Carefully he increased the range of his experiments—and his power requirements. He reached for a puppy that he remembered from his childhood, the pet of a nurse's daughter who had sent him videotaped "letters" for a while, until she grew tired of speaking to the taped image of a friend she would never see in the flesh. The puppy appeared in the special isolation chamber in Konda's apparatus, a ball of wriggling fur with a dangling red tongue. Konda watched it for a few brief moments, then returned it to its natural spacetime, thirty years in the past. His eyes were blurred with tears as the puppy winked out of sight. Self-induced allergic reaction, he told himself as he wiped his eyes.

He spent the next several days meticulously examining his encapsulated world, looking for changes that might have been caused by his experiment with the puppy. The calendar was the same. The computer programs he had set up specifically to test for changes in the spacetime continuum appeared totally unaffected. Of course, he thought, if I changed history, if I moved the flow of the continuum, everything around me would be changed—including not only the computer's memory, but my own.

Still, he scanned the news media and the educational channels of hundreds of TV stations all around the world that he orbited. Nothing appeared out of place. All was normal. His experiment had not changed anything. He still had the wasting immunodeficiency disease that his mother had bequeathed him. His body was still rotting away.

He thought of bringing the puppy back and killing it with a painless gas, to see what effect the change would make on history. But he feared to tamper with the spacetime continuum until he actually had Yamamoto in his grasp. He wondered idly if he could kill the puppy, then told himself angrily that of course he could; the dog must be long dead by now, anyway.

He knew he was ready for the climax of his experiments: snatching Yamamoto from nearly a century in the past. The time for hesitation is over, Konda told himself sternly. Set up the experiment and do it, even if it destroys this world and everything in it.

So he did. Making arrangements for the necessary power from Greater Nippon Electric took longer than he had expected: blacking out most of Asia for several hours was not something the corporate executives agreed to lightly. But at last they agreed.

As a final step in his preparations he asked the commander of the space station to increase its spin so that his isolation area would be at almost a full Earthly gravity.

"Will that not be uncomfortable for you?" the station commander asked. She was new to her post, the first woman to command one of Japan's giant orbiting stations. She had been instructed to take special care of the guest in the isolation module.

"I am prepared for some inconvenience," Konda replied to her image in his comm screen. He was already seated in his powered wheelchair. The low-g of the station had allowed him to move about almost normally, despite the continued atrophy of his limbs. His body spent most of its energy continually trying to destroy the fast-mutating viruses that were, in their turn, doing their best to destroy him. The lifelong battle had left him pitifully weak and frail—in body. But he had the spirit of a true samurai. He followed the warrior's path as well as he was able.

In truth he dreaded the higher gravity. He even feared it might put such a strain on his heart that it would kill him. But it was a risk he was prepared to take. Yamamoto would find his sudden emergence into the twenty-first century startling enough; there was no need to embarrass him with a low-gravity environment that might make him physically ill or overwhelm his spirit with sudden fear.

The moment finally arrived. The great power satellites turned their emitting antennas to the huge receiver that had been built near the space station. Half of Asia, from Beijing to Bangkok, went dark.

Grand Admiral Isoroku Yamamoto, commander in chief of the Japanese Imperial Fleet, suddenly appeared in the middle of Konda's living quarters. He had been seated, apparently, when the wave harmonics had transported him. He plopped unceremoniously onto the floor, a look of pain and surprise widening his eyes. Konda wanted to laugh; thank the gods that the field included the admiral's flawlessly white uniform. A naked Yamamoto would have been too much to bear.

Konda had divided his living quarters in two with an impervious clear-plastic wall. Both sides were as antiseptic as modern biotechnology could make them. Yamamoto, coming from nearly a hundred years in the past, was undoubtedly carrying a zoo of microbes that could slay Konda within days, if not hours.

For a frozen instant they stared at each other: the admiral in his white uniform sitting on the floor; the scientist in his powered wheelchair, his face gaunt with the ravages of the disease that was remorselessly killing him.

Then Yamamoto glanced around the chamber. He saw the banks of gauges and winking lights, the gleaming robots standing stiffly as if at attention, the glareless light panels overhead. He heard the hum of electrical equipment, smelled the mixed odors of laboratory and hospital.

Yamamoto climbed to his feet, brushing nonexistent dust from his jacket and sharply creased trousers. He was burly in build, thickset and powerful. His heavy jaw and shaved scalp made him look surly, obtuse. But his eyes gleamed with intelligence. Two fingers were missing from his left hand, the result of an accident during the battle of Tsushima, young ensign Yamamoto's first taste of war.

Konda bowed his head as deeply as he could in his wheelchair and hissed with respect.

Yamamoto granted him a curt nod. "I am dreaming," he said. "This is a dream."

"No, this is not a dream," said Konda, wheeling his chair to the clear partition that divided the room. "This is reality. You, most revered and honored admiral, are the first man to travel through time."

Yamamoto snorted with disdain. "A dream," he repeated. But then he added, "Yet it is the most unusual dream I have ever had."

For hours Konda tried to convince the admiral that he was not dreaming. At times Konda almost thought he was dreaming himself, so powerful was Yamamoto's resistance. Yet he persisted, for what Konda wanted to do depended on Yamamoto's acceptance of the truth.

Finally, after they had shared a meal served by the robots and downed many cups of saké, Yamamoto raised a hand. On the other side of the partition, Konda immediately fell silent. Even through the plastic wall he could feel the power of Yamamoto's personality, a power based on integrity, and strength, and limitless courage.

"Let us arrange a truce," Yamamoto suggested. "I am willing to accept your statements that you have created a time machine and have brought me here to the future. Whether I am dreaming or not is irrelevant, for the time being."

Konda drew in a breath. "I accept the truce," he said. It was the best that he would get from the utterly pragmatic man across the partition.

He felt terribly weary from trying to convince the admiral of the truth. He had deliberately wrapped his entire module in a stasis field, making it a small bubble of spacetime hovering outside the normal flow of time. He wanted true isolation, with not even a chance of interference from the space station crew or the doctors. He and Yamamoto could live in the module outside the normal time stream for days or even years, if Konda chose. When he was ready to turn off the field and the bubble collapsed, no discernible time would have elapsed in the real world. He would return himself to the instant the experiment began, and Yamamoto would return to his writing desk in 1941. Not even his three friends would know if the experiment had worked or not.

If his friends still existed when Konda ended the experiment.

They slept. The robots had prepared a comfortable cot for Yamamoto, and suitable clothing. Konda slept in his chair, reclined in almost a horizontal position. His dreams were disturbing, bitter, but he suppressed their memory once he awoke once again.

Time within the windowless chamber was arbitrary; often Konda worked around the clock, although less and less as his body's weariness continued to erode his strength. When Yamamoto awoke, Konda began the admiral's history lessons. He had painstakingly assembled a vast library of microform books and videotapes about the events of the past century. Konda had been especially careful to get as many tapes of boastful American films from the World War II years. This would be a delicate matter, he knew, for he intended to show Yamamoto his own death at the hands of the murderous Yankees.

Slowly, slowly Konda unreeled the future to his guest. Yamamoto sat in stolid silence as he watched the attack on Pearl Harbor, muttering now and then, "No aircraft carriers at anchor. That is bad." And later, "Nagumo should have sent in a third attack. The fool."

By the time the viewing screen at last went dark, Yamamoto looked through the partition toward Konda with a new look in his eyes. He is beginning to believe me, Konda told himself.

"This dream is very realistic," the admiral said, his voice dark with concern.

"There is more," Konda said. Sadly, he added, "Much more."

Konda lost track of time. The two men ate and slept and watched the ancient tapes. Yamamoto put away his uniform, folding it carefully, almost reverently, and wore the comfortable loose kimono that Konda had provided for him. The admiral had far more energy and endurance than Konda. While the scientist slept, the admiral read from the microform books. When Konda awakened Yamamoto always had a thousand questions waiting for him.

He truly believes, Konda realized. He sees that this is not a dream. He knows that I am showing him his own future. The admiral watched the disastrous battle of Midway in stoic silence, his only discernible reaction the clenching of his heavy jaw whenever the screen showed a Japanese ship being sunk.

To his surprise, Konda felt enormous reluctance when it came time to show Yamamoto his death. For a whole day he showed no further videos and even cut off the power to the microform book reader.

"Why have you stopped?" Yamamoto asked.

From behind his impermeable plastic screen, Konda grimaced with pain. But he tried to hide it by asking the older man, "Do you still believe that all this is a dream?"

Yamamoto's eyes narrowed into an intense stare. "All of life is a dream, my young friend."

"Or a nightmare."

"You are ill," said the admiral.

"I am dying."

"So are we all." Yamamoto got to his feet, walked slowly around his half of the room. In his dark blue kimono he needed only a set of swords to look exactly like a samurai warrior of old.

Slowly, haltingly, Konda told him of his disease. The gift of his unknown parents. He had never spoken to anyone about this in such detail. He cursed his whore of a mother and damned the father that had undoubtedly spread his filth to many others. An American. He knew his father had to be an American. A tourist, probably. Or a miserable businessman come to Tokyo to ferret out the secrets of Japanese success.

He railed against the fate that kept him confined inside a diseased body and kept the dying body confined inside this chamber of complete exile. He raged and wept in front of the man he had plucked from the past. Not even to his three best friends had he dared to speak of the depth of his hatred and despair. But he could do it with Yamamoto, and once he started, his emotion was a torrent that he could not stop until he was totally exhausted.

The older man listened in silent patience, for many hours. Finally, when Konda had spent his inner fury and sat half dead in his powered chair, Yamamoto said, "It does no good to struggle against death. What a man should seek is to make his death meaningful. It cannot be avoided. But it can be glorious."

"Can it?" Konda snapped. "You think so? Your own death was not glorious; it was a miserable assassination!"

Yamamoto's eyes flickered for an instant, then his iron self-control reasserted itself. "So that is what you have been hiding from me."

Almost snarling with searing rage, Konda spun his chair to the console that controlled the video screen.

"Here is your glorious death, old man! Here is how you met your fate!"

He had spent years collecting all the tapes from libraries in the United States and Japan. Most of the tapes were re-creations, dramatizations of the actual events. Yamamoto's decision to visit the front lines, in the Solomon Islands, to boost the sagging spirits of his men who were under attack by the Americans. The way the sneaking Americans broke the Japanese naval code and learned that Yamamoto would be within reach of their longest-range fighter planes—for a scant few minutes. Their decision to try to kill the Japanese warrior, knowing that his death would be worth whole battle fleets and air armadas. The actual mission, where the American cowards shot down the plane that carried Grand Admiral Isoruku Yamamoto, killing him and all the others aboard.

The screen went dark.

"If your flight had been late by five minutes," Konda said, "the Americans would have had to turn back and you would not have been murdered."

The admiral was still staring at the blank screen. "I have always been a stickler for punctuality. A fatal flaw, I suppose."

Yamamoto sat silently for a few moments, while Konda wondered what thoughts were passing through his mind. Then he turned to face the younger man once more. "Show me the rest," he said. "Show me what happened after I died."

Still seething with anger, Konda unreeled the remaining history of the war. The Imperial Fleet destroyed. The home cities of Japan firebombed. The kamikaze suicide attacks where untrained youths threw away their lives to no avail. The ultimate horror of Hiroshima and Nagasaki.

The humiliating surrender signed aboard an American battleship in Tokyo harbor.

The robots offered meals at their preprogrammed times. Neither Konda nor Yamamoto ate as they watched the disastrous past unfold on the video screen, defeat and slaughter and the ultimate dishonor.

"Does Japan still exist?" the admiral asked when the screen finally went blank. "Is there an emperor still alive, living in exile, perhaps?"

Konda blinked. "The emperor lives in his palace in Tokyo. Japan not only exists, it is one of the richest nations on Earth."

For the first time Yamamoto looked confused. "How can that be?"

Reluctantly, grudgingly, Konda showed the old man more recent history tapes. The rise of Japan's industrial strength. Japan's move into space. Yamamoto saw the Rising Sun emblem on the Moon's empty wastes, on the red deserts of Mars, on the giant factory ships that plied among the asteroids, on the gleaming Solar Power Satellites that beamed electrical power to the hungry cities of Earth.

At last the admiral rubbed his eyes and turned away from the darkened screen.

"We lost the war," he said. "But somehow Japan has become the leading nation of the world."

Konda burst into a harshly bitter laughter. "The leading nation of the world? Japan has become a whore! A nation of merchants and tradesmen. There is no greatness in this."

"There is wealth," Yamamoto replied drily.

"Yes, but at what price? We have lost our souls," Konda said. "Japan no longer follows the path of honor. Every day we become more like the Americans." He almost spat that last word.

Yamamoto heaved a heavy sigh. Konda tapped at the control console keypad again. The video screen brightened once more. This time it showed modern Japan: the riotous noise and flash of the Ginza, boys wearing Mohawk haircuts and girls flaunting themselves in shorts and halters; parents lost in a seductive wonderland of gadgetry while their children addicted themselves to electronic and chemical pleasures; foreigners flooding into Japan, blackening the slopes of Fujiyama, taking photographs of the emperor himself!

"My father was one of those American visitors," Konda said, surprised at how close to tears he was again. "A diseased, depraved foreigner."

Yamamoto said nothing.

"You see how Japan is being destroyed," Konda said. "What good is it to be the world's richest nation if our soul is eaten away?"

"What would you do?"

Konda wheeled his chair to the plastic partition so close that he almost pressed his face against it.

"Go back to your own time," he said, nearly breathless, "and win the war! You know enough now to avoid the mistakes that were made. You can concentrate your forces at Midway and overwhelm the Americans! You can invade the west coast of the U.S. before they are prepared! You can prevent your own assassination and lead Japan to victory!"

The admiral nodded gravely. "Yes, I could do all of those things. Then the government that launched the war against America would truly dictate surrender terms in the White House—and rule much of the world afterward."

"Yes! Exactly!"

Yamamoto regarded the younger man solemnly through the clear plastic partition. "But if I do that, would that not change the history that you know? Such a Japan would be very different from the one you have just shown me."

"Good!" Konda exulted. "Excellent!"

"Your parents would never meet in such a world. You would never be born."

Konda gave a fierce sigh of relief. "I know. My miserable existence would never come to be. For that I would be glad. Grateful!"

Yamamoto shook his head. "I have sent many warriors to their deaths, but never have I deliberately done anything that I knew would kill one certain individual."

"I can follow the warrior's path," Konda said, barely able to control the trembling that racked his body. "You are not the only one who can live by the code of Bushido."

The older man fell silent.

"I want to die!" Konda blurted. "I want to have never been born! Take my life. Take it in exchange for your own. For the greatness of Japan, you must live and I must never have come into existence."

"For the greatness of Japan," Yamamoto muttered.

They ate a meal together, each of them on his own side of the partition, and then slept. Konda dreamed of himself as one of the kamikaze pilots, a headband proclaiming his courage tied across his forehead, a ceremonial sword strapped to his waist, diving his plane into an American warship, exploding into a blossom of fire and glory.

He woke to find himself still alive, still dying slowly.

Yamamoto was back in his stiff white uniform. The old man knew that his time here was drawing to its conclusion.

With hardly a word between them, Konda directed the admiral to the spot in the room where the wave harmonics converged. Yamamoto stood ramrod straight, hands balled into fists at his side. The generators whined to life, spinning up beyond the range of human hearing. Konda felt their power, though; their vibrations rattled him in his chair.

Only seconds to go. Konda forced himself to his feet and brought his right hand to his brow in a shaky salute to Japan's greatest warrior. Yamamoto solemnly saluted back.

"Go back and win the war," Konda said, his voice shaking with emotion.

Yamamoto muttered something. Konda could not quite hear the words; he was too intent on watching the display screens of his equipment.

The admiral disappeared. As suddenly as a light blinking out, one instant he was there staring solemnly at Konda, the next he was gone back to his own time.

"Banzai," Konda whispered.

His finger hovered, trembling, over the key that would break the stasis and return him to the mainstream of spacetime. *If all has gone well, this will be the end of me. Saito Konda will no longer exist.* He pulled in a deep, final breath, almost savoring it, and then leaned savagely hard on the key.

And nothing happened. He blinked, looked around. His chamber was unchanged. His equipment hummed to itself. The display screens showed that everything was quite normal. The comm unit was blinking its red message light.

A terrible fear began to worm its way up Konda's spine. He called out to the comm unit, "Respond!"

The station commander's face took form on the screen. "When will you begin your experiment, sir?" she asked.

Konda saw the digital clock numbers on the screen: hardly ten seconds had passed since he had first put his chamber in stasis.

"It didn't work," he mumbled. "It's all over for now. You can return my module to the low-gravity mode."

The commander nodded once and the screen went dark. Konda felt a lurch in the pit of his stomach and then a sinking, falling sensation. He floated up out of his chair like a man in a dream.

Was I dreaming? he asked himself. Did it actually happen? Why hasn't the world changed? Why am I still alive?

Puzzled, almost dazed, he activated the tape rewind of the cameras that had recorded every instant of his experiment. When the recorder stopped, he pressed the PLAY button.

And there was Yamamoto in the chamber with him. Konda stared, put the tape in fast forward. Their voices chittered and jabbered like a pair of monkeys', they sped through their days together in a jerky burlesque of normal movement. But it was Yamamoto. It had really happened.

Konda sank onto his bed, suddenly so totally exhausted that he could not stand even in the low gravity. The experiment had worked. He had shown Yamamoto everything and sent him back to win his war against the Americans and save Japan's soul. Yet nothing seemed changed.

He wanted to sleep but he could not. Instead, in a growing frenzy he began to tune in to television broadcasts from Earth. One channel after another, from Japan, China, the Philippines, Australia, the United States, Europe. Nothing had changed! The world was just the way it had been before he had snatched Yamamoto out of the past.

Konda beat his frail fists on his emaciated thighs in utter frustration. He tore at his hair. Why? Why hasn't anything changed?

Frantically he searched through his history tapes. It was all the same. The war. Japan's defeat. The humiliation of achieving world economic power at the sacrifice of all that the Japanese soul had held dear in earlier generations.

I still live, Konda cried silently. My mother was born and grew up and plied her filthy trade and gave birth to a diseased, unclean son.

In desperation, he went back to the tapes of Yamamoto's assassination. It was all the same. Exactly, precisely the same. Either the experiment had not worked at all, and Konda had hallucinated his days with Yamamoto, or . . .

He saw one thing on one of the tapes that he did not recall being there before. The screen showed the twin-engined plane that would carry the admiral and his staff from the base at Rabaul to the island of Bougainville. The narrator pointed out Yamamoto's insistence on punctuality, ". . . as if the admiral knew that he had an appointment with death."

A moment or two later, while the screen showed American planes attacking the Japanese flight, the narrator quoted Yamamoto as saying, "I have killed many of the enemy . . . I believe the time has come for me to die, too."

"He did it deliberately!" Konda howled in the emptiness of his chamber. "He knew and yet he let them kill him!"

For hours Konda raved and tore through his quarters, pounding his fists against the walls and furniture until they bled, smashing the equipment that had fetched the greatest warrior of history to his presence, raging and screaming at the blankly immobile robots.

Finally, totally spent, bleeding, his chest heaving and burning as if with fever, he sat in the wreckage of his laboratory before the one display screen he had not smashed and called up the tape of Yamamoto's visit. For hours he watched himself and the doughty old admiral, seeking the answer he desperately needed to make sense out of his universe.

He should have gone back and changed everything,

Konda's mind kept repeating. He should have gone back and changed everything.

For days he sat there, without eating, without sleeping, like a catatonic searching for the key that would release him.

He came to the very end of the tape, with Yamamoto standing at attention and gravely returning his own salute.

He heard himself say to the admiral, "Go back and win the war."

He saw Yamamoto's lips move, and then the old man disappeared.

Konda rewound the tape and replayed that last moment, with the sound volume turned up high enough to hear the admiral's final words.

"Go back and win the war," his own voice boomed.

Yamamoto replied, "We did win it."

Haggard, breathless, Konda stared at the screen as the old admiral disappeared and returned to his own time, his own death. Willingly.

Tears misted his eyes. He went to his powered chair and sank wearily into it. Yamamoto did not understand anything. Not a thing!

Or perhaps he did. Perhaps the old warrior saw and understood it all. Better than I have, thought Konda. He sees more clearly than I do.

In the warrior's code there is only one acceptable way for a man to deal with the shame of defeat. Konda leaned his head back and waited for death to take him, also. He did not have to wait very long.

Thy Kingdom Come

In 1991 Charles Sheffield, Frederik Pohl, Jerry Pournelle, and I were commissioned by *The World & I* magazine to write nonfiction scenarios depicting what the world might look like in the year 2042. The scenarios were to be based on reports written by world-recognized leaders in various technological fields such as transportation, energy, space exploration, oceanography, etc.

Each of us was asked to slant his scenario either positively or negatively. I was given the "slightly pessimistic" slant. The scenario I wrote is included in this book, after the story that follows this introduction.

"Thy Kingdom Come" is a work of fiction based on my scenario for *The World & I* assignment. Charles Sheffield got the idea of combining our nonfiction scenarios with four novelettes by the four of us and packaging the whole shebang in a book titled *Future Quartet*. Fine idea, and a good example of how professional writers use the materials they generate to develop new markets (i.e., money) for themselves.

While the original scenario was based on a global view, and inputs from top technologists, I decided that the story would work best if it showed the same world of 2042 from the bottom of the heap: a worm's-eye view, if you will. For that, I returned to my roots.

I grew up in the narrow streets and row houses of South Philadelphia. Born at the nadir of the Great Depression of the 1930s, I saw as early as junior high school that there were some guys who preferred stealing to honest work, preferred violence to cooperation.

We return to what I told you earlier in this book: Write about what you know. "Thy Kingdom Come" is about some of the wiseguys I grew up with. Most of them are dead now; most of them died young. More than that, though, the story is about the longing that even the snottiest of these wiseguys have for a normal, decent life. And it's about how some of them struggle to break free of the vicious circle of ignorance and violence, to climb out of the cesspool and into the sunlight. A few succeed. Very few.

"Thy Kingdom Come" is about two of those kids: one who succeeds (maybe) and one who comes close, but misses. In a way, it's a true story. At least, it's as true as I could make it.

Audio transcript of testimony of Salvatore (Vic) Passalacqua

I knew it wouldn't be easy, but I figured I hadda at least try. Y'know? The [deleted] Controllers had grabbed her in one of their swoops and I hadda get her back before they scrambled her [deleted] brains with their [deleted] sizzlers.

Her name? Oh yeah, I forgot you're tapin' all this. How do I look? Not bad for a guy goin' on twenty, huh? Yeah, yeah. Her name's Jade Diamond, keenest-looking piece of— No, that ain't her real name. 'Course not. Her real name was Juanita Dominguez. I knew her before she changed it. And her eyes. Like I said, she was real beautiful. Naturally. Without the implants and the eye job. They changed her eyes 'cause most of the big spenders are Japs.

Anyway, she was supposed t'be protected just like all the hookers. Except that the [deleted] [deleted] Controllers don't take nobody's payoffs—that's what they say, at least.

So there was Jade in the holdin' jug down at city hall and here was me makin' a living out of old TV sets and tape players, anything to do with electrical stuff. Where? In the junkyards, where else? You don't think I stole anything, do you? Why would I have to risk my butt goin' into the tracts and breakin' into people's houses when they throw away their stuff every year and it all winds up in the junkyards?

Yeah, I know the stuff is all supposed to be recycled. That's what I do. I recycle it before the [deleted] recyclers get their [deleted] claws on it.

Look, you wanna know about the Chairman and Jade and me or you wanna talk about business?

Okay. I was in love with Jade, that's why I did what I did. Sure, I knew she was a pro. You'd be too if you'd grown up in the city. We don't exist, y'know. Not legally. No records for any of us, not even the [deleted] police bother to keep records on us anymore. Not unless we done somethin' out in the tracts. As far as your [deleted] mother-[deleted] computer files are concerned, we weren't even born. So of course we don't die. If we don't bury our own, the [deleted] sanitation robots just dump our bodies into a pit and bulldoze 'em over. After they've taken out all the organs they wanna use for transplants, that is. And we sure don't get nuthin from your sweetheart of a government while we're alive. Nuthin but grief. Lemme tell ya—

Okay. Okay. Jade and the Chairman.

None of it would've happened if the Controllers hadn't picked up Jade. I guess they picked her up and the other girls 'cause the Chairman was comin' to Philly to make a speech and they wanted the streets to look clean and decent. First time I saw a sanitation robot actually cleanin' the [deleted] street. First time in my life! I swear.

Anyway, there Jade was in the tank and here I was at the junkyard and all I could think of was gettin' Jade out. I knew I needed help, so first thing in the morning I went to Big Lou.

His name's kind of a joke. You know? Like, he's even shorter than me, and I been called a runt all my life. His face is all screwed up, too, like it was burned with acid or somethin' when he was a kid. Tough face. Tough man. I was really scared of Big Lou, but I wanted to get Jade outta the tank so bad I went to him anyway.

The sun was just comin' up when I got to the old school building where Big Lou had his office. He wasn't there that early. So I stooged around out in the street until he arrived in his car. It was polished so hard it looked brand new. Yeah, a regular automobile, with a driver. What's it run on? How the hell would I know? Gasoline, I guess. Maybe one of those fancy other fuels, I don't know.

At first Lou told me to get lost, like I figured he would. I was just small-time, a junkyard dog without the teeth, far as he was concerned. See, I never wanted to be any bigger. I just wanted to live and let live. I got no hatred for nobody.

But while I'm beggin' Big Lou for some help to spring Jade he gets a phone call. Yeah, he had a regular office in the old school building in our neighborhood. I know, they shut down all the schools years ago, before I was even born. They're supposed to abandoned, boarded up. Hell, most of 'em were burned down long ago. But not this one. It's still got a pretty good roof and office space and bathrooms, if you know how to turn the water on. And electricity. Okay, sure, all the windows were smashed out in the old classrooms and the rest of the building's a mess. But Lou's office was okay. Clean and even warm in the winter. And nobody touched his windows, believe me.

Y'know, down in South Philly, from what I hear— Oh yeah, you people don't know Philly that well, do you? Where you from, New York? Washington? Overseas? What?

Okay, okay. So you ask the questions and I do the answerin'. Okay. Just curious. Where was I?

Big Lou, right. He had an office in the old school building. Yeah, he had electricity. Didn't I tell ya that already? There was a couple TVs in the office and a computer on his desk. And he had a fancy telephone, too. I had put it together myself, I recognized it soon as I saw it. Damned phone had its own computer chips: memory, hunt-and-track, fax—the works. I had sold it to Lou for half a peanut; cost me more to put it together than he paid for it. But when you sell to Big Lou you sell at his price. Besides, who the [deleted] else did I know who could use a phone like that?

Anyway, I'm sittin' there in front of his desk. Big desk. You could hold a dance on it. I had figured that Big Lou could talk to a couple people, put a little money in the right hands, and Jade could get out of the tank before the [deleted] Controllers fried her brains and sent her off to Canada or someplace.

Lou gets this phone call. I sit and wait while he talks. No, I don't know who called him. And he didn't really do much talkin'. He just sort of grunted every now and then or said, "Yeah, I see. I gotcha." His voice is kinda like a diesel truck in low gear, like whatever burned his face burned the inside of his throat, too.

Then he puts down the phone and smiles at me. Smiles. From a face like his it was like a flock of roaches crawlin' over you.

"I got good news for you, Vic," he says. "I'm gonna help you get your spiff outta the tank." All with that smile. Scared the [deleted] outta me.

"The hearings for all the bimbos they rounded up are three o'clock this afternoon. You be there. We're gonna make a commotion for you. You grab your [deleted] and get out fast. Unnerstand me?"

I didn't like the sound of that word *commotion*. I wasn't sure what it meant, not then, but I figured it would mean trouble. All I wanted was for Big Lou to buy Jade's way out. Now it sounded like there was goin' to be a fight.

Don't get me wrong. I've had my share of fights. I'm on the small side and I'm sure no jock, but you can't even exist in the city if you can't protect yourself. But I didn't like the idea of a fight with the city police. They like to beat up on guys. And they carry guns. And who knew what in hell the Controllers carried?

"You unnerstand me?" Big Lou repeated. He didn't raise his voice much, just enough to make me know he wanted the right answer outta me.

"Yeah," I said. My voice damned near cracked. "Sure. And thanks." I got up and scooted for the door.

Before I got to it, though, Big Lou said, "There's a favor you can do for me, kid."

"Sure, Lou," I said. "Tonight, tomorrow, when? You name it."

"Now," he said.

"But Jade—"

"You'll be done in plenty time to get to city hall by three."

I didn't argue. It wouldn't have done me no good. Or Jade.

What he wanted was a fancy electronic gizmo that I had to put together for him. I knew it was important to him because he told one of his goons—a guy with shoulders comin' straight out of his ears, no neck at all, so help me—to drive me all the way downtown to the old navy base. It had been abandoned before I was born, of course, but it was still a treasure island of good stuff. Or so I had been told all my life. I had never even got as far as the electrified fence the Feds had put up all around the base, let alone inside the base itself. You had to go through South Philly to get to the base, and a guy alone don't get through South Philly. Not in once piece, anyway.

But now here I was bein' taken down to that fence and right through it, in a real working automobile, no less! The car was dead gray with government numbers stenciled on the driver's door. But the driver was Big Lou's goon. And Little Lou sat on the backseat with me.

Little Lou was a real pain in the ass. Some people said he really was Big Lou's son. But he sure didn't look like Big Lou. Little Lou was only a couple years older than me and he was twice Big Lou's size, big and hard with muscles all over. Good-lookin' guy, too. Handsome, like a video star. Even if he hadn't been a big shot he could've had any girl he wanted just by smilin' at her.

He was smart. And strong. But he was ugly inside. He had a nasty streak a mile and a half wide. He knew I wanted to be called Vic. I hate the name my mother gave me: Salvatore. Little Lou always called me Sal. Or sometimes Sally. He knew there wasn't a damned thing I could do about it.

I tried to keep our talk strictly on the business at hand. And one eye on my wristwatch. It was an electronic beauty that I had rebuilt myself; kept perfect time, long as I could scrounge a battery for it every year or so. I kept it in an old scratched-up case with a crummy rusted band so nobody like Little Lou would see how great it was and take it off me.

It was noon when we passed through a gate in the

navy-base fence. The gate was wide open. No guard. Nobody anywhere in sight.

"So what's this gizmo I'm supposed to put together for you?" I asked Little Lou.

He gave me a lazy smile. "You'll see. We got a man here with all the pieces, but he don't know how to put 'em together right."

"What's the thing supposed to do?"

His smile went bigger. "Set off a bomb."

"A bomb?"

He laughed at how my voice squeaked. "That's right. A bomb. And it's gotta go off at just the right instant. Or else."

"I—" I had to swallow. Hard. "I never worked with bombs."

"You don't have to. All you gotta do is put together the gizmo that sets the bomb off."

Well, they took me to a big building on the base. No, I don't remember seein' any number or name on the building. It looked like a great big tin shed to me. Half fallin' down. Walls slanting. Holes in the roof, I could see once we got inside. Pigeon crap all over the place. Everything stunk of rust and rot. But there were rows and rows of shelves in there, stacked right up to the roof. Most of 'em were bare, but some still had electronic parts in their cartons, brand new, still wrapped in plastic, never been used before. My eyes damn near popped.

And there was a guy there sittin' in a wheelchair next to a long bench covered with switches and batteries and circuit boards and all kinds of stuff. Older guy. Hair like a wire brush, a couple days' beard on his face, grayer than his hair. One of his eyes was swollen purple and his lip was puffed up, too, like somebody'd been sluggin' him. Nice guys, beatin' on a wheelchair case.

I got the picture right away. They had wanted this guy

to make their gizmo for them and he couldn't do it. Little Lou or one of the others had smacked the poor slob around. They always figured that if you hit a guy hard enough he would do what you wanted. But this poor bastard didn't know how to make the gizmo they wanted. He had been a sailor, from the looks of him: face like leather and tattoos on his arms. But something had crippled his legs and now he was workin' for Big Lou and Little Lou and takin' a beating because they wanted him to do somethin' he just didn't know how to do.

He told me what they wanted. Through his swollen, split lips he sounded strange, like he had been born someplace far away where they talk different from us. The gizmo was a kind of a radar, but not like they use in kitchen radar ranges. This one sent out a microwave beam that sensed the approach of a ship or a plane. What Little Lou wanted was to set off his bomb when whatever it is he wanted to blow up was a certain distance away.

Electronics is easy. I heard that they used to send guys to school for years at a time to learn how to build electronic stuff. I could never understand why. All the stuff is pretty much the same. A resistor is a resistor. A power cell is a power cell. You find out what the gizmo is supposed to do and you put together the pieces that'll do it. Simple.

I had Little Lou's gizmo put together by one o'clock. Two hours to go before I hadda be in city hall to take Jade away from the Controllers.

"Nice work, Sal," Little Lou said to me. He knew it got under my skin.

"Call me Vic," I said.

"Sure," he said. "Sally."

That was Little Lou. If I pushed it he would've smacked me in the mouth. And laughed.

"I got to get up to city hall now," I said.

"Yeah, I know. Hot for that little [deleted], ain'tcha?"

I didn't answer. Little Lou was the kind who'd take your girl away from you just for the hell of it. Whether she wanted to or not. And there'd be nuthin I could do about it. So I just kept my mouth zipped.

He walked me out to the car. It was hot outside; July hot. Muggy, too. "You start walkin' now, you'll probably just make it to city hall on time."

"Walk?" I squawked. "Ain't you gonna drive me?" I was sweatin' already in that hot sun.

"Why should I?" He laughed as he put the gizmo in the car's trunk. "I got what I want."

He shut the trunk lid real careful, gently, like maybe the bomb was in there, too. Then he got into the car's backseat, leaving me standin' out in the afternoon sun feelin' hot and sweaty and stupid. But there wasn't a damned thing I could do about it.

Finally Lou laughed and popped the back door open. "Come on in, Sally. You look like you're gonna bust into tears any minute."

I felt pretty [deleted] grateful to him. Walkin' the few miles uptown to city hall wouldn't have been no easy trick. The gangs in South Philly shoot first and ask questions afterward when a stranger tries to go through their turf.

About halfway there, though, Little Lou lets me know why he's bein' so generous.

"Tonight," he says, "nine o'clock sharp. You be at the old Thirtieth-street station."

"Me? Why? What for?"

"Two reasons. First we gotta test the gizmo you made. Then we gotta hook it up to the bomb. If it works right."

He wasn't smilin' anymore. I was scared of workin' with a bomb, lemme tell you. But not as scared as I was at the thought of what Little Lou'd do to me if the gizmo didn't work right.

So I got to city hall in plenty time okay. It's a big ugly

pile of gray stone, half fallin' apart. A windowsill had crumbled out a couple months ago, just dropped out of its wall and fell to the street. Solid hunk of stone, musta weighed a couple tons. It was still there, stickin' through the pavement like an unexploded bomb. I wondered what would happen if the statue of Billy Penn, up at the top of the Hall's tower, ever came loose. Be like a [deleted] atomic bomb hittin' the street.

Usually city hall is a good place to avoid. Nobody there but the suits who run what's left of the city and the oinks who guard 'em.

Oinks? Pigs. Helmet-heads. Bruisers. Cops. Police. There are worse names for them, too, y'know.

Well, anyway, this particular afternoon city hall is a busy place. Sanitation robots chuggin' and scrubbin' all over the place. A squad of guys in soldier uniforms and polished helmets goin' through some kind of drill routine in the center courtyard. Even a crew of guys with a truck and a crane tryin' to tug that windowsill outta the pavement. Might as well be tryin' to lift the [deleted] Rock of Gibraltar, I thought.

They were goin' through all this because the Chairman of the World Council was comin' to give a speech over at Independence Hall. Fourth of July and all that crap. Everybody knew that as soon as the Chairman's speech was over and he was on his way back to New York or wherever he stayed, Philly would go back to bein' half empty, half dead. The sanitation robots would go back to the housing tracts out in the suburbs and Philly would be left to itself, dirty and hot and nasty as hell.

I felt a little edgy actually goin' *inside* city hall. But I told myself, What the hell, they got nuthin on me. I'm not wanted for any crime or anything. I don't even exist, as far as their computers are concerned. Still, when I saw these guys in suits and ties and all I felt pretty crummy. Like I should have found a shower someplace or at least a comb.

I didn't like to ask nobody for directions, but once I was inside the Hall I didn't have a [deleted] idea of where I should go. I picked out a woman, dressed real neat in kind of a suit but with a skirt instead of pants. Even wore a tie. No tits to speak of, but her hair was a nice shade of yellow, like those girls you see in TV commercials.

She kind of wrinkled her nose at me, but she pointed up a flight of stone stairs. I went up and got lost again right away. Then I saw an oink—a woman, though—and asked her. She eyed me up and down like she was thinkin' how much fun it'd be to bash me on the head with her billy. But instead she told me how to find the courtroom. She talked real slow, like I was brain-damaged or something. Or maybe she was, come to think of it.

I went down the hall and saw the big double-doored entrance to the courtroom. A pair of oinks stood on either side of it, fully armed and helmeted. A lot of people were streamin' through, all of them well dressed, a lot of them carrying cameras or laptop computers. Lots of really great stuff, if only I could get my hands on it.

Then I saw a men's room across the corridor and I ducked inside. A couple homeless guys had made a camp in the stalls for themselves. The sinks had been freshly cleaned up, though, and the place didn't smell too bad. I washed my face and hands and tried to comb my hair a little with my fingers. Still looked pretty messy, but what the hell.

Taking a deep breath, I marched across the corridor and through the double doors, right past the oinks. I didn't look at them, just kept my eyes straight ahead.

And then I saw Jade.

They had her in a kind of a pen made of polished wood railings up to about waist-level and thick shatterproof glass from there to the ceiling. She was in there with maybe three dozen other pros, most of 'em lookin' pretty tired and sleazy, I gotta admit. But not Jade. She looked kind of scared, wide-eyed, you know. But as beautiful and fresh as a flower in the middle of a garbage heap. I wanted to wave to her, yell to her so she'd notice me. But I didn't dare.

You gotta understand, I was in love with Jade. But she couldn't be in love with me. Not in her business. Her pimp would beat the hell out of any of his whores who took up with anybody except himself. I had known her since we were kids together runnin' along the alleys and raiding garbage cans, keepin' one jump ahead of the dog packs. Back when her name was still Juanita. Before she had her eyes changed. I had kissed her exactly once, when we was both twelve years old. The next day she turned her first trick and went pro.

But I had a plan. For the past five years I had been savin' up whatever cash I could raise. Usually, you know, I'd get paid for my work in food or drugs or other stuff to barter off. But once in a while somebody'd actually give me money. What? Naw, I never did much drugs; screwed up my head too much. I usually traded whatever [deleted] I came across. I seen what that stuff does to people; makes 'em real psycho.

Anyway, sometimes I'd get real money. That's when I'd sneak out to the housing tracts where they had automated bank machines and deposit my cash in the bank. All strictly legitimate. The bank didn't care where the money came from. I never had to deal with a living human being. All I had to do to open the account was to pick up a social security number, which I got from a wallet I had found in one of the junkyards when I was ten, eleven years old. Even that young, I knew that card was better than gold.

So I had stashed away damn near a thousand dollars over the years. One day I would use that money to take

Jade outta the city, out of her life. We'd buy a house out in the tracts and start to live like decent people. Once I had enough money.

But then the [deleted] Controllers had arrested Jade. What I heard about the Controllers scared the [deleted] outta me. They were bigger than the city oinks, bigger even than the state police or the National Guard. They could put you in what they called International Detainment Centers, all the way out in Wyoming or Canada or wherever the hell they pleased. They could scramble your brains with some super electronic stuff that would turn you into a zombie.

That's what they were goin' to do to Jade. If I let them.

I sat in the last row of benches. The trials of the pros were already goin' on. Each one took only a couple minutes. The judge sat up on his high bench at the front of the courtroom, lookin' sour and cranky in his black robe. A clerk called out one of the girls' names. The girl would be led out of the holding pen by a pair of women oinks and stood up in a little railed platform. The clerk would say that the girl had been arrested for prostitution and some other stuff I couldn't understand because he was mumblin' more than speakin' out loud.

The judge would ask the girl how she pleaded: guilty or innocent. The girl would say, "Innocent, Your Honor." The judge would turn to a table full of well-dressed suits who had a bunch of laptops in front of them. They would peck on their computers. The judge would stare into the screen of his computer, up on the desk he was sittin' at.

Then he'd say, "Guilty as charged. Sentenced to indeterminate detention. Next case." And he'd smack his gavel on the desktop.

I remember seein' some old videos where they had lawyers arguin' and a bunch of people called a jury who said whether the person was guilty or innocent. None of that here. Just name, charge, plea, and "Guilty as charged." Then—*wham!*—the gavel smack and the next case. Jade wouldn't have a chance.

And neither did I, from the looks of it. How could I get her away from those oinks, out from behind that bullet-proof glass? Where was this commotion Big Lou promised, whatever it was supposed to be?

They were almost halfway through the whole gang of girls, just whippin' them past the judge, bang, bang, bang. Jade's turn was comin' close; just two girls ahead of her. Then the doors right behind me smack open and in clumps some big guy in heavy boots and some weird kind of rubbery uniform with a kind of astronaut-type helmet and a visor so dark I couldn't make out his face even though I was only a couple feet away from him.

"Clear this courtroom!" he yells, in a deep booming voice. "There's been a toxic spill from the cleanup crew upstairs. Get out before the fumes reach this level!"

Everybody jumps to their feet and pushes for the door. Not me. I start jumpin' over the benches to get up front, where Jade is. I see the judge scramble for his own little doorway up there, pullin' his robe up almost to his waist so he could move faster. The clerks and the guys with the laptops are makin' their way back toward the corridor. As I passed them I saw the two oinks openin' the glass door to the holding pen and startin' to hustle the girls out toward a door in the back wall.

I shot past like a cruise missile and grabbed Jade's wrist. Before the oinks could react I was draggin' her up the two steps to the same door the judge had used.

"Vic!" she gulped as I slammed the door shut and clicked its lock.

I said something brilliant like, "Come on."

"What're you doing? Where're we going?"

"Takin' you outta here."

Jade seemed scared, confused, but she came along with me all right. The judge was nowhere in sight, just his robe thrown on the floor. Somebody was poundin' on the door we had just come through and yellin' the way oinks do. There was another door to the room and the judge had left it half open. I had no way of knowin' if that toxic spill was real or not, but I knew that the oinks would be after us either way so I dashed for the door, Jade's wrist still in my grip.

"You're crazy," she said, kind of breathless. But she came right along with me. And she smiled at me as she said it. If I hadn't been wound so tight I would've kissed her right there and then.

Instead we pounded down this empty corridor and found an elevator marked JUDGES ONLY. I leaned on the button. Somebody appeared at the far end of the corridor, a guy in a business suit.

"Hey, you kids," he yelled, kind of angry, "you're not allowed to use that elevator."

Just then the doors slid open. "Emergency!" I yelled back and pulled Jade inside.

When we got down to the street level everything seemed normal. Nobody was runnin' or shoutin'. I guessed that the toxic spill was a phony. I couldn't imagine Big Lou doin' something like that just for me, but maybe he needed his bomb gizmo bad enough after all. Anyway, I told Jade to act normal and we just walked out into the central courtyard nice and easy, me in my shabby jeans and sneakers and her in her workin' clothes: spike heels, microskirt, skintight blouse. They had washed off her makeup and her hair looked kind of draggled, but she was still beautiful enough to make even the women out there turn and stare at her.

The work crew was still tryin' to tug that fallen windowsill outta the cement when we walked past. I steered Jade toward the boarded-up entrance to the old subway.

"We're not going down there!" she said when I pushed a couple boards loose.

"Sure as hell are," I said.

"But—"

"Hey, you!" yelled a guy in a soldier uniform.

"Come on!" I tugged at Jade's wrist and we started down the dark stairway underground.

The steps were slippery, slimy. It was dark as hell down there and it stunk of [urine]. The air was chilly and kind of wet; gave you the shakes. I could feel Jade trembling in my grip. With my other hand I fished a penlight outta my pocket. What? I always keep a light on me. And make sure the batteries are good, too. You never know when you're gonna need a light; trouble don't always come at high noon, y'know.

"Vic, I don't like this," Jade said.

"I don't either, honey, but we gotta get away. This is the best way to do it." I clicked on my penlight; it threw a feeble circle of light on the filthy, littered tiled floor. "See, it ain't so bad, is it?"

Jade was right in a way. The subway tunnels really were dangerous. We had heard stories since we were little kids about the hordes of rats livin' down there. And other things, monsters that crawled outta the sewers, people who lived down there in the dark for so long they'd gone blind—but they could find you in the dark and when they did they ate you raw, like animals.

I was kind of shakin' myself, thinkin' about all that. But I wasn't gonna let Jade be taken away by the Controllers and I wasn't gonna play with no bombs for Little Lou or Big Lou or anybody. I was takin' Jade and myself outta the city altogether, across the bridge and out into the housing tracts on the other side of the river. I'd take my money from the bank and find a place for us to live and get a regular job someplace and start to be a real person. The two of us. Jade and me.

Okay, maybe it was just a dream. But I wanted to make my dream come true. Wanted it so bad I was willin' to face anything.

Well, there ain't no sense tellin' you about every step of the way we took in the subway tunnels. There were rats, plenty of 'em, some big as dogs, but they stayed away from us as long as the penlight worked. We could see their red eyes burnin' in the dark, though, and hear them makin' their screechy little rat noises, like they was talkin' to each other. Jade had a tough time walkin' on those spike-heel shoes of hers, but she wouldn't go barefoot in the sloppy goo we hadda walk through. My own sneaks were soaked through with the muck; it made my feet burn.

Jade screamed a couple times, once when she stumbled on something squishy that turned out to be a real dog that must've died only a few hours earlier. It was half eaten away already.

No monsters from the sewers, though. And if there was any blind cannibals runnin' around down there we didn't see them. The rats were enough, believe me. I felt like they were all around us, watchin', waitin' until the batteries in my light gave out. And then they'd swarm us under and do to us what they had started to do to that dog.

All the subway tunnels meet under the city hall, and I sure as hell hoped I had picked the right one, the one that goes out to the river. After hours and hours, I noticed that the tunnel seemed to be slantin' upward. I even thought I saw some light up ahead.

Sure enough, the tracks ran up and onto the Ben Franklin bridge that crossed the Delaware. It was already night, and drizzling a cold misty rain out there. No wind, not even a breath of air movin'. And no noise. Silence. Everything was still as death. It was kinda creepy, y'know. I been on that bridge lotsa times; up that high there was always a breeze, at least. But not that night.

At least we were out of the tunnel. On the other side of that bridge was the housing tracts, the land where people could lead decent lives, safe from the city.

I knew the bridge was barricaded and the barricades were rigged with electronic chips that spotted anybody tryin' to get through. Those people in the tracts didn't like havin' people from the city comin' over to visit. Not unless they drove cars that gave out the right electronic ID signals. But I had gotten past the barricades before. It took a bit of climbin', but it could be done. Jade could take off her spike heels now and climb with me.

But in front of the barricade was a car. A dead gray four-door with government numbers stenciled on the driver's door. Only the guys standin' beside the car weren't government. They were Little Lou and his goon driver.

Lou was leanin' against the hood, lookin' relaxed in a sharp suit and open-collar shirt. His hair was slicked back and when he saw Jade he smiled with all his teeth.

"Where you goin', Sal?" he asked, real quiet, calm.

I had to think damned fast. "I thought we was in the tunnel for the Station! I must've got mixed up."

"You sure did."

Lou nodded to the goon, who opened the rear door of the car. I started for it, head hung low. He had outsmarted me.

"Not you, stupid," Lou snarled at me. "You sit up front with Rollo." He made a little half bow at Jade, smilin' again. "You sit in back with me, spiff."

Jade got into the car and scrunched herself into the corner of the backseat, as far away from Little Lou as she could. I sat up front, half twisted around in the seat so I could watch Lou. Rollo was so big his elbow kept nudgin' me every time he turned the steering wheel.

"You was supposed to be at the Thirtieth-street station at nine o'clock," Little Lou said to me. But his eyes were on Jade, who was starin' off at nothing.

I looked at my wristwatch. "Hell, Lou, it's only seven-thirty."

"Yeah, but you were headin' in the wrong direction. A guy could lose some of his fingers that way. Or get his legs broke."

"I just got mixed-up down in the tunnels," I said, tryin' to make it sound real.

"You're a mixed-up kid, Sally. Maybe a few whacks on your thick skull will straighten you out."

There wasn't much I could say. If Little Lou was waitin' for me at the bridge he had me all figured out. I just hoped he really needed me enough to keep me in one piece so I could set up his bomb gizmo for him. What would happen after that, I didn't know and I didn't want to think about.

We drove through the dead, empty city for a dozen blocks or so. I had turned around in my seat and was lookin' ahead out the windshield. Everything was dark. Not a light in any window, not a street lamp lit. I knew people lived in those buildings. They were supposed to be abandoned, condemned. But nobody bothered to tear them down; that would cost the taxpayers too much. And the people who didn't exist, the people whose names had been erased from the government's computers, they lived there and died there and had babies there. I was one of those babies. So was Jade.

"Are those tits real?" I heard Lou ask.

Through the side-view mirror I saw Jade turn her face to him. Without a smile, with her face perfectly blank, she took his hand and placed it on her boob.

"What do you think?" she asked Lou.

He grinned at her. She smiled back at him. I wanted to kill him. I knew what Jade was doin': tryin' to keep Lou happy so he wouldn't be sore at me. She was protectin' me while I sat there helpless and the dirty [deleted] [deleted] bastard climbed all over her.

"Thirtieth-street station comin' up," said Rollo. His voice was high and thin, almost like a girl's. But I bet that anybody who laughed at his voice got his own windpipe whacked inside out.

Lou sat up straight on the backseat and ran a hand through his hair. Jade edged away from him, her face blank once again.

"Okay, Sally, you little [deleted]. Here's where you earn your keep. Or I break your balls for good."

Lou, Rollo, and me got out of the car. Lou ducked his head through the open rear door and told Jade, "You come too, cute stuff. We'll finish what we started when this is over."

Jade glanced at me as she came out of the car. Lou grabbed her by the wrist, like he owned her.

If Lou had been by himself I would have jumped him. He was bigger than me, yeah, and probably a lot tougher. But I was desperate. And I had the blade I always carried taped just above my right ankle. It was little, but I kept it razor sharp. Lou was gonna take Jade away from me. Oh, I guess he'd let her come back to me when he was finished with her, maybe. But who knew when? Or even if. I had only used that blade when I needed to protect myself. Would I have the guts to cut Lou if I could get him in a one-on-one?

But Lou wasn't alone. Rollo was as big as that damned city hall windowsill. There was no way I could handle him unless I had a machine gun or a rocket launcher or something like that. I was desperate, all right. But not crazy.

The Station was all lit up. Cleaning crews and robots

were crawlin' all over the old building, but I didn't see any oinks or soldiers. Later I found out that they would be pourin' into the area in the morning. The Chairman was due to arrive at eleven A.M.

Lou took me and Jade to a panel truck marked PUBLIC WORKS DEPARTMENT. Two other guys was already sittin' up front. And there was my gizmo, sittin' on the bare metal floor. All by itself. No bomb in sight. That made me feel better, a little.

They hustled us into the truck and made me sit on the floor, big Rollo between me and the back door and Lou across from me. He made Jade sit beside him. She kept her legs pressed tight together. We drove off.

"Where we goin'?" I asked.

Lou said, "There's a maintenance train comin' down the track in half an hour. You set up your gizmo where we tell you to and we see if it can spot the train at the right distance away and send the signal that it's supposed to send."

"What're you guys gonna do, blow up the Chairman?"

I got a backhand smack in the face for that. So I shut my mouth and did what they told me, all the while tryin' to figure out how in hell I could get Jade and me outta this. I didn't come up with any answers, none at all.

When the truck stopped, Rollo got out first, then Lou shoved me through the back door. The other two guys stayed in their seats up front. Lou pushed the gizmo across the truck's floor toward me. It was heavy enough so I needed both hands.

"Don't drop it, [deleted]head," Lou growled.

"Why don't we let Rollo carry it?" I said.

Lou just laughed. Then he helped Jade out the back door. I thought he helped her too damned much, had his hands all over her.

We was parked maybe ten blocks away from the station. Its lights glowed in the misty drizzle that was still comin' down, the only lights in the whole [deleted] city, far as I could see. Some of the people livin' in the buildings all around there had electricity, I knew. Hell, I had wired a lot of 'em up. But they kept their windows covered; didn't wanna let nobody know they was in there. Scared of gangs roamin' through the streets at night.

All those suits and oinks and everybody who had been at city hall was all safe in their homes in the tracts by now. Nobody in the city except the people who didn't exist, like Jade and me. And the rats who had business in the dark, like Little Lou.

I saw why Lou didn't want Rollo to carry the gizmo. The big guy walked straight up to a steel grate set into the pavement. It must have weighed a couple hundred pounds, at least, but he lifted it right up, rusty hinges squealin' like mad. I saw the rungs of a metal ladder goin' down. Lou shone a flashlight on them. They had been cleaned off.

Rollo took the gizmo off me and tucked it under one arm. I followed him down the ladder. Down at the bottom there were three other guys waitin'. Guys like I had never seen before. Foreigners. Dark skin, eyes like coals. One of them had a big, dark, droopy moustache, but his long hair was streaked with gray. They were all kind of short, my height, but very solid. Their suits looked funny, like they had been made by tailors who didn't know the right way to cut a suit.

The two clean-shaven ones were carryin' automatic rifles, mean-looking things with curved magazines. Their jackets bulged; extra ammunition clips, I figured. They looked younger than the guy with the moustache; tough, hard, all business.

"This is the device?" asked the one with the moustache. He said "thees" instead of "this."

Lou nodded. "We're gonna test it, make sure it works right."

"Bueno."

We were in a kind of—whattaya call it, an alcove?— yeah, an alcove cut into the side of the train tunnel. The kind where work crews could stay when a train comes past. This wasn't one of the old city subways; it was the tunnel that the trains from other cities used, back when there had been trains runnin'. The Chairman was comin' in on a train the next morning, and these guys wanted to blow it up. Or so I thought.

Rollo carried the gizmo down to the side of the tracks. For an instant I almost panicked; I realized that we needed a power pack. Then I saw that there was one already sittin' there on the filthy bricks of the tunnel floor. I hooked it up, takin' my time; no sense lettin' them know how easy this all was.

"Snap it up," Lou hissed at me. "The train's comin'."

"Okay, okay," I said.

The guy with the moustache knelt beside me and took a little metal box from his pocket. "This is the detonator," he said. His voice sounded sad, almost like he was about to cry. "Your device must make its relay click at the proper moment. Do you know how to connect the two of them together?"

I nodded and took the detonator from him.

"Tomorrow, the detonator will be placed some distance from your triggering device."

"How'll they be connected then?" I asked.

"By a wire."

"That's okay, then." I figured that if they had tried somethin' fancy like a radio link, in this old tunnel they might get all kinds of interference or echoes. A hard-wire connection was a helluva lot surer. And safer.

It only took me a couple minutes to connect his detonator to my radar gizmo, but Lou was fidgetin' every second of the time. I never seen him lookin' nervous or flustered before. He was always the coolest of the cool, never a hair out of place. Now he was half jumpin' up and down, lookin' up the tunnel and grumblin' that the train was comin' and I was gonna miss it. I had to work real hard to keep a straight face. Little Lou uptight; that was somethin' to grin about.

Okay, so I had everything ready in plenty time. The maintenance train musta been doin' two miles an hour, max, scrapin' down the tracks and scoopin' up most of the garbage in the tunnel as it dragged along. I turned on my gizmo. The readout numbers on the little red window started tickin' down slowly. When they reached the number already set on the other window beside it, the relay on the detonator clicked.

"Bueno," said the moustache, still kneeling beside me. He didn't sound happy or nuthin. Just, *"Bueno."* Flat as a pancake.

I looked over at Jade, standin' with Rollo and the other strangers off by the tunnel wall, and I smiled at her.

"Does that means it works okay?" I asked. I knew the answer but I wanted him to say it so Little Lou could hear it. Lou was bendin' down between the two of us.

"Yes," he said, in that sad heavy voice of his. "It works perfectly." He said each word carefully, like he wasn't sure he had his English right.

I got to my feet and said to Lou, "Okay. I done my part. Now Jade and me can go, right?"

"No one leaves this tunnel," said the moustache. Still sad, but real strong, like he meant it. He had unbuttoned his suit jacket and I could see the butt of a heavy black revolver stickin' out of a shoulder holster. [Deleted], it would've taken my both hands just to hold that pistol up, let alone fire it off.

"Hey, now wait a minute—" I started to say.

Lou grabbed me by the shoulder and spun me around, his fist raised to smack me a good one. The moustache grabbed his upraised arm and held it in midair. Just held it there. He must've been pretty strong to do that.

"There is no need for that," he said to Lou, low and firm. "There will be enough violence in the morning."

Lou pulled his arm away, his face red and nasty. The moustache turned to me and almost smiled. Kind of apologetic, he said, "It is necessary for you and your lady to remain here until the operation is concluded. For security reasons. Do you understand?"

I nodded. Sure I understood. What I was startin' to wonder about, though, was whether these guys would let us live after their "operation" was finished. I knew Lou was goin' to want to take Jade with him. If these foreigners didn't whack me tomorrow, probably Lou would. Then he'd have Jade all to himself for as long as he wanted her.

So we sat on the crummy tunnel floor alongside the tracks and waited. The foreigners had some sandwiches and coffee with them. Moustache offered a sandwich to Jade, real polite, and one to me. It was greasy and spiced hot enough to scorch my mouth. They all laughed at me when I grabbed for the coffee and burned my mouth even more 'cause it was so hot.

I tried to sleep but couldn't. I saw that the two younger guys had curled up right there on the floor, sleepin' like babies with their rifles in their arms. Lou took Jade off down the tunnel a ways, where it was dark, far enough so I couldn't see them or even hear them. I sat and watched Rollo, hopin' he'd nod off long enough for me to follow Lou down the tunnel and slice his throat open. But Rollo just sat a few feet away from me, his chin on his knees and his eyes on me. Big as a [deleted] elephant.

Moustache wasn't sleepin', either. I went over to where he was sittin' with his back against the wall.

"Why's the Chairman comin' in on a train?" I asked him, hunkering down beside him. "There ain't been a train through here since before I was born."

Moustache gave me his sad smile. "It is a gesture. He is a man given to gestures."

I couldn't figure out what the hell he meant by that.

"Why do you want to whack him?" I asked.

"Whack?" He looked puzzled.

"Kill him."

His eyes went wide, a little. "Kill him? We do not intend to assassinate the Chairman." He shook his head. "No, it is not so simple as that."

"Then what?"

He shook his head again. "It is none of your affair. The less you know about it the better off you will be."

"Yeah," I said. "Until this thing is over and Lou whacks me."

He shrugged. "That is your problem. Not mine."

A lot of help he was.

My wristwatch said seven twenty-seven A.M. when Lou came walkin' back up the track toward us. His hair was mussed and he had his suit jacket thrown over one shoulder. He grinned at me. Jade came followin' behind him, her face absolutely blank, starin' straight ahead. I figured she was tryin' *not* to see me.

What the hell, I thought. Why don't I kill the mother-[deleted] [deleted] right now. Stick my blade in his nuts and twist it hard before Rollo gets a chance to move. They was gonna whack me afterward anyway. I knew it.

I was even startin' to pull up my pants leg when I felt Moustache's hand on my shoulder. "No," he whispered.

I must have looked pretty sore to him. He said, low and

soft, "I am a man of honor. I will see to it that you and the girl go free after our operation is concluded. You can trust me."

Lou had already passed me by then. Rollo got up on his feet, towerin' over us all like a mountain. I let my pants leg slide down to my ankle again. I just hoped Lou and Rollo didn't notice what I had started to do.

A little while later three more guys came down the same ladder we had used, two of them carryin' big leather suitcases, the third carryin' a little metal case and climbin' down so careful that I figured he had the bomb in it. They were foreigners too, but they looked different from Moustache and his men. They had dark skins, all right, but a different kind of dark. And they were taller, slimmer, with big hooked noses like eagle's beaks. Like Moustache and his men, they were wearin' regular suits. But they looked like they were uncomfortable in them, like these weren't the kind of clothes they usually wore.

Anyway, after talkin' a few minutes with Moustache they went up the tracks with the little metal case. They came back again without it, but trailin' a spool of wire. Which they connected to my radar gizmo. I noticed that the detonator was gone; they had taken it with the bomb, I figured. Then they set the gizmo right in the middle of the tracks and waited.

"Won't the oinks see it there?" I asked Moustache. "The police," I added before he could ask what *oinks* meant.

In that sad way of his he said, "Your Mr. Lou has been well paid to see to it that the security guards do not come down the tunnel this far." He kind of sighed. "It always surprises me to see how well bribery works on little men."

Bought off the security guards? I wondered if even Big Lou could cover all the Federal oinks that must be coverin' the Chairman. I mean, this guy was the Chairman of the World Council. They must be protectin' him like they protect the president or some of those video stars.

Moustache must've understood the puzzled look on my face. "There is a full security guard on the train itself, and entire platoons of soldiers at the station. The responsibility for checking the security of the tunnel was given to your city police force. That is why we decided to do our work here. This is the weak link in their preparations."

He talked like a general. Or at least, the way I thought a general would talk. No, I never did get his name. Nobody spoke to him by his name; nobody I could understand, at least. I did find out later on that he had another half dozen men farther down the tunnel, also waitin' for the train. Twelve guys altogether. Fourteen, if you count Little Lou and Rollo.

Okay, so the time finally comes. Little Lou is almost hoppin' outta his skin he's so wired up. Jade was sittin' as far back in the alcove as she could, legs tucked up under her, still starin' off into space and seeing nuthin. I started to wonder what Lou had done to her, then tried to stop thinkin' about it. Didn't work.

Moustache is as calm as a guy can be, talkin' in his own language to his two men. The other three strangers are bendin' over their suitcases, and I see they're takin' out all kinds of stuff. I'm not sure what most of it was, but they had little round gray things about the size of baseballs, weird-lookin' kinds of guns—I guess they were guns, they looked kind of like pistols—and finally they pulled out some rubbery gas masks and handed two of 'em to Moustache's men.

Lou and Rollo both are lookin' down the track toward the station, and I see they both have pistols in their hands. Rollo's hands are so big his pistol looks like a toy. Little Lou is sweatin', I can see the beads comin' down his face, he's so [deleted] scared. I keep myself from laughin' at him out loud. He's worried that the oinks he bought off won't stay bought. Be just like them to take his money and then double-cross him by doin' their job right anyway.

But then I figured that maybe Big Lou was the one who paid off the oinks. Screwin' Little Lou is one thing; if they mess around with Big Lou they'd regret it for as long as they lived. And so would their families.

Moustache sends off all five of the strangers up the track. I wonder how close to the bomb they can get without bein' blown up themselves. I wonder if the bomb will bring down the roof of the whole [deleted] tunnel and bury all of us right where we are. I wonder about Moustache sayin' they ain't tryin' to whack the Chairman. What're they gonna do, then?

I didn't have to wait long to find out.

Moustache is starin' hard at his wristwatch, that big pistol in his other hand. I hear a dull *whump* kind of noise. He looks up, runs out to the middle of the tracks. I go to Jade, who's gotten to her feet. Lou and Rollo are still starin' down the track toward the station, Moustache is lookin' the other way, toward where the train is comin' from. Nobody's watchin' us.

"Come on," I whisper to Jade. "Now's our chance."

But she won't move from where she's standing.

"Come on!" I say.

"I can't," she tells me.

"It's now or never!"

"Vic, I can't," she says. I see tears in her eyes. "I promised him."

"[Deleted] Lou!" I say. "I love you and you're comin' with me."

But she pulls back. "I love you too, Vic. But if I go with you Lou will hunt us down and kill you."

"He's gonna kill me anyway!" I'm tryin' to keep whispering. It's makin' my throat raw.

"No, he told me he'd let you alone if I stayed with him. He swore it."

"And you believe that mother-[deleted] lying [deleted]?"

Just then we hear gunfire and guys yelling. Sounds like a little war goin' on up the track: automatic rifles goin' *pop-pop-pop*. Heavier sounds. Somebody screamin' like his guts've been shot out.

Moustache yells to Lou and Rollo, "Quickly! Follow me!" Then he waves at me and Jade with that big pistol. "You too! Come!"

So with Moustache in front of us and Lou and Rollo behind, we go runnin' up the track. There's a train stopped up there, a train like I never seen before. Like it's from Mars or someplace: all shinin' and smooth with curves more like an airplane than any train I ever saw. Not that I ever saw any, except in pictures or videos, y'know.

I see a hole in the ground that's still smokin'. The track is tore up. That was where the bomb was. It was just a little bomb, after all. Just enough to tear up the track and make the train stop.

We run past that and past the shining engine. Even in the shadows of the tunnel it seemed to shine, like it was brand new. Not a scratch or a mark on it. No graffiti, even. Where I come from, we don't see much that's new. It was beautiful, all right.

Anyway, there are three cars behind the engine. They all look spiffy too, but a couple windows on the first car were busted out, shattered. The car in the middle had a blue flag painted on its side, a flag I never seen before.

Moustache climbs up onto the first car and we're right behind him. We push through the doors. There's a bunch of dead bodies inside. Flopped on the floor, twisted across the seats. Not regular seats, like rows. These seats were more like big easy chairs that could swivel around, one next to each window. You could see there'd been plenty of bullets flyin' around; the bodies was tore up pretty bad, lots of blood. I heard Jade suck in her breath like she was gonna scream, but then she got control of herself. I almost wanted to scream myself; some of those bodies looked pretty damned bad.

One of the tall guys came through the door up at the other end of the car. He had his gas mask pushed up on top of his head. His rifle was slung over his shoulder, makin' his suit jacket bunch up so I could see a pistol stuck in the belt of his pants. He looked kind of sick, or maybe that was the way he looked when he was mad.

Moustache went up and talked with him for a minute, lookin' kind of pale himself. Lou told Rollo to pick up all the loose hardware lyin' around the car. What? Hardware. Guns. Must've been six or eight of 'em on the floor or still in the grip of the dead guys. Oh yeah, two of the dead ones were women, by the way. Far as I remember, neither one of 'em had a gun in her hand.

We got through the connecting doors and into the middle car. Not everybody in there is dead. Only a couple guys in blue suits that Moustache's men are already draggin' down into the third car, at the end of the train.

There was one guy alive in there, a little guy no bigger than me with eyes like Jade's. Otherwise he looked like a regular American. I mean his skin wasn't dark even though it wasn't exactly light like mine. And the suit he was wearin' was a regular suit, light gray. Right away I figured he was the Chairman of the World Council.

C. C. Lee.

He was sittin' there, his face frozen with no expression on it, almost like Jade's when Little Lou had been pawin' her. I looked at him real close and saw his eyes weren't exactly like Jade's; they were real oriental eyes, I guess. Hard to tell how old he was; his hair was all dark, not a speck of gray in it, but he didn't look young, y'know what

I mean? Straight hair, combed straight back from his forehead. Kinda high forehead, come to think of it. Maybe he was startin' to go bald.

Anyway, Moustache sat down in the chair next to his and swiveled it around so they were facin' each other. Jade and I stood in the aisle between the rows of chairs. The others moved out to the other two cars.

"This is not what I wanted," Moustache said. He talked in English, with that accent of his.

"It is what you should have expected," said the Chairman. His English was perfect, just like a newscaster on TV.

"I regret the killing."

"Of course you do."

"But it was necessary."

The Chairman looked at Moustache, *really* looked at him, right into his eyes like he was tryin' to bore through his skull.

"Necessary? To kill sixteen men and women? How many of your own have been killed?"

"Four," said Moustache. "Including my brother."

The Chairman blinked. "I am sorry for that," he said, almost in a whisper.

"He knew the risks. Our cause is desperate."

"Your cause is doomed. What can you possibly hope to achieve by this action?"

"Freedom for the political prisoners in my country. An end to the dictatorship."

"By kidnapping me?"

"We will hold you hostage until the political prisoners are freed," said Moustache. "The people will see that we have the power to bend the dictator to our will. They will rebel. There will be revolution—"

The Chairman shook his head like a tired, tired man. "Blood and more blood. And in the end, who is the winner? Even if you become the new head of your nation, do you really think that you will be better than the dictator who now resides in the presidential palace?"

"Yes! Of course! How can you ask such a question of me? I have dedicated my life to overthrowing the tyrant!"

"Yes, I know. I understand. Just as Fidel did. Just as Yeltsin did. Yet, if the people are not prepared to govern themselves, they end up with another tyrant, no matter how pure his motives were at the start."

Moustache gave him a look that would have peeled paint off a wall. "You dare say that to me?"

The Chairman made a little shrug. "It is the truth. You should not be angered by the truth."

Moustache jumped to his feet, yelling, "The truth is that you are our hostage and you will remain our hostage until our demands have been met!" Then he stomped up the aisle toward the front car.

I told Jade to stay there and hustled after Moustache. I caught up with him in between the two cars, out on the platform connecting them.

"Hey, wait a minute, willya?"

He whirled around, his eyes still burnin' with fury.

"Uh, excuse me," I said, tryin' to calm him down a little, "but you said it'd be okay for us to leave once the job was over, remember?"

The anger went out of his face. He made a strange expression, like he didn't know whether to laugh or cry. "The job is far from over, I fear."

"But I did what you wanted—"

He put a hand on my shoulder. "We had intended to take the Chairman off the train and drive him to a helicopter pad we had prepared for this operation. Unfortunately, the truck we had stationed at the emergency exit from the tunnel has already been seized by your soldiers.

We are trapped here in this tunnel, in this train. The Chairman is our prisoner, but we are prisoners, too."

"[Deleted] H. [deleted] on a crutch!" I yelled.

"Yes," he said. "Indeed."

"Whattaya gonna do?"

"Negotiate."

"What?"

"As long as we hold the Chairman we are safe. They dare not attack us for fear of harming him."

"But we can't get out?"

"Not unless they allow us to get out."

I got this empty feeling in my gut, like I was fallin' off a roof or something. I guess I was really scared.

Moustache went through the door to the car up front. I went back into the middle car. Jade was sittin' where Moustache had been. She was talkin' with the Chairman.

"I had wanted to bring a message of hope to the people of America, particularly to the disenfranchised and the poverty classes of the dying cities," he was tellin' her. "That is why I agreed to make this speech in Philadelphia on the anniversary of the Declaration of Independence."

"Hope?" I snapped, ploppin' myself down in the chair across the aisle from the two of them. "What hope?"

He didn't answer me for a second or two. He just looked at me, like he was studyin' me. His eyes were a kind of soft brown, gentle.

"Do you know how many people there are like you in the world?" he asked. Before I could think of anything to say he went on. "Of the more than ten billion human beings on Earth, three-quarters of them live in poverty."

"So what's that to me?" I said, tryin' to make it sound tough.

"You are one of them. So is this pretty young woman here."

"So?"

He kind of slumped back in his seat. "The World Council was formed to help solve the problems of poverty. It is my task as Chairman to lead the way."

I laughed out loud at him. "You ain't leadin' any way. You're stuck here, just like we are."

"For the moment."

Jade said, "We could all be killed, couldn't we?"

I knew she was right, but I said, "Not as long as we got this guy. They won't try nuthin as long as the Chairman's our hostage."

The Chairman's eyebrows went up a fraction. "You are part of this plot? From what your friend here has told me, you were forced to help these terrorists."

"Yeah. Well, that don't matter much now, does it?" I said, still tryin' to sound tough. "We're all stuck in this together."

"Exactly correct!" says the Chairman, like I had given the right answer on a quiz show. "We are all in this together. Not merely this"—and he swung his arms around to take in the train car—"but we are all in the global situation together."

"What do you mean?" Jade asked. She was lookin' at him in a way I'd never seen her look before. I guess it was respect. Like Big Lou wants people to behave toward him. Only Jade was doin' it on her own, without being forced or threatened.

"We are all part of the global situation," the Chairman repeated. He was lookin' at her but I got the feeling he was talkin' to me. "What happens to you has an effect all around the world."

"Bull[deleted]," I said.

He actually smiled at me. "I know it is hard for you to accept. But it is true. We are all linked together on the great wheel of life. What happens to you, what happens to a rice farmer in Bangladesh, what happens to a stockbroker in Geneva—each affects the other, each affects every person on Earth."

"Bull[deleted]," I said again.

"You do not believe it?"

"Hell no."

"Yet what you have done over the past twenty-four hours has brought you together with the Chairman of the World Council, hasn't it?"

"Yeah. And maybe we'll all get killed together."

That didn't stop him for even a half a second. "Or maybe we will all change the world together."

"Change it?" Jade asked. "How?"

"For the better, one hopes."

"Yeah, sure. We're gonna change the world," I said. "Jade and me, we don't even [deleted] exist, far as that world out there's concerned! They don't want no part of us!"

"But you do exist, in reality," he said, completely unflustered by my yellin' at him. "And once we are out of this mess, the world out there will have to admit your existence. They will have to notice you."

"The only notice they'll ever take of the likes of Jade and me is to dump our bodies in a [deleted] open pit and bulldoze us over."

"Hey, stop the yellin'!" Little Lou hollered from the front end of the car. He had just come in, with Rollo right behind him like a St. Bernard dog. Lou looked uptight. His jacket was gone, his shirt wrinkled and dark with sweat under the armpits. His hair was mussed, too. He was not happy with the way things were goin'. Rollo looked like he always looked: big, dumb, and mean.

Moustache pushed past the two of them. Jade got up

from her chair and came to sit next to me. Moustache took the chair and leaned his elbows on his knees, putting his face a couple inches away from the Chairman's.

"The situation is delicate," he said.

The Chairman didn't make any answer at all.

"We are unfortunately cut off here in the tunnel. The security forces reacted much more quickly than we had anticipated. They are now threatening to storm the train and kill us all. Only by assuring them that you are alive and unharmed have I persuaded them not to do so."

The Chairman still didn't budge.

Moustache took in a deep breath, like a sigh. "Now the chief of your own security forces wants to make certain that you are alive and well. He demands that you speak to him." Moustache pulled a palm-sized radio from his jacket pocket.

The Chairman made no move to take it from his hand.

"Please," said Moustache, holding the radio out to him.

"No," the Chairman said.

"But you must."

"No."

We all kind of froze. Everybody except Little Lou. He stepped between Moustache and the Chairman and whacked the Chairman in the mouth so hard it knocked him out of his chair. Then he kicked him in the ribs hard enough to lift him right off the floor. He was aimin' another kick when I went nuts.

I don't know why, maybe it was like watchin' a guy beat up on a kitten or some other helpless thing. I knew the Chairman was just gonna lay there on the floor while Lou kicked all his ribs in and none of these other clowns would do a thing to help him and I just kind of went nuts. I didn't think about it; if I had I would've just stayed tight in my chair and minded my own [deleted] business.

But I didn't. I couldn't. Before I even knew I was doin' it I jumped on Lou's back, wrapped my legs around him, and started poundin' on his head with both my fists. If I'd wanted to really hurt him I woulda taken out my blade and slit his [deleted] throat. I didn't even think of that. All I wanted was for the big [deleted] to leave the Chairman alone.

So I'm bangin' on Lou's head, he's yellin' and swingin' around, tryin' to get me off him. And then something explodes in the back of my head and everything goes black.

When I wake up, I'm seein' double. Two Chairmen, two Jades. But nobody else.

"That was a very brave thing you did," says the Chairmen.

I'm lyin' flat on my back. Jade is bendin' over me, two of her kind of fadin' in and out, blurry-like. The Chairman is sittin' on the floor beside me, both his arms wrapped around his chest. Otherwise the car is empty. Everybody else is gone.

"What happened?" I said.

"Rollo knocked you out," Jade answered.

I shoulda guessed that. Musta hit me like a truck. I tried to sit up but I was so woozy the whole [deleted] car started whirlin' around.

"Lay still," Jade said. Her voice was soft and sweet. I thought I saw tears in her eyes, but I was still seein' double so it was hard to tell.

"You okay?" I asked the Chairman.

"Yes, thanks to you." His lip was split and his face was kinda pale, like it was hurtin' him to breathe.

"Where'd they go?"

"They are in the rear car," the Chairman said. "More of them in the front. We are all trapped here. The Council's security forces have sealed off this tunnel. American army troops have taken over the station and are patrolling the streets above us."

"But they won't make a move on us because Moustache says he'll whack you if they do."

The Chairman nodded. And winced. "We are their hostages. He is trying to convince them that he has not already killed me."

"Why didn't ya talk to your people on the radio?" I asked him. "Lou woulda beat you to death."

He almost smiled, split lip and all. "They can't afford to kill me. Your friend Lou is a barbarian. Even Moustache, as you call him, would have stopped him if you hadn't."

"So I got slugged for nuthin."

"You were very brave," said the Chairman. "I appreciate what you did very much. To risk one's life for the sake of another—that is true heroism."

"You're a hero," Jade said. And she really did smile. Like the sun shinin' through clouds. Like the sky turnin' clean blue after a storm.

I reached for her hand and she took mine and squeezed it. Her hand felt warm and good. I mean, don't get me wrong, I busted my cherry when I was twelve years old. Had my first case of clap not much later. I ain't no Romeo like Little Lou, but I got my share. But Jade, she was special. I didn't wanna just screw her, I wanted to live with her, make a home with her, even have kids with her. Yeah, I know she was fixed so she couldn't have kids. They do that to the pros. But I thought maybe we could find a doctor someplace who could make her okay again.

But first I hadda get her outta her life before she came down with somethin' that'd kill her or got herself knocked off by some weirdo. Okay, it was crazy. Stupid. I know. But that's how I felt about her. And I don't give a [deleted] what you say, I know she felt that way about me, too. I know. In spite of everything.

Anyway, there I was, lyin' on the floor of the train car and holdin' on to Jade's hand like I was hangin' off the edge of a ninety-nine-story building. I asked the Chairman, "So what happens now?"

He started to shrug, but the pain in his ribs stopped him. "I don't really know."

"I still don't see why you wouldn't talk to your people on the radio."

"We do not make deals with terrorists. I know that every government official of the past seventy-five years has said that and then gone on to negotiate when their own citizens have been taken hostage. You must remember that the World Council is very new. Our authority is more moral than military or even financial—"

"I don't unnerstand a word you're saying," I told him.

He looked kinda surprised. Then he said, "Let me put it this way: We do not deal with terrorists. That is the official policy of the World Council. How would it look if I, the Chairman himself, broke our own rules and tried to negotiate my way out of this?"

"Beats gettin' killed," I said.

"Does it?"

"Hell yeah! You want Lou to go back to work on you?"

He closed his eyes for a second. "I am prepared to die. I don't want to, but if it comes to that—it comes to that."

"And what about us? What about Jade and me?"

"There's no reason for them to kill you."

"Who the [deleted] needs a reason? Lou wants to whack me, he's gonna whack me!"

"That . . . is unfortunate."

It sure the [deleted] was. For a couple minutes none of us said anything. Finally curiosity got to me.

"What's this all about, anyway? Why's Moustache want

to take you hostage? What's in it for him? Who're those other guys with him? What the hell's goin' on around here?"

So he told me. I didn't understand most of it. Somethin' about some country I never heard of before, in South America I think he said. Moustache is the leader of some underground gang that's tryin' to knock off their government. The Chairman told me that their president is a real piece of [deleted]. No freedom for nobody. Everybody's gotta do what he says or he whacks 'em. Tortures people. Takes everybody's money for himself. Sounds like Big Lou's favorite wet dream.

So Moustache and his people want the World Council to get rid of this bastard. The World Council can't do that, accordin' to what the Chairman told me. "We are not permitted to interfere in the internal affairs of any nation." That's the way he put it. And besides, this dictator was legally elected. Okay, maybe the people had to vote for him or get shot, but they did vote for him.

And guess who Moustache wants to make president if and when the dictator gets pushed out? Good old Moustache himself. Who else?

So the Chairman tells Moustache he can't do nuthin for him. So Moustache decides to kidnap the Chairman and hold him until the World Council does what he wants. Or somethin' like that. Other guys from other countries who also want pretty much the same kind of thing from the World Council join Moustache's operation. Arabs or Kurds or somethin', I forget which. So they kidnap the Chairman. Big [deleted] deal.

So there we are, stuck in the train in the tunnel. They got him, but the U.S. Army and god knows what the [deleted] else has got us trapped in the tunnel. Standoff.

By the time he had finished tellin' me this whole story—and it was a lot longer than what I just told you—I was feelin' strong enough to sit up. At least the room wasn't spinnin' around no more and I wasn't seein' double.

"So what happens now?" I asked the Chairman.

"We wait and see."

I saw a junkyard dog once, a real four-legged dog, get his paw caught in a trap the junk dealer had set for guys like me who like to sneak in at night and steal stuff. Poor damned dog was stuck there all night long, yowlin' and cryin'. Dealer wouldn't come out. Not in the dark. He was scared that if his dog was in trouble it meant a gang of guys was out there waitin' to whack him.

I felt like that dog. Trapped. Bleedin' to death. Knowin' there was help not far away, but the help never came. Not in time. By morning the dog had died. The rats were already gnawin' on him when the sun came up.

"You're just gonna sit here?" I asked him.

"There's nothing else we can do."

I knew that. But I still didn't like it.

The Chairman put out his hand and rested it on my shoulder. "You may not realize it, my young friend, but merely by sitting here you are fighting a battle against the enemies of humankind."

I wanted to say bull[deleted] to him again, but I kept my mouth shut.

It was Jade who asked, "What do you mean?"

"This man you call Moustache. The men with him. Your friends Lou and Rollo—"

"They ain't no friends of mine," I growled.

"I know." He smiled at me, kind of a shy smile. "I was making a small joke."

"Nuthin funny about those guys."

"Yes, of course. Moustache and Lou and the rest of them, they are the old way of living. The way of violence. The way of brute force. The way of death. What the human race needs, what the *people* want, is a better way, a way of sharing, of cooperation, of the strength that comes from recognizing that we must all help one another—"

I was about to puke in his face when he smiled at me again and said, "Just the way you tried to help me when Lou was beating me."

That took the air outta me. I mumbled, "Lotta good it did either one of us."

"Have you ever thought about leading a better life than the one you now live?" he asked.

"Well, yeah," I said, glancin' at Jade. "Sure. Who doesn't?"

"There are Indians living in the mountains of Moustache's country who also have a dream of living better. And nomads starving in man-made deserts. And fishermen's families dying because the sea has become so polluted that the fish have all died off. They also dream of a better life."

"I don't care about no fishermen or Indians," I said. "They don't mean nuthin to me."

"But they do! Whether you know it or not, they are part of you. We are all bound together on this world of ours."

"Bull[deleted]." It just popped out. I mean, I kinda liked the guy, but he kept talkin' this crazy stuff.

"Listen to what he's trying to tell us," Jade said. That surprised me, her tellin' me what to do.

"The reason the World Council was created, the reason it exists and I serve as its Chairman, is to help everyone on Earth to live a better life. Everyone! All ten billions of us."

"How're you going to do that?" Jade asked. She was lookin' at the Chairman now with her eyes wide. She wasn't holdin' my hand anymore.

"There's no simple answer," he said. "It will take hard work, for decades, for generations. It will take the cooperation of all the nations of the world, the rich and the poor alike."

"You're dreamin'," I said. "The United States is one of the richest countries in the whole [deleted] world and we still got people livin' like rats, people like me and Jade and who knows how many others."

"Yes, I understand," he said. "We are trying to convince your government to change its attitude about you, to admit that the problem exists and then take the necessary steps to solve it."

"Yeah, they'll solve the problem. The [deleted] Controllers swoop in and take you away, scramble your brains and turn you into a zombie. You wind up as slave labor in some camp out in the woods."

"Is that what you believe?"

"That's what I know."

"What would you say if I told you that you are wrong?"

"I'd say you're fulla [deleted]."

"Vic!" Jade snapped at me.

But the Chairman just kinda smiled. "When all this is over, I hope you will give me the opportunity to show you how misinformed you are."

"If we're still alive when this is over," I said.

"Yes," he admitted. "There is that."

He was quiet for a minute or so. I didn't like the way Jade was starin' at him, like he was a saint or a video star or somethin'. But I didn't know what I could say that would get her to look back at me.

Finally the Chairman pipes up again. "You know, I was born of a poor family also."

"Yeah, sure," I muttered.

"My grandmother escaped from Vietnam in an open boat with nothing but the clothes on her back and her infant son—my father. They went from Hong Kong to

Canada. My grandmother died of pneumonia her first winter in Vancouver. My father was barely two years old."

"You're breakin' my heart," I said. Jade hissed at me.

"My father was raised in an orphanage. When he was fourteen he escaped and made his way into the United States, eventually to Houston, Texas." The Chairman was lookin' at me when he was sayin' this, but it was a funny look, like I wasn't really there and he was seein' things from his own life that'd happened years ago.

"My mother was Mexican. Two illegal immigrants for parents. We moved around a lot: Houston, Galveston, the cotton fields of Texas, the orchards of California. I was picking fruit almost as soon as I learned to walk."

"You never went hungry, didja?" I said.

"I have known hunger. And poverty. And disease. But I have known hope, also. All through my childhood my mother told me that there was a better way of life. Every night she would kneel beside me and say her prayers and tell me that I would live better than she and my father. Even when my father was beaten to death by a gang of drunken rednecks my mother kept telling me to keep my eyes on the stars, to work hard and learn and aim high. She worked very hard herself.

"After my father died we settled in California, in a little city called Modesto, where she worked twelve to fourteen hours a day cleaning people's homes by day and office buildings at night. By the time she died, when I was sixteen, she had saved enough money to get me started in college."

"At least you had a mother," I muttered. "I was so young when mine died I don't even remember what she looked like."

"That is very sad," he said. Real soft.

"Yeah."

"I remember the prayer my mother taught me to say: she called it the 'Our Father.' "

"Oración al Señor," whispered Jade.

"Yes. Do you know it? And the line that says, 'Thy kingdom come?' That is what we must aim for. That is what we must strive to accomplish: to bring about a new world, a fair and free and flourishing world for everyone. To make this Earth of ours as close to heaven as we can."

"Thy kingdom come," Jade repeated. There were tears in her eyes now, real big ones.

Me, I didn't say nuthin. I kept my mouth shut so hard my teeth hurt. I knew that prayer. The one thing I remember about my mother is her sayin' that prayer to me when I was so little I didn't know what it meant. That's all I can remember about her. And it made me want to cry, too. It got me sore at the same time. This [deleted] big shot of a Chairman knew just where to put the pressure on me. I sure wasn't gonna start bawlin' in front of him and Jade. Not me.

And I had lied to them. I did remember my mother. Kinda hazy, but I remember what she looked like. She was beautiful. Beautiful and sweet and— I pulled myself up short. Another minute of that kinda thinkin' and I'd be cryin' like a baby.

The Chairman kind of shook himself, like he was comin' out of a blackout or somethin'. He looked at me again. "Education is the key, my young friend," he said to me. "If we are to build a new world, we must educate the people."

"You mean, like school?" I asked him.

"Schooling is only a part of it," he said. "If we survive this, will you allow me to get you started on a decent education?"

"School? Me? You gotta be kiddin'!"

Jade said, "But Vic, he's giving you a chance—"

She never got no farther. Moustache came in, with Lou and Rollo behind him.

Moustache looked funny. Like he was real tired, all wiped out. Or maybe that was how he looked when he was scared. He stood in front of the Chairman, who stayed in his seat lookin' up at him. I kept my eye on Lou; he was watchin' Jade like he was thinkin' what he'd do with her later on. Like he already owned her.

"We are at an impasse," Moustache said to the Chairman. "Your security forces seem perfectly content to sit and wait for us to give up."

"They have standing orders for dealing with terrorists," said the Chairman. "This is not the first time someone has attempted to kidnap a Council member."

"They will not attack us?"

"There is no need to, as long as they are certain you will not harm your hostages."

Moustache said, "We have only one hostage, but a very important one."

"Then all the others who were with me are dead?"

"Unfortunately, yes."

The Chairman seemed to sag back in his seat. "That is truly unfortunate. It means that you will not be allowed to escape. If no one had been killed . . ." His voice trailed off.

"Are you telling me that the troops will risk your life in order to punish us for killing a few of your bodyguards?"

"Yes." The Chairman nodded slowly. "That too is their standard operational procedure. No negotiations with terrorists. And no leniency for murderers."

"They were armed! They killed four of my men!"

"Only six of them were armed. There were nineteen all together, most of them harmless administrators and my personal aides. Five of them were women."

Moustache sank into the empty chair across the aisle

from the Chairman. "It was those Moslem madmen. When the shooting started they killed everyone, indiscriminately."

"They were under your command, were they not?"

"Yes, but not under my control."

"That makes no difference."

"You leave us no course, then, but to use you as a shield to cover our escape."

"The security forces will not allow it. Their orders are quite specific. Their objective is to capture the terrorists, irrespective of what happens to the hostages."

"They will let you be killed?"

"I am already dead, as far as they are concerned."

"You will pardon me if I fail to believe that," Moustache said.

"It doesn't matter what you believe," said the Chairman back to him. "That is our standard operational procedure. It is based on the valid assumption that there are no indispensable men. The Chairman of the World Council can be kidnapped or even assassinated. What difference? Another will take his place. Or hers. You can do what you want to me, it does not matter. Violence will not deter us. Threats will not move us. The work of the Council will go on regardless of the senseless acts of terrorists. All you can do is create martyrs—and damage your own cause by your violence."

Moustache looked up at Lou, who'd been standin' there through all this talk with a kind of wiseguy grin on his face.

With a sigh, Moustache said, "We will have to try your way, then."

I got to my feet, facin' Lou. Without even thinkin' about what I was doin'. Like my body reacted without askin' my brain first.

"Don't try to be a hero again, Sal," Lou said to me. And

Rollo took a step toward me. But Lou went on, "We ain't gonna use any rough stuff—not unless we got to. We're just gonna sneak him out through the tunnel."

"But the soldiers got the tunnel blocked off," I said. "All the entrances—"

"Not all of 'em," said Lou. "There's a side passage for the electric cables and water pipes and all. It's big enough for maintenance workers to crawl through. So it's big enough for us to get through, too."

Lou yanked a map of the tunnel system outta his back pants pocket. It was all creased up and faded, but Moustache pulled a little folding table outta the wall and Lou spread his map on it. Then he pointed to where we was and where the nearest door to the maintenance tunnel was. Moustache decided that only the six of us would go. The rest of his men would stay with the train and keep the soldiers thinkin' we was all still in there.

While Lou and Moustache were talkin' all this over, Jade leaned over to me and whispered, "Vic, you gotta do something."

"Do? What?"

"You can't let them sneak him outta here! You gotta figure out a way to save him."

"Me? What the [deleted] d'you think I am, Superman?"

She just looked at me with those eyes of hers. Beneath the fancy surgery that had made her Jade Diamond her deep brown eyes were still Juanita's. I loved her and I'd do anything for her and she knew it.

"You've gotta do something," she whispered.

Yeah. What the whole [deleted] World Council and half the U.S. Army can't do she wants me to do.

So Moustache calls in a couple of his men and gives them their orders. You can see from the looks on their faces that they don't like it. But they don't argue. Not one word. They know they're gonna be left hangin' out to dry, and they take it without a whimper. They must've really believed in what they were doin'.

Me, I'm tryin' to look like I'll do whatever they tell me. Rollo is just waitin' for Lou to give him the word and he'll start poundin' me into hamburger. And I figure Lou will give him the word as soon's we got the Chairman outta this trap and someplace safe. Lou wants Jade, so he'll give me to Rollo to make sure I'm not in his way. Moustache wants the Chairman so he can get what he wants back in his own country.

And the Chairman? What's he want? That's what I was tryin' to figure out. Was he really willin' to get himself smacked around or whacked altogether, just for this dream of his? A better world. A better life for people. Did he mean he could make a better life for Jade and me?

Well, anyway, all these thoughts are spinnin' around in my head worse than when Rollo had slugged me. We get down off the train with Lou in the lead, Moustache with his big pistol in his hand, the Chairman, me and Jade all in a bunch, and Rollo bringin' up the rear. Lou's kinda feelin' his way through the tunnel, no light 'cause he don't want the soldiers to know we're outta the train.

So we're headin' for this steel door in the side of the tunnel when I accident'ly-on-purpose trip and fall to my knees. Rollo grabs me by the scruff of the neck hard enough to make my eyes pop and just lifts me back on my feet, one hand. But not before I slip my blade outta the tape on my ankle. It's dark so Rollo don't notice; I keep the blade tucked up behind my wrist, see.

All of a sudden my heart's beatin' so hard I figure Rollo can hear it. Or maybe the army, a couple hundred yards up the tunnel. Half my brain's tellin' me to drop the blade and not get myself in any more trouble than I'm in already. But the other half is tellin' me that I gotta do somethin'. I keep hearin' Jade's voice, keep seein' whatever it was that was in her eyes.

She wants a better life, too. And there's no way we can get a better life long as guys like Lou and Rollo can push us around.

So I let myself edge up a little, past Jade and the Chairman, till I'm right behind Moustache. It's real dark but I can just make out that he's got the gun in his right hand.

"Hey! Here it is," Lou says, half whisperin'. "Rollo, come and help me open up this sucker."

Rollo pushes past me like a semitrailer rig passin' a kid on a skateboard. My heart is whammin' so hard now it's hurtin' my ears. Moustache is just standin' there, watchin' Lou and Rollo tryin' to open up that steel door. They're gruntin' like a couple pro wrasslers. It's now or never.

I slash out with the blade and rip Moustache's arm open from elbow to wrist. He grunts and drops the gun and it goes off, *boom!,* so loud that it echoes all the way down the tunnel.

"Run!" I yell to Jade and the Chairman. "Get the [deleted] outta here!"

The Chairman just freezes there for a second, but Jade shakes his arm and kind of wakes him up. Then the two of them take off down the tunnel, toward the soldiers. I can't see where the [deleted] gun landed but it don't matter anyway 'cause Lou and Rollo have spun away from the door and they're both comin' right at me. Moustache is holdin' his arm with his left hand and mumblin' something I can't understand.

"You dumb little [deleted]-sucking [deleted]," Lou says. "I'm going to cut off your balls and feed 'em to you one at a time."

I hear a click and see the glint of a blade in Lou's hand. I shoulda known he wouldn't be empty-handed. Rollo is comin' up right beside Lou. He don't need a knife or anything else. I'm so scared I don't know how I didn't [deleted] myself.

But I'm standin' between them and Jade and the Chairman.

"Never mind him," Moustache yells. "Get the Chairman! Quickly, before he makes it to the soldiers!"

Everything happened real fast. Lou tried to get past me and I swiped at him with my blade and then Rollo was all over me. I think I stuck him pretty good, but he just about ripped my arm outta my shoulder and I musta blacked out pretty quick after that. Hurt like a bastard. Then I woke up here.

So I'm a big shot hero, huh? Saved the Chairman from the terrorists. He came here himself this morning to thank me. And now that the TV reporters and their cameras are all gone, you guys are gonna send me away, right?

Naw, I didn't do anything except set up the gizmo for them. And they made me do that. Okay, so grabbin' Jade outta the tank was a crime. I figured you mother-[deleted] wasn't gonna let me go free.

But what'd they do with Jade? I don't believe that [deleted] [deleted] story the Chairman told me. Jade wouldn't do that. Go to a—what the [deleted] did he call it? Yeah, that's it. A rehabilitation center. She wouldn't leave here on her own. She wouldn't leave me. They musta forced her, right. The [deleted] Controllers must be scramblin' her brains right now, right? The [deleted] [deleted] bastards.

Yeah, sure, they're makin' a new woman outta her. And they wouldn't do nuthin to her unless she agreed to it. Sure. Just like she agreed to have her eyes changed. Big Lou said to change 'em and she agreed or she got her [deleted] busted.

You bastards took Jade away and don't try to tell me

different. She wouldn't leave me. I know she wouldn't. You took her away, you and that [deleted] gook of a Chairman.

Naw, I don't care what happens to me. What the [deleted] do I care? I got no life now. I can't go back to the neighborhood. Sure, you nailed Little Lou and Big Lou and everybody in between. So what? You think that's the end of it? Whoever's taken Big Lou's place will kick my balls in soon's I show up back on the street again. They know I saved the Chairman. They know I went against Big Lou. They won't give me no chance to go against them. Not a chance.

Sure, yeah, you'll take care of me. You'll scramble my brains and turn me into some [deleted] zombie. I'll be choppin' trees out West, huh? Freezin' my butt in some labor camp. Big [deleted] deal.

I know I got no choice. All I want is to find Jade and take her away with me someplace where we can live decent. Naw, I don't give a [deleted] what happened to Moustache. Or the dictator back in his country. Makes no difference to me. All I want is Jade. Where is she? What've you [deleted] bastards done with her?

Note: Juanita Dominguez (Jade Diamond) graduated from the Aspen Rehabilitation Center and is now a freshman at the University of Colorado, where she is studying law under a grant from the World Council.

Salvatore (Vic) Passalacqua was remanded to the Drexel Hill Remedial School to begin a course of education that would eventually allow him to maximize his natural talent for electronics. He was a troublesome student, despite every effort at counseling and rehabilitation. After seven weeks at the school he escaped. Presumably he made his way back to the neighborhood in Philadelphia where he had come from. His record was erased from the computer files. He is presumed dead.

2042: A Cautionary Pessimistic View

There is a pseudo-scientific field called futurology. Like real scientific disciplines, futurology has an international organization, the World Future Society. Members of the World Future Society are called futurologists. Most of them work for government agencies or major corporations, trying to use scientific methods to make limited predictions about the future: what the market for petroleum will be five years from now, how the introduction of new technology may affect an existing industry, stuff like that.

Quite often, at public gatherings, science-fiction writers are introduced as "futurologists." I wish they wouldn't do that. To me, a futurologist is a science-fiction writer who's had the imagination kicked out of him. Or her.

This is not the place for me to go into details on the shortcomings of futurology. However, I do want to point out that one of the major tools of futurology has been lifted—lock, stock, and barrel—directly from science fiction. Futurologists call it "scenario writing": pulling together a lot of details about the period you are examining, then trying to put them all together to form a coherent picture of that future society.

Science-fiction writers have been doing that since at least
H. G. Wells' time.

The essay that follows was written for *The World & I* magazine, a publication of the Unification Church. Yes, Rev. Sun
Myung Moon, of ill repute. His church is a very successful
operation, however. Among other things, it publishes *The
Washington Times*, a daily newspaper in our nation's capital,
and sponsors international multidisciplinary conferences
that attract many top scientists.

As I said in the introduction to "Thy Kingdom Come," this
scenario was based on inputs from leaders in various technological fields. When it came to combining their ideas with the
social evolution that I foresee, it became clear to me that the
most effective way to present my "cautiously pessimistic
view" of A.D. 2042 was in the form of a speech by a world
leader.

That is what the futurologists call scenario writing. I call it
the background for a science-fiction story.

*A*ddress by the Hon. Chiblum C. Lee, Chairman of the
World Council, 2 February 2042

My fellow citizens of the world:

It is both an honor and a grave responsibility to assume
the task of chairman of this newly formed World Council.
The burdens that face us are immense, as you are all
aware. Our resources seem barely adequate to deal with
the massive dislocations forced upon the world's people by
population growth and climate shift.

Famine stalks much of the southern hemisphere. Even
in the industrialized nations, life expectancies are declin-
ing. Civilization stands on the brink of a precipice, in
danger of a fall from which it may never recover.

If I may have your indulgence for a few moments, I

want to review the most significant problems that beset us. You are all as familiar with them as I am, I realize. But I want to demonstrate, if I can, how the interrelated nature of these problems has created a negative synergy that actually makes their totality much more difficult to solve than they would be as individual predicaments.

First, and foremost, is the continued explosive growth of world population. Ten point seven billion human beings occupy Planet Earth, according to this morning's computer-monitoring data. More than sixty percent of them live in urban areas. Cities all across the world are bursting with overpopulation that is outstripping their transportation facilities, their water supplies, and their food and waste removal systems. From New York to São Paulo, from Cairo to Tokyo, the great cities of the world have become festering ghettos rife with crime, drugs, and despair.

By today's end, some three hundred thousand additional babies will have been born. Each of these human beings requires food, shelter, education, and a means of self-support. Each of these factors, in turn, demands a share of the planet's natural resources and energy. As long as population continues to grow unchecked, all our efforts to increase the Earth's productivity will continue to be swallowed up by the rising tide of hungry mouths.

Exacerbating this problem of population is the problem of climate shift. It is as if the punishment for the sins of our fathers has been visited upon us. Two and a half centuries of industrialization have so polluted the atmosphere of our world that global temperatures have risen into true greenhouse levels. Lands that were once fertile and abundant are turning into deserts. Sea levels are rising all around the world, threatening inundations that will force the relocation of hundreds of millions of families. Annual monsoons and tropical storms have increased in ferocity, as almost everyone who lives in a coastal area knows, to his or her sorrow.

The seven-decade-long Petroleum Wars have come to an end, at last, thanks in large part to the dedicated men and women of the International Peacekeeping Force—although perhaps even larger thanks should go to the scientists and engineers who have given us practical and efficient nuclear fusion power.

I want to dwell a moment on the IPF. When it was created, more than a generation ago, most of the world viewed the Peacekeepers with intense skepticism, if not outright hostility. An international organization dedicated to the prevention of war, authorized by the old United Nations to serve as a standing army—small but highly mobile—armed with the most modern and sophisticated defensive weapons that science can produce. It was unprecedented, even though ad hoc peacekeeping forces had been assembled by the UN as early as 1950!

To the astonishment of almost everyone, including many here in this great assembly hall this morning, the International Peacekeeping Force has worked. The Peacekeepers did not prevent aggressors from launching attacks on their neighbors—at first. But slowly, the world's national leaders learned that *any* attack by *any* nation upon any other nation would swiftly be met by powerful defensive forces, in the name of the united human race. Gradually the International Peacekeeping Force convinced would-be aggressors that the price for military assault was higher than any possible reward might be.

The Peacekeepers can serve as a model of how we can work together for the betterment of the human race. They have been able to virtually eliminate the scourge of war; we must work together to eliminate the potential causes of future strife.

The Petroleum Wars, of course, were not entirely military in character. Economic warfare, political maneuvering, even public relations tactics, were all a part of this seventy-year-long struggle. Much like the old Cold War between the North Atlantic nations and the former Soviet Union, the Petroleum Wars were fought at many levels. They have exacted a terrible toll of human lives wasted, resources squandered, and environmental degradation.

As I said, today we stand at the edge of a precipice. The human race has reached a turning point, one of those moments in history where the decisions we make now will determine the fate of humankind for centuries to come—perhaps forever. I see the fundamental problem that faces us as nothing less than the choice between the survival of civilization or its extinction—perhaps forever, certainly for longer than the lifetime of any human being alive today.

Our civilization has achieved great things, technologically. We can fly through space and build habitats at the bottom of the ocean. Our medical sciences have extended the average life expectancy in the industrialized nations to the point where difficult legal and ethical questions are being argued over the state's right to impose a limit on human life spans, as opposed to the individual's right not only to live for many more decades than a century, but to have one's body preserved at the point of death in the hopes of being revived at a later time, cured of the "fatal" disease, and then resume living.

But these wonderful achievements have been restricted to the rich alone. The overwhelming majority of the world's peoples are poor. They live and mate and die as they have for untold generations. Their numbers grow almost exponentially. And each generation they grow poorer, both in absolute terms and in relation to the growing wealth of the rich. Meanwhile, the rich control their family sizes; the wealthy nations have stabilized their population growth and have erected virtually impassable barriers against immigration, to prevent poor people from entering their countries.

How long can this planet continue to exist with a steadily growing population of extremely poor people and a small, stable population of extremely wealthy people? How long can we have one-quarter of the world's people consume ninety percent of its natural resources and energy, while the other three-quarters tries to eke out a precarious living in growing squalor, misery, and frustration?

As an American president said nearly two hundred years ago, "A house divided against itself cannot stand."

The Petroleum Wars were a symptom of this fundamental problem. Behind the politics and the military combat was the desperation of poor people struggling to obtain some scant slice of the world's riches. The Wars have ended, but the underlying problem remains. If we fail to solve it, new fighting will break out: revolutions and terrorism that even the Peacekeepers will be helpless against.

Let me emphasize this point: Unless we achieve some means to alleviate the poverty and hunger that haunt three-quarters of the world's population, our civilization will crumble and collapse into a new Dark Age of incessant warfare and chaos. The rich will be swept under by the growing tide of the desperately poor. The world's population problem will be solved by the Four Horsemen of antiquity: Famine, Disease, War, and Death.

I will not accept such an end to our noble dreams of freedom and plenty for all. I believe that we can and we will solve the problems that beset us, no matter how difficult they are or how agonizing the solutions may be. It is the sacred duty of this World Council to find these solutions, and to implement them.

We have the tools. We have the knowledge, the technology, the understanding to build a new world society that is fair, and free, and flourishing. But do we have the will, the courage, to create fundamental changes in the world's existing political and economic structures?

That is for you to decide. This World Council is a recognition by all the nations of the world that the old order must be replaced by something new. National efforts have not solved the world's problems. Not even multinational efforts have been effective. The problems we face are global; our solutions must be global as well.

How do we narrow the vast and growing gap between the rich and the poor? How can we avert the famines and end the poverty that already hold in their pitiless grasp three out of every four human beings on Earth?

I can see two possible approaches: coercion or cooperation. Of these two, I much prefer cooperation. But allow me to say a few words about the concept of coercion.

There are two possible ways to use coercive tactics in our attempts to increase the wealth of the poor nations. One: force the rich nations to give up enough of their wealth so that the poor nations may advance economically. Two: force the poor nations to limit their population growth and adjust their economies for long-term growth rather than the stop-gap measures they now employ to struggle through their most immediate problems.

I think you can see the difficulties with each of these tactics as well as I. The rich nations will resist a drastic redistribution of wealth. They will fight such measures politically and economically, and, failing all else, they will resort to force of arms. If all—or even most—of the industrialized nations took up arms against our World Council, not even the International Peacekeeping Force could prevent them from sweeping us into the dustbin of history. We cannot coerce the rich nations, but they can coerce us if they so choose.

Coercing the poor may sound easier, but how do we go

about enforcing population limits for entire continents? Do we have the right—to say nothing of the power—to enter the bedchambers of three-quarters of the world's peoples and intervene in their most intimate acts? Do we have the moral superiority to tell literally billions of men and women that they must ignore the dictates of their religions and their social customs in the name of *our* vision of what the world should be?

The poor will resist such attempts, if we should be foolish enough to try them. They will not battle us with military weapons. They will simply ignore us and continue to have babies. What would we do then: slaughter the innocents in the name of global economic progress?

My friends, coercion will not work. Not only is it wrong, it is ineffective.

That leaves us with the tactics of cooperation. There is no other choice.

A very wise man once observed "The problem with the world is not that there are so many poor people; it's that there are not enough rich people." The difference is subtle, perhaps, but very real. We cannot force the rich to give their wealth to the poor. We cannot even expect them to voluntarily give up large portions of their treasure to their needy brothers and sisters.

The alternative, then, is to somehow make the poor richer *without* pauperizing the rich.

As I said a moment ago, I believe that we have the tools to do this. We have a panoply of technologies that can generate abundant wealth, if they are effectively employed. It is up to us, this World Council, to lay out a long-range plan for the effective use of our best and most productive technologies.

Some of you who make up this Council are scientists and engineers. Most of you are not. To all of you, I say that technology—toolmaking—is the way human beings adapt to their environment. We do not grow wings, we invent airplanes. We do not have the muscular strength of the gorilla nor the fleetness of foot of the antelope. Yet we lift tons of weight at the touch of a button and race across land and sea faster than any gazelle or dolphin.

Yet technology is not, and should not be, an end in itself. Toolmaking for the sake of making tools will never solve our problems. Tool-*using* has been the salvation of the human race time and again, since the Promethean days when our ancestors first tamed fire. Our task is to use the bright, shining tools that the technologists have produced for the betterment of the human race's economic and social condition.

Let me give you an example of how some of our best and most sophisticated tools are being poorly used today.

In the industrialized nations, the work force consists of almost as many robots as human workers. This is especially true in the manufacturing and extractive industries, where robots "man" the factories, the mines, and the farms. A generation ago, when truly useful and adaptable robots began to enter the work force in Europe and North America, there was a great surge of labor unrest. Human workers feared that they would be replaced by robots.

It was the Japanese who showed the way around this problem. In one form or another, human employees formed partnerships both with their robot co-workers and with the owners of the firms that employed them. In essence, the human workers began to draw their incomes not from their own labor, but from the wealth generated by the robots who labored for them. In the United States, for example, employees now buy robots the way they buy shares of corporate stocks. The robot works in place of the human, while the human receives the income that the robot has produced.

This system of employee-ownership has allowed ever

more sophisticated robots to enter the work force of the industrialized nations smoothly, with a minimum of labor strife and a maximum of profitability for employee and employer alike. But the increasingly roboticized work force of the industrialized nations has had devastating effects on the economies of the poorer nations.

Robots in England, for example, now produce clothing more cheaply than the lowest-paid human workers in Angola or Bangladesh. Robots in California do the "stoop labor" of harvesting that was formerly done by migrant farm workers. California grows richer; Mexico grows poorer. Robots are widening the gap between the rich and the poor. Indeed, robots are even replacing domestic servants among the very rich.

Researchers are today developing robots that will rival human thinking power. They enthusiastically report that it will be merely a matter of a decade or so before robots are so intelligent and so flexible that they will be able to replace human workers in virtually every task we now undertake. Perhaps at that time some very intelligent robots will be able to solve all our problems for us, and we poor, slow-witted humans can at last relax and enjoy the fruits of our machines' cogitations. [Pause for laughter.]

But that day is not with us yet. We must face our own problems and produce our own solutions.

Can robots help to make the poor nations wealthier? Can, for example, a team of robots turn a squalid farming village in Guatemala into a thriving and prosperous community? No. Not by themselves. The people of that village are unprepared for such a leap into the modern world. They lack the education and the social framework to deal with machines that move and work and think. Their village, their entire nation, lacks the economic foundation to employ robot labor usefully.

But robots can help the poor nations indirectly by helping to produce the wealth needed to start those nations on the road to riches. It is inevitable, inescapable, that the rich nations must devote some portion of their growing wealth to the salvation of the poor.

I propose that we, the World Council, establish a tax upon all nations, based on the ratio of each individual nation's Gross Domestic Product in comparison to the mean GDP of all the nations. Thus, the very richest nations would pay the largest amount. The very poorest nations would have a negative tax: they would receive income from the tax fund.

The income that any nation receives, however, must be devoted to long-term programs that will improve that nation's economy. Thus the rich nations will pay to make the poor nations richer. In essence, the roboticized work force of the rich nations will help to increase the wealth of the poor.

This proposal smacks of the coercion I spoke against just a moment ago. But I ask the leaders of the rich nations to undertake this small sacrifice willingly. I have no intention of coercing any nation, and this World Council certainly does not have the power to be coercive. We need your cooperation, rich and poor alike.

No one likes to pay taxes. The rich nations may vote against this program. They may refuse to support it even if the Council passes it. That would mean the dissolution of this World Council and a step backward toward the chaos of previous years. But all the nations that worked so hard and so long to bring about this new World Council of ours have known from the outset that there would be new taxes to be paid. To quote the vernacular, "There ain't no such thing as a free lunch."

I propose that we set a tax rate that is as low as possible, commensurate with producing a fund that can adequately help the poor. I further propose that we fix this tax rate for five years, so that all the nations can make economic plans that need not fluctuate annually. And, of course, I want to see the best and brightest economists, anthropologists, and business managers put to work to help the poor nations begin to build their economies toward self-sufficiency.

I am not here merely to propose new taxes, however. I realize that if all we intend to do is to shift wealth from the rich to the poor, our efforts will be resisted and ultimately fail. We must, therefore, develop wherever possible the means and the opportunity to generate new wealth. It should be our primary goal to enlarge the human race's supply of real wealth: natural resources, energy, and human potential.

The place to find new resources is on the frontiers of our existing habitat. Obviously, we have physical frontiers in the world's vast oceans and the even vaster deeps of outer space. Yet there are mental frontiers, as well. Research laboratories are frontier country.

Perhaps the best news that we have received in this century is that a practical, efficient nuclear fusion power system has at last been developed to the point where it can leave the laboratory and begin to deliver reliable and safe electrical energy. After nearly a century of research, our scientists and engineers have harnessed the energy of the Sun and the stars themselves. We owe our everlasting thanks to the perseverance of the brilliant men and women who have given us this inestimable gift. In my mind, it ranks with the original gift of fire, back in the mists of prehistoric times.

Nuclear fusion power offers us the opportunity of moving away from all types of fossil fuels, with their inevitable outpouring of greenhouse gases, and away from the highly radioactive fissionable fuels of old-style nuclear power plants, as well. There are many who still fear the idea of nuclear power of any sort. We must convince them that fusion power is far safer than the old fission plants of the twentieth century. The fuel for fusion comes from ordinary water. Its major by-product is helium, an inert gas. There is no buildup of radioactive wastes, although the fusion equipment itself becomes radioactive over the course of its half-century-long useful lifetime.

The fusion process is so energetic that there is enough fusion fuel in an eight-ounce glass of water to equal the energy content of five hundred thousand barrels of petroleum! And less than one percent of the water is consumed! The rest is available for drinking, irrigation, or other uses.

I dwell on the prospects of fusion power because it is the key to the ultimate solution of the tremendous problems we face. With clean, efficient, and ultimately cheap fusion power we will be able to bring safe and reliable energy to the poorest of nations. We will have the energy to desalt sea water economically, in those growing areas where groundwater supplies are either disappearing or have become contaminated. We will have the energy to pump desalted water long distances for irrigation, to counteract the growing desertification of formerly productive farm lands.

Another important use for fusion energy will be in recycling waste materials. For fifty years and more we have looked to recycling metals and plastics as a means of cleaning the environment. Recycling has been seen as an alternative to landfills or dumping our garbage into the sea. But recycling requires energy, and our efforts in this environmental-protection area have been limited by the costs of the energy required. Fusion power will make recycling profitable. Moreover, when fusion-driven recycling centers are reducing practically all our waste materials into highly refined elements, we will have opened a new source for raw materials. Recycled metals and chemicals will be cheaper, in many instances, than digging new ores out of the ground or the sea bottom.

Fusion energy can also power our explorations and developments on the ocean floor and in outer space.

But before I turn to these physical frontiers, there is another intellectual frontier that we must consider carefully. I speak now of the tremendous opportunities and problems created by the biological sciences and their offspring biotechnologies.

Biologists have delved into the very core of living cells. They have learned the secrets of our genes so well that it is possible to extend healthy human life spans far beyond a century. There is even the faint chance of literal immortality glimmering in the latest reports from the research laboratories. With the population problems we already face, we have scant need for longer life spans. Yet, who would reject such an opportunity?

Of more immediate import is the enormous impact that biotechnology is making in agriculture and medicine. New strains of food crops, genetically engineered to withstand drought, heat, frost, insect pests, or other hostile conditions, can greatly increase the world's food supply. Genetically engineered bacteria now "fix" nitrogen for many food crops, eliminating or greatly reducing the need for artificial fertilizers.

These are powerful aids to our efforts to feed the world's hungry people. Yet these advances are not entirely without their risks. The temptation to plant nothing but these new "supercrops" could lead to disaster if some factor has been overlooked and the crops ultimately fail. Diversification must be the watchword among the world's farmers, not uniformity.

Biotechnology, like all technologies, is a two-edged sword. The very breakthroughs that produce cures for genetic diseases such as diabetes and cystic fibrosis are also capable of producing biological agents of unparalleled virulence. Biological-warfare weapons have been justly called "the poor man's nuclear bomb." I am not suggesting a Frankenstein scenario, but I do insist that biotechnology laboratories must be under the continuing scrutiny of World Council monitoring agencies, just as nuclear facilities are. The benefits to come from new biological developments are immense; so are the possible dangers. Our aim must be to reap the benefits while minimizing the risks.

Now to the physical frontiers.

We have seen that there are immense resources in the world's seas: resources of food, energy, and raw materials. We are today consciously reproducing in the oceans the Neolithic Revolution that our prehistoric ancestors produced on land some ten thousand years ago: that is, we are moving from merely gathering food from the sea to deliberately growing food there. Fish farms, algae farms, carefully tended beds for shellfish—these and more can eventually produce far more food, per hectare of sea surface and per calorie of energy input, than farms on land.

There is energy in the sea, as well. By tapping the difference in temperature between the cold deep layers of the ocean and the sun-warmed surface layers, it is possible to produce abundant electrical power without harm to the environment. Thus, industrial facilities and human habitats on the sea can be self-sufficient in energy, and will even be able to sell energy to consumers on land.

Seabed mining is already contributing to the world's supply of important metals such as magnesium, manganese, copper, and molybdenum. Future efforts will bring more of these resources to us, and increase humankind's supply of wealth even more than today.

Outer space is also a source of unimaginable wealth. More energy and raw materials exist in space than our entire planet Earth can provide, by many orders of magnitude. However, the costs of operating in space are still so high as to be prohibitive for all but the most profitable endeavors.

Today, three Solar Power Satellites provide half the electrical energy used by Japan. As large as Manhattan Island, placed in high orbits where sunlight constantly drenches their broad panels of solar cells, they beam energy in the form of microwaves to receiving "antenna farms" built off the coasts of two major Japanese islands, Honshu and Kyushu. A multinational consortium is attempting to raise capital for two more Solar Power Satellites, one each for Europe and North America. Furthermore, Moonbase, Inc. has recently announced plans to build solar-power "farms" on the surface of the Moon and offer the electrical energy they produce to consumers either on Earth or in the growing number of manufacturing and research stations in orbits between the Earth and the Moon.

The old dream of mining the asteroids for their metals and other raw materials has not yet been realized. The asteroids lie twice the distance of Mars, for the most part, and there is as yet no economic necessity to go that far for metals that can be obtained on Earth. Indeed, asteroid mining, if it ever becomes practicable, may threaten the economies of resource-rich nations that depend on exporting raw materials.

However, the space frontier is expanding, steadily if slowly. Thirty-two thousand people are working off-Earth as of this morning's census. Most of them are in near-Earth orbital facilities. Eight thousand are on the Moon, at the various government and private bases established there. And, of course, there are fifty men and women carrying out the continuing exploration of the planet Mars.

Outer space is a harsh and dangerous frontier. It will never serve as an outlet for the Earth's growing population. There will not be mass emigrations to space; not in our lifetime, nor in any foreseeable future. However, space *is* rich in energy and raw materials. And it offers unique environments in which inventive humans can produce goods and services that are impossible to produce on Earth.

The highest-quality metal alloys are manufactured in zero-gravity orbital facilities. The best crystals for our electronics industry are made there, as well. Much of the pharmaceutical industry is moving to space manufacturing facilities, where there is abundant solar energy, the ultraclean environment of high vacuum, and the availability of zero gravity. And a small but apparently lucrative tourist industry has sprung up in Earth orbit—for those few rich enough to afford it.

Outer space, the deep oceans, the research laboratories at universities and corporate centers around the world: these are the frontiers from which we may generate the new wealth that can bring the poor nations out of their deepening crises of poverty and hunger.

But all that we do, all that we hope to achieve, everything we plan will come to naught if the world's climate continues to deteriorate. You know the terrifying facts as well as I do. Every year in this century, thousands of square kilometers of productive land have turned into desert or useless scrubland. More thousands of square kilometers have been inundated by rising sea levels.

The global climate is warming, heated by greenhouse gases that we ourselves produce. For the first time in history, the actions of the human race are overshadowing the natural processes of climate and weather. We are overburdening the atmosphere, the oceans, and the land with our own filth. The result is contaminated drinking water, desertification, and a growing greenhouse warming of the planet.

We must mend our ways. We must reverse the man-made trends that are altering our environment so swiftly that natural processes are being overwhelmed.

We have the tools to accomplish what must be done. As I have pointed out to you, modern technology has given us cheap fusion energy, solar power, and energy from the oceans. All of these systems are essentially renewable and produce no environmentally degrading greenhouse gases. Superconducting motors and batteries, which can be made small and powerful enough to rival existing petroleum-burning engines for automobiles and other forms of transport, can end the smog problems that still plague the world's major cities. Such electrical vehicles will make a huge contribution to lowering the amount of greenhouse gases being pumped into the atmosphere.

Our biotechnologies offer the opportunity of using biological means of increasing farm productivity and controlling insect pests, rather than brute force methods of artificial fertilizers and pesticides.

We have the tools. Do we have the intelligence and the courage to use them wisely? Military men speak of "friction," meaning the thousand-and-one individual misunderstandings and resistances that arise in the heat of battle. "Friction" is what comes between the general's brilliant plan and the actual outcome of the combat. You and I face "friction," also.

The sad fact is that human beings change their attitudes only slowly.

A villager who owns a petroleum-powered tractor has very little incentive to go into debt for a new electrically powered one, especially if he must learn to deal with superconducting machinery that requires liquid nitrogen.

A corporate executive who oversees the operation of a

petrochemical plant is not going to endorse a shift to biotechnology that will replace everything he knows and leave him feeling useless.

A factory worker who controls several robots will not endorse a tax increase that is earmarked for assisting people of different lands, different skin color, and different social values.

And, saddest of all, there are still too many politicians who think nothing of siphoning off funds from aid projects for their own personal use. How many earlier attempts to assist the poor merely served to make certain political leaders rich?

This is the kind of friction we must overcome. As I said earlier, we stand at the edge of a precipice. All of us, rich and poor alike, are staring at the extinction of our civilization. Let there be no mistake about that. We have fouled our environment and overstrained our social systems to the point where civilization's continued existence is very much in doubt. Sooner or later—and I fear it will be sooner than we dare think—the cumulative effects of climate shift, burstingly crowded cities, and growing hunger and poverty will combine to tear apart the very fabric of society. Chaos and bloodshed such as the world has never seen will sweep across the face of the Earth.

Then it will be too late to change. Too late to mend our ways. The bright hopes of our sciences and technologies will have been washed away in blood. Nowhere will there be the energy, the capital, the human brain power to reinvent civilization. Humanity will sink into savagery while the climate continues to deteriorate, fed now by the raging fires of our destroyed cities and the decaying bodies of the dead.

That is the nightmare we must avoid. Our policy must point toward the good dream of a free, fair, and flourishing world society, where we fight with all our strength and all our wisdom against humankind's ancient and remorse-less enemies: poverty, hunger, ignorance, and despair.

It is far from certain that we can win this battle. But we must try, for if we do not, then the end of civilization is at hand and the legacy we give to our children will be endless savagery and pain.

You can start a lovely fight by asking any two science-fiction people to define what "science fiction" is. Doesn't matter if they are writers, readers, editors, publishers, illustrators, or fans. Hardly anyone agrees on what *is* science fiction and what *isn't*. As you will see in the essay that follows, some practitioners have tried to avoid the term altogether and call it "speculative fiction" or even "scientific fantabulation."

You will also see my definition of science fiction. It is a narrow definition. It excludes most of what you will find in the average bookstore under the SF heading.

To publishers, science fiction is a catchall category that includes *my* definition of what is science fiction and an enormous lot of other material that falls outside my definition: fantasy, horror, and certain types of social commentary. Publishers are not terribly concerned about definitions; they are almost totally concerned about making money. Over the years they have found that they can sell books best by categorizing them into discreet little genres and getting the bookstores to group the books in those categories.

Thus, when you enter a bookstore you see titles above the shelves: romance, westerns, mysteries, science fiction.

When you send a manuscript to a publisher, the first question the editor wants answered is "What category is this book?" If it is not in a clearly defined category, it has little chance of being published.

As I said, however, to publishers the category of science fiction includes a wide range of material. Interestingly, some books that I would call science fiction are not published under that rubric. Tom Clancy's novels, starting with *The Hunt for Red October*, are as much science fiction as anything else. Yet the publishers have a new category—technothrillers—for novels that employ high-tech gadgetry, alternate political history, and highly suspenseful plots.

Me, I think that the only stories you can call science fiction are those that deal with some aspect of future science. That is what makes science fiction interesting, and gives it such power.

As the following essay explains in more detail.

Originally, "SF" meant "science fiction." Not "speculative fiction." Not "scientific fantabulation." *Science* fiction.[1]

Why *science* fiction? What does science have to do with fiction, anyway? And who cares?

You care. Or you would not be reading this essay. You would not be holding this book if you did not care, at least subliminally. And I care. I care a lot. I have devoted my life to science fiction—writing it, reading it, editing and publishing it, and helping to make some of it come true.

For science fiction is concerned with the real world, more than any other branch of contemporary literature. If you think of science fiction as escapism, remember Isaac Asimov's dictum: "Science fiction is escape—into reality."

1. At one time the term "scientifiction" was bruited. We won't go into that.

Because it deals with science and the technologies that spring from scientific research, science fiction has the capability of dealing with the most powerful driving engines of modern society: science and technology.

Other forms of literature either ignore science and technology altogether or show an active distrust of them. The subject matter of science fiction is how scientific advances and technological breakthroughs change the lives of individuals and the course of whole societies.

However, not all SF is science fiction. In the modern marketplace of publishing, the term SF actually covers an enormously wide range of subject material, from the meticulously crafted alien worlds of Hal Clement to the galloping barbarian swordsmen of Robert Howard to the wizards and gnomes of Terry Brooks. That is why many practitioners of SF prefer to use the term "speculative fiction" rather than "science fiction."

I want to talk about that portion of SF that is truly science fiction. Therefore, a definition is in order:

When I say *science fiction* I mean fiction in which some element of future science or technology is so integral to the tale that the story would collapse if the science or technology element were removed.

The archetype of such fiction is Mary Shelley's *Frankenstein*. Take away the scientific element and the story collapses of its own weight. There is no story without the science.

How does this make science fiction different from other fields of literature? Is science fiction inherently better, more worthwhile, than other kinds of fiction? Or does its preoccupation with science and technology doom science fiction to being inherently inferior to other forms?[2]

---

2. Science-fiction aficionados/aficionadas often refer to non-SF as "straight" or "mundane" fiction.

There are two major differences between science fiction and all other forms of literature.

The first, of course, is the subject matter. To the uninitiated, it might seem that focusing on science or technology would be terribly limiting for an author of fiction. Yet just the opposite is true. For science is an open door to the universe, and technology can be the magic carpet to take us wherever we wish. Properly used, science and technology are the great liberators that allow the imagination to roam the length and breadth of eternity.

Human beings are explorers by nature. The descendants of curious apes, we have something in us that thrills at new vistas, new ideas. By using scientific knowledge to build the background for their stories, science-fiction writers can take us to places no human eye has yet seen. The excitement of discovery, what science-fiction aficionados/aficionadas call "the sense of wonder," is both primal and primary in science fiction.

John W. Campbell, most influential of all science-fiction editors, fondly compared science fiction to other forms of literature in this way: He would spread his arms wide (and he had long arms) and declaim, "This is science fiction! All the universe, past, present, and future." Then he would hold up a thumb and forefinger about half an inch apart and say, "This is all other kinds of fiction."

All the other kinds of fiction restrict themselves to the here and now, or to the known past. All other forms of fiction are set here on Earth, under a sky that is blue and ground that is solid beneath your feet. Science fiction deals with all of creation, of which our Earth and our time is merely a small part. Science fiction can vault far into the future or deep into the past. In my own work I have written stories of interstellar adventure and of time-travelers who go back to the age of the dinosaurs.

Is this mere tinsel, nothing more than cheap stage props

to make a dull story look more interesting? I do not think so. The best works of fiction are those in which the human heart is tested to its limits. We write fiction, and read it, to learn about ourselves. By stretching the artist's canvas from one end of the universe to the other, by spreading it through all of time itself, science fiction allows the artist to test the human heart in crucibles of new and tougher make, in fires hotter than anything planet Earth can provide.

Yes, at the core of every good science-fiction tale is a story of human emotion, just as in any good story of any type. In science fiction, though, the characters may not always look human; they may be tentacled alien creatures or buzzing, clanking robots. Yet they will act as humans do, if the story is to be successful.

The second difference that science fiction offers is its relationship to the real world around us. While pretending to amuse us with stories of the future, the best science-fiction stories are really examining facets of the world that we live in today. I have often said that no one actually writes about the future; writers use futuristic settings to throw stronger highlights on the problems and opportunities of today.

The assumptions here are that: (1) science and technology are the driving forces in modern society; and (2) because science fiction deals with science and technology it can—and often does—have something important to say to its readers.

More than that. In the best of science-fiction stories, the scientific element can be used as a metaphor that reaches into the heart of the human condition.

In Frank Herbert's *Dune,* for example, the desert world of Arrakis is carefully presented as a metaphor for the environment of Earth. At one level of this complex novel Herbert is telling his readers, subconsciously, subliminally, not only that human actions can change the nature of an entire planet, but that these changes will have effects that will be both good and bad, simultaneously, inescapably.

Robert A. Heinlein touched on this truth in *The Moon Is a Harsh Mistress*. His phrase TANSTAAFL, "There ain't no such thing as a free lunch," is actually a slang restatement of the Second Law of Thermodynamics. You can't get something for nothing; never, no time. The universe just is not built that way, and we human beings are part of the universe, like it or not.

Arthur C. Clarke's *2001: A Space Odyssey* (one of the rare examples of excellent science-fiction moviemaking, thanks to Stanley Kubrick) speaks to humankind's relationship with its tools, and asks whether our increasingly sophisticated technology makes us more human or less.

Cyril Kornbluth's "The Marching Morons" takes a sociological observation—poor people have more babies than rich people—and extrapolates this into a ghastly future that is becoming truer with each passing day.

I can give a more detailed explanation of how deeply science/technology is used by referring to one of my own works, *The Kinsman Saga*.

The central science/technology idea in this novel is the possibility of building satellites that can shoot down ballistic missiles. The tale began in this way:

In the 1960s I was employed at a research laboratory where the first high-power lasers were invented. I helped to arrange a top-secret briefing in the Pentagon in early 1966 to reveal to the Department of Defense that such lasers existed. It quickly became apparent that high-power lasers, placed in satellites, could someday shoot down H-bomb–carrying ballistic missiles within minutes of their being launched.

I had been a published science-fiction author for nearly

ten years. I cast this very real technological breakthrough into a novel set in the last month of the year 1999. The novel, first published in 1976, was titled *Millennium*.[3]

Its central figure is an astronaut who realizes that if the small band of Americans and Russians living on the Moon dare to take control of their respective nations' antimissile satellites, they can enforce a lasting peace on the world.

Science as metaphor. By creating a fictitious but technically plausible Moonbase, I was able to place the pivotal characters in isolation, away from the world yet in daily communication with it. At such a distance from Earth, in the dangerously hostile lunar environment, both Americans and Russians see clearly the necessity to cooperate rather than fight. By postulating a technological means of enforcing peace I was able to emphasize the central political problem of our age: national governments do not want to give up their right to make war. And more. The novel shows that the tools for war can also be used as tools for peace. The tools are morally neutral. The people are not.

The entire story hinges on the personality of the American astronaut, Chester A. Kinsman. Like so many science-fiction protagonists, he becomes a messiah figure, with all that that entails.

In the mid-1970s such a story was science fiction. Today it is the stuff of newspaper columns: the Strategic Defense Initiative, SDI, "Star Wars." And the central issue of this new technology is precisely the same as the central issue of the novel: will this new tool be used for peacemaking or war-making?

Yet to this day no novelist outside the science-fiction field has attempted a serious work on this subject. Nor will they, because they do not have the interest, or knowledge,

3. Later I wrote a "prequel," *Kinsman*, and a decade later rewrote both novels and combined them to form *The Kinsman Saga*.

that science-fiction writers have. Only when the technology of SDI is as commonplace as nuclear weapons or corporate takeovers will "straight" writers begin to explore the subject. If then.

Which brings us to another pair of questions. Do science-fiction writers try to predict the future? And, whether they do or not, should their stories be taken as serious social commentary?

No, to the first question. Yes (with reservations) to the second.

I do not know of any science-fiction writer who deliberately set out to predict the future in any particular story. Yet, as I have often pointed out to the World Future Society and the U.S. government's Office of Technology Assessment, science fiction has a better track record at prediction than any other method.

Generally, science-fiction writers initiate stories by asking themselves, "What would happen if . . ." Professional futurists, men and women who get paid to make forecasts for government and corporate clients, call this technique "scenario writing."

What the science-fiction writer is trying to do is to examine the possibilities that might unfurl, given a set of starting conditions. What would happen if it became possible to shoot down ballistic missiles from laser-armed satellites? What would happen if intelligent aliens sent us unmistakable evidence of their presence? What would happen if we pollute this planet so terribly that the ice caps melt and the continents are flooded?

You can find hundreds, thousands of science-fiction stories that deal with such possibilities, and myriads more. In reading them, you are giving yourself a sort of kaleidoscopic view of many, many possible futures. Most of those scenarios will never come to pass. But those that do will have already been examined in science fiction.

That is why Alvin Toffler recommended science fiction as the antidote to "future shock." Very little that has happened in the twentieth century was not written about in science fiction. All the major thrusts of the century—world wars, nuclear power, biomedical wonders, space flight, civil rights, decolonization, the computer revolution, and more—have been examined in great detail in science fiction, decades before they reached general public awareness.

Science fiction, then, is truly the literature of *change*.

Again, my thesis is that science and technology are the main driving forces in our society, the major engines of change. Therefore a literature that makes science and technology its special subject matter is a literature that no thinking person can afford to ignore.

If you doubt this thesis, glance at the front page of today's newspaper. Headlines about political upheavals, pollution, drug trafficking, medical care, global economic competition—they are all based on new technological capabilities. Television and VCRs have cracked authoritarian regimes around the world; once people can see the good economic life that they are missing, they topple their government. Scientific discoveries in medicine and biology lead to new ethical dilemmas about defining an individual's right to life—and death.

And (as one writer is prone to say) so it goes.

The way the modern world works is this: scientists discover something new; engineers develop this new knowledge into a new capability—a medicine or a machine, usually; business leaders begin to make profits from the new thing; some workers find new jobs, others are laid off from jobs made obsolete; social and religious leaders ponder the significance of the change; and finally politicians start to make laws about it.

Science and technology are the major forces for change

in society because they are inherently forward-looking. All the rest of our institutions are backward-looking, by design. The law, religion, government, social customs, education—all such institutions exist to preserve society's status quo, to try to make tomorrow exactly like yesterday. That is the nature of institutions.

Except for science and its offspring technologies. By its very nature, science is constantly uncovering new knowledge, new concepts. Often these new ideas are stoutly resisted by society. You have only to think of the battles over Galileo, Darwin, Freud, even Einstein.

Technology keeps presenting us with new tools, some of which force enormous changes in society. The birth-control pill, for example, which led to the modern feminist movement. Computers, which have revolutionized industries as diverse as banking and animal husbandry, and forced Soviet Russia onto the path of *perestroika*.[4]

For each of these changes there have been loud and sometimes massive protests by those who fear change. In a nation as enlightened as the U.S., laboratories have been attacked and new technologies assailed in courts of law.

These are central issues to our society. This is the subject matter of science fiction. There is not a single issue confronting our society today that was not the subject of science-fiction stories ten, twenty, fifty years ago.

Does this make science fiction more worthwhile than other forms of contemporary literature? Is sculpture more worthwhile than painting? Comparisons among art forms are best left to academics who have nothing better to do. All I will say is this: Everyone *should* read science fiction, if for no other reason than to get a better understanding

---

4. The USSR had to give up its Stalinist, centrally controlled economy if it wished to be economically competitive in the global marketplace.

of the changes that will inevitably rock our society tomorrow.

This is not to say that all of science fiction is elegantly written, or even that all of it is worth the time it takes to read. Decades ago, Theodore Sturgeon coined what is now known as Sturgeon's Law:

"Ninety percent of science fiction is crud. But then, ninety percent of *everything* is crud."

Much of science fiction is written for specialized markets, where graceful prose is still secondary to interesting ideas. Even so, too much of science fiction is made up of tired retreads of old ideas.

Yet that good ten percent is about as good as contemporary writing gets. The subject matter can be exciting, exalting, mind expanding. The relationship to here and now is strong and very real. Do not let the alien settings and strange backgrounds fool you; most of these stories are dealing with ideas and problems that will change your life, for better or worse.

Strangely, comparatively few science-fiction stories actually deal with scientists themselves or scientific research. As one who has been involved in research programs for a fair portion of my life, I can tell you that most scientific research is about as glamorous as ditch digging, except for those rare moments of breakthroughs. And even then, the language and behavior of the scientists involved is highly specialized—rather like a tribal meeting of some small, isolated band of hunters.

Science-fiction tales tend to deal with the *consequences* of research. How wonderful it will be when this new idea actually comes to fruition! Or how terrible it might be. Good fiction deals with what happens when the change occurs, seldom with how the change came to be.

Does this concentration on technical subject matter

doom science fiction to an inferior position in the world's literature? That is for future generations of readers to decide. A hundred years from now, will people still read *The Left Hand of Darkness* or *Pride and Prejudice?* I see no reason why they will not read both.

Because its roots are in commercial publishing rather than literary academia, science fiction has yet to gain the appreciation of the self-appointed literati. Yet its popularity among the masses is growing. And any unprejudiced study of the field will show that the literary quality of science fiction has, in general, risen steeply over the past twenty-five years.

I feel sure that as more of the world's population understands the crucial relationships between science and the quality of life, more people will turn to the kind of fiction that speaks to those relationships.

They will read science fiction. They will read it for all the same reasons that ancient Greeks listened to the tales of Homer: Because it is important to their understanding of the world and their place in it. Because it links them to their fellow humans of the past, present, and future.

Mostly, though, they will read science fiction because it truly is exciting, exalting, mind-expanding fun.

Will Writing Survive?

Pythagoras said, "Things equal to the same thing are equal to each other."

People who are interested in writing or reading stories about the future must, therefore, be interested in the future. QED, as they say in geometry texts.

People interested in stories about high technology must be interested in high technology, too.

I started thinking about the impact of high technology on the publishing industry back in the early 1970s, when I was editing *Analog Science Fiction/Science Fact* magazine. Every year, almost, increases in the price of paper forced an increase in the price of the magazine. Other costs were going up, too, in the inflation-ridden '70s, but the costs of paper seemed to be the biggest burden.

That was about the time that the personal computer first arrived on the scene. It was very clear that the power and speed of computers were increasing rapidly, while the price for computers was falling dramatically. Computer enthusiasts were fond of pointing out that if the automobile improved as much as the computer, you would be able to buy a Rolls

Royce for a few hundred dollars and get a hundred miles to the gallon of gasoline.

Hmm, I thought. Price of paper keeps going up. Price of computers keeps going down. There must eventually come a crossover point where it will be cheaper to publish books electronically than on paper.

I envisioned an electronic book, a special-purpose computer small enough to hold in your hand with a high-definition display screen that could show a page of text or illustration at a time. A *Cyberbook*, I dubbed it. Then I tried out my brilliant idea on everyone I knew. To a man, and woman, they each replied: "Read books off a computer screen? Never! A book ought to be printed on paper."

"No," I would counter. "It should be carved in clay tablets."

Even science-fiction people reacted in that disgustingly backward way. Eventually I wrote a novel, *Cyberbooks*, that is as much a satirical poke at the hidebound publishing industry as it is an examination of the advent of the electronic book.

Even after *Cyberbooks* was published, though, the impact of electronics on publishing kept preying on my mind. I began to think of how electronic publishing might affect education. So when Bill Brohaugh of *Writer's Digest* asked me to do a piece about writing in the twenty-first century, the following essay is what came out.

Writers write for readers who read. As we hurtle along toward the year 2000, however, fewer and fewer people are reading. How will this affect the ancient and honorable profession of the writer?

The civilized skill of reading is under attack from two directions: from new technologies that offer information without the need to read, and from old educational systems that allow students to go all the way through public school without learning how to read. Or caring to.

Videotapes and functional illiterates are realities today. By the year 2000, voice-activated computers and three-dimensional television may make both writing and reading obsolete.

National surveys show that more than a million American youngsters graduate from high school each year with only the barest reading skills. Already this horrifying statistic is making itself felt in bookstores around the land. Where once the average bookstore carried only hardcover books, paperbacks, and perhaps a few magazines, today increasing shelf space is devoted to nonbook items such as audiocassette "books on tape," videotapes, posters, and comic books.

Many publishers have entered the "graphic novel" marketplace. They are producing comic books based on novels or shorter works of fiction. Classic Comics was the harbinger of this move, some four decades ago. High school students who did not have the inclination (or reading skills) to tackle *Dr. Jekyll and Mr. Hyde* as Robert Louis Stevenson wrote it could get a rough idea of the tale from the comic-book version. They might even pass a test on the subject, especially when the test was graded by a teacher who had never read the original either.

Today "graphic novels" are being generated not only from existing works of literature, they are also being commissioned specifically as new pieces of fiction. Instead of characterization and depth we get cartoon figures. Instead of powerful prose we get "oof!" and "aargh!"

Many "graphic novels" have been generated from works of short fiction, especially science-fiction stories. Even here, the "graphic novel" version lacks the power and finesse of the original story. The comic-book format *cannot* produce works of the same dimensions as a printed story or novel. The comic book, by its very nature, must emphasize its pictures, the graphics. It has limited space for printed words and a strictly limited number of pages.

"Graphic novels," after all, are not intended for an audience of readers. Comic books are for people who can't read, or don't much enjoy reading.

While publishers are already catering to audiences of nonreaders, potential readers of all ages are spending more and more of their time in front of cathode-ray tubes—TV and computer screens—and less time reading books and magazines. While the audience for network commercial television is slowly dwindling, viewers of cable TV have increased enormously in the past decade. Add videotapes that can bring to your living room everything from *National Geographic* documentaries to Hollywood's latest epics, and the competition against reading gets even fiercer.

Then too there are many literate men and women who spend most of their working hours peering at computer screens. They evince no great desire to read once they leave their workstations. On the other hand, millions of people have become hooked on computer networking and "interact" long into the night through their home computers with persons whom they have never met in the flesh. They are not reading literature either, not even pop literature.

Lest you think I am being an alarmist, sit down next Sunday morning with your local newspaper and count how many column inches are devoted to books as compared to how much space TV and movies get. Not advertising space, column inches of news.

In my local Sunday paper's entertainment section this week there were forty-three column inches devoted to reviews of two books, plus a list of best-sellers reprinted from *Publishers Weekly*. TV coverage got sixty-five column inches, including forty-one devoted to updates of the major soap operas. Motion picture coverage received seventy-nine column inches. And, of course, there was a complete television guide for the week in a separate section of its own.

These trends away from books and toward nonreading forms of entertainment and education show every sign of accelerating over the next decade. By the year 2000, writers of books and magazine pieces may well be on the endangered-species list.

If you are a devoted reader of science fiction, much of this may sound quite familiar to you. More than thirty years ago the late Cyril Kornbluth wrote a horrific novelette titled "The Marching Morons." The basic idea behind the story was simple: idiots tend to have more children than geniuses. The result, in Kornbluth's story, was a grossly overpopulated world of morons in which a handful of despised geniuses were desperately trying to stave off the inevitable collapse of civilization.

Again, that may sound too dreadful to be believed. Even if illiteracy is growing in the U.S. and elsewhere, the situation is not *that* bad, is it?

It can be fairly said that someone must write the prose for the "graphic novels," flat and shallow as that prose may be. Someone must write Hollywood's motion pictures and even the *National Geographic*'s specials. And the participants in an electronic network must tap out their messages on their computer keyboards; that's a form of writing, isn't it?

Well, so are graffiti.

You and I are interested in the forms of writing that can be grouped together under the headings of literature and journalism. The stuff of good fiction and good reporting. The kind of work that has been done by the likes of Ernest

Hemingway, Ernie Pyle, James Michener, Red Smith, John Steinbeck, Norman Mailer—to name merely a half dozen Americans who have worked in those fields in this century.

Writers. Whether it's a report on a World Series game or a novel about the Vietnam War, we are interested in that kind of writing. And we should be concerned about whether it can endure into the twenty-first century.

Pervasive illiteracy could dry up most of the writers' markets. Who will publish novels for a public that cannot read beyond a fourth-grade level? James Michener's novel *The Novel* examined just that question in considerable depth. How can a writer tell a story of some depth and complexity to "inquiring minds" whose attention span is about the length of a TV commercial?

Illiteracy is not new to the world. Indeed, it has been only in the past couple of centuries that civilized nations have made it a point of importance to teach their citizens to read and write. Modern industrialized democracies could not be run, it was felt, by an illiterate work force. Public schooling became mandatory not because of abstract good-heartedness by the upper echelons of society, but because those upper echelons needed workers who could read, write, and do basic arithmetic.

Wise, brave, resourceful Odysseus would have been a total bust in Bob Cratchit's job. Odysseus could neither read nor write.

Literacy was not always important. Up to the Industrial Revolution, literacy was the privilege of the upper classes alone. Prior to the Renaissance, only the priestly classes were taught to read and write. The common folk existed to do manual labor, go to church, and serve as cannon fodder in wartime.

The very ability to write was looked on askance in

ancient times. Plato recounted in his *Phaedrus* how a mythical king of Egypt, Thamus, rejected the god Toth's offer to teach the Egyptians how to write. "It is no true wisdom that you offer your subjects," said the churlish king to the god, "but only its semblance . . . with the conceit of wisdom, they will be a burden to their fellows."

Recognize that a king of ancient Egypt would have no reason to want his subjects to be able to read and write. What he wanted from his subjects was obedience, not erudition.

In our modern industrial democracy, illiteracy is a real and painful fact of life today, a problem that is growing worse with every graduating class. Moreover, the inexorable flow of technological progress may be aiding and abetting the growth of illiteracy.

It may seem strange that technology is working to a considerable extent against literacy. But it is.

When I was a youngster just starting to try to write seriously, professional writers carried on passionate arguments about the merits of the pencil (or fountain pen) over the typewriter. I remember reading articles in writers' magazines to the effect that typewriters were too mechanical, too intrusive, too danged *noisy,* to allow a true writer to think and create as he or she should.

Today writers argue over which word-processing program is the best. In the thirty-some years since my first novel was published I have progressed from a Smith-Corona portable (literally supported on an orange crate), through various electric typing machines with self-correcting tapes and cartridge feeds, to word-processing computers. I can, and do, carry a notebook computer with me wherever I travel. Inside its six-pound case I can fit all my files and the drafts of several novels, and still have room for correspondence and essays such as this one. In fact, this article was written with my faithful Japanese companion. (On WordPerfect software, if you must know.)

Still, I had to learn how to type, even with merely two fingers, and how to compose readable English prose. That day may well be on its way out.

Voicewriters. Computers with voice-recognition circuits in them that can understand what you say and put it into printing, either on a display screen or on paper. In laboratories all across North America, Europe, Japan, and the Pacific rim nations, researchers are working hard to produce practical voicewriting machines. IBM has been trying to produce such a system for the People's Republic of China—no mean feat, since each sound in Chinese has several different possible tones, and each tone gives that sound a different meaning and therefore must be written with a different symbol.

I recall sitting in the office of a Bell Labs vice president several years ago while he explained how difficult it is to develop microchips that can recognize human speech patterns. "We all talk differently," he said, in a soft Viennese accent. "No two people speak the same way."

Just considering problems such as distinguishing "two" from "too" from "to"—let alone "do"—makes the problems of a practical voicewriter seem daunting. But the engineers will succeed, undoubtedly. By the year 2000 you will be able to buy a machine that can be trained to understand your particular accent and word patterns, and faithfully reproduce them in print.

There have always been writers who dictated their words rather than type or scribble. The renowned Sir Winston Churchill rarely wrote his own first drafts of anything. He dictated to teams of secretaries, then rewrote the drafts they typed, using a fountain pen and red ink.

I myself have done a fair amount of work by dictation.

But only letters and company reports, in those bygone days when I worked in the aerospace industry. I found that it was fairly simple to dictate a formularized memorandum or business letter. But writing prose that I cared about—fiction or nonfiction—took another set of muscles altogether.

The new technologies that will produce practicable voicewriters by the year 2000 will have at least three enormous impacts on writers.

First, of course, they will make it possible to compose entirely by dictation. How this will affect writing styles remains to be seen, but the temptation to "write the way we speak" will probably overwhelm many writers. Voicewriters will make it easier to write quickly, easier to toss off a few thousand words and send them to market without the sweat and painful self-analysis of rewriting.

I realize that similar warnings against "easier" writing tools were made when the typewriter became a practical instrument. They were probably made when paper and ink replaced clay tablets and styluses. But where these earlier writing implements introduced quantitative differences in writers' abilities, the advent of voicewriting technology ushers in a qualitative difference.

Carving on stone or typing onto a display screen, all our writing implements so far have still involved the manual—and mental—act of *writing*. Dictation, as I mentioned above, uses a different set of muscles. We all have two different, though overlapping, vocabularies: our reading vocabulary and our speaking vocabulary. The words we use when we are communicating through our eyes, as in reading and writing, are considerably different from the words we use when we are communicating through our ears, as in speech.

Voicewriters will undoubtedly tempt writers to use their speaking vocabulary in preference to their reading vocabulary. Our literature will change. The change may be an improvement, although I suspect the change will be in the direction of simpler, flatter, less beautiful prose. We will move in the direction of everyday, commonplace conversation, and away from the elegance and power that the written word can produce.

If you doubt that the differences between our reading and speaking vocabularies are big enough to worry about, try two experiments.

First, take a page of conversation from a Hemingway novel. When you read it silently it "sounds" in your mind like the actual conversation that real people use. Now read it aloud. Nobody really talks that way. It was Hemingway's genius that produced a written scene that fooled your mind into thinking the characters were speaking just as they would in a real café or bedroom.

Now, turn on a tape recorder in your home or office and let it run for an hour while people are speaking to one another. Then listen to the result. We do not converse in the same vocabulary or style that we use for writing.

I fear that writers will move in the direction of the flat, banal, "natural" vocabulary of speech partly because of the second effect that voicewriting technologies will create. That effect will be to replace reading material such as books and magazines with material that you can watch and listen to.

Today you can listen to dramas on radio or audiocassettes, or watch them on TV and movie screens. By the year 2000 we may very well have what I call the Cyberbook: a hand-sized electronic viewer that will allow you to read or listen to, or perhaps even watch, virtually any book in print.

I invented the term for my satirical novel about the

publishing industry, *Cyberbooks*[1]. The concept of an "electronic book" is real, though, and already on its way.

Imagine a piece of electronic hardware small enough to fit into your palm, about the size of a paperback book. Most of its front face is a high-definition video screen. It is a Cyberbook reading machine.

Now imagine books being "printed" not on paper, but on thumbnail-sized electronic chips. You buy a chip and insert it into the reader. Its screen will show you a page at a time. Illustrations can be of higher quality than the best printing presses can achieve. If you don't want to read the book, or can't read, the device will read it aloud to you, just as your mother did when you were a baby.

Imagine one thing further. Imagine that Cyberbooks cost less than a dollar apiece.

Ninety percent of publishers' costs today come from hauling tons and tons of paper across the continent, from paper mills to printing plants to warehouses to distribution agencies to bookstores. Electronic books could be telephoned from publisher to store. You could even place a direct order to the publisher and receive your book over your home phone, transcribing it on a blank chip. Or, if you *must* have a book printed on paper, you could use a fax machine.

Books will become very cheap once electrons replace paper. Publishers will at last realize that they are actually in the information business, not the wood pulp and paper industry.

In my slightly futuristic novel, the publishing industry resists the idea of Cyberbooks with all its stubborn might, fearing that electronic books will spell the doom of wholesalers, distributors, even sales personnel. In reality, Cyber-

1. Published by Tor Books in 1989.

books will probably produce *at least* that big an upheaval.

Already today, manuscripts go directly from the word processors of certain writers to the typesetters' computers. Many publishers, mass market houses in particular, do practically no editing at all. Electronic books will make it easier to do away with editors—except, perhaps, for electronic editing programs that scan incoming manuscripts for spelling, punctuation, and grammar.

Secondly, a world of inexpensive electronic books might mean more markets for writers. But if electronic books fragment the existing book market, it might also mean lower prices paid to writers for their books, unless the books sell much better than they are sold today, thanks to the lower retail prices of electronic books.

Which brings us to the third area on which these new technologies will have an impact: copyright protection.

How can you protect your rights to your own prose when it can be duplicated electronically? Certainly safeguards can be built into a Cyberbook system, but as we have already seen, teenaged hackers have cracked the security of highly sophisticated computer systems.

When copying machines such as the first Xerox copiers came on the market several decades ago, many magazines aimed at professional audiences went out of business.

I worked in the late 1950s in an aerospace company where every second engineer (and there were thousands of them at that one plant alone) subscribed to several technical magazines. Came the Xerox machine and magazine subscriptions plummeted. Why subscribe when you can copy from somebody else's subscription?

In an era of electronic books, will the copiers outnumber the buyers? If so, what happens to the publishing industry? And its writers?

The world of A.D. 2000, less than a decade away, poses tremendous challenges for writers. Between growing illiteracy and modern technologies that make literacy unnecessary, will writing survive?

As we noted above, no matter how pervasive illiteracy becomes, no matter how low publishing and the other entertainment industries sink, someone must still write the prose for the "graphic novels," for Hollywood's motion pictures and PBS's TV specials.

Some markets will continue to exist even under the worst of circumstances. New markets may arise, such as self-publishing, where writers distribute their own work over electronic networks or by using home computers to print limited editions of their own poetry or prose.

The quality of the markets will be lower, however. The filtering process imposed by the costs of printing books and magazines, a process that forces editors to be selective, will be largely lost. We will be flooded with material "written" on voicewriters and distributed electronically.

There is a form of Gresham's Law[2], I think, about writing: Bad writing drives out good. We have seen this occur in mass-entertainment media such as motion pictures and television. When entertainment is aimed at the largest possible audience, it also aims at the lowest possible common denominator.

Will writing go this route? Will illiteracy and technology combine to lower the quality of today's professional writing? Will the best of our efforts be swamped in a wave of low-cost hacking, the electronic equivalent of "graphic novels," or worse?

I think the most powerful trends in today's society are heading *exactly* in that direction.

Yet . . .

---

2. Sir Thomas Gresham (1517–1579) pronounced that when two forms of currency have equal face value but unequal *real* value (one contains more gold than the other, for example), people will tend to horde the more valuable coins, which takes them out of circulation. Hence, "bad money drives out good."

Storytelling will survive. No matter what, every human society has always needed men and women who can create stories. Whether the stories are spoken out of memory, as Homer told his tales of Troy and Odysseus, or read from illuminated manuscripts, or played upon a three-dimension television projection, human societies want and need storytelling.

My favorite photograph in all the world shows the people of an African village gathered around a bonfire at night, gazing raptly at an old man who is telling a story—withered arms raised above his head, eyes wide with the excitement of his tale. And every other person in the photo is staring at the storyteller, mouth hanging open with suspense.

That's storytelling.

Writing as we know it may not survive much beyond the year 2000. But people will always need storytellers. Prepare.

Science-fiction and Fantasy Writers of America (SFWA) publishes a quarterly *Bulletin* that is filled with articles and reviews of interest not only to SFWA's members, but to writers in general. Among the types of thing the *Bulletin* publishes is a "What Works for Me" feature, in which established writers talk about—well, what works for them.

The following essay is my contribution to the ongoing feature. Mostly it is about the challenges of writing the thematic novel. And the powerful responsibility the science-fiction writer has to present rational thought as well as stirring emotions.

Science fiction should be *about* something.

It's been a long time since I've heard anyone describe our field as "the literature of ideas." To me, the idea content of science fiction is very important.

What first attracted me to science fiction, back when the only magazine on the newsstands was *Astounding* and *The Martian Chronicles* was a mint-new hardcover, was that here were stories that not only excited the sense of wonder; they also had some relevance to the world we lived in.

Partly because of my science-fiction reading I eventually became involved in the first American program to put an artificial satellite into orbit, Project Vanguard. Ever since, I have written fiction that deals with the interplay of high technology and high politics.

In other forms of fiction the writer must create believable characters and set them into conflict to generate an interesting story. In science fiction the writer must do all this and much more. In science fiction the writer has the opportunity—and perhaps the responsibility—to offer a powerful commentary on the world of today by showing it reflected in an imaginary world of tomorrow (or, in some cases, of distant yesterdays).

Think of the science-fiction tales that have made the most lasting impression on the field. And their authors. Robert Heinlein was certainly not offering bland pastorals. Frank Herbert gave a major impetus to the environmentalists. Ray Bradbury showed the evil that lurks within our own hearts in those *Chronicles* about Mars, as he did in *Fahrenheit 451*. Arthur Clarke, Ursula LeGuin, Gregory Benford, Harlan Ellison—their stories have something to say far beyond the requirements of mere entertainment.

In my own work I have dealt for the most part with the juncture where science and politics meet. The *Voyagers* novels begin with the world as it was in the late 1970s and then examine the changes that would be caused by the certain knowledge that other intelligent races exist in the universe. *Privateers* looks at an America that has given up on space and, consequently, on itself. Even the *Orion* novels, fantastic adventures that delve into the distant past, deal at heart with the relationships between human beings and their gods.

My dear friend Gordy Dickson calls such works "thematic novels," meaning novels that have a strong point of view that the author wants to impart to the reader. Sometimes, when the author goes too far, such works can slip into propaganda. Done properly they can be powerful statements that make readers *think*.

To me, science fiction should encourage people to think. God knows we have enough forms of amusement that discourage or actively prevent rational thought.[1] Even in most of contemporary literature the emphasis is on emotional reaction rather than rational thought. Science fiction is a fertile ground for the thematic novel; SF can and should be for the thinking reader.

The classic methods for generating thematic stories are well known. The writer asks, "What would happen if . . . ?" and fills in the rest of the sentence. Alternatively, the writer can look at a certain idea or trend and ask, "How will the world look if this goes on?"

Many of my novels begin with a theme, a point of view, an *idea* that I want to explore. This does not mean that I sit down to write the fictional equivalent of a political pamphlet, where I want to support a certain position that is well established in my mind before the first word is put down. I am not in the diatribe business; neither am I a partisan of any fixed political formula.

I regard these thematic novels as true explorations, wherein the author and reader investigate a certain concept or group of ideas, examine a mindset, look at a world that might actually come into being within the lifetime of the reader.

The danger of the thematic novel is that it can slide into propaganda, as noted above. There are two things that the author can (must!) do to avoid falling into this pit:

1. Is there the plot for a paranoid novel there?

First, do your own thinking. *Never* sit down to write a story that supports an existing political position. Develop characters that represent powerfully opposing views and let them work out their own positions as the story progresses. If all goes well, those characters will soon enough take over the story and carry it to conclusions that you the author were not aware of when you began writing.

Second, eschew the pleasure of creating a villain. Every story needs a protagonist and an antagonist, even if the antagonist is nature itself or the inner conflicts within the protagonist's soul. In thematic novels the antagonist tends to be a person, a character. The author must know that character so well that the novel could be turned around 180 degrees, written from the antagonist's point of view, making the "villain" into the "hero."

To make a thematic novel work well, the story must have a strong relationship to the real world. This is why I set most of my novels in the near future, the years that most readers can confidently expect to see for themselves. The world that I usually start with is the world as it exists today, or will exist in the next decade or so. Then I begin to examine what would happen if . . .

This technique has served many writers quite well over the years. For example, it was H. G. Wells' standard operating procedure.

If you begin your creative work with the real world, you must then populate such stories with real people. These characters should behave as people normally do, at least at the outset of the story. They must be people whom the reader can recognize and sympathize with.

The protagonist, in fact, should be someone that the reader wants to *be*. Every work of fiction is an exercise in psychological projection.

Stories must be consistent, otherwise the reader stops suspending his or her disbelief. It is perfectly possible to lead the reader from the here and now to the mines on the Moon or the cloning of the President of the United States or the struggles of a religious sect to establish a colony on the planet of another star. But it must be done in a way that does not jar the reader so badly that he or she stops reading.

I want to use my own double novel *The Kinsman Saga* as an example of what I have been talking about.

In 1966 I was working at the laboratory where the first high-power lasers were invented. It became clear to me then that such lasers could eventually lead to a system of satellites in orbit armed with lasers that could destroy ballistic missiles.

I examined that possibility in the novels *Millennium* and *Kinsman*. Years later I rewrote them, in the light of unfolding history, and combined them into the *Saga*.

I had no political ax to grind. What I wanted to accomplish, as an author, was to examine how the advent of this new technology would affect global politics—and the life of a certain human being whom fate casts into a pivotal role in this arena.

Chet Kinsman was a character I knew very well, from stories I had been writing over the years. He became the pivotal character for the novels. All the other characters were drawn from life, including one friend who happens to be a well-known science-fiction writer and another who is a world-famous folk singer.

The technology dictated the time frame for the novel. The characters drove the plot to its climax.

Interestingly, when the individual novels were originally published, in the 1970s, they were reviewed very kindly. When *The Kinsman Saga* was published in 1987—the same two novels, slightly rewritten—it was attacked on political grounds. The "science-fictional" dream of an orbital defense against nuclear missiles had become the real-life Strategic Defense Initiative, and *The Kinsman Saga* found itself in the midst of a highly politicized controversy.

Which brings us to the risks that the thematic novel presents to the author.

The first risk is that history catches up with near-future novels. Much of the *Saga* is history now, and some of it is history that never happened in the real world. By the turn of the century we will see if the technologies that are now called "Star Wars" lead to a more peaceful world in which no nation's missiles can threaten anyone. By then the *Saga* will have to stand on its own as literature without any prophetic overtones, just as *1984* and a myriad of "first men to the Moon" novels have had to face the music.

The second risk, and this surprised me, is that so many science-fiction readers want nothing to do with realistic stories. They seem to be especially frightened of stories populated by characters who are realistically portrayed as human beings. Apparently a sizable fraction of the hard-core audience for science fiction is afraid to read about characters human enough to bleed, or sweat, or stumble. They want to avoid dealing with real human emotions and frustrations.

Decades ago, Kurt Vonnegut, Jr., pointed out that most science-fiction characters behave as teenagers, regardless of their alleged age in the story. To some extent the field is still bedeviled by this attitude among its most faithful readers.

Fortunately, an honestly written realistic novel can find legions of readers outside the hard-core SF aficionados/aficionadas. Much of the market for thematic novels lies among readers who pick up little, if any, other types of science fiction.

Finally, the thematic novel runs the risk of political prejudice. As noted above, *The Kinsman Saga* was attacked by critics as "hawkish"—even when the story concluded with an international organization's rising from the ashes of the United Nations to maintain world peace. The very same novel led some real hawks to denounce the *Saga* for its liberal, internationalist flavor!

Once certain critics have pigeonholed an author in their pigeon-sized brains, no matter what the author writes those critics will review their conception of the author rather than the fiction the author has produced. In my case, thematic novels such as *Privateers* and the *Saga* have convinced some critics that I am a hawk. They report on my unsatisfactory (to them) political orientation first, and then might offer a commentary on the novel under consideration. Or might not.

Those are the risks of writing thematic novels. I think that science fiction is ideally suited to such work, which is why I am in this field. It's not the gadgetry that's important. I've been called a "hard science" writer for decades now, even though I've been writing about politics and sociology.

What is important is that this field of contemporary literature that we call science fiction, or speculative fiction, or SF—this field allows a writer the scope to examine real ideas and the real world. Which in turn offers a writer the chance to say something worthwhile, to write fiction that can have an impact on readers.

As I said above, science fiction should be *about* something. To throw away that opportunity is a criminal waste of time and talent.

John Campbell and the Modern SF Idiom

It saddens me to realize that an entire generation of science-fiction writers and readers has now grown up without knowing John Campbell.

John W. Campbell, Jr., as he insisted on being bylined, died in 1971. From 1937 until then, he was *the* towering figure in the field of science fiction. The following essay goes into some detail on that subject, so I will not try to justify my statement here.

When Florida State University asked me to write a piece about Campbell for their *Fantasy Review,* I was flattered and delighted. A thousand memories of John flooded through my mind. I will burden you with only two of them:

Scene 1: The lobby of a hotel that is hosting a science-fiction convention. Dozens of fans and writers (many were both) milling around, talking, exchanging jokes, looking for the bar. John Campbell, editor of *Analog* magazine, is surrounded by a shining-faced group of worshipers. At this time, *Analog* was published by The Condé Nast Publications, Inc., a very powerful New York–based magazine house.

One young man worms his way through the crowd and says, with studied diffidence, "I wrote a science-fiction story once. But I didn't send it to you because I knew you'd reject it."

Campbell, an imposingly large man with broad shoulders and white hair crew-cut militarily flat, looms over the kid and says in a crack-of-doom voice: "And since when does The Condé Nast Publications, Incorporated pay *you* to make editorial decisions for *Analog?*"

The kid disappeared into the carpeting.

John's point was that if you took the trouble to write a story, he wanted you to send it to him. Let him judge if it was good enough to be published. If he thought not, he would send you a detailed letter explaining his reasons—and giving you a hatful of ideas for new stories.

Unfortunately the youngster did not stay around to get the explanation.

Scene 2: A midtown Manhattan restaurant. John Campbell is taking six or seven (I forget the exact number) writers to lunch. John was fond of posing mental puzzlers; he liked to see how bright his writers were.

He asks us: "In the year 1910 there were two railroad stations in the city of Boston. One of them was the largest railroad station in the United States. But as every proper Bostonian knew, it was not the largest railroad station in Boston."

Talk about challenges! We had to explain that conundrum. Over lunch. If memory serves, I believe it was Joanna Russ who finally cracked it. Think about that as you read about John W. Campbell, Jr. There will never be another like him.

When he died unexpectedly in 1971, John W. Campbell, Jr., was the towering editorial figure who had dominated the field of science fiction for more than three decades. In recent years, Campbell's reputation has been eclipsed by the continuing evolution of the field.

Even so, to a considerable extent, modern science fiction is the creation of Campbell's editorial genius. What we call science fiction today is a literature that reflects Campbell's ideas of what the field ought to be.

Forgotten in today's dynamic, growing science-fiction realm is the fact that it was Campbell, starting in 1937, who insisted on high-quality writing for science-fiction stories. The first steps in leading science fiction out of the formulas and dreadful writing of the pulp-magazine industry were taken—forcibly, at times—by John Campbell.

The title of the magazine he edited from 1937 until his death reflects his own goals, and the evolution of the field. When the twenty-four-year-old Campbell was given the editor's job, starting with the December 1937 issue, the magazine was titled *Astounding Stories.* By February 1938, Campbell had changed the title to *Astounding Science Fiction,* and over the next twenty-two years insisted on cover type that emphasized "Science Fiction" and downplayed the melodramatic "Astounding." Finally, in 1960, when publisher Street & Smith was bought out by The Condé Nast Publications, Campbell was at last allowed to change the title to the one he had wanted for decades: *Analog Science Fiction/Science Fact.*

Many contemporary writers think of Campbell as an eccentric who championed a variety of crank ideas, from dianetics to libertarianism. A chain-smoker, he refused to believe the surgeon general's report on the links between smoking and heart disease—a refusal that may well have cost him his life. He was a great arguer, in the Socratic sense, and enjoyed nothing more than convincing a skeptical audience of his point of view.

His editorial crotchets, especially in his later years, are

well remembered. Few now recall, however, that his primary goal—stated boldly early in his career and then more and more by implication as the years rolled by—was to fill his magazine with what he considered to be "good stories."

How did Campbell define a "good story?" I believe he used three main criteria: technical background, mood, and writing quality.

Clearly he insisted that the technical background of each story be based firmly on what is known of scientific fact and principles. In this, he set the basic rule of modern science fiction: the writer can invent anything so long as no one can demonstrate that it is physically impossible.

To cite one famous example of the result of Campbell's policy, stories dealing with nuclear weapons began appearing in the pages of Campbell's *Astounding* long before the first atom-bomb test at Alamogordo in 1945. The most famous of these was Cleve Cartmill's "Deadline," published in May 1944.

> He stopped before the bomb, looked down at it. He nodded, ponderously . . . "Two cast-iron hemispheres, clamped over the orange segments of cadmium alloy . . . and a small explosive powerful enough to shatter the cadmium walls. Then . . . the powdered uranium oxide runs together in the central cavity. The radium shoots neutrons into this mass—and the U-235 takes over from there. Right?"

Not *exactly* the way the first atomic bombs worked, but close enough so that the FBI investigated the genesis of Cartmill's story, fearful of a security leak in the Manhattan Project.

Many latter-day critics have decried what they believed to be Campbell's insistence on "gadget" stories. They claim that "hard" science fiction, concentrating on stories that deal with technology and the physical sciences, limits the writer too much. The claim is true, but the implication that Campbell restricted the pages of *ASF*[1] to nothing but gadget stories is demonstrably false.

Consider the atomic-bomb case again. More than four years before Cartmill's description of an atomic bomb was published, Robert Heinlein wrote "Solution Unsatisfactory," which appeared in the May 1941 *ASF.*

"Well," I answered, "what of it? It's our secret, the atomic bomb, and we've got the upper hand. The United States can put a stop to this war, and any other war. We can declare a *Pax Americana,* and enforce it."

"Hm-m-m—I wish it were that easy. But it won't remain our secret; you can count on that. It doesn't matter how successfully we guard it; all that anyone needs is the hint . . . and then it's just a matter of time until some other nation develops a technique to produce it. You can't stop brains from working . . .

"It's like this: Once the secret is out—and it will be if we ever use the stuff—the whole world will be comparable to a room full of men, each armed with a loaded .45. They can't get out of the room and each one is dependent on the good will of every other one to stay alive. All offense and no defense. See what I mean?"

Heinlein (once described by Algis Budrys as "the hand of John Campbell's mind") correctly described the political implications of nuclear weaponry: the Cold War stalemate between the superpowers, the state of nuclear terror that has held the world in its thrall since 1945.

---

1. *ASF* will be used as an abbreviation for both the *Astounding* and *Analog* magazine titles.

Few critics have seen beyond the gadgetry in the pages Campbell edited to understand that *ASF* pioneered the way for stories dealing with the social, political, and human consequences of new technology. Far from restricting the pages of *ASF* to "hard" science fiction, Campbell educated the readers—and writers!—to consider the "softer" sciences of sociology and politics, as well.

It is no secret that Campbell did prefer "upbeat" stories. He had little tolerance for weaklings or failures. His preference was based on his belief that the human animal is admirable, that rational thought—as exemplified by science and engineering—is our main method for dealing with the environment in which we find ourselves. He was certain that Man is the toughest critter in the forest, and to those who did not believe it, or who felt there was something wrong or evil in such an attitude, he showed scant patience.

In this, Campbell clearly fell into the ranks of the philosophical optimists. He would have laughed at the myth of Sisyphus and immediately started to sketch out a system of pulleys that would allow the tragic mythical figure to get his stone over the top of that damned hill.

Does this mean he automatically rejected "downbeat," pessimistic stories? No, as a glance at Tom Godwin's "The Cold Equations" (August 1954) will show.

In this story, a young woman stows away on a spaceship carrying desperately needed vaccine to a plague-stricken planet. She wants to reach her brother, who is one of the plague victims. The ship's pilot, its only crew member, discovers the stowaway and realizes that her extra weight will prevent the ship from reaching its destination. He decides that the lives of millions of plague victims outweigh the life of the stowaway, and forces her out of the airlock, to die in the vacuum of space.

A cold equation had been balanced and he was alone on the ship. . . . It seemed, almost, that she still sat small and bewildered and frightened on the metal box beside him, her words echoing hauntingly clear in the void she had left behind her:

I didn't do anything to die for—I didn't do anything—

The theme of the story is classical: The universe (or what the ancient Greeks would have called Destiny) does not care about our petty loves and desires. One and one inexorably add up to two, no matter how desperately we would have it otherwise.

Years after "The Cold Equations" was published, Campbell laughingly recalled the story's evolution. "He [Godwin] kept wanting to save the girl." The editor had to insist on the "downbeat" ending. To do otherwise would have been to turn a memorable story into merely another "gadget" tale.

Beyond his insistence on scientific plausibility and his philosophical attitude, Campbell demanded writing quality much higher than that of the pulp fiction that preceded his reign at *ASF*. There were only a few science-fiction magazines being published in the late '30s and throughout the years of World War II. Campbell consistently paid the best rates in the field and consistently was the first editor to whom a writer sent each new manuscript. He used this powerful position to pick the stories that he considered best, and the quality of the writing was an important criterion, although usually an unspoken one.

Yet consider what was published in *ASF* before Campbell. I picked two stories at random: "Redmask of the Outlands" by Nat Schachner, and "Star Ship Invincible" by Frank K. Kelly. They were the lead stories in the January 1934 and January 1935 issues of *ASF*. The magazine at that time was considered among the best in the field. Schachner was a regular contributor who had fifty-seven stories published in *ASF* between 1931 and 1941, several of them under pen names because he often had more than one story in an issue. Kelly had only three stories in *ASF* in 1934 and '35.

The opening lines of Schachner's "Redmask of the Outlands":

> The city-state of Yorrick was a huge cube of blackness on the shores of the ocean. On one side stretched the interminable Atlantic, billowing and sun-bright; on the other, the almost interminable forests of the Outlands. In between lay a sudden cessation of light, of matter itself—a spatial void of smoothly regular outlines.
>
> The oligarchs of Yorrick had builded well to protect themselves and their millions of subjects against attack. Against the warped, folded space that inclosed [sic] the three levels of the city, powered as it was by the gravitational-flow machines, the most modern offense was impotent. No weapon conceived by man could breathe through.

And the opening of Kelly's "Star Ship Invincible":

> He had been sitting hunched on the high stool of the operator's chair, elbows on the smooth ledge of metal that encircled him, when the receptor tube spat a harsh sound in his ears, a sibilant warning note. He thought, "What now!" but straightened with alacrity, his stiff back shaping a tense angle.
>
> He jerked his head upward in an arc, nostrils widened, his thin nose slightly trembling, as if he could

smell what was vibrating through the receptor channel. He forgot how cold he was, and how his stomach ached faintly from many days on a diet of compressed-food tablets, and how he wished his relief would come, because he was lonely, the universe seemed strange and hostile all around him.

It took many months before Campbell used up the inventory of stories that his predecessor (now his boss) had accumulated, and even longer before he began to get the kind of stories he wanted to publish. Here are the opening lines from the lead stories of the January 1940 and January 1941 issues of *ASF*.

The first is "Neutral Vessel," by Harl Vincent:

In the captive military observation sphere a hundred miles above the outer cloud layer of Venus, Tommy Blake idly punched a location spot on the calculating board. He was not greatly impressed by the alarm indication of this body's approach. Seven million miles it was off, at the limit of the sensitive magnetic pickup system. From its direction, it could hardly be a Martian battle fleet, and even if it were, they would be several days getting here. Plenty of time.

The January 1941 lead story was "Sixth Column" by Anson MacDonald (Robert A. Heinlein), an acknowledged masterpiece. Its opening lines:

"What the hell goes on here?" Whitey Ardmore demanded.

They ignored his remark as they had ignored his arrival. The man at the television receiver said, "Shut up. We're listening," and turned up the volume. The announcer's voice blared out, "—Washington destroyed completely. With Manhattan in ruins, that leaves no—"

There was a click as the receiver was turned off. "That's it," said the man near it. "The United States is washed up." Then he added, "Anybody got a cigaret?"

The contrast between the stiff, stilted prose of 1934–35 and the more naturalistic and engaging style of 1940–41 is no accident. Schachner and Kelly were still writing in the early 1940s, but Campbell did not buy their work.

Instead, he sought writers who not only had real experience in science and engineering, but who could also write smoothly and naturalistically. He wanted writers who had "been there," at the edge of modern research and engineering, and who could write out of personal experience of the kinds of people and situations that existed at those frontiers.

As he himself often put it, "I'm looking for stories that could appear in the 'slicks' [i.e., *Collier's, The Saturday Evening Post,* et al.] two hundred years from now."

The "slick" magazines have died away, but Campbell's science fiction is a powerful, dynamic field of contemporary literature.

The pantheon of science fiction's 1940–1960 Golden Age is filled with writers Campbell published in *ASF*: Poul Anderson, Isaac Asimov, Hal Clement, L. Sprague de Camp, Lester del Rey, Gordon R. Dickson, Harry Harrison, Robert A. Heinlein, Henry Kuttner, Murry Leinster, C. L. Moore, Clifford Simak, Theodore Sturgeon, A. E. van Vogt, Jack Williamson, and many others.

The prolific Robert Silverberg started his career in *ASF*. While every book publisher in New York rejected Frank Herbert's novel *Dune,* Campbell serialized it despite the fact that it was twice as long as ordinary magazine serials of the time. The tremendous reader response to the novel

created the audience for the book's eventual publication—
by a textbook publisher in Philadelphia.

No one read the manuscripts submitted to *ASF* except
Campbell himself. There was no "first reader"; he read
them all, those sent in by agents, those from the best-
known writers in the field, and those from the unknowns.
It was particularly that enormous flow of manuscripts
from previously unpublished writers, called in the trade
"the slush pile," that Campbell mined for gold. There he
discovered the new talent that made his magazine—and
the field—great. He gave up his own not-inconsiderable
writing career and spent the rest of his life reading manuscripts, frequently for twelve hours a day or more. For
thirty-four years.

He was inordinately kind to young writers. His letters,
even his rejection letters, are legendary for their richness of
helpful ideas and encouragement to "try again." The most
famous example, of course, is his treatment of the teenaged Isaac Asimov, who all his life gave Campbell the
major share of the credit for his success as a writer.

Campbell often said, "The real job of an editor is to find
a good writer in a bad story." That is, to recognize talent
in a beginner's clumsy efforts. And then to encourage the
beginner until he begins writing publishable stories.

By the 1950s, new science-fiction magazines such as
Galaxy and *The Magazine of Fantasy and Science Fiction*
began to appear on the newsstands. Book publishers
started to take science fiction seriously. They all built on
the foundations that Campbell had constructed. Even
those editors and writers who decried "Campbellian" science fiction as too restricting and old-fashioned were (perhaps unknowingly) taking advantage of Campbell's many
years of labor and the audience he had built up.

The quality of science-fiction writing was unquestion-
ably higher in 1950 than it had been in 1937. More than

that, the readers had been trained in the pages of *ASF* to expect and demand writing that was much better than the earlier prose of the pulp magazines. These expectations and demands increased as the decades rolled on. The "New Wave" of the late 1960s and the burgeoning of science fiction in the seventies and eighties were the inevitable consequences of the evolution of science fiction away from the pulp magazines and toward a true contemporary literature. Campbell played a pioneering role in that evolution.

Perhaps the most revealing incident in Campbell's long career came immediately after he was appointed editor of *Astounding*. He asked a senior editor at Street & Smith, "What happens if I don't get enough stories to fill the magazine?" The older man fixed him with a stern eye and said, "A *good* editor does."

From that moment on Campbell spent his enormous energies making certain that he could fill the magazine. His hackles-raising editorials, his voluminous correspondence, his long hours of reading manuscripts, his marathon arguments over everything and anything from quantum physics to slavery to the Dean Drive—all were aimed at making certain there would be no blank pages in *ASF*.

More than that, he wanted to fill the magazine with *his kind* of stories: technically acute, upbeat, and well written. He succeeded far better than anyone before or since. What we call "science fiction" today is what John W. Campbell, Jr., determined the field should be.

Science, Fiction and Faith

Writing is a lonely occupation, but writers cannot be hermits. The very act of writing is an attempt to communicate with others, and a communication is not complete until someone receives and understands it. The writer does not work in a vacuum, therefore, nor does the reader exist as a solitary individual. As John Donne put it, we are all a part of the whole.

This final essay is my attempt to put science-fiction writing in context with today's society, and in particular to show that science fiction may be in the process of developing a mythology for our modern age.

A very large claim. But then, science-fiction people have always thought large.

Knowledge is always based on faith. The verb *to know* depends on the verb *to believe*.

In the misty beginnings of human society, knowledge and faith were so closely intertwined that the tribal wise man was the tribal shaman. Even in sophisticated societies such as those of ancient Egypt, China, and the Middle East, the men who watched the stars and predicted the seasons were priests, servants of the gods whom they fully believed were responsible for the stars and their motions in the sky, as well as the seasons here on earth.

In 1620, the year that the Pilgrims set foot on Plymouth Rock, Francis Bacon published in England a book that changed the world. It was titled *Novum Organum*, meaning "The New Method." This book signaled the beginning of a new era in human thought—the organized and self-checking system of observing and measuring that we now call the scientific method.

"Man is the servant and interpreter of Nature," wrote Bacon. "About Nature, consult Nature herself."

Early in the seventeenth century a detailed investigation of nature was a new and daring idea. Most learned men of that era were content to discuss "natural philosophy," as physical science was called then, in much the same way that they discussed politics: from the safety of a comfortable chair. There were dangers involved in examining nature. In Italy, Galileo was hauled before the Inquisition and kept under house arrest for the remainder of his life because he espoused scientific investigation rather than bow to the authority of the Church. People were tortured and executed horribly for allegations of witchcraft.

Bacon titled his book *Novum Organum* in reaction to Aristotle's *Organon*, which had been written some twenty centuries earlier. During the intervening eighty human generations, Aristotle's word had been the final authority on nearly every question concerning the natural world throughout Christian Europe.

The flowering of modern science broke the authority of Aristotle and the Church. In ways that most historians still do not appreciate, it was the scientific revolution of the seventeenth century that made possible—even inevitable—the political revolutions that followed.

Yet the scientific method, for all its rationalism and insistence on unbiased measurement and experiment, is based on faith. Not necessarily on a belief in a deity, but on the faith that nature is absolutely indifferent to human actions. The scientist believes, without even thinking consciously about it, that one and one *always* add up to two, that hydrogen atoms behave the same way in distant stars as they do in earthly laboratories, that the universe is predictable—no matter who is making the measurement, no matter what the investigator's religion or color or politics. Or gender. The universe plays fair; it is governed by a set of rules that human beings can discover and understand.

Albert Einstein expressed that faith in these words: "The eternal mystery of the world is its comprehensibility."

It is no coincidence that the first science-fiction stories—tales that dealt with the wonders of science and exploration of other worlds in space—were written in the seventeenth century. In 1657, Cyrano de Bergerac (the real one, not the romantic figure of Rostand's nineteenth-century play) wrote his *Voyages to the Sun and the Moon,* in which he "invented" the idea of using rockets to travel to other worlds.

Fantastic tales had been a mainstay of the world's literature since long before the invention of writing. But unlike these earlier stories, which depended on the supernatural interventions of gods and goddesses, the new "scientific romances" based their adventures on what was known of the real world—plus some informed speculation about what might be discovered in the future.

Like the scientists themselves, the science-fiction writers

have been guided by a basic tenet of faith: the belief that the universe is knowable, and that what human beings can understand, they can eventually learn to control and harness.

Not everyone shares this belief. Since Galileo's time, and right up to this day, many people have feared science and scientists. Since the neolithic tribal shamans first arose, the power of knowledge has frightened the ignorant. Most people have held an ambivalent attitude toward the shaman-astrologer-wizard-scientist. On the one hand they envied his abilities and sought to use his power for their own gain. On the other hand, they feared that power, hated his seeming superiority, and knew that he was in league with the forces of evil. And it was always easier to blame one's troubles on a witch and have some poor woman killed or driven out of the village.

Even today many still fear the so-called "Faustian bargain," the mistaken idea that knowledge can only be bought at the price of eternal damnation—or one of its modern equivalents, nuclear holocaust or ecological despoliation.

There are basically two kinds of people in the world: Luddites and Prometheans—those who fear science and its offspring technologies, and those who embrace them.

History has not been kind to Ned Ludd, the unwitting founder of the Luddite movement of the early nineteenth century. *Webster's New World Dictionary* describes Ludd as feebleminded. The *Encyclopedia Britannica* says he was probably mythical.

The Luddites were very real, however. They were English craftsmen who tried to stop the young Industrial Revolution by destroying the textile mills that were taking away their jobs. Starting in 1811, the Luddites rioted, wrecked factories, and even killed at least one employer who had ordered his guards to shoot at a band of rioting workmen. After five years of such violence, the British government took harsh steps to suppress the Luddites, hanging dozens and transporting others to prison colonies in far-off Australia. That broke the back of the movement, but did not put an end to the underlying causes that had created it.

Slowly, painfully, over many generations, the original Luddite violence evolved into more peaceful political and legal activities. The labor movement grew out of the ashes of the Luddites' terror. Marxism arose in reaction to capitalist exploitation of workers. The Labour Party in Britain, and socialist governments elsewhere in the world, are the descendants of that early resistance against machinery.

Today the progeny of those angry craftsmen live in greater comfort and wealth than their embattled forebears could have dreamed in their wildest fantasies. Not because employers and factory owners suddenly turned beneficent. Not because the labor movement and socialist governments have eliminated human greed and selfishness. But because the machines—the machines that the Luddites feared and tried to destroy—have generated enough wealth to give common laborers houses of their own, plentiful food, excellent medical care, education for their children, personally owned automobiles, television sets, refrigerators, stereos—all the accoutrements of modern life that we take so much for granted that we almost disdain them, but which would have seemed miracles beyond imagination to the original Luddites.

We still have the Luddite mentality with us today: people who distrust or even fear the machines that we use to create wealth for ourselves. The modern Luddites are most conspicuous in their resistance to high technology such as computers and automated machinery, nuclear reactors, high-voltage power lines, airports, fertilizers, and food additives. To today's Luddites, any program involving high technology is under immediate and intense suspicion. In their view, technology is either dangerous or evil or both, and must be stopped. Their automatic response is negative; their most often used word is *no*.

Opposing the Luddite point of view stands a group of people who fear neither technology nor the future. Instead, they rush forward to try to build tomorrow. They are the Prometheans, named so after the demigod of Greek legend who gave humankind the gift of fire.

Every human culture throughout history has created a Prometheus myth, a legend that goes back to the very beginnings of human consciousness. In this legend, the first humans are poor, weak, starving, freezing creatures, little better than the animals of the forest. A godling—Prometheus to the Greeks, Loki to the Norse, Coyote to the Plains Indians of North America—takes pity on the miserable humans and brings down from the heavens the gift of fire. The other gods are furious, because they fear that with fire the humans will exceed the gods themselves in power. So they punish the gift giver, eternally.

And, sure enough, with fire the human race does indeed become the master of the world.

The myth is fantastic in detail, yet absolutely correct in spirit. Fire was indeed a gift from the sky. Undoubtedly a bolt of lightning set a tree or bush ablaze, and an especially curious or courageous member of our ancestors overcame the very natural fear of the flames to reach out for the bright warm energy. No telling how many times our ancestors got nothing for their troubles except burned fingers and yowls of pain. But eventually they learned to handle fire safely, to use it. And with fire, technology became the main force in human development.

Technology is our way of dealing with the world, our path for survival. We do not grow wings like the eagle, or fur like the bear, or fleet running legs like the deer. We make tools. We build planes, we make clothing, we manufacture automobiles. The English biologist J.B.S. Haldane said, "The chemical or physical inventor is always a Prometheus. There is no great invention, from fire to flying, that has not been hailed as an insult to some god."

In a broader context, we might say that the basic difference between the Luddites and the Prometheans is the difference between an optimist and a pessimist. Is the glass half full of water or half empty?

Many human beings see themselves, and the entire human race, through the weary eyes of ancient pessimism. They see humankind as a race of failed angels, inherently flawed, destined for eternal frustration. Thus we get the myth of Sisyphus, whose punishment in Hades was to struggle eternally to roll a huge stone up a hill, only to have it always roll back down again as soon as he got it to the summit. It sounds very intellectual to be a pessimist, to adopt a world-weary attitude; at the very least, no one can accuse you of enthusiasm or youthful naïveté.

The optimists tend to see the human race as a species evolving toward immortality. We are perfectible creatures, they believe. Optimists may be accused of naïveté, but they can also point to recent history and show that human thought has improved the human condition immensely within the few short centuries in which science has come into play. Certainly there are shortcomings, pitfalls, drawbacks to every advance the human race makes. But the optimists look to the future with the confidence that humankind can use its brains, its hands, and its heart to constantly improve the world. And itself.

It is this difference between the pessimists and optimists that causes a fundamental resistance among the pessimists to science fiction. Especially among those who concentrate on the literature of the past, the optimistic literature of a brighter tomorrow is anathema. They simply cannot fathom it; they are blind to what science fiction says. Even within the science-fiction field itself, some of its practitioners often fall prey to this ancient schism, regarding darkly pessimistic stories as somehow more "literary" than brightly optimistic ones.

There is a bit of the pessimistic Luddite in each of us, and each of us is something of an optimistic Promethean.

The great poet and historian Robert Graves revealed a decidedly Luddite side of his personality some twenty years ago when he wrote in the British journal *New Scientist:*

> Technology is now warring openly against the crafts, and science covertly against poetry.

Graves apparently feared that the machines that had replaced human muscle power and handiwork—the machines that the Luddites tried to wreck two centuries ago—are now giving way to electronic systems that threaten to replace human brainpower.

He went on to contrast science with poetry, stating that poetry has a power that scientists cannot recognize because poetry is usually the product of intuitive thinking, which "scientists would dismiss . . . as 'illogical.' "

Graves apparently pictured scientists as sober, plodding, soulless thinking machines that do everything rationally and never take a step that has not been carefully examined beforehand. As a historian, he should have known better.

Because scientists have an inherent faith in the "fairness" of the universe (one and one always equals two) they frequently feel free to make leaps into the unknown confident that they will not find themselves in a region where the basic rules of the universe have changed.

James Clerk Maxwell's brilliant insight that visible light is a form of electromagnetic energy; Max Planck's notion that all forms of energy come in discrete packages, or quanta; Wolfgang Pauli's faith in the conservation of energy, so strong that it led him to predict the existence of an unseen particle, the neutrino—the history of science is dotted with examples of great "leaps of faith."

Scientists are just as human, just as intuitive, just as emotional as poets. They have just as strong a need for belief in the basic justness of the universe as any monk or minister. But the scientist's belief is in a rational, understandable, predictable universe, rather than a universe created and governed by a personality.

The science-fiction writer goes one step farther. Not only do the writers share the scientists' belief in an understandable universe, the writers also tacitly believe that humanlike intelligence is a permanent fixture in the universe.

Even in the darkest, most dystopian science-fiction stories, intelligent life somehow endures. Despite nuclear holocaust, environmental disaster, devastating invasions from other worlds, science-fiction stories always show that life goes on. Intelligent life persists, somewhere, somehow.

The intelligent life may not be human. In some stories the human race may perish, but that is not the end of the universe, nor of intelligence. There can be intelligent creatures from another world, or intelligent machines left behind by their creators who have died away or vanished.

In actuality, what the science-fiction writers are doing is creating a modern mythology. Science fiction is slowly, almost unconsciously, codifying a system of beliefs tailored to our modern scientific society.

Joseph Campbell, late professor of literature at Sarah Lawrence College, spent his long lifetime studying and writing about mythology. His *Hero with a Thousand Faces* and his four-volume *The Masks of God* are classic books on the world's mythologies.

Campbell has pointed out that modern scientific society has no mythology of its own, no psychological underpinning. The old myths are dead, and no new mythology has arisen to take its place.

Human beings need mythology, he insists, to give an emotional meaning to the world in which we live. A mythology is a codification on the emotional level of our attitudes toward life, death, and the entire vast and often frightening universe.

The Prometheus myth is an example of what Campbell is driving at. It explains, at the deepest emotional level, not merely our mastery of fire and its resulting technology, but the price that must be paid for such a gift.

Much of today's emotion-charged, slightly irrational urge toward astrology and mysticism is actually nothing more than a groping for a new mythology, a search for a set of beliefs that can explain the modern world on the emotional, intuitive level to people who are frightened that they are too small and too weak to cope with the world in which they find themselves.

Campbell's work has shown that there are at least four functions that a mythology must accomplish, if it is to be helpful to the individual.

First: a mythology must induce a feeling of awe and majesty in the people. Science-fiction stories often do this, especially when they strike the reader with new and stunning visions of the universe. In the science-fiction community, this is called "a sense of wonder," and it is something that writers strive to achieve.

Second: a mythology must define and uphold a self-consistent system of the universe, a pattern of believable explanations for the phenomena of the world around us. Virtually every science-fiction tale takes as a "given" the universe revealed by scientific investigation. While most science-fiction writers feel free to extrapolate from what is known today in an effort to produce fresh insights, the writers almost always try to stay within the confines of what is known to be possible. The rule of thumb is: the writer is free to invent anything, as long as it cannot be proven to be physically impossible by today's knowledge.

Third: a mythology usually supports a specific social establishment. For example, the body of mythology that originated in ancient Greece apparently stemmed from the Achaean conquerors of the earlier Mycenaean civilization. Zeus was a barbarian sky god who conquered the local goddesses as the Mycenaean cities fell to the invading Achaeans. Many a lovely legend was started this way. Science-fiction stories tend to support the social system we call Western Democracy. The concept that the individual person is worth more than the Organization, even when the Organization might be an all-conquering interstellar empire, is one of the basic tenets of science fiction. Especially in Western science fiction, nothing is as important as human freedom.

Fourth: a mythology serves as a crutch to help the individual member of society through the emotional crises of life, such as the transition from childhood to adulthood, and the inevitability of death. It is important to realize, in this context, that science fiction has a large readership among the young, especially teenagers eager to find their places in society. And much of science fiction's tales of superheroes, time travel, and immortality are nothing less than thinly veiled attempts to deny the inevitability of death.

Without intending to, without even consciously realizing it until very recently, science-fiction writers across the world have been slowly building up a mythology suitable for our modern scientific age. Like the scientists themselves, the writers share the rock-bottom faith in the power and beauty of rational human thought.

MORE SCIENCE FICTION
BY BEN BOVA

☐ 53219-8 PROMETHEANS $2.95
                                            Canada $3.75

☐ 53231-7 STARCROSSED $2.95
                                            Canada $3.95

☐ 53208-2 TEST OF FIRE $2.95
                                            Canada $3.50

☐ 50735-5 THE TRIKON DECEPTION $5.99
           with Bill Pogue   Canada $6.99

☐ 53161-2 VENGEANCE OF ORION $3.95
                                            Canada $4.95

☐ 50076-8 VOYAGERS $4.95
                                            Canada $5.95

☐ 51337-1 VOYAGERS II: THE ALIEN WITHIN $4.95
                                            Canada $5.95

☐ 53236-8 VOYAGERS III: STAR BROTHERS $4.95
                                            Canada $5.95

☐ 53227-9 WINDS OF ALTAIR $3.95
                                            Canada $4.95

Buy them at your local bookstore or use this handy coupon:
Clip and mail this page with your order.

Publishers Book and Audio Mailing Service
P.O. Box 120159, Staten Island, NY 10312-0004

Please send me the book(s) I have checked above. I am enclosing $ _____
(Please add $1.25 for the first book, and $.25 for each additional book to cover postage and handling.
Send check or money order only—no CODs.)

Name _____
Address _____
City _____ State/Zip _____
Please allow six weeks for delivery. Prices subject to change without notice.

BESTSELLERS FROM TOR

☐	51195-6	BREAKFAST AT WIMBLEDON *Jack Bickham*	$3.99 Canada $4.99
☐	52497-7	CRITICAL MASS *David Hagberg*	$5.99 Canada $6.99
☐	85202-9	ELVISSEY *Jack Womack*	$12.95 Canada $16.95
☐	51612-5	FALLEN IDOLS *Ralph Arnote*	$4.99 Canada $5.99
☐	51716-4	THE FOREVER KING *Molly Cochran & Warren Murphy*	$5.99 Canada $6.99
☐	50743-6	PEOPLE OF THE RIVER *Michael Gear & Kathleen O'Neal Gear*	$5.99 Canada $6.99
☐	51198-0	PREY *Ken Goddard*	$5.99 Canada $6.99
☐	50735-5	THE TRIKON DECEPTION *Ben Bova & Bill Pogue*	$5.99 Canada $6.99

THE BEST IN
SCIENCE FICTION